The Curse of
Treasure Island

—

The Curse of Treasure Island

—*—

Francis Bryan

Viking

VIKING
Published by the Penguin Group
Penguin Putnam Inc., 375 Hudson Street, New York, New York 10014, U.S.A.
Penguin Books Ltd, 80 Strand, London WC2R 0RL, England
Penguin Books Australia Ltd, 250 Camberwell Road, Camberwell,
   Victoria 3124, Australia
Penguin Books Canada Ltd, 10 Alcorn Avenue, Toronto, Ontario, Canada M4V 3B2
Penguin Books India (P) Ltd, 11 Community Centre, Panchsheel Park,
   New Delhi–110 017, India
Penguin Books (N.Z.) Ltd, Cnr Rosedale and Airborne Roads, Albany,
   Auckland, New Zealand
Penguin Books (South Africa) (Pty) Ltd, 24 Sturdee Avenue,
   Rosebank, Johannesburg 2196, South Africa

Penguin Books Ltd, Registered Offices:
Harmondsworth, Middlesex, England

First American edition
Published in 2002 by Viking Penguin,
a member of Penguin Putnam Inc.

1   3   5   7   9   10   8   6   4   2

Originally published in Great Britain as *Jim Hawkins and the Curse of Treasure Island* by
Orion, a division of Orion Publishing Group Ltd.

Library of Congress Cataloging-in-Publication Data

Bryan, Francis.
    [Jim Hawkins and the curse of Treasure Island]
    The curse of Treasure Island / Francis Bryan.
       p. cm.
    Previously published as : Jim Hawkins and the curse of Treasure Island, 2001.
    ISBN 0-670-03089-9
       1. Treasure Island (Imaginary place)—Fiction. 2. Treasure trove—Fiction.
    I. Stevenson, Robert Louis, 1850-1894. Treasure Island. II. Title.

PR6102.R93 J56 2001
823'.92—dc21   2001056828

This book is printed on acid-free paper. ∞

Printed in the United States of America
Set in Bembo with Johann Sparkling display
Designed by Carla Bolte

For

J.O.N.V.

with affection

CONTENTS

The Curse of
Treasure Island

—

Prologue—

Grown to Man's Estate

Seven years after I returned from the sea I became twenty-one, a man's majority. My mother told me I should now become my father's successor beneath the sign of the Admiral Benbow. I embraced my inheritance and took over the running of the inn.

My ambition to become a good landlord was helped by the riches for which I had risked my life, and which we now began to use a little. With my dividend from Treasure Island I improved the inn, fitting brass and glass from Bristol, and purchasing tables and chairs made of Somerset yew. The old sea dog, Captain Billy Bones, whose fatal map caused us our misery and our adventure, said when he first came to us that the Admiral Benbow was "a pleasant sittyated grog-shop." I meant to make it more than that and I believe I have done so.

In those unhappy days we had lacked business. Our remoteness was foremost among the old pirate's reasons for coming to us. Yet, although his vile presence had brought great hardship to my mother and me, we acknowledged that Billy Bones had also been the cause of our wealth. His oilskin packet, with its map marked OFFE CARACCAS, brought us the treasure, and it helped to increase our trade—because upon my return the men of the district crowded the inn to hear my account. Whatever my youth and excitability, I believe I did not decorate the story too much; it needed no ornament. And my listeners drank much ale as they smacked their lips at the adventure.

Word of my yarns spread and we acquired customers from far beyond our boundaries. As the months and soon the years passed, almost every day brought a new visitor. Many of these were sailors, bound for Bristol or Plymouth with their haversacks. They sought out our inn because its young host had a wonderful tale to tell of pirates and treasure!

My mother felt unease at my stories and thought me immodest. I replied that she must think too of our trade, and how it had grown. The Admiral Benbow, once a lacklustre tavern in lonely Black Cove, had become a busy port of call. We often smiled—that Billy Bones, having chosen our inn as a quiet place to hide, became the cause of making it bustle. At such a moment my mother would murmur again that she prayed for his departed soul but feared it too blackened to be saved.

Whenever I thought of him and the other pirates, I was comforted by the feeling that it had all passed. No more would we hear Blind Pew and his dreadful tapping in the clear air of a frosty night. Nor would I wince again at the crushing force of his grip upon my arm; nor shudder at the great green shade over his empty eyes; nor ever more endure the sound of his cruel, cold, ugly voice. Nor should I need to scan the headlands for Long John Silver, the sea cook with one leg, whose spectre so frightened Billy Bones.

As we grew in substance, I hired sufficient help. This brought to an end my mother's daily burdens. She rested her body a little more, but not her mind—nor her tongue; her pronouncements from her upstairs parlour became more vigorous than I had known, yet she still guided rather than forced me towards good decisions. I bought two horses, one for me and one for our general purposes, and some land by the inn for the horses to graze upon, and against a day when we might think it necessary to build anew. (Indeed, we built straightaway—a stable, which we had never before been able to offer travellers.) The parish, which formerly pitied us behind their hands, looked to the young landlord of the Admiral Benbow and his dignified mother with interest and, I think, pride.

Our new fortunes also helped to honour my dear father. He lies in the churchyard overlooking the waves at Kitts Hole where I honoured him with a fine headstone. My mother shall lie beside him in the same plot, but not, I hope, for many years yet. Old Taylor, the gardener, who died during my absence in the South Seas, was buried nearby during the stormiest day my mother believes she ever saw.

That windswept little graveyard will be my last resting place too and I hope I will not be carried there until generations have passed. But that will be a vain hope unless I can cease taking risks, such as the adventure I am now about to relate.

My part in this new story still baffles me. Why would any sensible man, especially having known such fearful experiences as I had, ever leave our haven? Yet I did. Again I travelled to that island where I killed Israel Hands. Again I climbed those slopes where my friends once thought I had deserted them in favour of cutthroat mutineers. Indeed, were it not for the great bravery and loyalty of my comrades in those adventures, Dr. Livesey, Squire Trelawney and the redoubtable Captain Smollett, I might have died on Treasure Island—yet I revisited those frightful shores. It seems to go against the credible: why did I return to a place I hated and which haunted my worst dreams?

That is a question which you, my reader, may rightly ask. It was no desire to repeat such exploits that drove me back. Yes, we had left some treasure there—a considerable amount, because we had not had men enough to heave it nor space enough to stow it. But the lure of that trove played little part in my return. The truth is—new and powerful feelings drove me.

These began as compassion and soon grew to something more difficult to describe or name, something exciting, warm, overwhelming. There was also fear; one day, I found myself, of a sudden, trapped in circumstances where I was accused and in danger of the law's worst penalty. If I must be honest, my natural foolishness (which I try to control) also played a part.

Perhaps I hoped also to lay the ghosts of the old nightmares. Often, as I lay in my bed, the wind came up from the cove and raved near the chimneys. The windows rattled and as the inn sign swung and creaked, I heard in my dreams the surf along the island's horrid shore. On such nights the wretched words of Long John Silver's parrot cackled and droned across my brain: "Pieces of Eight! Pieces of Eight!"

So here I am, taking up my pen again. While I set down every awful thing that took place, I seek your judgement. Place yourself where I sat on a certain summer day in the year of grace 17——. Direct your thoughts towards the assistance asked—implored—of me. As you read my account, measure me against your own thoughts— judge me according as you think you, yourself, would have acted in such unexpected and difficult matters.

———✦———

Part One

—❧—

The Bright Face of Danger

Ch. 1—

A Mysterious Arrival

It began on the first Saturday of August last year, at another inn, the Royal George up on the heath. I had gone there to await the mail coach. Many of its weekly visits brought from Bristol and farther away articles and goods we had sent for.

The landlord of the Royal George is John Culzean. He was a sound neighbour and good friend to my mother in that time I first went abroad. John is an easy man and I like his company. As I waited, he and I spoke of local things, as neighbours do.

A bugle blew from the hilltop; soon we heard the rattle of wheels coming into the yard. John left me to go out and greet the coachman and I saw something quicken between them. The coachman asked some strong question. John nodded his head and listened for a further moment. Then he pointed, first towards the direction of the distant Admiral Benbow and next indicated me through the open door of his own parlour. I sensed that my name had been invoked. The coachman walked around to the door of his vehicle and spoke to someone within. John Culzean stood by and watched—and I waited in a puzzle.

Then the coachman wrenched open his door. A boy stepped down; he was aged, I thought, twelve or so. He looked all around him, tried to peer in at me, then looked at John Culzean and stepped back. Instantly he was followed by a tall woman in a brilliant green, embroidered cloak. The hood of this rich garment enveloped her head and hid her face.

The boy walked forwards, peering all round him. He came nearer the door and saw me. I smiled at him; he did not return my smile. He looked away and then looked at me again as Culzean pointed and said to the woman, "Madam, that is Mr. Jim Hawkins."

On that side door of the Royal George sits a brass door knocker, in the form of a hand. The boy looked at it, then reached up and rapped it very hard. At first I thought he did it out of politeness, to announce that strangers had come. But then he did it again, much louder and irregularly.

As the noise faded, the coachman pointed towards the sun, indicating that he wished to resume his journey. John Culzean restrained him and led the woman in the green cloak towards where I sat. Caution filled my brain, yet I was excited as I rose from my chair. John walked to me, his face grave yet excited.

"Jim," he said, and he hesitated. The boy rapped at the door knocker again and John glanced at him in an irritation which I shared.

I waited, not knowing why I felt apprehensive.

"Jim, you've been asked for by name."

"By name?"

John nodded. "The coachman asked where you live. And she, the lady—"

At this he was interrupted, brushed aside by the great green cloak. The boy followed and this odd, urgent pair stood before me.

"Are you Mr. Jim Hawkins," the woman asked, "of the inn called the Admiral Benbow?"

"Indeed I am, Madam."

She revealed her face—and I caught my breath. Until that moment I had only seen such pure loveliness in the tall portraits owned by fine houses.

"I am called Grace Richardson," she said. "You will not have heard of me. This is my son, Louis."

I nodded my respects. To regain my senses for a moment I distracted myself by looking away, then saying mildly to the boy, "I see you like the door knocker."

He turned his back on me and leaned his elbows backwards on the table at which I sat. His gesture lacked respect, yet his mother did not correct him—but pressed on.

When I looked at her again, she said, "I have heard your name, Mr. Hawkins. I have heard of the tale you tell. Of an island. And treasure on it."

She drew the boy to her arm and he turned around unwillingly. Then he turned back again and began to whistle at John Culzean's dog who had appeared near the doorway. In general his mother showed, to my mind, insufficient desire to restrain him.

"Madam," I said. "May I ask where or how you heard my name?"

"People know of you," she answered, in a manner vague enough to discourage enquiry. "Your inn is well spoken of."

I paused, wishing she might have told me, then asked, "Is there perhaps a person whose acquaintance we share—"

She interrupted. "There is a person. He is not the one who spoke of you. But he is the reason I sought you. I am told you certainly know him."

These words came from her bluntly, accompanied by a stare into my eyes.

"His name, Madam? If I know his name I am sure—"

"His name is Joseph Tait."

Shock forced the politeness from me. With the lady and her son still standing before me, I sat down hard on my chair.

"Joseph Tait?" I gasped the name.

"Joseph Tait," she repeated. "I see you do know him. He's a gentleman of fortune, is he not?"

Momentarily I wondered if she knew that "gentleman of fortune" meant "pirate"—because she gave no impression that she understood the implicit disrepute.

"Madam, I did know him. Ten years ago. But I don't know anything of him now." My voice was hesitant; I was telling the truth, yet I was also withholding.

Some feeling, which may have been fear, hooded her eyes. "Do you say that he's dead?"

Although she lowered her voice from the boy, she did not say "passed away," or "ceased to be." He whistled at the dog and seemed not to have heard.

"I can't know, Madam," I replied. Then, more freely than I wished to (which measures how she took me aback), I added, "But he wasn't a man ready to die. Nor, from the evidence of my eyes, willing to."

"Where is he now?" she asked. Her words had the ring of something between a request and a demand.

I looked dumbly at her, transfixed by this Grace Richardson. She had the complexion of fine breeding and good health. Her eyes were as dark as our cliffs and she gave out an air of being generally angry, as well as afraid. In a movement as fast as a knife she grasped at her left hand with her right. Something flashed and before me on the table she placed a gold ring. On it sat four identical gems the colour of clouds.

"They are opals and this is the Richardson family's greatest heirloom. Given to my great-grandfather by the King himself after the coronation at Oxford. I offer it to you so that my son may sleep of nights."

She stepped back a pace, staring at me and her look held as much challenge as entreaty. The boy darted from the room towards the door and the dog fled his path. I know John Culzean's dog, a placid creature.

John looked at me and I looked at him, then I looked to the woman. I picked up the ring, weighed it in my hand and gave it back.

"Madam, I'm not a man in need of payment," I said, meaning to sound neither gallant nor churlish.

She spoke again. "But will you help me? Please, Mr. Hawkins?"

"Madam," I replied. "As I say—it's ten years since I saw Joseph Tait . . . I don't know . . . this needs to be talked about." My confusion and reluctance must have been plain.

But now I began to have difficulty holding her attention. She looked behind her all the time. At first I thought she was watching her son, seeking to check him as he ran about the yard. Then I realised she was looking into the greater distance as though she feared pursuers. I pressed on.

"But let me first ask, Madam—when did you last eat? This isn't business for an empty stomach."

She grew ever more agitated. "I can't wait."

"I propose that you and your boy enjoy Mr. Culzean's hospitality here. At my expense. And I promise you we shall speak at length."

She repeated, "I can't . . . I can't wait."

The way she said the words, strong at first, then forlornly, touched me deeply. My face felt hot.

She turned and looked at the coachman who paced the yard. He was a small, foxy man with a side tooth askew. I watched him as he surveyed with displeasure the boy (who was now fiddling with the water pump) and then shaded his eyes with his hand to tell the time by the position of the sun. More than once he looked firmly into the inn as if to hasten his mysterious passengers.

Grace Richardson turned her face towards me again.

"This is terrible," she said. "I'm in a dreadful bind. Mr. Hawkins— I need the help of a brave man."

She placed the tips of her fingers to the bridge of her nose and shook her head a little, clearing some painful thought or affliction. Her whole being conveyed distress—but she had a determination that seemed to grow as she stood there. Finally, she turned to face me. She had taken a decision.

"Mr. Hawkins, I shall not leave this place until you agree to help me."

John Culzean, standing a yard away, interrupted.

"Madam, it's plain that you're burdened with some fear. May we help? This is a safe and quiet place."

This released something in her.

"I must conceal us!" She called with sudden loudness, "Louis!" Then she looked from John to me. "Where do you live, Mr. Hawkins? You're in a more remote place, are you not? The coachman didn't know where."

The boy walked in. He saw me look at him and I believe he flinched; so far, I had not enjoyed his behaviour.

John Culzean said, "Madam . . . you . . . and your boy? Something or someone . . . has made you frightened?"

No answer came and I spoke. "Madam, you must tell us. If we're to help you."

She hesitated still and John Culzean said, "I have a private parlour—upstairs. Nobody can enter without my knowledge or permission," and he patted a great key at his belt. "It has an oak door."

But still Grace Richardson made no move.

I, being the son of my father and mother and therefore bound forever to a sense of what is right, spoke strongly with a view to consoling her.

"Madam, I'll discuss your request with you. I promise. But you'll talk better if you're rested. Your son too—he must be hungry."

This speech seemed to do the trick. I fancy she even sagged somewhat, as if lapsing into a safety she had not lately known. She stood there, motionless, looked up and spoke to me.

"Kindness is the greatest of virtues—" but, as though in pain, stopped herself from saying more. Until that moment I had never encountered a more vulnerable or needful human being.

The boy came to the door and peered in. He turned away again. To my great annoyance he bent and picked up a stone which he then shied after John's peaceful dog. The animal was not struck but it ran and hid with its tail between its legs. John and I exchanged glances and I moved towards the door.

The boy saw my face and my look of disapproval.

I said, with some asperity, "That is a kind dog. And he's old, he needs care."

The boy looked at the cowering dog, then at me. He next did a thing I found remarkable—he came towards me, leaned his head upon my arm and put his thumb in his mouth like a baby. I took it for a gesture of apology and we stood there for a moment, until he ran off again, all lively and swift.

Silently but with tenderness, John in his big, kindly bulk, guided the woman towards the staircase. The boy followed her and as they climbed past the portrait of the King, he looked back at me and waved. The flash of his sudden young smile seemed to light the dark stairwell.

I called. "And your luggage, Madam? Shall I have it brought to you?"

No answer. I waited. The woman fought with embarrassment. She halted on the staircase and spoke down between the banisters. "We foundered at Yeovil," she said. "We have no bags. I am sorry."

The coachman, who suprisingly requested no ostling for his team, stood impatiently at the door, listening to this exchange. I produced a coin.

"Thank you for waiting," I said. "The lady and the boy won't be travelling onwards."

"There was no bags at Yeovil," he murmured. "Nor before Yeovil, neither."

He was a bandy-legged man, surly and unpleasant, of a sort often sits astride the box of a coach. I looked closely at him. He had a hooky nose and his eyes were too beady for my liking. Or was it the case that my suspicions had in general begun to run high, like a sudden tide along a reef?

"But where did they join you? And where did she say they were bound?"

"I answer few questions these days," he said.

To which I replied, "Then you'll oblige me by answering no questions to anyone else. Did you bring any goods for me?"

The coachman replied, "Nothing for no one, except some bottles for a Squire Trelawney."

"He's my good friend," I said. "I'll take them to him."

This disobliging little man turned to his coach, extracted the squire's goods, handed them to me gracelessly and climbed up. Within a moment he was wheeling his team from the yard of the Royal George.

Some impulse made me look up towards the window of the private parlour. I saw there, as in a framed picture, the face of the boy who gazed down towards the roadway. I thought: I shall not forget that look. Then I turned and followed his glance. Nothing was to be seen, just the departing coach and beyond it a distant horseman, and some sea birds wheeling in the blue sky.

—❦—

Ch. 2—

Violent Encounters

When I am beset with any difficulty I seek a quiet space in order to think. I strapped the squire's parcel to my saddle and set out to The Hall.

My heart jangled. I found myself in a state of dreadful excitement, in a way I had never known. Since Treasure Island, fear was long familiar to me and I felt some of that—but there was tenderness mixed in with it, and optimism and sudden uncertainty. No woman had so caught my attention. But then I had never seen a woman whose face and presence seemed so perfect, so exciting. She had the neat and beautiful ears I have often observed in people of high breeding, and her eyebrows formed winsome arches. I knew by her voice and speech that she came from people who possessed an admirable place in the world.

Ordinarily I met few women—farmers' daughters or other parish girls. They had little to offer outside of giggles or unseemly boldness. None of them met my mother's aspirations and therefore I had not yet thought seriously of marriage. Once or twice, a girl from one of the inland parishes, or from as far away as Bristol or Exeter, was brought to the inn by a female relative seeking to fasten the girl's future. But my mother believed we might now, with our new wealth and success, move in different circles and she conveyed discouragement to such callers. She would, I expected, my heart leaping at the thought, take a different view of the woman in the green cloak.

Oh, that lovely face! And the bearing, the shapeliness, the fine, proud head and neck! It became my profound belief that no woman so exquisite had ever been in our parish until that day. And the need in her, her requirement for kindness, for bravery! I was in a mood nobody had ever caused in me. All around, the countryside seemed daz-zlingly bright.

I forced myself away from these brilliant sensations in order to think about this stranger's request and the contradictions it provoked. She wanted to find Joseph Tait. Impossible! And profoundly unwise!

Yet—I felt instantly moved to think I would help this woman as mightily as I could. My heart rose to her situation. She and her son travelled with only the clothes they wore. We must remedy that at once! And I felt sad and clumsy that I had embarrassed her when I asked about her baggage.

But—how shall I answer her questions? Must I be truthful and tell her how I last saw Joseph Tait? Kneeling with the other two pirates, Tom Morgan and poor, foolish Dick Johnson by that final spit of sand on Treasure Island as the *Hispaniola* cleared the North Inlet? They were calling and wailing, begging us not to maroon them. One of them—was it Tait?—cursed us and our generations to come and sent a musket ball whistling over my head and through our mainsail. Is she not too frail to hear such truths?

And what must I ask her? Must I ask her how such an ill-starred pi-rate and such a remarkable woman had once related to each other? I felt thankful that she had not used the word "husband." But why did her son not sleep easy at night? Could the boy be Tait's son? That consideration led me towards thoughts I did not want. As for "gentle-man of fortune"—shall I leave her in the innocence she seemed to ex-hibit? Or shall I disclose the irony of the term?

Squire Trelawney professed himself pleased to see me and thanked me for fetching his mail coach delivery. We repaired to his dining room for luncheon and I was reminded of his capacity for food. Halfway through a meat pie—or, rather, the squire was three-quarter-way through, and I a quarter—I began to tell him of the day's awk-ward but exciting event.

"Tait?!" he exploded in a spray of crumbs. "We should've hung him. Blackhearted lout! I hope he's come to coral by now!"

"I don't know what to do regarding this woman," I said. "The boy's face pulled at my heart."

I did not mention my surprise that his mother took no account of her son's unruliness. The squire is robust on discipline of the young. A drop or two of red wine splashed on the back of his hairy hand. He reflected on my words. After a moment he said, "Get rid of her. If needs be, fund her in the next stage of her journey. Anything to do with Tait is bound to be trebly bad."

"What's strange," I offered, "is that although she seems to have no natural place with such a villain, she's had a son by him. Or so I judge."

"What d'you say her name was? Sarah something?"

I replied. "Grace. Grace Richardson. I feel from her speech she may be Scotch. And of good family, I think."

Squire Trelawney said, "No such thing as a Scotchman of good birth. Who can trust 'em? I've never transacted business with a Scotchman. Never shall. 'Cept with a sabre."

The squire's heated opinions on the Scotch gave me room to think some more. Already I was observing that I could not concentrate on anything but this strange, vital woman. I tried to imagine what she looked like, waiting now in the upstairs parlour of the Royal George. Her face would not come back clearly to my mind and I quickened as I tried to recollect it, remembering only the spray of freckles at her throat.

"How's your mother?" asked the squire.

Into my head leapt the crazy notion that I had known Grace Richardson for a long time. I also knew this to be untrue. And, as I now understand myself somewhat more clearly than I then did, I recognise that when I think I have known someone, even though I have never met them before, it means I am taking an especial interest in them.

"She's very well," I said.

I left The Hall to ride back to the Royal George. Unless John

Culzean had learned anything contradictory in my absence I proposed to bring the woman and the boy to the Admiral Benbow. We now had a set of rooms good enough for any visitor of any station in life. There, my shrewd mother might, as one woman sympathetic to another, discover useful truths. Then, in a few days, I could advance gently my opinion that Joseph Tait ought never be sought.

Of those three castaways, Tait was the buccaneer I had least known. In Dr. Livesey's opinion, Dick Johnson could not have lasted more than a further week or two, given the marsh fever he had contracted. Tom Morgan had the symptoms of apoplexy. Tait was the roughest, the hardest of the three.

My worried thoughts were interrupted.

"Ho, now!" came a cold voice right beside me. My horse started.

Within a gateway under a tree, almost concealed from the road, sat a horseman of unusual appearance. He was a big man, as burly as the squire—but most deformed; a severe hunchback.

"Ho, there!" he called again, although I had stopped a few feet from him. His tone had the ugliness of mockery.

"Good-day," I replied.

"Where's a man to get work round here?" he asked—and added, "sir!"

I do not like insolence. And I do not like eyes that glitter.

"What kind of work?" Answering him civilly was difficult.

"Masoning. Where 'ud there be a stone quarry in these parts—sir?"

"Twenty miles away the nearest, I believe."

"And where 'ud that be at—sir?"

"Place called Otterford," I said.

"Where 'ud that be—sir?"

"Past Clovelly. By Horns Cross." A shortness came into my tone—and my skin shrivelled at the sight of this fellow.

"No stone-carvin' then, round about here? No gravestones needed 'n that? See! I be well fitted—sir."

He drew from a saddlebag a small, thick leather pouch and from it took three hammers. Their silver heads shone like weapons.

"The work these a' done—sir. Oh, some work! Crack anythin', these 'ammers. Like it was eggs—sir."

"In that case," I said, "Otterford's the place for you. It lies that way," and I pointed him in the general direction.

"Ale 'ouses on the way—sir?" he asked.

"There are many," I said. "No traveller need go thirsty." I did not want this creature in the Benbow.

He gripped my gaze with his nasty eyes. When he turned in his saddle to restore his hammers to the saddlebag his hump seemed to shift a little on his back, as though made of loose flesh.

"Good-day," I said, "and good luck go with you."

"Oh, I aww-l-ways 'as good luck—sir."

The hump and the way he drawled "aww-l-ways" gave me a shiver. Before I rounded the turn I glanced back. He had ridden to the middle of the roadway and was sitting there, staring after me like some dangerous, misshapen bird.

After the hunchback, thoughts of Joseph Tait felt almost sweet. Tait had been a handsome, though surly, man. He never led any event, but he followed every bad thing with vigour and bile. Yes, I thought, I do believe he was the one who fired on the *Hispaniola* for, although I could not see closely enough to identify which was which, the others seemed too feeble—or too drunk—for such vicious energy.

Was Tait still alive? That was going to become the heaviest question of all. Of the three, he seemed the best bet to survive. Might he not have made a raft? Hailed a passing ship and spun them some untruth about shipwreck? Recovered Ben Gunn's coracle, rebuilt it and caught the tide? Or did he stay and establish himself out there? Bought favours with silver bars from curious explorers? In this back-and-forth reverie I reached the Royal George—but I had made up my mind what to do.

Nothing afterwards, on that lovely afternoon, fell out as I expected. First, John Culzean told me he had gleaned no fresh details of the strangers' story. He said that neither woman nor boy could eat quickly enough—as though they had not eaten for some time. Perhaps, he thought, they also ate rapidly in order to move onwards as soon as possible. But after eating, neither could then stay awake, he said.

"My heart's touched by them, Jim. But Jim, isn't he the wild lad, eh? No good behaviour there—and she don't hold him back. And yet, there's a softness to the boy."

"I know what you mean"—but Grace Richardson heard our voices and appeared on the staircase. The boy came running down, whizzed past John and me without a word and out into the sunshine. I issued an invitation for mother and son to stay at the Admiral Benbow and she accepted.

As we prepared to leave I asked John quietly, "Has a hunchback come past here lately?"

"No, Jim. No reports of such."

"I met one on the road," I said. "Unpleasant fellow."

"They be mainly harmless poor little things."

"Not this one," I said. "This one's even bigger than you, John. If he should call, keep an eye to him."

My little party set out for the Admiral Benbow, a mile and a half away. I gave Grace Richardson my horse and walked alongside, holding the bridle. The pair seemed refreshed but she still looked sombre with anxiety. I wondered by what name I should think of her: "Grace" felt too familiar as yet; "Miss" Richardson felt unseemly, given that she had a son; and she could not be thought of as "Mrs." Richardson were she the partner of Joseph Tait. I resolved to think of her by her full name until, as I hoped, the familiarity caused by acquaintance should draw me closer—in every way—and I might then call her "Grace."

The boy, Louis, had been renewed in energy. He ran ahead seeking a view of the sea. From a point in our hilly little lane one may see down to the coast of Cornwall. Louis's mother entreated him to stay within sight and looked all about her constantly.

"Madam, this is a quiet place," I assured her. "Let him run, it will make him feel well."

Suddenly, my bones froze to hear a terrible scream somewhere in the road below. I looked up at Grace Richardson and saw terror scrawled across her face.

"God-and-honour!" she gasped. "Louis!"

"Don't move!" I commanded her and ran onwards with all my speed.

Around the corner, by the roadside, stood a richly harnessed horse. Nearby, half on the grass margin, half on the lane's hard ground, lay Louis. A young man was kicking him brutally, and I must say my thought was that Louis had provoked his anger. But this was too dangerous. A dandy by his clothing, the man towered above the boy. Each kick landed to an oath of foul abuse. In that blurred moment it seemed to me he meant to kill Louis, now crumpling under the savage boots.

The assailant turned at my shouts. He was dressed as fancily as any man I had ever seen, more suited to the fopperies of Bath than this quiet country track. I shouted again, some words of abuse. It worked; I drew his attention upon me and the dandy reached for his sword. To lure him further from the boy, who now lay stock-still, I backed away, taunting. I was unarmed; men around these parts only wear their swords when travelling far.

At this moment Grace Richardson rode into view, in wild distress. Her screams distracted the attacker from me and he rushed towards her, shouting oaths and dragging his own horse by the reins. My judgement of the incident changed—because he evidently knew her and knew her well enough to have some reason for hatred. This was no random attack provoked by a boy's impertinence.

The black-wigged fop was squat and fat but he was agile. I ran after him. He raised his sword to cut the woman from the saddle. Thin and light though I am, I hurled myself at the backs of his legs, intending to bring him low and then, I thought, sit upon him in some fashion until help might be summoned.

My arms made contact with his legs and I achieved my aim; I tripped him and the fellow came down. His horse's hooves flurried near my head and retreated. The fop's head met loudly with the small rocks that scatter this ground. He grunted and rolled back half upon me; his clattering sword fell past my face. Then he rolled forwards again like a lugger unsafely anchored. And next he moved no more. His horse pranced, slamming its hooves again on the ground near my head and then it bolted.

There were some seconds of silence. I knew my hands had been grazed, my knees, elbows and a part of my cheekbone torn. I also knew my opponent was dead. Hauling myself out from under him, I saw Grace Richardson dismount.

That scene is a picture in my mind today—the sunshine, the blue sky, the body on the road, his shiny buckled shoes, the curly wig askew, the kicked and silent boy, the mother wild with distress, the echoing hooves of the riderless horse. And me, rising, one knee on the hard lane, with the coldness of dread striking my face like ice.

Grace Richardson raced to where her son lay. I rose and followed, my breath short with fear and effort. Then I felt her relief—the boy had remained motionless out of instinct rather than injury. No mark showed of any kick having landed directly upon his bare head. Being young and elastic he had suffered little other than fright. His mother cradled him, crooning his name.

"Are you safe, oh, Louis, are you safe?!" she cried. Her words, her pain, ripped into me.

"Is he safe?" I heard myself echo.

"Yes he's safe, yes, yes, he is, yes, you are safe, you are safe! Dearest Louis! Dear, dear one!"

With some dread I returned to the prone body of the fop. His face lay sideways. A small line of his own black-red blood stained his lace collar. I tried to feel for his heartbeat. The gold on his ring had been severely scratched against the rock where he met his death. In desperate events we often observe small details.

As I stood from the corpse, my hand brushed his blue silken coat. The fabric's excellent quality jolted me. I tried to make my thoughts follow a straight line. My mind said fiercely, "The next thing! Decide the next thing!"

"Madam," I called. "Who is he? D'you think he was alone?"

Louis was now standing, confused and tearful.

"Who is he?" I cried again. All of me now wished to scream and roar.

She hesitated then answered desperately, "I cannot say . . . I, I do not know. But he is often with companions."

"Companions? Will they be following?" I now knew that she must have expected hostile pursuit, hence all her anxious behaviour and her desire to move on, to hide. Therefore, for the third time, I asked, "Madam, who is he?" I must have known that his name would prove significant.

She caught my firmness and gave in.

"I have been part of great trouble between his family and mine. He hoped to be my husband. If he is now dead I need no longer conceal his name. He is the Duke of Berwick."

I knew the name. Favourites of the King; raisers of militia; heroes of foreign battles. I had been involved in the death of a prominent man. Danger. Confusion. I did not know whether to go back whence we came or forwards to my own home.

The boy, Louis, settled matters. With a strange turn of his head he said to me, "There are others nearby."

I looked at his mother, as if to ask her how he knew.

She stroked his head and murmured, "You may believe him. Louis often knows what's going to happen."

———✦———

Ch. 3 —

Under Siege Again

We raced from that fatal spot. My mind raced too. First, in confusion, I thought: we must go back to the Royal George—as I had no wish that my mother's life should be disturbed. Then I changed my mind. None of this violence was my doing. The man brought it upon himself. I had witnesses. Anyway, whoever found him would think he had fallen off his horse. But no, I reasoned—he had drawn his sword, it lay on the ground beside him. That would indicate a fight—and his horse had gone. But—if he hoped to marry the lady, why did he wish to cut at her and her boy?

My next thought was of safety—for myself, for all of us. That decided me upon my own inn. I could not hide Grace Richardson and her son from a troop of soldiers, but I could create some kind of shelter, or send for help.

Helter-skelter, we reached the Admiral Benbow. Louis had recovered quickly and his mother did not bother to remount. I led our jingling horse and Louis clung to my arm. His mother's beauty seemed heightened, that cream-and-gold skin improved (were that possible) by the flush of this agitation. Though we had entered frightful straits her face fascinated me more than before.

At the door we saw my workman, Tom Taylor. When his father died, my mother hired Tom; since then, I had taken on his wife and their son, a youth of seventeen or so. Tom saw our bruises and the air of distress we carried.

"We may be followed, Tom," I said. "I fear we've run across a violent gang."

Tom Taylor's quick intelligence was different from the snail's pace at which he usually worked. He immediately dispatched his son, Joshua, to fetch Dr. Livesey. Then Tom bolted all the doors and bar-shuttered the windows. The inn was empty; this was scarcely yet four o'clock, with all tranquil. But in my sinking heart I knew that fear and danger had once more come to the Admiral Benbow.

I still retained the double-barrelled pistols Long John Silver gave me the day the pirates turned upon each other. Tom Taylor had his own fowling piece. Tom's wife, Clara, took charge of Grace Richardson and Louis. As they went upstairs, I urged them to sit quietly and told Clara to advise my mother that I would soon explain the whole tale.

However, when her curiosity is roused, no force in the world restrains my mother. Within moments I heard her footstep on the stair. Tom and I sat, our weapons charged on the table in front of us.

"What have we here?" my mother asked, in the unexpected gloom of the parlour. "Not another siege?"

My mind's ear heard again the *tap-tap* of blind Pew's awful stick upon the frozen road. That night long past, when she and I trawled through the dead captain's sea chest, Pew's blackguards hammered down the inn door moments after we'd fled.

"Mother," I said, a touch sharply, for at that moment I wanted none of her blame. "This wasn't any of my doing. We've sent for help."

She disregarded my words.

"There are two more guns," she said. "In the linen press upon the staircase. I'll fetch them."

I began to resist. Tom Taylor shook his head at me: don't object. She returned, drew up a chair, sat down and inspected the weapons she had brought.

"Mother," I said, a little impatiently. "I'd feel easier if you—"

"I've no doubt you would," she interrupted. "But if hard times come, who's to reload for you?"

Once I thought my mother a frail creature. On the night of the buccaneer's destruction of the inn she had seemed about to faint.

Since my return from Treasure Island, though, I felt she had taken a new lease on life. Others saw it too.

Dr. Livesey said to me, "Many women flourish in widowhood, Jim. She'd too much respect for her husband to permit herself to be seen as stronger than him. I often observe that quality. Always indicates an excellent woman."

The "excellent woman," with, I saw, a small smile in these grim circumstances, said to me, "And I'll greatly look forward to hearing about this lady you've brought to meet me. How," she asked, her tone growing drier, "did she hear of you?"

I blushed. It must be the case, I knew, that my boastful tales of Treasure Island had reached Grace Richardson—and thus had my wide mouth brought trouble.

Our cat, Christmas, painted my legs with his tail, strolled away, then stiffened and hissed. Hooves rang in the lane. It was too soon for help to be here. We had been followed.

Tom Taylor held up his fingers to count. One. Two. Three. Christmas leapt for the stairs, arching there at bay.

"Three," Tom whispered. He listened again. "No." He changed his mind. "Four," he decided.

The hooves stopped; a horse snickered; metal clinked. We sat in silence. The wooden pistol butts grew damp in my hand. A gull cried overhead. Some conversation took place outside, too low to hear the words. One set of hooves sauntered closer. A powerful knuckle rapped high on the door, at the height of a horseman still in the saddle. We did not reply.

"Oy-up in there!" came a voice, not a local man. He breathed heavily.

Silence.

Another man swore. My hands began to tremble. Oh—the many nights of waking, sweating with the island's fear! Had terror left me weakened? I blinked. My stomach burned.

"In there!" called the man again. "Hark! Come out someone.

Out!" And there followed another knock high up on the door and another oath.

"They be vile," whispered Tom.

A thought arrived, a thought I feared. It made me ask: why am I doing this? Why have I let this happen to me, to all of us? The answer was plain. But I knew that if I formed the words in my mind I might begin to blame her who had brought this to us. Yet I could neither escape nor deny the fact. All this trouble came from the woman who, a few hours ago, had so urgently disturbed my pleasant life.

The hooves clinked away from the door and around to the side of the inn. A breeze creaked the sign a little. The silence continued. Then, like a sudden storm, a murderous pounding rattled the wooden shutter right beside my head. I all but discharged my pistol in the fright it gave me.

"Come out you!—" and more imprecation followed.

Some talk happened among them. Again, I could not catch the words. Then came another oath, and another.

"How they charm us," whispered my mother.

"Who's in there?" called a different voice, as tough as the first. But they were yet smooth voices. Whatever their state, or habitual behaviour, these riders had been raised among gentlemen.

Once more that strange, dark silence fell. I looked at my companions-at-arms. Tom was as calm as marble, his musket lying gently across his forearm, right hand near the trigger. My mother seemed the very portrait of alert serenity, listening intently to every move outside. Suddenly she hissed at us: "Down! Down!"

A fusillade of three musket balls struck the shutter nearest us. We threw ourselves from our seats and sent chairs crashing across the floor.

Their shots did not penetrate, but the thick old wood splintered; the acrid stench of the gunpowder floated slowly in and watered our eyes as we lay beneath the tables. There was a *ching!* of their reloading. I raised my head. Tom pointed: they had aimed their fire at one concentrated place. It seemed plain that they meant to punch a hole in the shutters through which they might discover what—or who—lay within.

The next fusillade hit the very same spot and one musket ball penetrated. It broke through the glass and trickled to the floor beneath the window. My mouth and lips had turned bone-dry. I looked at the splinters high up in the shutter and the small round hole in the glass pane. They were firing from horseback and from no more than a yard's distance. The next salvo might well make an opening large enough to see through. My hair filled with sweat.

Tom and I knelt to face the besieged window and my mother crawled to a post behind us, to my left and out of the line of fire. That part of the parlour still seemed as neat as ninepence. The whole situation, of such a peaceful room under attack by powder and shot, felt beyond belief.

Now my measure of their strategy was confirmed. At the point where the musket balls had weakened the wood, a regiment of swordsmen, or so it sounded, hacked and cut and hammered. They beat the timbers with their hilts, they slashed with their blades, they shouted and cursed and then they attacked again. The noise was as loud as a mob. Failing to prise the shutters apart they drove deep cuts into the wood. With oaths and grunts they withdrew their blades and cut again. Now we all lay flat on our faces and I felt my water nearly burst from me.

I heard another horse come forwards. Suddenly, a pounding like the end of the world hit our shutters—a barrage of blows that made the ground tremble. A pause was taken, broken by a scream.

"Hell's hounds, I'll do it—I *will*!"

That voice—it snarled in my brain. Where had I heard it? And lately?

The hunchback with his hammers! That figure on the horse! The word "vile" can be rearranged to make the word "evil." My mind danced in panic. He must be their hired man—to travel with them and use his awful force and presence in their interests!

A voice sought to restrain him but the hunchback, and it was he, screamed and launched himself and his hammers again and again at our old shutters. He bent the boards in far enough to hit and break some panes of glass. The noise became awful. Mixed in with it came his screams. But our old wood resisted him—my grandfather built this inn.

The hunchback subsided. I heard a muttering from him; he had murder in his voice. That frightening silence fell again, slow and black. What now? Our determination to defend ourselves did not keep our dread at bay.

Long minutes passed by, minutes full of fear. Tom Taylor sniffed the air and looked uneasy. He harked with a hand to his ear. I shook my head in uncomprehending annoyance.

"They be making something of a bomb," he whispered.

Outside, the whole world was still; the birds had been frightened away by the gunshots. A horse snickered again, another jingled its harness, and once or twice one of the men grunted as if asking for something to be handed to him.

In a crisis, which is worse: noise or silence? I fancy silence is; stillness can aggravate fear.

The spokesman, the one whose voice we first heard, called again. This time he chose to make almost an oration.

"Halloo! Halloo in there! We believe you are harbouring murderers. The corpse of a nobleman, freshly killed, lies near here. Nobody has passed us in the opposite direction and we must deduce from your fortification of yourselves that you have something to hide. Release them who did the deed and we will ride away content. If you don't, we will oblige you to come out!"

As before we never answered. Next we heard a flame being struck. Directly beneath the nearest window sounded the fizzing of a spark along a fuse. Then came the receding clink of hooves as of horses being hauled back along the roadway. The fuse hissed.

But over all these sounds rang a new noise—of other hooves, galloping hard down our lane. Many riders, a small troop by their sounds, thundered towards the Admiral Benbow. Our besiegers out-side swore again. But the fuse fizzed its deadly course, stemming the rise of joy in our hearts.

My mind raced. What should I do?

First, I listened. The fuse, from its smell and noise, ran along the windowsill outside the shutter. I looked at Tom but he knew less than I did how to cope with this danger. At the same time, the galloping outside seemed to draw ever nearer. Were we to be blown to pieces at the very moment we were being rescued?

Not fully knowing what I was doing and yet with thoughts as clear as a bell, I slid across the floor avoiding the shards of broken glass. I pinched open the window; then I squeezed the shutter outwards, but only by an inch. No hostile face, no gun barrel greeted me. Our ene-mies had turned to face the oncoming riders.

I looked down. A thin string of smoke rose from the window ledge and there, beneath my face, snaked the fuse. Never did a serpent spit such venom as that red tip of fizzing cord. The box towards which it raced now stood no more than two inches from the little running flame. Not only that—if our attackers turned to watch their bomb and saw me, I might expect to receive a musket ball in the eye.

I squeezed open the shutter another inch. Nobody shouted. I next brought the butt of my pistol down slowly and, pressing hard, sought to extinguish the fuse. But when I took the pistol away, the flame still hissed and burned along the tarred cord. I stopped, stepped back a moment. Luck seemed to be with me and when I next went to the window nobody swore at me—and nobody fired because the galloping hooves had clattered to a halt. A loud commotion began in the lane.

Wetting my fingers, I doused the cord by gripping it tight between thumb and forefinger. The burn of that fuse stung for days.

———— ⚓ ————

Ch. 4—

The Majesty of the Law

Our rescuers were not led by Dr. Livesey. Tom Taylor's son had not found him and had therefore raced to The Hall. It was Squire Trelawney who bellowed, "To order, gentlemen! To order!"

"Do you dare, sir?" came one of the voices that moments ago had terrified us.

"I do dare. Put down those weapons."

"I beg you to know who I am!"

"And be you the King's son himself," retorted the squire, "you'll yet obey His Majesty's law in our parish. Now dismount, sir, and ready yourself to answer questions."

"I *am* the law," replied the man. "I am such law as you shall ever meet."

Something in his manner caused the squire to stall. He asked, "Explain yourself."

"Our companion, a most distinguished nobleman and my kinsman, has been foully killed."

"Aye. Two of my men are removing his corpse," butted in the squire.

Our chief besieger retorted, "And this inn here harbours the murderer. As well as two fugitives."

The squire grunted. "Any man may say those things. That gives no proof you're the law."

"I am Sir Thomas Maltby. My dead cousin is—was—the Duke of Berwick."

Another of the besiegers spoke; he had a trace of the foreign in his accent. Judging by his voice he sought to ease matters by explanation, while yielding no ground.

"Sir Thomas Maltby is one of His Majesty's court counsellors. As such he has the brief to impose the King's law wheresoever he finds it needed in the realm. I am his clerk."

My heart froze over. A court counsellor had the right to hold an immediate investigation, call a trial and pass judgement—judge, jury and, by all accounts, executioner. I had heard travellers to the inn speak with dread of the summary law practised by such figures. This man had the power to try me and hang me in my own yard! This very day!

Squire Trelawney understood the matter too. His tone cooled a little.

"Our local magistrate will be of great assistance to you, sir," he boomed. "I can vouch for him and I expect him presently."

"Your local magistrate isn't here, however," said Sir Thomas Maltby, not far off contempt. "And I doubt he is known personally to the King. In which case, I judge we need the administration of the law."

Squire Trelawney fell silent. This was unusual enough to alarm me further. All the squire's solutions contain more action than thought. In the quiet of the moment something was once more rapped fiercely hard upon our door.

"In there?! Come out! It's against the King's law to harbour criminals. Out, murderers! Out!" It was Maltby.

My mother, pink in the cheeks with indignation, whispered, "Murderers? I shall become one if he uses such names again."

The squire intervened, but he was somewhat quiet.

"I know this inn as well as I know my own fireside. There's no murderer here, either in residence or visiting."

"Well, then," rang the voice of another of the attackers, a voice I had not heard before, a drinker's voice. "Let them come out and show they have nothing to fear from the law."

The three of us inside held a silent council of war with our eyebrows. Then I slowly opened the shutter half-wide and looked out without showing myself.

My view was at an angle but I could still observe. The scene in our yard looked like the prelude to a small but fierce battle. Our attackers sat their horses in a line, guns held pointed at the squire and his riders; he had armed several of the men working in his estate. A little way back, the hunchback watched them all from his saddle, his eyes as cold as black stones.

While staring straight at Squire Trelawney, Maltby called to me from the side of his mouth, "The window won't do. People enter and leave their houses by the door. Unless they be thieves as well as murderers."

Behind me I heard my mother's angry gasp. At that moment I saw a swift movement outside and something flashed through the air. A small hammer, thrown by the hunchback, struck the open shutter, banging it back upon my fingers, bruising several knuckles. As I slammed the shutter closed, the squire fired his pistol in the air above the hunchback's head.

The squire roared. "Next it'll be your eye, sirrah. And you, Maltwich, or whatever your confounded name is—restrain that cripple or he'll die!"

The hunchback screamed an oath so foul I blushed that my mother, even though accustomed to the rough words of drinking sailors, should have it in her ears.

"Make them open the door and we shall take no more action," cried Maltby.

In a reluctant voice the squire called, "All square, Jim?"

Slowly, Tom Taylor and I opened the heavy door a foot or so. I watched through the crack of the jamb but could only see the squire and his men. Some of them now quickened, as if the strangers had given a sign they meant to rush the door or fire upon us.

"Stay where you are, Jim," called the squire. "Don't come out—"

Maltby interrupted him. "We'll rest our weapons. And we'll expect all who call themselves 'gentlemen' to do the same."

I heard the slow clang of a gun being lowered on the ground. Other clangs followed. The squire stood all his men at ease. He beckoned at the door for us to throw forth our arms. Tom Taylor walked out and laid down his fowling piece.

But I made no move to walk out. I retained one pistol and pitched the other out onto the flagstones. All they saw of me was the hand and arm which threw my gun. I stepped back again. In the months ahead I would thank repeatedly those friendly shadows behind the Admiral Benbow's heavy door: they saved my life more than once.

Maltby moved forwards and now I saw him better. He bore a strong resemblance to the man who died in the lane. Less foppish but of obvious wealth, he also ran to fat, with a jowl of bacon, hands like small hams and large, clever eyes. One of his companions looked a learned man; the clerk, I reckoned. The other, to judge from his complexion, took his pleasure from hunting, soldiering and drinking. These three dressed ornately. And there too sat the hunchback, still as a vulture, his eyes never blinking.

Maltby roared towards the inn door, "Did you kill the Duke of Berwick?"

"Jim, don't speak," shouted the squire.

"You are harbouring a fugitive and her brat," roared Maltby again. "And you, sir"—to the squire—"are aiding and abetting them."

He walked forwards and gathered his companions closer to him. "By the power vested in me by His Majesty King George, I call a court into session."

This was a most dangerous kind of adversary—a man of swift, accurate thought, who took strong decisions quickly but still had the gift of adjusting to his opponents' responses.

When the authority of the moment had fallen upon everyone, Maltby's clerk said in his thin French voice, "We shall need to be seated."

"Very well," replied Squire Trelawney slowly, and called towards our door, "A bench, if you will, Jim." The squire seemed baffled and anxious.

Tom's son, Joshua, approached from behind the squire's troop. With his father he began to set out some benches in the air.

"And we shall need a table to write upon," demanded the clerk.

Tom and Joshua rolled an empty barrel to a point between the benches. Maltby and his clerk seated themselves with some officiousness. The third man of their company joined them, and this trio, who, minutes before, had been attempting to destroy our lives and property, established themselves as a bench of the King's law. The hunchback's eyes flickered upon everything.

At that moment an apple landed on the top of the empty barrel with such force that the skin burst and splashed juice on Maltby. He roared in fury. I knew who had thrown the apple from the upstairs window and although I smiled I wished fervently he did not do so again. Useless to hope that; another apple flew, all but hitting the thin clerk. Maltby rose in something of a rage.

I said to my mother, "Go up and tell the boy to stop throwing apples."

She smiled too, despite the gravity of the moment and tiptoed up the stairs.

Maltby stood there, deciding whether to attack again; he changed his mind; he meant to waste no time and he sat down.

"In the name of His Majesty, King George (how he rolled the words), I call forth—now, this moment—the landlord of this inn."

But a voice that I knew and I loved called clearly through the still afternoon air.

"Not, sir, without my permission!"

Dr. Livesey walked calmly round the gable of the inn. He stood by the large tub of bright flowers my mother maintains beneath the bow windows.

"Who the devil are you?" snarled Maltby.

"I'm the true law in these parts," said Dr. Livesey.

"And I am the King's law," retorted Maltby.

"A fiddlestick's end," cried Dr. Livesey. "When a troop of my neighbours must ride hard on a peaceful day—I know that villains, and not the King's men, have come among us."

"I am Sir Thomas Maltby. Cousin to the murdered Duke of Berwick. I am a court counsellor."

Dr. Livesey raised an eyebrow. "Then, sir, you'd better learn the running of the King's law. And as it seems you don't know it, I'll cite it to you." He intoned, "'Where a magistrate sits or is available to sit, the court counsellor shall declare himself unnecessary to the occasion, *unless called upon* by such magistrate, as the magistrate is one of the four corners of English law.' And, sir, I *don't* call upon you."

Dr. Livesey clapped his hands vigorously, once, twice. "In other words, sir, as this is a local matter, it'll be judged locally and I'm the local judge. If you'll understand me, sir."

The sarcasm had changed hands; I recognised Dr. Livesey's wit, his playing with the word "sir." There entered upon Maltby and his party the first sign of confusion I had seen. His clerk made a general motion of his arm.

"I have not my law books with me, sir," began the clerk, "but I know that the court counsellor—"

"You know nothing of that. Or of any such sort," interrupted Dr. Livesey. "And you have shown us no proof of your standing."

"A murder has been committed," said Maltby. "A distinguished man from a noble family has been cut down. We believe the murderers to be here. I believe myself to be looking towards one—" he turned his gaze to the inn door—"and I believe the accomplices and accessories to that murder to be concealed within those premises."

"Do you intend to prove this?" asked the doctor. "Did you see this murder? Where are your witnesses? You throw accusations, gentlemen, and you set yourselves up as judge and jury. I don't know who the devil you are. You could be Diabolus himself. But whoever you are, sir, I'll arrest you if you breach our peace, I stake my wig on that. So do me the favour of stepping down. You'll defer, sir, to a known and sworn magistrate of the King. Namely myself, Livesey is my name."

Maltby and his clerk conferred. Then Maltby spoke.

"Very well, sir. But we make a serious complaint and therefore call for arrests to be made. Our companion, my cousin, has been murdered in your parish. His horse has been stolen."

"How d'you know 'twas murder?" asked the doctor. "Or horse stealing? I see you choose capital offences."

"We believe ourselves exact in making our accusations. Those we accuse lurk inside that inn."

"No," I cried out, "the truth is—"

Dr. Livesey cut me off. "Silence—all round! I'll conduct this investigation according to my position and experience. Above all, according to the law. I'll begin to take depositions immediately."

He walked forwards to Maltby.

"Give me your sword, sir. It isn't permitted for a plaintiff any more than a defendant to bear arms during an enquiry-at-law."

No man ever parted more reluctantly with a weapon. Dr. Livesey collected the other swords.

"Those men are armed," protested Maltby, indicating the squire's little troop.

"You haven't alleged against them," replied Dr. Livesey. "So they don't form part of this enquiry. Now sir, I remind you—you're not to leave this ground unless ordered by me," and the doctor swept past Tom Taylor, past me hidden behind the door and into the foreshadowed parlour of the inn.

Tom followed him and began to open the shutters. I saw him call Dr. Livesey's attention to the damage that had been caused, and he pointed out the unexploded box beneath the window. Dr. Livesey pressed his nose with a finger, a sign I knew to mean annoyance in him. In a moment or two Tom walked past me.

"Squire Trelawney," he called in a loud voice (there had long been a public official lying in wait inside Tom). The squire walked past my place of concealment and I closed the door behind him.

Soon, some change of mood began to take place in the parlour. Dr. Livesey ceased to glance at me, and he and the squire spoke in voices too soft for my hearing.

The afternoon fidgeted onwards, as the rooks tumbled about the sky, the gulls wheeled and the horses lowered their big necks towards the grass by our yard's edge. Nobody outside spoke.

Suddenly I heard my voice called. "Mister James Haw-kins!" I thought, Tom has begun to let his temporary court duties affect him too much.

Across the parlour, Squire Trelawney leaned back on a high settle. Dr. Livesey sat at one of our older tables, ironically the same one where Captain Billy Bones habitually drank.

"Jim," the doctor said. "You're to tell me as clearly as possible what occurred." His gaze did not waver.

I began and finished my tale without interruption. But my heart was stopped by the gravity of the doctor's expression. Then he spoke.

"Jim, I haven't formally constituted this as a hearing. You'll observe that you took no oath. I have my reasons for this. In this we have a bad business. I fear I hear the footsteps of the hangman."

Ch. 5—

Fugitives All

Dr. Livesey sighed; he had taken on a burden that disturbed him by its weight.

He continued, "I believe I haven't the legal power to contain these men. At the very least they'll demand that you be held as a suspect. If that must take place, then I fear higher courts will come upon us and these 'gentlemen' (he did not know what to call them) will use great influence. And they'll swear you killed their comrade."

"But I didn't!"

"They'll enquire about you. They'll hear of your tales. Of our adventure overseas. Of Israel Hands."

My voice grew shrill. "But I killed Israel Hands because Israel Hands was trying to kill me! He was climbing up the ship after me. And I didn't mean to kill him—the gun went off when he threw his knife at me!"

I must have seemed uncommonly distressed, for the doctor rose to his feet.

He said slowly, "In my opinion the matter couldn't be graver. You have no witnesses because they'll accuse those who were with you. It'll be easy for them to obtain a guilty verdict. That's how such things work."

"What am I to do?" My voice, and all my body, shook.

In a distant tone the doctor said to the squire, "I propose to conduct my enquiries to another location—the Royal George, or, John, if you'll permit it, The Hall—" and the squire nodded. The doctor continued, "I'll bind the gentlemen outside to go there immediately."

He turned away and Squire Trelawney murmured to me, "Should you fail to appear, Jim—"

I sensed my two friends had made some arrangement between them.

"But that will turn me into a fugitive!"

Squire Trelawney said, "All bad business needs time."

Dr. Livesey did not look at me. Both men understood my dilemma. To run would seem an admission of guilt. To stay and be held, probably in Exeter jail and gravely accused, offered no safety. My thought of myself as a man of honour confused me.

It also led me to my decision. The faces of the strange, lovely woman and her wilful boy upstairs caught at my heart. I remember thinking, "Some deeper story lies inside all this. And nothing can be resolved until that mystery is opened up. But I will not let down those two persons. Even if they have imposed themselves upon my care."

Therefore we never went to The Hall. Within the hour, when everyone had dispersed and all ways seemed clear, we left the Admiral Benbow, accompanied by Tom Taylor and endorsed by my mother.

Our arrangements were necessarily hasty. We gathered food and clothing for two days, but our burdens had to be as easy as possible. Some delay arose in trying to find clothing for our two fugitives who, after all, had come to us without possessions. My mother's wardrobe was called upon and if the clothes Grace Richardson would now wear did not match her accustomed finery, at least she and her son had sturdy garments for the uncertainties that lay ahead.

Warm southwesterly winds at our backs, we raced inland. We headed towards the high ridges of this county to make the most of the lingering summer evening light and we trusted the fine weather would give us enough warmth to pass nights in the fields.

Grace Richardson showed herself as someone accustomed to flight. When she and Louis came downstairs she attempted a speech of apology but I would not hear of it; in any case, we had no time to talk.

"Louis," I said, "I must compliment you on your aim."

He looked at me from under his eyebrows, then looked at my mother who smiled at him.

"I missed," he said. "Twice. Apples are not accurate."

Then he went to help his mother, who worked silently and quickly, packing clothing and food. I noted that Louis was also used to such activity.

Again that day, my mother astonished me. Our destination was her suggestion. "Make for Bristol," she said. "Many people stay there as birds of passage."

"But do our . . . our guests agree? They have just come from Bristol."

"All the more reason," said my mother. "Who will think of looking for them in a place they've fled?"

I had another concern. "Is it not improper for a young woman to, well—simply to take the roads with a young man her own age? Is not this somewhat—?"

Her glance told me I had erred in tact, that I had questioned both my own and my travelling companion's sense of principle. Mother ignored the question.

"You will stay with your uncle. He likes you and his opinion is sound."

"And then?" I asked, but more of myself than of her. "What shall we do then? Are we to run always? We can't hide with Uncle Ambrose forever."

She asked for time to think on this while our preparations moved on apace. Just before we departed, she called me.

"You know well that I didn't like it when you went to that island. And you know well that I didn't want you to go. But you did right. It has given you capabilities that fifty more years in this inn wouldn't give you."

I shifted a little at her praise, to which I was not often accustomed.

"This is what I think," she continued. "Let your honour guide you. You're the son of your father. You're not a murderer. Nor ever will you be, no matter how powerfully these ruffians may claim so.

But 'tis also true that their power can coat white with black. Such people can turn day into night. We're folk too modest to oppose them. We'd have no victory."

She hushed her tone and walked to the door, searching for listeners. In a whisper she finished. "I've learned there's a tale hidden within all this. We have been talking, as women do. You and I should reflect admiration and respect for what those two people have endured." She touched my arm. "And I *much* look foward to my next meeting with that *fine* young woman."

"Mother, I consider you fortunate to have learned something of what's been going on. I know nothing." My tone was dry.

"You'll find out. And you'll only resolve all the badness by discovering what lies behind it. So when you get to Bristol, be guided by what you think is necessary and by your uncle's judgements. So long as you mean to gain a good end of it all, you'll not go wrong."

Thus blest, I led my party from the Admiral Benbow. I now had new and frightening responsibilities.

The usual road to Bristol lies by the coast. We rode inland so that, by choosing lanes, farm tracks and drovers' trails, we should avoid being seen. One woman with a basket gathering herbs and some children playing in a tree waved to us. I hoped we did not seem remarkable to any of them; it cannot have been uncommon for a man, a woman, a boy and a servant to ride through these parts of a summer's evening. If questioners came along in our wake, we might perhaps have been singled out for the time at which we passed and the speed at which we rode. I allowed no slackening until we had put more than two hours behind us and long shadows were darkening the hedges.

Along the journey I tried to puzzle out our position. We had not been charged with murder, but we were suspects. No witnesses had been present during the horrid event; it would remain as our word against theirs. But, as the squire and Dr. Livesey clearly feared, our foes' accusations would carry great weight—Sir Thomas Maltby spoke so confidently of their position and connections. Our prudence in fleeing remained correct—except that all actions have their consequences.

Therefore, what was to happen now? Should we leave England? If so, how—and to where? And for how long? If we stayed, did we know of anyone to whom we might appeal? Such a person would need to have comparable or greater stature when set beside our accusers and former attackers. And what of Joseph Tait—the cause of my being drawn into all this? I did not even know, nor could I guess, whether he remained alive.

I had also been turning over my mother's remarks. She was right—the answers to my questions lay within the story of Grace Richardson, her young son and the pirate Tait.

The sky had turned red when I called a rest in a hollow on a ridge. No one followed us yet, but I reckoned that by now our antagonists knew we never meant to appear before Dr. Livesey at The Hall.

We all dismounted, with Tom handing the boy down carefully to me. Louis stretched, endearingly patted the horse in gratitude and went to talk to his mother. Each of us walked this way and that, easing our bones. I took the opportunity to study these two people, who had so lately made me responsible to them.

The boy looked like his mother, but I searched his face for other breeding traces. Was that the same strong nose as Tait? I all but shuddered at the thought. Tait remained in my mind as an object of fear. I wholeheartedly endorsed the squire's word that we should have hanged the fellow. If Louis were indeed his son, then to see Tait's features echoed in this innocent boy was to feel a kind of awful turn.

As for his mother, I saw again and more fully that here we had a person of true breeding. Even as she walked up and down this pasture, talking to her son, she had that curious mixture of refinement and strength present only in exceptional women.

Her step, even on grass, was strange to watch; she walked with firmness, yet picked her way as if a pool of water awaited each foot. The result gave her a high motion, like a stork or, in her case, a more exotic bird such as a desert ostrich, or the flamingos I have heard of in southern lands.

And her face kept changing, so frequently and so completely. It is said that this characteristic is true of beautiful women—perhaps that elusiveness is essential to the beauty. My heart became anxious again, and excited. The same confusing brilliance lit my mind. Shyness came over me so much that, had I needed to speak to her at that moment, I should have been gruff to the point of rudeness.

As it was, I reminded the others of our urgency and briskly made all remount. This time I took Louis upon my own horse and I said we would ride until dark.

Early stars came out. No night breeze sprang up and the fields offered no excess of dew, so that we felt no cold. The balm of the evening soothed much of the strain under which we travelled.

Across the tops of high fields and down into warm-hearted combes, by the edges of cornfields and over deep pastures, we rode our way. Only the munching cows observed us, as they lay in shadowy bulk on the grasses. Once or twice they felt obliged to move and if we rode too close to them, they clambered to their knees swinging their big heads.

Soon in our long, steady canter, the boy's head leaned back against my stomach and he fell asleep. I rearranged my reins in my hands so that I could give him the greatest safety.

After three hours or so, we rode down a steep, slanting field. Light never fully leaves these high places of the west until the nights reach September. It was about ten or eleven o'clock.

The farmer was evidently grazing both meadows, and had left a gate open. We rode into the next field and up a slope. Ahead, something jumped and fled, vaulting with fright; we had startled a deer. In the distance to my right I saw the shape of a lone building. Silently I bade the others to wait while I rode a substantial radius around. No farm appeared; this was an outside barn, used for the storing of hay and the birthing of calves.

Inside there was nothing but a bench, a fodder rack and some large piles of fresh hay. Along the ride I had reasoned with myself that such a woman would understand the necessity of spending nights in rough quarters. It is always the best people who are the most accepting—and

I judged that, as with all pursued people, she had probably been accustomed to uncushioned experiences.

To do her due respect, however, I now raised the matter with her.

"Madam, I fear it is only a barn."

"Please don't be troubled," she replied. "I grew up in the countryside. Nights under the stars have their own peace. No matter what the circumstances."

Thus was my anxiety soothed but not my heart: she had a manner that touched me, made me want to guard her.

Louis never woke as Tom fetched him down from my horse. His mother shook out two blankets and chose as congenial a corner as she could make out in the gloom. There, Tom lay the boy, who stirred a little.

Though still, I believed, asleep, he sat upright very fast and said, "We must stay here tomorrow as well. Until tomorrow night." Then he lay down again.

All of us heard him and were struck by the force of the remark. Tom Taylor was standing close enough for me to see his frown in the gloom. I thought of asking Louis his reason for saying that, but he was, I knew, in a deep and instant sleep. His mother looked at me anxiously and I nodded—we would stay here.

We opened the provisions. The milk still tasted sweet, dispersing my fears that the journey might have curdled it. How we managed to stow enough food and clothing for four fugitives and yet not be hazardously weighed down, I cannot know.

Amid occasional murmurs, we ate with hunger and enjoyment. Soon, Tom smoked a pipe, covering the bowl with his hand lest the glow be seen from a hill or a house. Then he too fell asleep, leaving me alone for the first time with Grace Richardson. After a while she rose and walked out of the barn. In the dusk outside the door I could see her taking her high steps, up and down, up and down, a little way off. Soon she returned and lay down by her son.

———✝———

Ch. 1 —

The Night Riders

The night moved into the deep period when creatures squeal in the
woods and the stars give the brightest of their silver pepper.

It may seem strange to say it, but the greatest alarm in me sprang
from the prospect of asking Grace Richardson some direct serious
questions. Whether it was the force of that frantic day I could not yet
say, but no woman had ever so affected me—that haze in my mind,
that panic around my heart.

She had no sleep either. After an hour or so, I heard her rise. She
walked past where I sat in the undoored entrance of the barn. I knew
I must speak to her and begin to discover the truth beneath this tu-
mult. She sat on the grass a few feet away from me. We had some
moments of silence in which I could hear but two sounds—her
breathing, and my own heart pounding. The darkness denied me the
pleasure of her face. I tried to overcome my confusion.

"Can you not sleep, Madam?"

She did not answer me. Perhaps she did not hear me? Perhaps she
had no wish to talk, merely to sit and watch the stars—and therefore
had I disturbed her? I felt disappointed and irked with myself when,
without a word, she rose, took herself back into the shadows of the
barn and again lay beside her son. Soon Grace Richardson fell asleep.

I began to feel a cramp in my legs—not for some time had I ridden
so long, or so continuously fast. Loosing my bootlaces, easing my
knees, stretching my thighs, I walked a little to and fro before the
barn. Our horses gurgled and huffed, gentle, comforting sounds.

The night allowed more visibility, as it always does when the eye grows accustomed. We had stopped halfway up a meadowed defile, thick with that rich grass after mowing. On the top of the hill it seemed lighter, a chance, I thought, to assess our surroundings.

The climb was stiff, over uneven ground, treacherous in the dark. On the crest stood a large, lone tree towards which I walked. As I reached it, the skin on my neck suddenly tightened and shrank with cold. Riders approached, travelling hard. Their hooves drummed the ground.

I was close to the outer branches of the large tree. Ahead, I saw the shapes rushing towards me. These were not riderless horses, in some wild herd. The stars looked down. Closer and closer the horsemen came. The night's shadows seemed to ride with them. Closer and closer the riders bunched. Through the soles of my boots I felt the hammers of their hooves upon the earth. At last, I dared to count them—one, two, three, four. But I had already expected that—because from the moment I heard the first hoofbeat I knew with certainty and dread who they were and what they wanted.

I believe the heart may halt from terror and the blood can turn to ice beneath the skin. They galloped by. Perhaps at that speed, in this dusk, they could scarcely see me.

Then—fifty yards away from me the leading rider suddenly reined in. I had been seen! Turning a small half-circle, he looped his horse tight and called his comrades to a halt. They stopped. All dismounted and there, thirty yards from me, conferred in the dark. My terror grew.

Yet nothing happened. Nobody moved towards where I stood, no voice called me, no gun barrel pointed me out. Had they seen me?

Maltby led the talk, as before; the others listened. I could see their shapes but not their faces, hear their voices but not their words—which made matters worse, as the imagination of something delivers a sharper fear than the reality. Worst of all I could discern the hump on that evil back.

Suddenly, my situation struck me like a fist. While they were approaching I had naturally chosen the farthest side of the tree from their oncoming direction.

Now that they had passed, I stood on the side most exposed to them.

I looked all around seeking other cover or a route of retreat, but only open ground offered itself. At any moment they must see me. Was the summer night's light, so kind to us otherwise, about to make me pay a savage price? My heart lurched with pain when I thought of my sleeping friends.

It is my belief that we can solve most problems with careful thought. Concentrating hard, I stared at the shadows of these restless, intent men. And then, almost without awareness, I began to give myself a hiding place. Slowly, very slowly, I reached up above my head and took hold of a branch. When mature, the elm is wide and leafy. Slowly, very slowly, I pulled down a twig that hauled down a branch, until a mass of leaves swayed gently in front of me. I pressed the branch down farther, almost to the ground. Seen from where they sat, it must merely appear that a large branch had grown in a curious direction.

One disadvantage—my hiding place reduced my clear view of them. I wanted to peer through the branches but there was no wind and thus a rustle of leaves would seem strange. So there I stood, trying to figure out their moving shapes but I could not see whether they looked in my direction. After some moments I gave up and resigned myself to wait for, I hoped, their departure.

But how had they found us? I could not believe that someone had informed. Only three people, my mother, Clara Taylor and young Joshua, knew we had fled. Unless we had been seen as we crossed the heath above the Royal George, or some innocent person somewhere had answered an ordinary question . . .

It was also possible that we had now crossed, or travelled near, a main droving trail to Bristol, one which any traveller might have used who chose the inland road. But I reckoned that no advantage lay in trying to puzzle their arrival. My brain should be used to keep myself and my companions safe, so I began to listen as I imagine wild animals do.

Occasional laughter or imprecations reached my ears. One man coughed, a short fit. Two of them lit pipes and I could smell their smoke. It was incongruent to find the pleasant aroma of tobacco associated with such menace.

Of a sudden, a new fear struck. Something came towards me, making odd noises. One of the horses had begun drifting towards my hiding place, cropping the grass and rattling the empty stirrups against his saddle. Horses smell fear and much dislike it. I should have thought the odour of my dread could be smelled in the stables of Plymouth.

The animal approached. I listened as he cropped, tearing up hanks of grass with his great, innocent mouth. At any moment would he sniff the night's breeze and find me upon it? And then rear as at a dragon?

Suddenly there came the rough call, "Thunder!" The comrade of Maltby's I took for a soldier was calling his horse to heel: "*Thunder!*"

But Thunder took no notice and now stood perhaps six or eight yards from my cold, sweated face.

"Thunder! Stand, you!—" and the customary vile words followed.

And still Thunder cropped on, a pace nearer to me with every mouthful. I looked down. Large abundant tufts grew a yard from my boots, just outside the tree's general shadow. Still, I thought, no horse eats in a straight line. My best hope was that he might pass by; my worst fear that he might begin to tear at the leaves that screened me.

Once again, when I thought my terror at its greatest, it heightened further. Thunder's rider detached himself from his companions. His pipe glowing in the dark like a vicious little red lantern, he strode towards the horse, muttering blasphemously. He rounded the creature and reached for the bridle. Thunder objected a little by throwing his head back and stepping forwards in my direction. His owner followed and grabbed the bridle at last, giving it a jerk to establish who was master. By now I could almost have stroked the animal's haunch.

Thunder then swung around and his master followed suit, trying to bring the bridle under control. His raised elbow brushed my screening branch; any closer or harder and he might have knocked the leaves from my hands.

When I think of that moment now I fancy that I must have given a small whimper. But that cannot be so, or the horse and rider would have heard the sound. However, I am certain my heart whimpered.

The soldier, having gained control of his mount, made some new arrangement with the bridle. Then he stopped, and listened. I know that he looked straight to where I stood, but the night defeated him. This black-hearted man was kept from my throat by a different blackness—the blackness of the tree's shadows.

He wrested the horse's head around and walked back to his companions, saying, "I'm for going on. I fear this place has spooks."

Although he spoke half-jocosely, neither of his companions laughed. One answered Nature's call, then the smokers kicked their pipes out against their heels. They mounted and rode hard away.

When their hoofbeats receded I released the branch and came forth from my shadows. For luck I walked to where they had been standing. On the grass lay the red embers of their smokes. The tiny piles of tobacco glowing in the grass seemed like the spawn of devils.

I made for the barn down in the cleft of the fields. When the mind, and on that night, the heart and soul, are affrighted, every other thing provides shocks. I half-shrieked as a shape bounded to my side.

"Jim, easy, easy! 'Tis me."

"Oh, Tom—" I nearly fainted at the touch of his arm.

"I woke and found 'ee gone. You be all right?" His anxiety picked up and mimicked my whispering.

"Down," I said. "Keep down."

He dropped like a cat to his haunches and squatted there, afraid and dependent.

"What's up, Jim?"

From the rim of this arching field I took one last look around the terrain. Not a sound to be heard, not an owl nor a small creature's night cry. Nothing to be seen either, except the high bulk of my friendly tree, the deeper darkness beyond and the stars in their little diamond points. I swept down the slope and Tom half-tumbled after me.

When we reached the barn I stayed him with my arm.

"They've been here," I whispered. "They've ridden through. I saw them. The four of them, and they were like men on a trail."

"You saw them?"

"I could have touched them. And one nearly touched me."

Tom shuddered and asked, "What about Madam?"

"I will tell her in the morning."

"Oh, Jim. What a long, bad day!"

I said, "They'll not be back. I think Bristol is what they aim at."

Tom said he would keep watch.

The next thing I knew was a bright morning and the clear voice of the boy, Louis. I opened my eyes and was able to study him without his observing me. He spoke earnestly to his mother of some sight or other they had seen together in their travels. She had evidently been awake and abroad some time. Her hair now pulled back in a ribbon of gold, she wore a grey cloak, one of my mother's best. Was it only noon yesterday that this pair had come to the Royal George? She and her son chatted pleasantly and then, feeling intrusive upon their privacy, I told them of my presence by a waking groan followed by a cough.

"Good-day," said Louis with a smile, and he stepped a little towards me.

His mother bade me "Good-day" also.

I returned their greetings with a civil enquiry as to how they had slept. She spoke of deep, refreshing sleep and Louis remarked, "I dreamed of horses, galloping and galloping, like this," and with a little canter he showed us.

We broke out some food. The sun lit us pleasantly as we sat in the mouth of the barn. Yet my limbs jangled to think of the night gone by.

Presently I said, "Madam, may we speak of some matters?"

We walked into the field.

"Madam—it is, there are . . ." I began, halted, then continued. "Madam, I need knowledge in order to decide some things."

She looked at me, a piercing, quick glance that gave an impression of mental strength and courage.

"They have been near, haven't they?" she asked.

In other circumstances, chivalry and good behaviour might lead to the concealment of such troubling knowledge from a woman. Not now—and not this woman.

"They rode through last night. Up there on the hill. I stood mere yards from them."

"Louis always knows," she said. "Oh, this is all so unsafe!" She took fright; her skin changed to the colour of whitened bone. "Mere yards? And they did not see you?"

"Fortune may be on our side," I murmured. "That is why I so much need . . . I need to know about Tait and—"

"No. I cannot speak today." For a moment she stopped in front of me and commanded me powerfully with her eyes. "I need to bring all this under some control and I shall do so better if I don't speak of it for some time." And then she walked away.

"Madam," I begged. "You must tell me something. This death, the Berwick gentleman, Sir Thomas Maltby—I am desperate to know. Mysteries are dangerous."

"No," she said. "Please don't press me."

I could not resist her request. She ran to meet her smiling son, leaving me adrift amid continuing danger and without enough knowledge to take the crucial decisions that surely faced me.

———✝———

Part Two

—✕—

To Travel Hopefully

Ch. 7 —

My Clever Uncle

We spent all day in that field, a day of sunshine and long thoughts. Grace devoted her time to Louis, or sat quietly on the margin of the hedgerow. She spoke to me infrequently and then with a face so withdrawn it seemed impossible to address her.

I saw that she looked at me and sensed that I did not displease her—but I felt unsettled by her reticence. Common sense declared that I, of all people, needed to have the fullest information, yet although she had confided in my mother, she was not prepared to tell her story to me.

Several theories crossed my mind. She was ashamed of her situation and by telling me feared she might risk my respect for her. But I could have reassured her. Or she was tired of telling this tale, knew she would have to tell it again to my uncle and wanted to include me in that telling. But I longed to be the only one hearing her voice, receiving her confidences. Or—she had observed my repulsion at Tait's name and she feared my disapproval of the details she harboured. My regret at her silence included the thought: but I could show her how I will never disapprove of her, or anything about her.

Tom Taylor showed Louis how to make a cat's cradle out of long stalks. I made him a whistle out of a wand of ash. This is done by easing the skin off, cutting the whistle notch into the naked, baby wood and then sliding the skin back on again—as my father had shown me. I allowed Louis one soft practice blow, to see that it worked and then told him it was his own private warning signal.

Towards late afternoon Grace Richardson—she seemed weary—said to me, "If we are to travel tonight, sleep needs to be taken."

In turns Tom and I sat watch. And when the night began to darken we all set forth again, having eaten for the journey. For the following days we repeated our new habit—of sitting quietly all day in a hidden field, far from any village or house, sleeping towards evening and riding by night. Past signs to Dodington and Fiddington and Cannington and then a swing north, past white fingerposts pointing to Cote and Cheddar and Chew, we heard no new alarms and saw no new frights.

Bristol appeared beneath us as another dawn broke. Tom said no party had ever travelled so fast but so leisurely. His early life as a drover gave us a valuable advantage; we came down into the city from a high hill by a quiet trail, our eyes out for our pursuers.

My uncle, Ambrose Hatt, has his house in a tall square of railings and ivy. His servants fussed about us as we stood in the hallway awaiting him. I have never seen my uncle surprised; he takes things calmly, perhaps because he practises law and it requires him to be capable of all human variety. When he came downstairs he greeted me as easily as though I had been passing by with some friends and decided to call in.

Daylight had not yet reached inside his house. Uncle Ambrose ordered a lamp to assist the servants' candles. When it came he asked his man to hold it high, and he looked at each of our four faces with interest and compassion. At Grace Richardson's face he lingered longest and then addressed her simply.

"Madam, you are most welcome in my house." He smiled at Louis. "And you, young sir, I like the look of you."

Louis smiled back and looked at me, seeming pleased and safe. My uncle continued.

"How fortunate that you call so early. I've been lying too late in my bed these past few weeks and my work has fallen behind." He spoke pleasantly to his servants. "Now, Wilfred, you too, Mrs. Wilfred, these travellers are hungry and would enjoy some warm water and warmer food."

The servants jumped to it and we dispersed in the manner correct to such a house. Tom disappeared with Wilfred, while Mrs. Wilfred led mother and son off in a different direction. I went to my uncle's study, following his lamp along the flagstoned corridor.

Many happy memories of that house came back to me, and I felt safe. My mother and I spent one summer there when I was eight or so; she had been unwell and my father, who liked my uncle Ambrose greatly, sent her to recuperate with him.

"Jim, how is your mother?"

"She is very well," I said.

"I often think of your father. I miss him still."

"We all do, Uncle."

He placed the lamp upon his desk and opened his shutters. Dawn, still a little grey, filled the garden.

"Forgive me. I have not yet put away yesterday's work. I think I am growing careless. When I was younger I did a day's work in a day and kept all my letters to one side of the page. As I was taught to do. Now my work goes into the night and my letters sprawl too much."

He walked to a small table and picked up a decanter.

"What I do find," he said, "is that growing older encourages me to break a rule now and then. So—we shall have some brandy."

He picked up a decanter and two glasses.

"Oh," he laughed. "To drink brandy at dawn again!"

We sat facing each other across his large desk. I gave him my mother's letter; he read it, said nothing and put it aside.

"Now," he said. "So that we may all enjoy our breakfast, tell me your story."

And so I told the tale again, as I had done with Dr. Livesey, adding afresh my adventures with the night riders. My uncle listened like a man hearing the most fascinating tale ever told, even though I know him privy to more confidences and reckless stories than any man in the southwest.

When I had finished he said, "But you're not satisfied?"

I smiled. He and my mother always race to the nub of any business.

"I'm puzzled, Uncle."

"Puzzle it out. That's what I always say."

"Well—" But as I began I fell silent, teasing out my difficulty. He waited, as all good listeners do.

"The lady gives me no details. Therefore I have no way of knowing what's right to do."

"What does she want?" he asked. "Is it only to see this pirate fellow?"

"That's what she says. But how," I questioned aloud, my brain irritated, "how did Tait—who is a villain, Uncle—how did he? . . ." I let myself run out of words—but Uncle Ambrose wanted me to say them.

"Go on."

"He's a pirate and she's plainly a well-born woman. Don't you agree, Uncle? So how did he gain such a place in her life?" I said. "And what must I do about it? I believe she's forcing me, by her silence, to accept what she wants to do."

"I think you should have been the lawyer and I the innkeeper," smiled my uncle. The lamp paled in the morning light.

I spoke on. "But perhaps not forcing me? No, I think not," I said. "More likely leading me." I paused again. "Uncle—this Tait, he was, I grant, a handsome man. He was very silent, though. I can't recall one sentence that he spoke."

My uncle continued to wait for me as I thought aloud.

"It's too difficult. What am I to do? Am I to sail again?" I shuddered. "And if so, how? Life is now very comfortable, I grant you, Uncle. We want for nothing. But I, acting alone, *I* do not have the resources to charter a ship—and I am unlikely to find a passage on one that will take me straight to Treasure Island! Added to this I'm a fugitive from justice, or so it seems, does it not?"

He smiled. "The word 'fugitive' is too loosely used."

"But Uncle, the matter has become very difficult now," I said.

My uncle wears a great scarab ring, the source of which he will never disclose and from which he will never be parted. The ruby at its core flashed as the early sunlight flowed into the room.

"She wants me to go back there. To the island. I know that, I know it from the way my stomach sinks." I shivered.

By simple listening Uncle Ambrose made it possible for me to unravel my puzzle.

"If I don't—what must I do? Stay away from my own inn forever? And be prey to those—those malefactors? If I go to Treasure Island at least I'll know the place." I laughed. "But Uncle, look how matters cancel each other. There's still some silver there which we had to leave behind. In all my tales of that adventure I have never disclosed that fact. But there was fever on that island, Dr. Livesey said so. And therefore Tait must be dead by now. With prudence it's possible we could have a clean voyage and return quickly. And by then the other matter will have had the attentions of Dr. Livesey. Yet, Uncle, other than the silver, I cannot think that anyone should undertake that voyage to find that ruffian."

My uncle smiled. "Jim, a good lawyer will tell you that to take a decision you must always separate thought from feeling."

I saw his meaning and blushed. "She's very brave, I can tell you that—" and I stopped, fearing my tongue would run away with me.

"And a good lawyer will also tell you," he smiled, "that he will often listen to his client at the expense of his own judgement."

"Meaning she may herself find a way of making that voyage? I could never allow—" The sentence faltered and my uncle ignored, or pretended not to hear, the passion with which I wished to protect her.

As if summing up, Uncle Ambrose said, "She has all but asked you to find this man. You fear he may be the father of her son—that, you think, can be the only reason powerful enough. And I agree, it is a powerful motive. She's aware you knew that man to be a base pirate, yet you feel she will press you. I agree—that requires courage from her. What I seek to measure is whether you *feel* more than you *think* in all of this. I know it has all been sudden—a vigorous few days indeed. But men *are* sudden." He beamed at me.

I fell silent, both from believing I should listen and from a fear that

I could not keep the strength of my feelings for Grace Richardson from being heard in my voice. Uncle Ambrose continued.

"Jim, let me put to you a question that requires as honest an answer as you may ever be called upon to give."

I knew and feared what he was going to say.

"Do you intend," he asked, with all the gravity of his profession, "to grant this woman's wish?"

I did not reply directly. Instead I said, "My mother—I mustn't bring my mother pain again—"

Uncle Ambrose laughed. "Oh, don't wager on that! Your mother's shrewder than any of us. Nobody knows better how our lives must be allowed to map themselves."

I groaned. "Uncle, it will turn my life into a heap. It may even prove dangerous. As the last journey did. It'll go against my grain. I swore that nothing would draw me back there."

My uncle looked at me. He smiled most benignly. I hadn't convinced him.

"Jim, you tell your story clearly," he said. He was about to say something more but changed tack and reached for his writing materials. "However—to be practical. From what you say, this fellow Maltby and his friends are combing Bristol for you. I think I'll write a letter." He paused, looked out of the window for a long, long moment and took a new decision. "No, not one letter, I'll write two." Then he began to write.

I sat there watching the sun on the old brick walls of his garden, observing his dear, grey head bent to his words, listening to the only sound in the house, the scratch of his pen across the page. He finished.

"My secretary doesn't arrive until quite late," he said. "He doesn't rise until the cock jumps on his bed and crows in his ear. Achssss!" he hissed as he burnt his fingers on the wax. I have never seen a man so clumsily seal a packet as my uncle, Ambrose Hatt. He rang the bell.

"Wilfred, please deliver these. But as you do, tell Mrs. Wilfred that we shall come by for breakfast presently."

Soon, with his long gown and his longer nightshirt flapping, he led me down the benign passages of his fine house to breakfast with him by the fire that, he claims, is never allowed to die winter or summer. I was glad of it that morning, even though the day outside promised well. The night air still chilled my bones—or was it the fear of the decision I thought I had just taken?

Mrs. Wilfred and her maid began to serve breakfast. I began to see why his servants so loved my uncle. He liked to listen to them and never cut them off while they spoke. In consequence they fussed about him as though he were somewhere between a baby and a respected parent. If he tried to dismiss them, they refused to leave him.

Mrs. Wilfred's maid now began to serve my uncle with special hot milk in his large yellow cup and the glass of tepid water he always had for his liver. He turned to me and exhorted me to eat. The servants departed. I waited some minutes and addressed him.

"What do you advise, Uncle?"

"Oh!" He started, as if prodded. "How unkind of me. I should've told you what I have done. You heard me instruct Wilfred to take two letters. In one I've asked our most respected judge in these parts, Lord Gibbon—whom I've the honour to think of as a friend—I've asked him to have your pursuers intercepted, have them found wherever they are and brought here. As my guests. That we may merrily discuss the administration of law in England. You see, Jim, one of the law's many advantages is that in its pursuit, certain shall we say, social barriers melt away."

It was my turn to start. For a moment I feared that his respect for the law had outweighed my uncle's family affections.

"But Uncle! Having escaped the lions' den—do you now bring the lions here?!"

He calmed me. "Jim, by then you shall be gone. My letter was most explicit as to when I wish to see this Sir Thomas Maltby."

"But where shall we have gone?" I asked. "There is no place we can go!" My agitation seemed to rise contrary to the comfort of the food.

"All this will take until tomorrow. I have said so. You will by then be safely on your way back to the Admiral Benbow. That's my advice."

This was a second shock and all I could manage to say in my apprehension was, "Uncle, I don't understand you."

My dear uncle smiled at me. "Jim, where's the one place nobody will think of searching for you? Also, the second letter I wrote—do you remember Mr. Blandly?"

How could I forget Mr. Blandly? From whom John Trelawney bought the *Hispaniola* for our fateful voyage? And whose slackness allowed Silver to get a place aboard and bring his own rotten, mutinous crew with him? I remembered Mr. Blandly!

My uncle said, "Blandly's a bit more honest these days. Odd what wealth can do to a man. And, as you know, he again owns the *Hispaniola*. It will reach you and your friends at Kitts Hole—as I have ordered—no later than a week hence."

In alarm, and, I have to say, some excitement, I half rose from my chair.

"Uncle! What are you proposing?! And who is to travel? Surely not—"

He interrupted. "Now, my dear Jim. Sit. Be calm. Eat first. Then sleep. Plenty of time for details in due course."

That is how I came to sail once more to Treasure Island. I took no decision to do so, nor to this day can I say accurately how the decision occurred.

———⚓———

Ch. 8—

Old Friends Are Best

We left my uncle's house much repaired. Yet the danger remained; my stomach told me so. I also fretted that by staying in his house we had perhaps drawn Uncle Ambrose into a difficulty that could threaten his very reputation.

But if he felt doubts they soon disappeared in his delight at the acquaintance he made with Grace Richardson. To the joy of them both it emerged that he had known her deceased uncle on her mother's side, also a lawyer, who owned land in Wiltshire. Thus, our luncheons and dinners with Uncle Ambrose became occasions of natural pleasure.

Judging from her animation, his company seemed to prove easier for her than mine so far had promised. I ascribed this to the fact that she, a stranger, was desirous of me undertaking on her behalf something very difficult, very threatening, and that she felt the weight of the encumbrance she placed on me.

Passionately though I longed for her conversation, I was gladdened in my heart to see her relax with my uncle. They held many long talks in private. She had then been delighted by the arrival of numerous women who improved her wardrobe, called to the house by Mrs. Wilfred at my uncle's command. The gowns validated her beauty and she became so animated I began to see what she could be like if generally untroubled: my heart went wild.

My uncle hosted her masterfully. When he knew she felt rested, he showed her his paintings and told her their stories; he opened his great collections of table silver, his many resplendent rooms and their gracious furnishings. (My mother once told me of her brother's pride when someone had said he owned "the finest house in Bristol": Mother, tartly, thought it wasted on a bachelor.)

At one moment during our stay I thought that Uncle Ambrose could help me in my dilemma, that he could ask Grace Richardson the questions I feared to ask and that she might not shut him off as she had done me. I approached him and made my request—but he merely smiled at me and said, "Women need to be indirect, Jim."

On the day of our departure my uncle supervised everything. From his drawing-room window he watched the long sloping street below. We had early been prepared, and we waited on his word.

"There," he cried at last. "See! That is my carriage and I have ordered it to be kept closed. It will take them ten minutes to reach the front door. I will watch them all the way—and you must now ride out by the coach gate."

He wanted us to feel no risk of being seen by our pursuers as we left Bristol; he had also given me a letter for my mother.

I looked quickly through the open window. His carriage, bearing Maltby and his dreadful companions, rolled like a beetle down the opposite hill. My eyes stung with fear and I took only a little comfort in knowing my uncle's plan to be a sound one. Maltby and his troop had to all intents and purposes been taken into his custody. Under the guise of the law and in the interests of its local practice, the reputable Bristol solicitor, Ambrose Hatt, had invited the court counsellor and his companions to come and stay with him, calling down the name of his good friend, Lord Justice Gibbon. If Maltby refused those circumstances, he snubbed significant people at a time when he would need to present an impeccable face to the world. Or so my uncle reasoned.

"Uncle," I said, not a little wryly, "when you die will you bequeath me your cleverness?"

We shook hands. Then Grace Richardson conducted her leave-taking as though Uncle Ambrose were her oldest and dearest relative.

The horses stood liveried and ready. Mrs. Wilfred had prepared a small mountain of food which we had already packed. For the sake of stealth we guided our horses along the grass margin beside the cobbled street at the rear of my uncle's house. Soon I felt stronger in my wits and in half an hour we had cleared the city and were back among the combes and pastures whence we had come.

We paused on a hilltop and looked back at Bristol. Sunshine's haze hung over the city. Ahead some sheep grazed and ran. My horse stood beside Grace Richardson's but I had tried to form the habit of not looking at her.

Now she defeated that momentarily, because she turned to me and said with heart-stopping shyness, "Mr. Hawkins, do not think I have not observed what you have been doing for Louis and me."

She spurred her horse and I floundered like a swain in her wake.

Our next days passed serenely. We were a calmer troop this time, perhaps because we had rested so much, in such warm care, or perhaps through the combining of relief and anticipation. The weather and the countryside blessed us under sun and under stars, until finally, late one morning, we reached the lane above the Admiral Benbow and watched the sea below us sparkle in the light.

Joshua, Tom Taylor's son, heard our hooves and ran to meet us. He seemed not in any way afraid. We learned that the pursuers had not been near the Benbow since we left, nor had any agent from them. In fact no stranger, of any sort, had come near the place. As I handed my mother his letter, I began to feel further assured by my uncle's shrewdness.

After I had eaten, I walked upstairs to my mother's parlour and there saw the two women together in conversation. The scene touched me. Louis, after his food, had fallen asleep on the long settle and my mother held his hand softly. Grace Richardson seemed more peaceful than even my uncle had caused her to be. I stood in the doorway and begged their leave of having intruded. On our return the greeting between them had been as warm and comprehensive as between old friends. The sun in the parlour made everything gold and mellow.

Clara Taylor appeared with linen and led Grace Richardson in the direction of the upper stairs. My mother beckoned me to sit down.

"Grace needs to bathe. And to sleep," she whispered.

The familiarity struck me—"Grace" was it?! My mother tended to keep people at the length of her arm. But—"Grace?"

This set up many enquiries in my mind, not least the hope that my mother's affection for her new young acquaintance would benefit me. Indeed, I thought of saying how different our guest proved from the hopeful girls who had travelled to see my mother—but at that moment my mother more or less took over all our matters.

She kept her voice low. "I understand that you've decided to sail. Then we must make our plans." I began to resist, to explain that nobody had told me outright this would happen—but she talked on. "That's the correct decision and I believe that a ship crewed at your uncle's behest will be a good ship. Grace must go with you, you understand that?"

"No, Mother," I whispered. "She must not!"

My mother ignored me. "She accepts that she doesn't know what she'll find, but she's a brave woman."

"Mother! Tait is scarcely a reason for anyone going back to that wretched place. Let alone a young woman with a young son. She *must* stay behind!"

"And I believe you'll all return safely."

I felt my anger rising and had difficulty in not shouting. "Mother, why do you encourage this? It's dangerous. And her reasons are so slender—not that I have been made privy to them."

My mother did not hear. "Shhh. You must remember too, Jim, that a trove of bar silver lies there. If you should recover it, shan't that be Grace's reward? For the difficulties in her life? It'll pay for the voyage too. And how fitting that you should be the one to recover it?"

"Mother! Joseph Tait was a pirate!"

She looked at me. "Many fine women have had unusual people in their lives."

"Unusual?! He's a villain! A brute. And Mother, she wishes me to do this but she'll tell me nothing."

"Just because she finds it difficult to speak openly about him doesn't make her a liar."

"But, Mother—"

"Keep your voice down, Jim. She now understands a great deal about life and she wants this fear lifted from her."

"But Mother, what caused this fear? Why do powerful men want her killed?"

"And she possesses very considerable qualities. Not least in her feeling for her son," at which my mother indicated the sleeping Louis. "We mustn't wake him," she whispered, and ever conscious of helpful interruption, warned, "Children may absorb things even though they be asleep."

I knew my mother when she was in this mood—there was no point pressing her. In something of a bate I left the room, reflecting that this did not represent the mother who had so wept in grief when first I set sail all those years ago.

As I went downstairs, I saw through the inn windows a face as welcome to me as Admiral Benbow's face on our signboard.

"Heard you were here, was going by, thought I'd see to things, those d——d ruffians left in a hurry."

Squire Trelawney can never confess to showing a concern for others, yet few men possess such kindness. We stood outside in the strong sunshine, where he and I marvelled at the holes made by those musket balls in the shutters. He naturally wanted information—and laughed in delight at my uncle's various stratagems.

To my surprise he raised no question over the plan of returning to Treasure Island.

"All business needs finishing. Livesey and I always say so."

"Will you be persuaded to join us, sir?"

He took so long to answer me that I began to ask again, thinking he had not heard me. Gazing towards the sea, a view I knew him to enjoy, he said, "No, Jim. I'll not be joining you."

As I made to press him he spoke again. "It'd be unwise, I'm told, to undertake anything so strenuous."

My distress showed. "But you seem so robust?"

He prevented me from speaking.

"Look here. Ship's doctor. You'll need one. Livesey can't go. You know that. Can't even see you, mustn't know you're here, otherwise he'll have to arrest you. You take my point? Anyway he must remain to deal with that scoundrel Malt-what's-his-name. So—my cousin, Jefferies. Staying with me just now. Lively fellow, a deal younger than me. Excellent physician, Livesey says so. Could do with an adventure, he's come into money, he's restless."

I did not respond. Squire Trelawney sensed I resented the sound of this man.

I said, "Sir, are you certain you can't come?"

He cut me short. "Those swamps, that infernal island—crew needs physic." He rose. "I'll send Jefferies here tomorrow."

The squire paused, his eyes still on the far waves. "There's someone else you should take with you," and he began to laugh a little.

For a moment or two I puzzled also and then, realising what, or rather who he meant, I began to laugh too.

"Ah, yes," I said.

"Plenty o' cheese," chuckled the squire and we enjoyed the joke. "Knows the island better than anyone. Better, I'll vouch, than the three ruffians we left behind there."

Ben Gunn was the man of whom we spoke: he could, I think, possess only one use in life, that of being a guide to Treasure Island. He had been marooned there by the first pirates, the ones who buried the treasure. Our arrival set him free and not just from his diseased abode—it also released him from the terror that somehow Flint and Billy Bones and Pew and all those old, bad ghosts of the isle would come back to claim his spirit.

On our return to England Ben squandered his share in nineteen days—gave much of it away or lost it at cards. On the twentieth he came to me asking help. Squire Trelawney found him a position as a lodge keeper on a cousin's estate. Poor Ben felt himself imprisoned there and was in frequent trouble. But everybody liked him, even though he annoyed all with whom he dealt.

I promised Squire Trelawney I would seek Ben that very day. The squire is awkward when he feels emotion and he rode away without a leave-taking. Did he fear he might not see me again? I did not like to hear of him being unwell and I watched wistfully until his horse vanished from sight. With him rode much of my lifelong safety.

To rid myself of my anxiety, I set out immediately to find Ben Gunn. The estate whose lodge he kept lies an hour's ride away, in a most beautiful part of our county, and I rode down narrow lanes high with flowers.

Ben must have been a sore trial to his employers. Earlier that day he had been set the task of trimming some hedges. A butcher with a cleaver could have clipped with more precision; under the old maroon's hand, the shrubs had begun to look like sheep who gnawed their own fleeces.

He was glad to see me; he would have embraced Lucifer himself for interrupting the hedge cutting.

"Ye'll not believe me, Jim." He had retained the habit of plucking at people's clothing as he spoke to them. "Only this morning I thought of ye. I thought, 'I wonder how that fine young man is?' that's what I thought. Ye were always square to me, Jim."

"How do you like it here, Ben?" I asked him. "Squire Trelawney sent you his good wishes."

"Jim, they feeds me and I gets enough cheese. That I confess I do. But if I tell ye that there be times when the old island speaks better to my mind, then ye'll not mistake me."

To which I replied, "So a voyage there might be a matter of some pleasure to you?"

He looked at me out of one eye. "There be silver bars there, Jim. An' we knows the only man—the only man who knows where they be, Jim. Don't we?"

I laughed. "Indeed, Ben."

He squinted at me again. "But I'll take ship with ye, Jim, ye were a good shipmate."

As I recalled it, I had spent much of our voyage home keeping him from the brandy. I gave Ben his instructions and told him how to find the Admiral Benbow.

As I rode home, I had much to think upon. This new doctor, Jefferies, would arrive tomorrow or after. Then the ship would come and our departure would remove us from England for a long, convenient while. My uncle said he believed that by the time we returned from our voyage the Maltby business would have been concluded and the truth told. From this I took the impression that he and Lord Justice Gibbon had made enquiries and intended to resolve all.

And then my mind went into patterns I had lately begun to enjoy. I fancied that Grace Richardson had become my wife, and that we lived a life of peace and comfort with young Louis and with other children of our own. But that reverie, as pleasant thoughts often do with me, led on into gloomy ideas.

I did not know what to expect when we reached the South Seas. What should happen were we to find Tait alive and well? Must we bring him back to stand trial for piracy? Or did Grace Richardson mean to marry him (a sea captain may conduct a wedding) and thereby give her son the respectability of wedlock? I could not believe that she, fine bred and fine born, might countenance marriage to a low buccaneer, who by all the laws should return and face the hangman. Nor should Louis go through his life as the son of a man who ended his days dangling from a rope in Execution Dock. With me as a chief witness to piracy, mutiny and murder.

If that were not to happen, it must mean that Tait would stay out there and she and Louis with him. On an island inhospitable at least with plagues and vapours, and now perhaps uninhabitable? Then, some other southern place perhaps—to which we could convey them? In which impossible case—in any case—must she soon be lost to me forever?

Downed by these thoughts, I turned at last down the lane to the sea and saw ahead of me two of Squire Trelawney's men. Each rode a cart and each urged his horse to do better. I caught up with them and found that the squire had sent (with his compliments) "provisions for the voyage." From the size of the loads, I judged there to be sufficient for three voyages.

Ch. 9 —

The Hispaniola

We closed the inn for some days and made a sign to this effect at the head of the lane. But I felt no relaxation, only a returned current of fear. Not an hour passed without my eye to the sea below us, or my ear to the land behind us. Who was to know if Maltby had instructed henchmen? Or whether the Berwick relatives might choose to visit the place where their kinsman had met his death? My mother told me that the body had been taken from our county for burial elsewhere. The runaway horse was never found.

I kept my pistols near me during that busy time. On three occasions I reached for them. The first alarm passed easily—when I heard Ben Gunn's amusing call, "Fetch aft the rum, Darby," the same ghostly cry which had struck terror into the pirates on the island. Ben wandered down our lane like a ragged emperor, dressed in a crazy assortment of liveries and a tricorne hat.

All at the Admiral Benbow loved Ben Gunn immediately. His exaggerated responses to any command made us laugh. He called everyone "Admiral" and lightened our mood.

My second alert was caused by a stranger on horseback. Louis ran to me, saying he heard hooves. By a crag up the lane, even though I myself heard no hooves, I waited. Tom Taylor, also armed, hid behind the small bridge.

Ten minutes later I marvelled again at Louis's senses: I walked forth to find a horseman arriving. He dressed uncommonly well and had a hat with a flat brim. His blue eyes shone with excitement and I disliked him on sight.

"Good-day, good man," he said to me like some versifier. "Where is your landlord?"

"And the name?" I asked, intending to disarm his pride.

"His or mine?" retorted the newcomer. "He, I am told, is Hawkins."

"And yours?"

"I am Jefferies."

"I am Hawkins."

"Are you now?"

This, then, was John Trelawney's nomination as our ship's doctor. I looked him over carefully—a man of smartness and ease, and he showed at least the manners of a gentleman. He dismounted immediately and grasped my hand.

"My good fellow! Of whom my relation speaks so well! I have just come from The Hall. John says—and, seeing you, I agree with him—that I am certain we shall be the best of shipmates, shall we not?!"

He was older than me by some years and was clearly a man who knew a wide world, but he bounded too much for my liking. He was too eager, too busy; I like folk a little steadier. And he gave me a difficulty which I sometimes encounter: how may one dislike those who show a liking for oneself? I am happy to say that I have known many men who liked me—but it has made me unhappy when I have not liked them in return.

"The ship will be here soon. Tomorrow, perhaps tonight," I said. "I think the wind has been a little contrary to them. Let me conduct you inside."

"I live in Falmouth," he cried. "And I have never been to sea. Is that not a curious thing?"

Indoors, Dr. Jefferies bowed low to my mother and Grace Richardson. His appearance and manner caught their attention. I have often observed that women do not seem to object when a certain kind of man exaggerates.

"Roger Jefferies, Physician," he said. "And, I beg leave to hope, Gentleman."

"May we judge that?" asked my mother, smiling as though in a banter—but I knew her well enough. Had it been me she addressed thus, I would have felt myself taken down some pegs. Grace Richardson said nothing, but Jefferies looked at her with, I fancied, a lively interest.

Our third alarm came in the early hours of next morning. Tom had come to me as I climbed the stairs for bed.

"I wants to keep watch," he said.

"But we are in no danger, Tom. Or do you feel we are?"

He looked at me. "Your father would say 'yes' to me, Jim, and I have it thought out. Joshua and me. We need no other."

"If danger should come, Tom—"

I did not have to finish my sentence.

"I shall rouse you, Jim, I promise."

I bade him goodnight and went to bed, expecting a full and un-troubled sleep.

But some time in the night I felt a hand on my bed and a voice urging, "Here! Here!"

My caller was Tom. "There be a horseman. On the lane."

"Some traveller, Tom. Someone who has not seen our CLOSED sign in the dark."

"No, no. He has stopped some time. He sits there and watches."

"Is he alone?" Now my heart did quicken. The hunchback was a man who sat and watched—and was alone when first I encountered him.

"So far. I have heard no other hooves. I think he watches us." Tom wore his grim voice.

I roused myself, not unafraid. "Only one thing to do, Tom. Beard him. Stay here. Mind the door."

I dressed, armed myself and with a deep, reluctant breath went out-side. The first glimmer of a dawn came into the sky with a lemon colour. I rounded the gable and walked up the shadowed lane. Right enough, there sat a dark and bulky horseman, still and erect. He hauled his horse's head upright when he heard my boots ring on the stones. I cocked and aimed my pistols.

"Who goes?" I called.

"Shhhhhhh!" came the voice.

"Who are you and what do you want?" I drew closer and fully intended to shoot if faced with a sudden action from this figure.

"Shhhhhhh," came the voice again. His shushing disconcerted me. "Gads, Jim, you're a noisy fellow tonight."

I laughed at first and then felt concern.

"Doctor Livesey! To what end—"

"Jim, will you please quieten?! People need their sleep!"

I lowered my voice too. "But why are you here?"

I saw that he wore a brace of pistols and had his flintlock strapped to his saddle.

"Jim, who knows what wind of your trip might have become known in Bristol or elsewhere along this tattletale coast. So—I set myself to stand guard."

"I've been thinking of you," I exclaimed.

"But I'm not here, if you take my meaning, I've not met you."

"I understand, sir."

"There's wonderful air tonight," he said. "Is your mother in distress at your leaving?"

"Not yet. But I expect that in the hour of departure she may show some feeling."

We stood silent for a moment or two.

"Sir, I'm greatly moved," I said.

Dr. Livesey coughed, but said nothing. I wished to stay and be with him, whatever the law said, and I attempted to make some conversation.

"The squire was here yesterday. I am sorry he's not well."

Dr. Livesey began to wheeze with laughter. "Is that what he says?" He laughed himself to helplessness. "No, Jim. He doesn't wish to admit of getting old, so he's invented some stomach ailment and I fear I've given him a vile powder. It'll cure him—" and we both laughed.

"This Jefferies?—" I began to ask.

"John's cousin? Yes, he spoke of him to me. Good physician. Looking for a wife too, I hear. Has the money now to call himself a gentleman."

I sucked in my breath. This did not suit me.

The doctor provoked another silence and I wondered if he perhaps meant me to leave him and not compromise his position. But I wanted to thank him by keeping him company.

I said to him, "Sir, I shall tell nobody I've seen you—but however this voyage turns out, I'll think constantly of this kind deed."

Dr. Livesey said nothing. We stayed near each other for some time, exchanging now and then pieces of local talk, but never for more than a word or two at a time. The night lightened in the east. When it had become bright enough for us almost to see each other's faces plainly, Dr. Livesey made a small motion with his hand. It might have been a gesture of dismissal, a wave of farewell or a blessing. He rode away.

I turned back down the lane and rounded the corner towards the inn.

Then I saw her! Out in the sea, along a path of dancing dawn light, the *Hispaniola* tacked towards our little bay like a ship in a dream.

For a long moment I stood in the inn yard and gazed. Aboard her, I had uncovered conspiracy and discovered companionship, had seen fear and valour, betrayal and death. Aboard her, the worst parts of Man had been made manifest to me. But she had saved my life, this ship, and I had saved hers; I stopped her drifting away when the last pirate had been overcome.

Inside the inn, everybody had come awake to the ship's arrival. We all flew into swift, silent and excited action. Soon Ben Gunn announced that the ship's jolly boat was sparkling across the little waves to our shore.

On the first leg of our embarkation, I departed with Grace Richardson and Louis, to help them take ship—but more than that, to see them safely off this threatening parish of ours. It was my intention to return and supervise all the remaining loading of provisions. After that we still had Tom Taylor, Ben Gunn and Jefferies to take aboard.

Quiet sailors assisted the woman and boy. The sun dazzled my eyes as I stood once more on the deck of the *Hispaniola*.

If ever there were a moment of turbulent feelings! I looked down to where Israel Hands killed the deckhand O'Brien in a long-drawn-out drunken fracas. My eye went straightaway to the mast where Hands then sought to kill me. The mast was unchanged. I believed I could still see the mark and I fancied I felt again the nip on my shoulder where Hands's knife had pinned me by my skin to the wood. And I shuddered again, the same kind of shudder that had released me from the blade.

Often I thought of Israel's eyes as he climbed up towards me, and too often I saw his face as I emptied both pistols into him. On my worst nights I looked again to the bottom of the clear sea where Hands and O'Brien lay by each other, stone dead on the seabed, their bloodied corpses rolling a little to larboard and then to starboard with the swirling of the waves. Or heard the hard *peg!peg!peg!* of Long John Silver's crutch upon the deck.

Then, my morbid thoughts were banished by a most pleasant surprise. From the aft companionway stepped my uncle, Ambrose Hatt.

"What—Uncle?!" I exclaimed. "Are you to sail with us? No! You've come to visit my mother? Surely that's it?!"

My uncle laughed. "Should I forego such an adventure, Jim? Think of how often you've lit up my mind with talk of the South Seas. I have to visit them for myself!" He laughed again, like a boy. "Jim, the law can be a dull dog. I may never get such a voyage again."

Then he bowed to Louis and kissed Grace Richardson's hand. We all smiled in delight at the comfort of my uncle's presence.

Another surprise arrived. The jolly boat's next journey brought Dr. Jefferies, Ben Gunn, Tom Taylor—and my mother. I felt in some kind of whirligig with such arrangements having been made outside my knowledge; she evidently knew from his letter that Ambrose meant to sail with us.

And my mother brought with her another deckhand as she announced, "Every ship must have its cat."

From her arms tumbled Christmas, who did as all tomcats do—claimed the ship as his kingdom and went off to look for a sunlit corner in which to preen.

I had not seen my uncle and my mother together for some years and I had forgotten how they liked each other. Within moments they had begun to laugh at some exchanged memory and even though their meeting was a fleeting one it warmed our entire company.

Much had been repaired and improved upon the *Hispaniola*. She had a new mizzen; several areas of decking had been freshly planked and she boasted new canvas universally. After our treasure hunt John Trelawney sold her back to Mr. Blandly (and, as was his custom, the squire lost money in the transaction).

An officer came forwards.

"Mr. Hawkins, so they say?"

"They say correctly."

"I am the mate, sir, Nathan Coll." A Scotchman, he had a face the colour of teak and a hand that was harder than that. "I am given to understand, sir, that when under way we shall receive full information."

I knew nothing of this and said so.

"Mr. Hatt, I believe, sir, has spoken to the captain."

I replied, "Then I'm sure that is what will happen."

Nathan Coll went about his business. I moved to take my mother ashore and complete the safe transfers of the provisions. On the land my mother gave no demonstration of affection, but walked a little away from me.

She turned and said, "I look forwards to your safe return, Jim."

She rarely addressed me by name—therefore I knew this to be an expression of some depth for her.

"We'll be back by the springtime, Mother," I assured her.

Then she smiled at me, in a warm special way I have only seen from her two or three times in my life. Even now I am made warm by that smile. When I think of it, I stop writing this chronicle for a moment and gaze through the window at the sea.

With powder, shot and myself, the jolly boat completed her last journey. I allowed my feet to feel the deck of the *Hispaniola* more fully and I can say now that no matter how frightful have been some of my days aboard her—I love that ship and I love the memory of her . . .

Ch. 10 —

The Black Brig

Presently we were ready to depart. Louis took great delight in watching the raising of the anchor. These sailors did not sing at their work, nor did they speak. Under the eye of a tall, thin officer they ran the capstan round in diligent and busy silence. The anchor rose dripping from the deep seabed. Then Louis came to me and clutched my arm tightly, as though afraid. I felt that familiar burst of discomfort that heralds fear—the fear, as I thought, of this great responsibility I had undertaken.

Behind us the land slipped away. I could see the white walls of the Admiral Benbow high on the foreland and I was surprised at the force with which my heart ached. Then I found, I believed, the source of my sudden fear—and it came from something other than my new burdens.

Kitts Hole has headlands of uneven length, the one to the east protruding much longer than the westward. As we cleared the last bluff of rock, I saw a brig lying at anchor in the next little bay. She was generally black, and smaller than the *Hispaniola*.

It seemed as if she had not rigged and so had not moved. I looked around. Uncle Ambrose had a telescope and he watched too. I took the glass from him and murmured, "Uncle, let her not see this." My uncle did not hesitate; he left me and soon I saw him walking with Grace Richardson on the decks to starboard.

I studied the black ship. From her quarterdeck someone now watched us with a spyglass. Soon, the brig's rigging swarmed. Her sailors broke out jet-black sails. Anchor aweigh, on she came after us, a beetle scudding across the green waters.

Did the brig mean to follow us? I asked myself the question, observing the suddenness with which she rigged. Did this mean also that she had followed the *Hispaniola* from Bristol? I had one of those moments of greatest discomfort that come when we know our fears have true foundations.

Our wake began to run. Soon the brig, if she intended a pursuit, would pick up our foamy path like a hound. I had not enough experience of the sea or ships to tell whether such a craft might catch us. I reckoned not—but I kept watching her, although I meant to conceal my worry.

Mr. Coll observed my telescope and came to stand by my side.

"I saw her too, sir. Because not many rig theirselves black."

"How fast is she, Mr. Coll?"

He found his own glass and looked at her.

"Fast enough, sir. And neat," and as if Mr. Coll guessed my thought he added, "But not apt to race or keep in sight a ship like this."

"Why not?" An appeal to a man's knowledge often produces vital information.

"Because—her spread of sail, sir. She's lean in the water, right enough. And she's light. She has no damage in her that I can see. But because also we carry, I should say, once-and-a-half her canvas, sir. Maybe more."

"Yet she seems to move swiftly."

"You'll see for yourself, sir. Because in some minutes we'll be under full sail." (Mr. Coll had an attachment to the word "because.")

The great noises of shipboard life continued to ring out across the *Hispaniola*—barked orders, running feet and the very loud snapping of canvas. As a mainsail, topsails and then two mizzens broke, our vessel lurched forwards like a carriage.

I continued to watch the black brig. Although now under full sail herself, she began to slip farther and farther behind. Soon we would be too far ahead for her to guess our course.

For'ards, I saw that Dr. Jefferies also walked with Grace Richardson. I could not immediately attend to that worry because I had much to ask my uncle, particularly about events in Bristol and how Maltby's visit had turned out. Uncle Ambrose saw my beckoning, left his companions and returned to my side.

To my question he answered, "They proved uncommon difficult, Jim. My friend Lord Gibbon was so sorely tried by their manners one evening that he said to me he felt they should be in irons, not in the comfort of my house."

My heart in my mouth I asked, "Did they discuss the death of their friend?"

I observed that, all the time we spoke, my uncle watched Grace Richardson as she walked with Jefferies. He, I felt, did not like the doctor either.

"No, Jim. Odd thing. Not a word about it. My own opinion is, they sensed some stratagem afoot but couldn't pin it. Twice they asked me whether I knew this country—" Uncle waved his hand towards our shore. "And Maltby, he asked me whether my legal works took me, he said, 'to that lovely land west of Minehead?' Jim, I disliked that man."

"What became of them?" I asked.

My uncle shook his head. "I don't know. I left them in my house, attended by my servants and having sworn Blandly to secrecy. But many people will have known the *Hispaniola* has slipped harbour, even though we sailed at night. She's a distinctive ship and well liked in Bristol."

"Was the hunchback with them?" I asked.

Uncle Ambrose replied, "I saw no hunchback." He began to count, using his fingers. "There was Maltby. There was his thin clerk and there was that red-faced, beery fellow you described. A fellow of good birth, I feel, but much caroused. Three of them." Uncle Ambrose raised his fingers. "No, Jim, no hunchback. I should think they would not wish a lawyer questioning that they kept such company."

At that moment Dr. Jefferies, from whom Grace was parting, hailed us. Accompanied by Mr. Coll, he approached and said that Captain Reid had called us to a conference. We went below.

How pleasant and yet not without distress to see again the large cabin. How long a time and how short a time since I last stood here—the years from boy to man! Here, trembling from excitement and fear, I had told Captain Smollett, Squire Trelawney and Dr. Livesey about the mutinous incitements of Silver, upon whom I had eavesdropped from my hiding place within the apple barrel. How strange, how thrilling, to see again the timbers, the nautical furnishings I had so often tried to recall.

Captain Reid, a Scotchman from Glasgow, was reddish of hair, clear of eye and plump. He possessed an almost fearfully imposing authority. His forehead bore a deep scar. I was unable to stop myself asking him if the ship had an apple barrel. Captain Reid looked at me hard and did not answer. My uncle whispered to me with a smile, "I think he found your question frivolous." When we had seated ourselves the captain began.

"Gentlemen. I will commence by informing you of the ship's strength. Mr. Coll's my first officer. My second mate's Dawson, he's a tall, thin man, you cannot avoid seeing him. The bo'sun's called Noonstock, likewise tall. We've twenty-two able-bodied seamen, three deckhands, a cabin boy, a cook and a cook's assistant. Watches'll be according to regulations. *Anybody* who flouts an order as to the safety of the ship will be taken to a near port and discharged. I've accepted Dr. Jefferies's medical credentials and he's been appointed ship's doctor. This gives him no formal attachment to the ship beyond the duty of these voyages out and home. In all things aboard I'm the last authority. In my absence, which'll be due to sleep or watch only, Mr. Coll'll act for me, assisted by Second Mate Dawson. This is a diligent ship. She'll continue so. As we near the destination charted to me, I'll call upon you to make plain your shore intentions. That'll be all."

I sought his attention. "Captain Reid? May I ask one or two things?"

He looked at me without friendliness. "I did not give permission for questions. If you require information, address yourself to Mr. Coll."

He rose and turned his back to us; we stood, dismissed. Only Jefferies seemed pleased by this countenance.

"By Jove! Direct, eh? Is he not a firm man? I shall enjoy having such a shipmate."

For a moment I feared Jefferies about to utter some other mariners' exclamation as "My hearties," or "Belay there!" or somesuch. In the days before our departure he had been irksomely testing seafaring expressions from a small book he carried with him.

On deck, I turned around and saw Nathan Coll ascend behind us.

"Mr. Coll, I must have a word," I said.

"And so must I," added my uncle.

Mr. Coll looked at us coolly and waited.

"Your captain's tone is too high for me, Mr. Coll," I said.

My uncle added, "And for me."

Nathan Coll, though firm, was a diplomatic man. He directed us in a pleasant way to the afterdeck and found a place where we might stand and discuss without being overheard.

"Gentlemen," he said. "I say three things. If you take exception to Captain Reid's manner and make this known to him, he will about ship now and return us to Bristol. For a second point, he is the only captain I know who, with only a few loyal hands left to him, quelled a mutiny and saw all the mutineers, who outnumbered his crew, hanged at Executioner's Dock. He inspected every man jack's body as they all swung from the gallows. My third point is, if I divine you well, you wish to brief him on the purpose of your voyage. Captain Reid is a man who does not wish information in advance of the time he needs it. Because when he believes the appropriate moment has come, he will ask you."

"But, sir," protested my uncle, "his courtesy wants much!"

"He is not at all courteous in a crisis either." Coll softened a little. "Captain Reid is a firm man, sir. Think you what age he might be, gentlemen?" When we did not answer, Coll said, "Because he has not yet reached thirty-five. He is a rare man."

"Thirty-five?!" gasped my uncle.

My jaw also dropped at this discovery. Although the captain's age was indeterminable from his appearance, I expected a certain venerability from a ship's master. My uncle and I spoke our thanks to Nathan Coll and he left us. I turned to face astern. In a vista crystal-bright to the horizon's line, I saw no trace of the black brig.

—✦—

Ch. 11—

Ocean Waves

Days at sea possess a mood very unlike days ashore. There is much time for thinking. I began to recall our first voyage with ever greater clarity, and without fear. How John Silver duped us all! He had heard of Squire Trelawney's loose talk around Bristol, talk of treasure and a map and a distant island. Silver then foisted his own gang of pirates on the squire: the selfsame bunch who raided the Benbow the night Billy Bones died, became a majority of the crew on the *Hispaniola*.

What became of Silver? As I gazed over the rail and the waters rushed by, I thought of him. From the outset of our fated voyage he had planned that he would never return to England. That inn of his, on Bristol docks, the Spy-Glass, with its large, low, smoky room and its neat red curtains—he had sold that before he embarked with us.

John Silver! He had a way of making you feel a rare importance in yourself. Long John! I saw him murder a man. I heard him plot foul crimes. I knew he lied on both sides of his face. Yet I missed him when he went, vanished one hot night in that gleaming, landlocked gulf where we put in for supplies.

But that was ten years ago. As my new voyage settled down, I was able to enjoy the blue sky and the wide solitude of the ocean without any of the fears of mutiny Silver had once caused this ship.

After five days among shipping lanes, we soon saw no other vessels come near, not a schooner, nor a man o' war, nor a brig, black or any colour. One afternoon a school of dolphins attached themselves to us and gambolled so close by we might have touched them. That was our most direct experience of other life. The sun grew hotter by the day.

The night Silver jumped ship, he took with him a helping of our treasure. The cargo was so mixed we could not fully ascertain what or how much—we thought he took one bag of coin; I believe he also grabbed some ingots when he cut through the bulkhead. If I knew Silver, he would claim he was doing no more than allocating himself a dividend—"a fair divvy, Jim"—but in any case we did not begrudge it. His place aboard had given us difficult thought. He had, after all, saved our lives and yet we were bringing him home to England to be tried as a pirate and mutineer—and almost certainly hanged. I remember the warmth of the air the night he disappeared; after ten days at sea that same strong heat now began to mantle my face in sweat.

We had wonderful fortune with the winds and Captain Reid's crew took full advantage. They also kept to a discipline I had never seen before. None of them paused to pass the time of day, nor to comment upon the weather, nor to make pleasantries. This strict demeanour did not impede their natural courtesy, which they displayed if encountered in, say, the close quarters of a companionway. Each crewman would stand aside and speak only when spoken to.

Of Captain Reid I saw little. I heard from my uncle once or twice that he had met the captain again and thought him "a much-concentrated man."

I began to rest considerably. Shipboard sleep being one of the greatest and deepest pleasures of life, I began to feel relaxed and capable again. At last my thoughts could dwell upon Grace Richardson. Before leaving home I had promised myself that, while at sea, I would try and bring my feelings for her under control. Should I speak to her what was in my heart? No, not yet, let us conclude our mission successfully—but I meant to ask her the most imperative questions to which I still needed answers.

My reflections ran like this: I am twenty-five years old and not without some experiences of life—but I feel more baffled by this woman now than when I first met her. And more deeply in thrall to her: I watched her when she walked, when she sat at table, when she talked. I imagined constantly of giving her a wondrous, troublefree life, where she would be my companion and I would dedicate to her everything I did.

This was all so new and disturbing to me that were I a man of prayer, I think I should have asked the Almighty to unchain me from this wild man who had come to dwell in my heart. Perhaps I could try and take my uncle's advice—separate my feelings from my thoughts? This might enable me to survey and judge what little I knew of her.

However, deep in these thoughts I began to learn one of the great lessons of my young life. Whatever Uncle Ambrose advised, the heart will not necessarily make itself subject to the brain. I found it impossible to pin down a clear judgement of her—and I could not pluck up the courage to press my questions.

As the days passed, our mood aboard grew quieter and quieter. Young Louis's behaviour since we set sail had been exemplary. He no longer behaved as excessively as when we first met. Now he became more watchful. He still ran about the decks and he still stared at the sailors swarming the rigging, but he had become a little solemn. His mother was sombre too; she appeared on deck less frequently; indeed, she withdrew much as she did in my mother's company at the Admiral Benbow.

The talkative Jefferies, everyone's friend, also stilled himself. Busy among his medical boxes, he spread out his powders, measuring and preparing. My uncle, untypically, brought silences to our conversations during our daily promenade around the decks. When I saw Ben Gunn from time to time, he too seemed changed. He still looked like a kind of man who has truly found his element, who is only comfortable with the timbers of a ship rolling beneath his feet. Now I thought him a little mad, jerking his head like a marionette and unsure of his own natural merriment.

From observing this general change of mood among my travelling companions, I knew one day that we had crossed over from the peacefulness of a long sea voyage to a sense of apprehension as we neared our goal. And I fancied the anxious mood had spread all through the ship; the officers and men seemed more concentrated than before, a development I should not have thought possible.

I myself grew as gloomy as any of them. Whether this air came from those around me, or from the remembrances caused by the original journey, or from the natural apprehensive fear of the circumstances, I could not be certain. Yet, however solemn the ship, I reflected many times upon how comfortable a mutiny-free voyage felt. This *Hispaniola*, unlike the squire's rebellious commission all those years ago, ran tight and orderly before the wind.

———t———

Ch. 12—

Treasure Island Again

Early of a hot evening, when sea birds began to drift and soar above the *Hispaniola*, Mr. Coll summoned my uncle Ambrose, Grace Richardson and me to attend upon Captain Reid. I, the last to arrive, found myself in the companionway behind the others. We waited in silence, fanning ourselves with our hands and kerchiefs to keep cool.

The boatswain, Noonstock, came down and, sliding past us in the narrow space, greeted us civilly. He knocked respectfully upon the captain's door and entered, closing the door behind him. We looked questions at one another, but had not long to wait. Noonstock reappeared and with a great display of courtesy invited us to enter and greet the captain.

With Mr. Coll and Noonstock standing behind him, Captain Reid rose from his chart table and indicated seats. Noonstock moved among us with a beverage; silence prevailed until all had been served. Then Captain Reid stated his business.

"Madam, Doctor, gentlemen."

He was born old, this captain of ours; I could not see in him any trace of the boy he must once have been; I expect he was grave at his schooling, and fierce. For the first time I observed in him a slight peculiarity of the eye. When formal, he seemed to squint a little. It was so moderate that I was slow to determine which eye was crooked. I also got the impression that when he was less pressed, the eyes reverted to a normal position. The captain's hands lay calmly upon his charts. In a man so evidently hard, it surprised me to see the girl-white softness of his knuckles and palms. He coughed a little.

"As we embarked I assured you that I would ask for a fuller briefing when the voyage proved it necessary. 'Tis necessary now." He had the uncomfortable habit of ending his words abruptly, leaving his listeners expecting more.

Ambrose Hatt, the most comfortable among us, spoke.

"May I enquire, sir, what has brought this necessity upon us?"

"I calculate that we're but a day and a half from this island you seek," replied the captain. A tremor ran through me and, I think, through the others. "Therefore I require to know what I must expect."

"Be more specific, sir," said my uncle. "Do you ask after anchorages? If so, my nephew will give you such knowledge as he has. So will Gunn. If you require details as to our purpose—" My uncle indicated Grace Richardson. "This lady—although there are other matters—will give an explanation."

Captain Reid gave no sign that he thought my uncle's words important.

"I require to know whether I must take passengers from this island. Whether I have cargo to take aboard. Whether the rule of law will apply—in other words, am I to use my powers of arrest?"

We all looked puzzled. Reid grew sharp.

"Are there pirates there? That's what I mean."

By this we were all dismayed. I could see the difficulty in my friends' faces. This was the point we had all avoided. Whatever I knew, were we openly to call Joseph Tait a pirate? But if we did not, given what I knew, should we be accused of concealing a criminal from the eyes of justice?

My uncle began a smooth rescue.

"Sir, we are aware that the gentleman we seek has, we understand, been on the island some time. Of course we do not know whether he has remained there. Or whether he is still alive. But the journey is being undertaken principally to meet him. Should the man wish to return I hope we can give him passage. It may prove that he wishes to remain here. Or go to another destination.

My uncle stopped.

Captain Reid looked up. "You use the word 'principally,' sir. Do you imply there may be secondary reasons for this voyage?"

"There is a matter, I believe, of some—" Uncle Ambrose hesitated as though he did not want to finish the sentence.

"Some what?" asked Captain Reid.

"Some silver," I spoke up. "The last of a contraband."

"Does it belong to His Majesty the King?" asked the captain.

"By which you mean spoils of piracy?" interjected my uncle.

"And from ships of which flag?" The captain was a relentless man.

"Spanish, I understand," I said. My manner was entirely hesitant—because I felt most uncomfortable in Captain Reid's society.

The captain then showed the Scotch side of his nature. He drew from beneath the chart table a small chest and from it took a document.

"Sir," he said to my uncle. "Do me the good favour of appraising this. This is my deed of contract, which I believe you had Mr. Blandly draw up. It will specify as to my profits should this voyage gain commercially."

My uncle sighed and I took it to be an expression of relief. He began to read the contract.

"I believe, Captain, that this entitles you to ten parts on a hundred."

"We have established that such trove as may still repose there is not the property of His Majesty the King. And I owe no allegiance to the King of Spain, nor shall I ever. Therefore," asked the captain, "what is the worth of this contraband silver?" He more or less spat the word "contraband."

I replied. "I am the one person in this cabin who has seen it. I don't know its value—but in bulk it's said to be only a third less than the hoard taken home and shared among those of us who came here previously."

Captain Reid became almost merry. "Why, then," he said, "we merely must discuss procedures. Mr. Coll, do you have plans in mind? And you, Bo'sun Noonstock?"

The mate spoke up. "I believe, sir, we must first establish the presence of the gentleman. Whether he still be on the island."

Grace Richardson spoke for the first time—and startled me. "I am given to believe he was seen there a year ago."

I spun my head. She had never said this before! I was riven with curiosity. How had she heard this information? My uncle also turned to look at her—by which I knew that he too was surprised.

"Do we know of his condition?" asked the captain.

"No," she said, and took on a look of not wishing to speak again. If my experience of her reticence could be drawn upon as a witness, I felt sure nobody would ever learn how she had heard so recently of Tait. At a stroke she had deepened by cubits the mystery of her life.

"In which case, sir," continued Nathan Coll to his captain, "I believe we should send a respectable party to find him. Because when he's apprised of the situation, meaning, sir, the personnel aboard this ship, we shall determine whether he come to us, or whether the lady and the boy go to him. Mr. Noonstock?"

The bo'sun took up the plan. "I propose one boat, cap'n. Of our finest hands. All armed and seen to be so. We'll show a firm position. Under colours too, sir."

Nathan Coll said, "Because we don't rightly know, sir, what faces us, sir. We don't know whether others will have landed on that island. Because there may even be a population there."

"They'll be having an ill time of it, if that is so," I interrupted. "You're forgetting, gentlemen—this is a very inhospitable place. I believe, Captain Reid, your orders will contain that information."

"Mr. Coll," asked the captain, "what arrangements have you made for the ferrying of the goods?"

"We have the strength to make good, quick expeditions, sir," replied the mate.

I intervened. "There are at least thirty chests."

"How far from the shore nearest the anchorage?" Captain Reid asked me.

"If carrying heavy loads—a good hour's march," I said. "In rough land."

The captain thought for a moment. "Do we know aught of the tides? If we are to take on cargo?"

I said, "There are reefs. The tides run unevenly. It can be difficult not to drift. She drifted much on our last voyage."

Silence fell in the cabin. The captain, at last, stood to his feet.

"I should like to think we shall face for home within two to three days. Mr. Hatt, I take it you'll oversee the personal business? Mr. Hawkins, I should be obliged if you make yourself available to Mr. Coll and to Bo'sun Noonstock. As guide and adviser. For the time think yourself an officer of this ship. You may take that regrettable fellow, Gunn, with you. But keep him on a leash."

Our interview was over. How he signalled it I cannot say, but all knew that we had ended our meeting. His hard, round face shone with confidence. I think he reckoned with relish the booty to come and the efficiency with which he meant to fetch it. Captain Reid was not a man who expected reversal—certainly not reversal so great and unusual as that which he was about to face.

After the crowded cabin I came up on deck to breathe the air. Night had begun its descent, so fast, I recalled, in these regions. A figure plucked at me from the shadows and I jumped back, until I recognised the style of plucking.

"Ben," I said. "Don't alarm me any longer."

He clung to me. "Two things, two things," he said, and I noted his anxiety, "Two things, Jim. Ben Gunn doan't want to go ashore."

"Nonsense," I said. "Why d'you think we've brought you here? You know this island like you know your own hand."

"Oh, no, Jim, no, pity's sake, no, Jim, Ben doan't want to go back to them bones and that."

I made light of it. "Think of it, Ben. Think of your goats. Their grandchildren will be bounding there now. Anyway, what was the second thing?" I walked briskly, hoping to shake him off; his aroma was sometimes too much for me, notwithstanding Dr. Jefferies's best efforts to make Ben use soap and water.

"Oh, Jim, the second thing is—reckon there's land. Reckon that's him up there."

We went forwards, Ben and I. Although the old moon was some hours away the night was bright. Where Ben pointed I could see the dark, low line of land—it seemed to wait for us, expecting us, as a beast watches prey and I found it more sinister than I could say, even to myself.

It terrified Ben Gunn.

"That's him, Jim." He clapped his hands over his head as I am told monkeys do when distressed. "Oh, Jim! That cursed place!"

I shivered. Now, such a long time after, I shiver again as I write these words.

———⌇———

Part Three

—⁊—

Black and Blacker

Ch. 13 —

A Mysterious Disappearance

That was a troubled night. Jarred by the sight of that wretched isle, my senses assailed me, asking me violent questions. I became wakeful and disturbed—as who would not be in my circumstances? Here I was, on the other side of the world, on the shores of an island of which I still had vile dreams, in a cause of whose true depths I knew nothing, for the sake of a woman to whom I believed I had lost my heart, yet who had already led to me being accused of murder!

I understand now that I seemed to have undertaken the whole enterprise in a kind of daze. But it was her power that had also persuaded my uncle to come here—the wealthy Bristol lawyer, Mr. Ambrose Hatt, whom I used to call my "cautious" uncle, widely consulted for his prudence by men of influence! What strength Grace Richardson must have, if she could draw us all here—and without ever having overtly asked.

When I sleep badly, I do not reach firm or useful conclusions and it is best, I find, to put the night to an end. I rose with the sun, shaved, dressed with as much care as if going to church and ascended to the already warm deck. There and then I felt the renewed and more powerful stabs—of anger at myself, stomach sickness at my own foolishness and of true fear. These sudden knives to my soul were brought on by my full sight of land and the onrush of fierce memories.

Treasure Island lay exactly as I remembered her in my thoughts, as fearfully as she had appeared in my nightmares. Low and evil at the shore, high and confusing as the eye progressed inland, she spoke to me of greed, betrayal and death. The trees on her slopes had multiplied so densely that the earliest landmarks we had used among them were long overwhelmed. Those groves with their haphazard growths—I once ran through them in fear of my life, across ground rough with roots and scrub.

I scanned the island with all the power I could bring to my eyes. I looked up to her peaks, I looked down to her foreshore, I looked left and right, here, there and everywhere, until my eyes hurt. But no people or buildings could I see anywhere; no boats squatted on the desolate shore or bobbed in the shallows; no human life seemed here.

A figure came to my elbow and grunted.

"Your island, Mr. Hawkins," said Captain Reid in his dry voice.

I made no answer, other than a sound to acknowledge his presence. The captain raised his telescope.

"What is that?" He lowered the glass and pointed.

"Spyglass Hill," I said. "And that"—pointing to my right—"is Foremast Hill. We stand before the North Inlet, Captain."

With some irritation he replied, "Yes, I too can read a map, Mr. Hawkins. Or so I have been told. I was not referring to the chart readings, I was asking about the building."

I strained my eyes. He handed me his telescope and said, "Sou' sou'west. Near the top of Spyglass Hill."

I looked. A half-built edifice had arisen, of poles and stakes. It seemed abandoned. We stood in silence for a moment. He gestured and I gave him back his glass.

"The men who raised that are no builders, Mr. Hawkins." He scanned. "Empty. Disused. There is nothing human here—that is my opinion."

Captain Reid blew loudly on a whistle. Noonstock appeared.

"Bo'sun, fetch Mr. Coll."

"Aye aye, sir."

Others gathered; Grace Richardson came last. By the time she arrived, Uncle Ambrose, Dr. Jefferies, Mr. Coll and Noonstock had gathered around Captain Reid. All of us deferred to her, almost as people do to a mourner. She stood in the place we cleared for her alongside the captain. He handed her the telescope and told her to scan the island.

After several moments she handed the instrument back to the captain and said quietly, "That is a wilderness."

"Madam, there is no sign of human life." He spoke directly, without feeling.

At the captain's invitation my uncle and Dr. Jefferies took turns with the telescope. While they fell into talk I looked intently at the incomplete building.

"They climbed high, at least," I said loudly.

Captain Reid took the glass again and viewed.

"Bo'sun, fetch Gunn."

Ben arrived, nervously covering his head again with his hands.

"What was up there?" asked the Captain.

"On Spyglass Hill? Ben Gunn's goats, Cap'n. They jumped higher'n any goat you ever seed."

"The terrain, man?!"

Ben looked even more stricken and I translated.

"What was the land like there, Ben? Could a man live that high up?"

"Ow, Jim, no, nobody could live there, our Almighty Himself, not He, no!"

"Is it rough, Ben?"

"Rough, Jim."

"Too rough for you, Ben?"

"Ow, Jim, sheer. An' high. An' hard. Any man'd fall. The goats nearly was afraid of it, Jim."

"Thank you, Ben," I said.

I longed to ask him what he made of the rude building we could see, but the moment was not right. He scuttled away.

"Captain?"

He gave me his attention.

"In the interests of a swift return," I said, "let us go ashore without Ben. I know the way."

Captain Reid said, "I always thought him a burden. But if he finds our cargo—"

"Let us do that once the first business is resolved," I argued.

Coll nodded his agreement, evidently relieved; I had merely been protecting Ben from the harshness of a brisk foray under harsh orders—while showing to Grace Richardson that I cherished the prior importance of her quest.

The captain summarised. "I view the matter in this way. Madam, gentlemen, we have here no changed circumstance, no prospect very different from our expectation. We see here no evidence of organisation. Or civilisation. Or daily human life."

"Indeed, sir, there's no road, no path," said Nathan Coll, waving the glass and indicating with his hand. We all scanned the lowlands, across the flat wide mouth of beige sand that wound into the trees.

"No harbour," said Uncle Ambrose, thinking aloud. "Not even a mooring."

"But in accordance with the commissioning of this voyage," continued Captain Reid, "we will find out. Mr. Coll, take six men. Arm them. Mr. Hawkins, I expect you to volunteer as a seventh. You'll find a way to the hill. I take it the other side of the island was equally inhospitable."

I nodded. "This ship saw every side. It is all diseased and dangerous."

"Depart immediately," said Captain Reid. "Make your way to that building. It is at least a sign that people once dwelt here—or tried to. If you find your man—Mr. Coll, bring him aboard. If that should seem imprudent for whatever reason—return so that we may think again. In general, achieve what you can. Return when you believe yourself satisfied."

Nathan Coll possessed the kind of competence that does not draw attention to itself. Within minutes we stepped into the lowered jolly boat. Grace Richardson watched as I moved to the ladder. She showed no emotion. Louis waved—both his hands: I had begun to feel a father's affection for that boy and this did not assist my attitude towards Joseph Tait. Ben Gunn did not appear.

The seamen under Mr. Coll's orders rowed with steady power. I stared at the island, as much to overcome my fear of the place as to figure out what lay immediately ahead. We reached the shoulder of North Inlet within half an hour. Now, I felt this soft spit of sand on Treasure Island beneath my boots again. To my surprise much of my apprehension abated and I felt excited.

With the boat moored to a high old crag, the eight of us formed up and marched silently along level ground, the King's colours in full view. Breezes cooled us in woods of scattered trees where birds crawked and whirred. Our only difficulty came from the roots which coiled like hard serpents near the surface of the earth and threatened to catch our ankles.

After about an hour or more, keeping the spring and the swamplands due southeast of us, to our left, we began to climb steeply. Once, we had to clamber across the bed of what must have been a torrent in rainy seasons. All was shaded and dry along its length, with not even a glint of water. The land levelled briefly and then rose again, this time steep as a mountainside. We halted, looking at the ruined hut far above.

Competent men I have known, even though they be men of action, possess a common property—they also take time to think. I saw the workings of Mr. Coll's mind in his broad face.

At length he said to me, "Mr. Hawkins, I b'lieve the cap'n's right, I don't think there's no human life here."

"I think the same, Mr. Coll," I said—but I knew I spoke as much from the wish as from the belief.

The wind blew. Not an animal howled and no bird sang. I had a child's fear that eyes watched us from the trees.

We rounded a precipice with the greatest care. My hands and face had become as wet as from washing; the sweat stood in my hair too. Mr. Coll gave a signal to halt and we waited while he advanced. No sound interposed, except the occasional *ching!* of metal upon rock from boot or musket. Then Mr. Coll reappeared from round a corner and beckoned us forwards: it took several minutes after his signal to reach him. We reached him, crowded together and looked up.

Above us stood the unfinished building. The climb to it had once been eased with some steps of rough stone. If ever again my heart pounds like that, I shall not ignore what it tells me. We clambered the last, near vertical thirty yards and stood on the plateau.

Whoever had chosen to build here had a black soul, a cold, bleak spirit. Yet they—or he—had some practical turn of mind. It could easily be defended. A dozen, two dozen men could stand here and have sufficient freedom of movement to repel attackers. Sheer drops fell on either side; the high cliff of Spyglass Hill stood at the back. Only one way led up to it, the steep path we took. Any advancing party stood completely at the mercy of those above.

In the centre of the plateau stood the timbered ruin, the only evidence we had so far seen that men had once been on the island. A crude door stood against a wall, never hinged, never hung. Other rough timbers rested against that thick, high cliff of grey stone, three-quarters clad with spiky vegetation.

Who could have built the hut? The three buccaneers whom we marooned? Could they have survived long enough, recovered well enough, to make this effort? If so, at least one did not endure to enjoy it. Inside, on the clay of what passed for the floor, squatted a human skull half-in and half-out of the earth.

I don't know from whom I learned this—but when faced with difficulties, of whatever proportion, I think it prudent to fall silent; then, I do not proceed until I have listened hard to the noises all around me. On that shelf of rock, no sound did I hear, not of whisper nor of thunder.

Behind me Mr. Coll murmured, "Mr. Hawkins?" and I stepped back.

"What now?" I asked.

"This is a burial, I think," he said. I waited. "Let us establish if you can say who it is."

"Not from a skull," I said.

"There may be clothing. Beneath the earth." I took Coll's point. Turning to the men he said, "A trenching tool. Go softly."

The men lowered their muskets and fell out, not making a sound. Most looked about and wrinkled their noses, as if struck by a bad odour. No one of us moved away from our group by more than a few feet; there was not room to do so. Two of them dug the space around the skull but, I saw, took care not to touch the thing itself. The rest of us became fixed upon the digging as raptly as if watching some dreadful game. A dank breeze swirled.

Mr. Coll, who also from time to time held a hand to his nose, interrupted my fearfulness.

"Mr. Hawkins, do you read a compass?"

"Captain Smollett taught me," I said.

Mr. Coll smiled at the reminder of a famous seafarer.

"There is nothing to be found here—but I want to leave no stone unturned. Take my compass," he said, "and while we dig, travel to the lower plateau, round that last rock there"—he pointed down—"and establish the direction to the cave where old Gunn says the silver must lie. Because if we assess it as we go back, we shall save time on our next expedition."

"What do you need?" I asked.

"A good impression," he said, "of how we should travel there, the shortest or best route to and from the jolly boat's mooring."

I took Mr. Coll's compass and started down the hard path, glad to turn my back on the digging. As so often proves true in life, the return had more difficulty than the advance. I almost fell across one narrow precipice and had to steady myself repeatedly. Eventually I stood at the point where, on our upwards march, we had noted a wide view of the island beneath us.

With care I took the compass readings, remembering Captain

Smollett's exhortation: "Read your compass three times. The first to make out, the second to prove, the third to retain."

I took my east-of-south reading, checked it and began to commit it to memory. For a moment or two I stood, looking at the vista far below me. Leaning hard and dangerously to my left, I could make out the *Hispaniola* at anchor in the green-and-blue distance. The sight of her cheered me and I turned back to my climb, murmuring the compass readings to myself.

As I manhandled myself around by the rock that led to the last reach upwards, I stopped. No man stood by the old shack. I could see right within the misfortunate building. Nobody stood there. That small plateau was as tight as a dish and a solid column of creeper-covered rock was its back. Mr. Coll and the six sailors had vanished.

But they had nowhere else to go. Mine was the only path. The other three sides of the place consisted of sheer drops to left and right; straight ahead rose that wall of stone and thorny growth. My heart almost stopped. I stood, not knowing what to do. My bladder slackened urgently. Then I reasoned to myself that another hidden path must lie behind the plateau and I climbed on, calling Mr. Coll's name.

When I reached the level ground and entered the old timbers I saw that some bones of a scattered skeleton had been exposed. A piece of faded red cloth lay spread on the ground; I thought I recalled the tunic of the apoplectic old pirate, Tom Morgan. The skull, when I could bring myself to look at it, reminded me of Morgan's bull head. Heavy footprints marked the burial place where the men had dug. But I found no other trace of them, although their digging had exposed the fact that Morgan had been placed vertically in his crude grave.

I walked outside and squeezed to the back of the rough building. No one could have stayed there—and there was no place to hide. I went to each sheer drop and forced myself to look down. No bodies, no trace of falls, no torn shrubs or broken branches. In each case the view down was long and clean and anybody falling must have died. Behind the ruin, I inspected the tall rock clad with growth. No trace of life could be seen, no sight of weaponry, no sign of warfare. The vegetation was clammy and forbidding.

I called and called. I hallooed, *"Mister Coll!"* The stones gave back some of my words and that echo was all I heard. Spyglass Hill was as empty as a new-made tomb.

Ch. 14—

Our Difficulties Increase

Once, when I was a boy visiting my uncle, the annual fair came to Bristol. A fakir made himself disappear and that night, in my childish excitement, I told Uncle Ambrose the story. Gently, with no disrespect to the magic, he tried to teach me reason.

"People cannot disappear into thin air, Jim," he said.

On Spyglass Hill I said to myself over and over, "People cannot disappear into thin air, Jim."

I trembled; fear had followed on the heels of my bewilderment, too much fear to allow me a prolonged search. Anyway, one man alone could not resolve this problem. I began to assess what must be done and why. Mr. Coll and his men must not stay there—wherever they were—prone to fever, prey to wild animals. I felt certain a good search party would retrieve them—and answer the puzzle.

For one last time I looked about the plateau and then set off down the path. At the big rock I halted and gazed back. Everything remained still and dank; the clamminess of the stone had spread, it felt, to my heart.

Best, when afraid, to busy oneself. I pressed on, head up, eyes ahead, feeling very much a lone soldier. When the ground levelled I rested a moment. I had crossed these lands before—rattling along in the band of pirates with Silver, as we raced to the treasure "X" marked on the map; then to find it empty save for a few coins. Near here, I had found Ben Gunn and the bones of a long dead pirate arranged like a sign. Across this arena I ran my breakneck rush back to the stockade. But this was a worse situation.

The ground has one last high undulation before it descends to the water. As I breasted it and saw the *Hispaniola* at anchor far out beyond the reef, another defeating thought came to me. This morning, the ship's jolly boat had needed four strenuous oarsmen.

No rest now. Half an hour's brisk march stretched between me and the water, enough time to think some solution of the rowing problem. Once before I had needed to get to this ship, anchored in more or less the same position. Then, Ben Gunn's coracle had followed the tides. I reasoned that the jolly boat, a sounder and larger craft, also floated. If I could manoeuvre her into the flow of the current she should bring me close enough to the *Hispaniola* for the watch to see me.

In the late morning heat and a filling tide I pushed the jolly boat out into the deepest water I could stand up in. Then I clambered aboard, held two oars and tried to haul like a giant; skill, if I possessed any, must now come into play. Soon, once I had clumsily mastered the art of keeping the tide from taking me back to shore again, the sea took over, with alarming strength.

Now I understood why the oarsmen had been so strained in the morning's crossing. Farther and farther, with each surging wave, the boat, with guidance from my oars which had become almost as rudders, was taken out to sea. That run of the tide was why Mr. Coll had chosen not to beach deep inside the North Inlet.

And then—I allowed her to be taken too far! My plan had been to place her in the current I could see running down to within a shout of the *Hispaniola*'s anchorage. Instead, the waves decided a different course and I began to be whipped away, far to the west of where I wanted to be. The waters up there are most rough and this was not what I had planned or sought. Worse—I heard a roar, sudden as an animal, behind me and knew I was almost upon the reef. All had gone wrong.

Did I close my eyes? Yes, I must have closed my eyes. In an instant, as if about to stop all its motion, the boat felt as heavy as lead; the oars had all but ceased obeying my feeble wrists. This was the lull that comes before all violent events—because my next movements took place in a kind of rushing blur and all I could do was hold still, sit straight and go along with the sea's wishes.

I still dream badly of that roaring reef. Louder and louder it grew and my eyes closed ever tighter. Water flared up on either side of me, in columns and spouts, white and then green and then black, and yet the spouts never fell upon me, though they did drench me with their spray and filled my face with salt. I opened my eyes once but they smarted to the glare of the white waters and my ears were drummed to deafness with the amazing roars.

Then—silence, or at least a dulling of the noise and I opened my eyes again. I saw what I had been through, a boiling cauldron of savage water, shiny and wild and foaming and climbing and falling. The ocean has hills in it, and troubling gullies and now I could look on the ravaging teeth of the reef I had defeated. Had I taken this cumbersome longboat through that? I felt no pride, only relief, and the beginnings of the familiar reproof at having put myself in foolish circumstances.

Nor was my problem resolved; how was I to get near the ship? I looked behind me. The sun danced on the waters and outside me, perhaps a hundred yards or so away, I could see another current, much like the one I should have used, also flowing parallel to the land. That would surely bring me to the *Hispaniola*, if to the seaward side.

I had no shore tide to help me but I figured that if I sat in the bows with my two oars, perhaps I could drive a yard or two of her length forwards; the boat's weight might do the rest. This proved a good judgement; I reached the running tide with no more cost to me than my aching limbs.

Now the current carried me so easily that I was able to turn and view the ship. No roof of home, no blazing hearth ever proved so warm in its welcome. I hallooed, settled and waited for the watch to find me.

It was not the watch; it was my young friend, Louis. He had been up in the rigging, in a safe place where he liked to squat athwart. I heard his cry and saw him wave. Soon faces came to the side; within minutes I heard splashes and three of the sailors swam to the longboat. I removed from my mind forever the old piece of lore claiming that sailors cannot swim! But this happy, relieved thought vanished when I climbed aboard and saw across the heat-whitened deck the grim presence of Captain Reid.

A most unpleasant time followed. Bo'sun Noonstock whisked me away from the eyes of all who were waiting—Uncle Ambrose, Jefferies, Grace Richardson and Louis, most of the crew. The captain saw me alone and in the space of half an hour asked me fewer than ten questions. Discomfort overcame me.

He made me stand before his table like a culprit. For several seconds he looked in my eyes, the greyness of his gaze containing cold disapproval. He then looked all over my person, at my dishevelled linen, my hose, my hands blistered from the oars, my face pinpricked with blood from the branches of shrubs. When his eyes returned to mine they rested again. This time contempt entered. And then came his opening salvo, cold as the sharpest blade.

"Mr. Hawkins, what have you done with my mate and my six able seamen exactly?"

My friends do not say that I babble. Dr. Livesey occasionally chides me for a touch of foolish pride. Squire Trelawney thinks me too cautious. My mother wishes me more humble. Uncle Ambrose (as my dear father did) loves me without judgement. But none of them has ever complained that I babble. When faced with Captain Reid and his questions, I babbled like a brook.

"It was, it is, well . . . the circumstances we found . . . Mr. Coll said . . . we found no one . . . and they disappeared . . . like phantoms . . . we found a skull, a skeleton . . . Morgan is dead, we do not have to think of him . . . but they vanished . . ." And on and on I went, making no sense.

Not an eyebrow did he raise. His few questions revolved around the strangeness, as he clearly saw it, of Nathan Coll's decision to go somewhere else without informing me. The fact that Coll had allowed me to return alone, with all those manoeuvres of the boat, struck Captain Reid as further beyond comprehension. In short, he did not accept that Coll had truly gone missing as mysteriously as I reported.

One of his questions ran, "And why, exactly, did you decide that you should return alone?"

Followed with another question: "With exactly no thought of the rowing complement needed? I might have lost my longboat as well as my men." (Captain Reid had a liking for the word "exactly.")

Eventually he dismissed me, but he ordered me to my cabin with instructions to describe my adventures to nobody. Food and drink came soon, brought by Noonstock. I washed, changed my clothing, ate, drank and stretched out on my bunk. My thoughts raced, and all understanding continued to elude me. I could not add up to anything reasonable what I had seen and heard on the island.

Or, I should say, "not seen and not heard." Now that my mind was restored to some logic by Captain Reid's brutal directness, I remembered most powerfully the silence on Spyglass Hill, that blankness in which nothing rustled or shook.

Where might they have gone? The time was so short—what? Fifteen minutes? At most? And this was a complete disappearance. Yet the captain did not seek my opinion. What did he think? Did he think they had fallen? Did he think they had found a pathway forwards and none back? Had I failed to perceive, say, a ledge leading around the massive stone outcrop that formed the rear of the little plateau where I had last seen them?

Seven men, all armed, all disappeared: had my brain come adrift in some way? When next I met Coll would he say to me, "Where did you go? We searched and searched for you."

About an hour after my interview, Noonstock came to my berth. He escorted me to the captain.

"Mr. Hawkins, I wish a detailed description of how to reach Mr. Coll and my men."

I told him the way in all its simplicity; he wrote it down. This time he asked me many questions, always in his cold tone. How many routes did I know to the hill? Did it have a seawards access? What were the pitfalls on the journey? Where stood the most dangerous points? How steep the drops? How sheer the climbs? This interview took almost as long as the first and when it ended he made an announcement to me.

"Mr. Hawkins, it now stands two hours past noon. The bo'sun will lead the ship's remaining complement—save a skeleton crew including the cook and the cabin boy—to the place you last saw Mr. Coll. When Mr. Coll and his party return, we will then, with Gunn's guidance, send forth again as many hands as are needed to recover the contraband. We will not search further for this gentleman who has clearly—by one means or another—quit the island. When all men are safely aboard again and our cargo stowed we sail for Bristol."

I began to speak in my own defence but he cut into me with his words.

"Mr. Hawkins, I will not have an officer of mine and six able-bodied seamen lost ashore. At sea is permissible—but only in the worst circumstances. Please remain below."

The look he gave me suggested he thought me a fool for losing his patrol, and a coward for not making a more diligent search. And he thought me reckless for my longboat exploit. I went back to my tiny cabin and endured the noise of great industry above on deck. Soon the ship fell to silence.

A long time later the cabin boy humiliatingly pushed open my door. Then he departed, having obviously acted upon orders. Up on deck I went straight to the rail and scanned the island. But Captain Reid had held me below until the men had reached the shore and disappeared into the trees.

The bell rang for an unexpectedly early mealtime. Captain Reid was evidently changing the ship's pattern of activity. I yet had to face the questions of Uncle Ambrose and worse, of Grace Richardson and feel her disappointment.

Cook served us and the cabin boy stayed near the door—instructed to listen, I suspected, lest I break the silence imposed on me by the captain. As I was seated before the others arrived, I could not divert their opening questions.

My uncle was first to the table and he asked, "Jim, Jim—what is all of this? Another party gone ashore—and a large party too?"

I replied, as kindly as I could, "I fear, Uncle, you must ask Captain Reid any questions."

"But has the voyage been concluded? Have we found our man? Have all purposes been fulfilled? What of the silver bars?"

"Uncle, I cannot say." Then in a lower tone I murmured, "I must not say."

Uncle Ambrose's mind is always that of a lawyer, seeking the meaning behind the fact.

"Must not say? Aha!" he said and looked at me with understanding.

I glanced in the direction of the door; my uncle grasped my implication and made a face as if to say, "We have a fine state of things—but I shall wait." He then put on a smile of warmth and kind support and I was grateful.

Grace Richardson gave no such succour. She arrived at the table of a rush. "What is happening? Have you found him?"

I said cautiously, "Madam, I cannot say."

She blazed. "Cannot say? Or will not say?"

I was so thankful that Louis had not arrived.

"Madam, I fear I am not at liberty to tell you—" I began and she fired again.

"Where is Joseph Tait? There is to be no great search for him, is there? I believe that you have found the silver and that is enough for you. That is the reason for your secrecy, is it not? That is why all the men have gone ashore. What can I not be told?"

She had said all this while standing, eyes aflame. I had not seen this enraged side of her.

My uncle restrained her and said softly, "Madam. Spare yourself. There are things here which we are not allowed to know. Be assured they will be matters concerning our safety. My nephew has clearly been placed under a vow of silence. That's my interpretation of the thing."

She allowed herself to be guided to her chair and was about to hiss at me again when Louis bounded in.

"Have we found him?" He was most excited.

I looked at him with tenderness and patted the bench beside me. His young presence would be a comfort. He came and sat down and, as children do, took his mood from that of the gathering; after another question or two had foundered, he asked no more.

The glum meal drifted to an end. I did not know what to do. My uncle's advice was not available to me because I could not tell him of the seven men missing—yet I knew how, liking answers so much, how he must be puzzling things. I feared Grace Richardson had taken a new and uncomplimentary view of me and this was a grievous wound. Even the company of dear old Ben Gunn had been taken from me. At least he would know how to be safe on the island—though, I reflected, I should love to have witnessed him guiding the rather uncompromising bo'sun.

I thought of setting myself to walk a given distance round the ship, say, thirty circuits. I also thought of rearranging my possessions, polishing my boots, an act that always gives me comfort. Any such decision was taken out of my hands by the day's next remarkable occurrence. With most of the crew gone ashore the ship was as silent as a mountain. On a calm sea the rigging hardly creaked. With all furled, we had no canvas to slap and crack like pistol shots. That is how we could hear the watch's voice call, "A sail! A sail!"

———✦———

Ch. 15 —
The Captain's Ruse

We trooped on deck. Off to my right I observed Captain Reid come to the bridge, his spyglass under his arm. He called to the watch (a wizened little man, too old and infirm to join the shore party), "Say you her course?"

The watch replied immediately, "As ours, sir. She's nor'nor'east now."

"Say you what she carries?"

"Full sail, sir, with little wind."

"Say you how long?"

The watch took a moment. "Maybe half, three-quarters of a day, sir, at that rate."

I watched Captain Reid digest this intelligence. He looked down to where we, recent diners together, stood in a knot. I knew he had seen me observe him. Then he turned and went below.

Our cat, Christmas, who enjoyed the living of a sultan aboard, being fed and fêted all ways and hours, began to show discomfort and ran away from Louis.

My uncle approached me. "Jim, I do not wish you to break any silence you have agreed."

"Thank you, Uncle."

"But tell me—why do I worry that a sail should appear?"

"Uncle, your fears will be mine." As though to stay away from my true suspicion, I added, "Pirates do travel these waters."

Uncle Ambrose nodded. "Yes, and the captain has made a grievous error. He has left the ship unprotected."

I said, "I wish, Uncle, I could tell you that you're being fanciful. But this is all most worrying."

"Let's not be sudden," said Uncle Ambrose. "This may be a passing merchantman or some such. Although she does seem bound straight to our bearings." He turned away from me and I knew he wanted time to think.

The hot afternoon became the warm evening. Grace Richardson took up a position far astern from where, alone and forbidding, she watched the shore. Whenever the *Hispaniola* swung around at anchor and cancelled her view, she crossed restlessly to the other rail.

Louis had returned to his vantage point in the rigging whence he had seen me. From there a mere turn of his head accommodated the views in all directions.

In the crow's nest the watch observed the distant sail, and he also observed the island. Captain Reid did not appear.

Presently, my uncle and I walked together but we spoke little. Our anxiety was visible only to each other. A stranger would have thought us a couple of friends who from time to time ambled to the other rail and continued our leaning and looking. Like everyone else aboard we waited for two matters to develop—the return of the crew and the arrival, if it intended to come our way, of that distant sail.

On the island—nothing happened. We were too far away to pick out details of activity beneath the trees. The foreshore shone clear enough to define a troop or a single man; a child would have been visible. Sound carries over water but we heard no human voice. I now remember the end of that long day for the raucousness of the birds in the trees at the edge of Treasure Island. Why did no birds sing farther in? I wondered—and the memory of that dark silence seemed to carry the same weight inside my spirit as that unpleasant sensation we call "foreboding."

As for the sail, haze covered the sea and even though the faraway vessel materialised from time to time, our view of her remained incomplete.

Before seven o'clock, when the light first dipped, I knew that our men would not return that evening. The shuddering in my joints called up the hardest suspicions and I thought: nor will they come back tomorrow. Nor perhaps ever. I had no evidence of any kind for this belief—but why did I feel so convinced?

I did not go to bed that unquiet night. At midnight I went below, washed and changed, and returned to my troubled watch.

Dawn came, in stripes of red and emerald green climbing from the eastern sky. In the slowly opening light I saw a shape not far distant and almost at the same time heard the watch (had he not slept either?) call, "Ship ahoy. Port astern."

The faraway sail of yesterday had become this morning's neighbour. To my horror but not to my suprise, she was the black brig and she lay about an hour distant from us.

A figure to my right alerted me. Captain Reid had come on deck. Another figure appeared—my uncle, but he held back, like a man hiding. Both men had dressed impeccably. Still the ship bore down.

My uncle beckoned me to go below and I heard him call to the captain. I followed my uncle's direction and we all met outside the stateroom.

"What is this, Mr. Hatt?"

"I worry about this ship, Captain."

"Is not this the brig we saw as we left Devon?"

"I believe it may be, Captain."

"Then, Mr. Hatt, we have been followed. Is that not a logical conclusion?"

"Indeed. In which case, I believe it might be prudent to expect grave danger, Captain Reid."

The little Scotchman bristled. "Grave danger? Will you tell me, Mr. Hatt, exactly what you wish to convey?"

As we stood there, and as my mind seized with chill after chill, my uncle succinctly told Captain Reid the story of the Berwick death, Maltby's siege and his own ensuing strategy. Captain Reid listened in silence.

Uncle Ambrose concluded, "And I believe these men or their

agents are our pursuers. They must have chartered or otherwise acquired this vessel."

When my uncle had finished, the captain said, "We will come later to the fact that I wasn't informed I harboured fugitives. Or that we sought a common pirate. I asked most particularly whether the man we had come to seek *was* a pirate. As I recall, you evaded the question." Reid was furious.

Uncle Ambrose fought back. "They're not fugitives. They've never been charged."

"Don't split hairs with me, sir. At this moment I have a choice of view. I am empowered to follow the law's course and see Mr. Hawkins here (he had clearly taken a great dislike of me) as a fugitive and you as his accessory."

"I assure you, Captain Reid, that my reputation in Bristol is not something I jeopardise lightly," said my uncle more coldly than I have heard him speak.

The captain continued his attack. "But you will comprehend my position, Mr. Hatt?"

"I comprehend this, sir. I comprehend that in my absence and at my behest, two of the most distinguished lawyers in England will have been making enquiries as to the previous behaviour of the dead Berwick, of Sir Thomas Maltby and their disreputable, murderous companions. Their findings will be presented to none other than my good friend, Lord Gibbon, and from his court will undoubtedly be given out the justice that is warranted. If you wish, Captain, to await events in order to see which side is victorious, then you must also take what the law brings."

The captain paused and turned away, thinking. When he turned back he said, "At the end of this business, sir, I will speak to you with some directness. I have been duped and made, possibly," (though clearly angry he spoke with great care) "an accessory to serious offences. For the moment I am placed in the intolerable position of having my ship thrust into danger."

He walked away, boiling with energy and rage.

Uncle Ambrose looked at me.

"We must all remain below, Jim."

Immediately I thought of Grace Richardson and Louis and made my way to their quarters. I met her near her cabin door as she made to go above.

She glanced at me, barely (I imagined) tolerant.

I said, "Madam. Don't go on deck. And restrain Louis. There's a ship. We've been followed."

I did not have to tell her more. Her eyes closed in horror.

"But how could they have known?" she whispered.

"These latitudes were known to every sailor in Bristol," I said.

She rejoined bitterly, "Your mother told me of your boastful tales to your inn guests and drinkers. Therefore we can expect no treasure left here either."

I bit my tongue from saying that until she appeared it had been my bounden intention never to return here! And that it was my tales brought her to find me! But I did say, "Madam, if I did tell my adventures, I always conveyed the impression of a foul place, full of deadly fever, where no treasure remained."

"Where are the crew? What are they doing? Are we without protection?"

"Madam, please. Remain below. I wish you and Louis to be safe."

"But if they board. We shall be caught like mice. What's to become of us?"

The first tears I ever saw in her eyes also melted her anger.

"They shall not board," I said, and I knew I spoke the truth, but did not know how or why.

Head bowed, she returned to her cabin. I heard her close the door and engage with Louis.

When I cannot influence events that have a great bearing on me I become restless. I turned away from Grace Richardson's cabin door, not knowing what to do with myself. Practical things always help. I needed to find a place from which I could establish what would happen between Captain Reid and the brig.

With much delicate treading below decks, and many blind alleys, I found myself aft in a tight companionway that had a secluded hatch. From there I could hear if not see.

In events I fared better. The hatch stood concealed behind two tarpaulined stacks of stores; these rose some four feet by six feet with a small space between. Through this gap I had a perfect view.

The brig's crew now hauled her in with speed. I could not see her port of registration nor any colours. The morning sea was calm, with a gentle tide running. Even the reef seemed watchful. Nearer she came. A lump in my mouth stopped my breath, made me breathe shallow and quick. And nearer. Now trimming her sails, the brig hove to and dropped anchor. Nearer still. Not one of her mariners looked towards our schooner. A swimmer could have reached her within minutes.

I heard but did not see Captain Reid's hail.

"Who are you, sir? You fly no colours."

His voice could have been heard ashore. No reply came. The brig turned slowly, yawing slightly.

The captain called again. "Sir, it is a crime of the sea to sail without colours. Who are you?"

Still no reply came. By now all her hands had finished their tasks and were no longer visible. I raised my head in fear of a boarding party, but no boat left her. Nor did any such activity begin that I could see.

Captain Reid shouted, "Make your name and your colours known to us, sir. You are too close."

There followed a period of silence. I thought that these had been days of such silences. Yesterday I had the deadened quiet of the island's interior, and the muteness of the plateau. Following that, I had dumbness imposed upon me by the captain. Now were we to have something more sinister yet?

In a crisis, time cannot be measured accurately: an hour can last but a minute and a minute an hour. I tried to guess how Captain Reid thought. Not knowing him well I could not divine his game. I knew he dare not show the stranger what little strength we had aboard.

The stranger, for his part, did not seem about to try anything upon us. We sat there—and sat there, in a doldrum, a stalemate. Who would be the first to break it?

Reid shouted again and the black brig broke her silence. A voice, whose face I could not see, called, "But who are *you*?" with an insolent emphasis.

I knew the voice!

Captain Reid replied, "Under the King of England's colours we are *Hispaniola* out of Bristol. Your voice tells me, sir, you are English."

Silence fell again for another long period. I felt this business unbearable.

"We *are* English."

Yes, I knew the voice, the voice of fear itself—it was Maltby! My gut turned inwards and my nostrils flared in cold terror.

He spoke again. "And are *you* English, sir?"

This was mockery: Maltby had picked up Captain Reid's distinctive Scotch speech and clearly sought to provoke.

This time Captain Reid said nothing. His policy worked and changed the boot to the other foot. Maltby had to press, although still in a mocking tone.

"I ask again. Are you an *English*man, sir?"

The captain played a good card next.

He called, "If you sail under no colours you must be pirates."

In this retort the captain showed evidence of strong and careful thought. He estimated that whatever guise he had temporarily adopted to pursue us, and whatever illegal appearance he might present to any legitimate sea captain, a man with such a good opinion of himself as the Sir Thomas Maltby we had told him of, would neither accept nor risk being called "pirate."

The black brig yet showed no activity on board. We waited longer. Then a noise of brass came from them, as of a gong struck somewhere. As the sound reverberated across the seas I saw Maltby appear, as purple and evil as before. He took care to stand by a mast fearing, I supposed, a shot from us. I myself ducked my head, but soon understood he could never see me.

Maltby called, "It is my intention to board, sir, in the name of the King."

"Welcome, sir."

Captain Reid astonished me. He surprised Maltby too, who halted.

"Welcome, sir? I do not need your welcome. I know you are harbouring fugitives."

"I don't know what you mean," replied the captain.

"Nor I you," replied Maltby. "With your 'welcome'—what mean you, sir?"

"Doubly welcome if you bring your physician, sir."

What game was this? I did not know—but was much intrigued.

"And some able men with shovels if you can spare them?" Captain Reid added, then coughed loudly.

Maltby hesitated, then spoke. "You mean to confuse me. But you will not confound me. We will board you and have done with it."

"And take the ship with you," called Captain Reid.

He turned and paraded down the deck as if about to go below. Now I could watch him and Maltby both. The captain pressed a white kerchief to his mouth. The very moment he turned his back Maltby roared again.

"Sir, you shall have need of a physician when we reach you."

Captain Reid stopped and cried out, "You cannot harm us more than we have been harmed. Stop to think, man. Where are my sailors? My officers? What work can you do that the fever has not already done? Go back whence you came, you fool. There is a plague in these parts."

The wonder of his ploy—I almost laughed! He gambled that Maltby knew Treasure Island's reputation for disease.

"I do not believe you!"

"That is business for you, sir. But why are my decks so empty? And look to your west. Why is my jolly boat ashore? That is our fifth burial party in three days. Below I have eight others, two dead, three dying, three heading that way. So—*welcome aboard*, sir."

He uttered the last words sarcastically.

Maltby's clerk appeared; he had been in hiding. They conferred. Maltby called again, less crudely this time.

"Where is the murderer, Hawkins?"

I bristled and thought of my mother's fierceness.

"Second to die. We buried him Wednesday."

"And his lying relative?"

They meant my uncle—this angered me comprehensively.

"Dead too."

"The woman? The brat?" I could scarce keep calm.

"One dead, one dying," said the captain. "All these were weakened by not knowing the life of the ocean. My men are my worry now." Then he laughed a bitter laugh as he pressed his kerchief to his lips again. He took it away and cried, "Do you have any spare crew, sir? Or perhaps you'd like to enlist yourself. I am in need of a bo'sun. Or a cabin boy."

"Confound you," roared Maltby and he and his clerk looked thoroughly adrift of matters.

Captain Reid made a show of temper and strode to the rail where the ships almost touched. He balled the white handkerchief in his hands and flung it at the brig. It naturally fell short and opened in the wind; there were what appeared like bloodstains on it and I saw Maltby recoil.

"Curse you! May you rot and rot!" he shouted at Reid. "Curse you! Curse you!"

The captain walked away and went below. He must have arranged his departure so that Maltby could see him.

Again we entered a silence. I had a good view of our decks. Nobody could be seen, a sight unthinkable in a ship as fine as the *Hispaniola*.

Suddenly, crewmen swarmed all over the black brig and prepared to haul. Every unfurling of every sheet drew her a few welcome feet farther from us. I had not seen such frantic industry at sea, not under Captain Smollett nor under Captain Reid.

But then, even as the sails were hauled up, a sinister party assembled on her foredeck. Approximately ten men turned and marched astern. By now the brig had yawed again and her poop deck stood before my eyes. Five of the men stood there blindfold and wretched. The other five guarded them and marched them to the rail where a boy thrust a plank five feet out over the ocean. From behind them Maltby called.

"Sir! You need crew! Have these dogs!"

One by one the men's hands were untied—but not their blindfolds. One by one each was guided to stand on this narrow platform to eternity. Maltby came forwards and, one by one, pushed the five into the south seas. They fell like unfortunates dropping into damnation.

Captain Reid appeared and called in an enraged voice, "Sir, I took you for a scoundrel at twenty knots' distance. If these souls reach me at least they will receive Christian burial."

The last action I saw the captain take was to throw a line overboard. At that I knew he had not only won a brilliant ruse but had gained more than he could have hoped—five extra crew if they took the line and survived. Reid concluded his trickery by leaning on the rail like a man defeated but resigned.

———❧———

Ch. 11—

I Argue My Case

Four of the men hauled themselves aboard. The one who drowned had been too badly beaten and had no grip in his hands for our rope. While treading the water the others tore off their blindfolds. Held below in the brig, none had been privy to the exchanges between Maltby and Captain Reid. Now they fell upon our aft deck; each bore traces of severe injury. They lay there, wordless and spent.

I heard Captain Reid call in a low voice to them.

"You—men! Don't move. You're safe. But you're still being watched by your recent master. Don't come 'til I call you."

Maltby observed us from his receding ship. I think he tested Captain Reid's story. When the men made no move Maltby puzzled awhile, talked it over and continued to watch. Ere long, he needed a glass to focus on the place where the four men had come aboard. He saw nothing. There was nothing to see. The wretches, still in the shock of near death, obeyed Captain Reid's command.

Stepping down a rung and leaning back in my narrow hiding place, I sighed. A vast danger had been averted.

I peered out again and looked at the men. They seemed unthreatening, not fighting men. The *Hispaniola* was swinging gently; a light wind had sprung up. When my view of the island came to me I peered in that direction but saw nothing whatever of our missing crew.

I grew impatient with sitting quietly. What would happen now? Where did our best chance lie? To sail a little away, if we could, and await the relief ship some four months hence? No. To sit and hope? But for how long? What good action could we undertake? I knew not.

Her movements said that the *Hispaniola* had swung me again towards the departing Maltby. How quickly ships go when bearing away a loved one: how slowly when bearing a foe! Maltby's brig remained well within the scrutiny of a glass and there we all were, taken prisoner by the invention of the telescope! Hours of hot sun lay ahead.

In the relief from terror I fell asleep, wedged upright. To judge from the sun, almost an hour must have passed when I awoke. My view was neither of island nor departing brig. Soon it would resolve into one or the other; the sea had begun to run a little. Matters must have generally improved, I felt, if I could have taken the liberty of sleeping. The wretched men lying not fifteen feet from me had crawled into a shaded place.

Also, I began to hear again the sounds of the ship. I had never forgotten them, and I never will. Despite all the dreadful incidents to which I was party in the two voyages, the sounds of the *Hispaniola* stay with me like the voices of old friends. I know the noise of her strain upon the anchor; of her creaks at yard and masts; of the soft whistles the wind makes in her lines. And I well know why a ship is "she." To those who love her she is a beloved woman; mother, sweetheart, wife.

Soon I observed the wide sea. The brig had diminished. But I never believe danger has gone until I am told so. Therefore, although I thought it safe to approach the four strewn wretches, I crept beneath the level of the rail.

"You're secure," I murmured to each. "This is a good ship with a good captain. Your tormentors have gone away."

One seemed healthier than the others, lips less swollen.

"They have given us no water," he murmured.

"You shall have food and water in abundance," I said. "But how did your bad state come about?"

The question was perhaps ill timed (my curiosity has no tact) but it brought an answer.

"We were pressed at Bristol. They gave us foul ale. Two of us are not seamen and the other two are ship's officers. I am a clerk and he (indicating the man next him) a manservant."

I promised to return and crawled for'ards to the main companion-way, where my uncle Ambrose stood as calm as a man who had been there all day. He greeted me profusely.

"Would you have thought of that, Jim?! Wish I had! What a ruse! The captain should be a lawyer. A 'plague ship,' less, a *plague* ship! We must revise our view of Reid. That stiff manner hides a brain for more than seafaring. Would you have thought of that, Jim?! Would you?!"

His delight fired me with hope.

"Uncle," I said, "if a moment such as that can pass—or be dismissed—then we must be capable of all we came to do."

"And the kerchief, Jim, the kerchief! Goodness!" Were he a man given to slapping his thigh, Ambrose Hatt would have bruised both legs that moment. "Let us find him, let us give him our congratulations!"

My uncle's jubilation infects all around him—but Captain Reid had returned to his old self. He is a man who resists hope, praise or delight.

"Captain, I congratulate you!" My uncle's effusions lit the state-room like a sunburst. Captain Reid looked at him.

"Not all life must be action, Mr. Hatt. You must know that."

My uncle's good spirits would not be doused.

"How did you think of it, sir? How? I mean—how? I've been saying to my nephew that had I thought of it I should have been double proud of myself."

The captain caught me smiling. His eyes lightened for a second, no more. "Mr. Hatt, sit down. And you, Mr. Hawkins. I ask you not to interrupt me until I have said one or two things."

Courtesy and asperity when placed together have great force.

"Gentlemen," began the captain. "May we now establish some clarity?"

I looked across at my uncle who seemed nonchalant but watchful.

Reid continued. "I take it that you gentlemen understand by now what an ill-starred venture may come from a woman."

My uncle said, "But such a remarkable woman, sir?"

"Not for me to say," said the captain. He rapped his table with a brass rule. "But I can ask—what is this pirate's relationship to this woman?"

Uncle Ambrose and I looked at each other.

I said, "I believe he is the father of her son. She once said to me that she needs to find this man so that her son 'can sleep at night.' But—she will not be specific."

My uncle added nothing to my words.

Captain Reid did not soften, as I hoped he might.

"If this pirate comes aboard he comes back to England in irons. Be clear in that."

"Is there no other?—" my uncle began.

"If you ask me to take him on board and then, out of charity or pity or any such motive, leave them all three in some hospitable port, you're asking me, sir, to commit a crime. Assisting a criminal to escape justice. And I will not do that—and I will treat any who ask me as an accessory."

I wished to speak but I was so bound by the captain's ferocity I knew I would never find the words. My uncle seemed about to speak too, but also held his tongue.

"Now we come to the next and more immediate conundrum," continued the captain. "I speak more mildly than I feel. Gentlemen, your venture has so far cost me almost my entire crew. This is what I have decided."

This captain had in him something of the actor. We had already perceived that much, from his kerchief performance. Now he paused as actors do when creating expectation or power.

"Your pursuers would have done for us all and taken the ship. Of that I have no doubt. I know a villain when I see one. That is why, Mr. Hatt, I've decided to accept your description of the legal situation. You say that the lady, her son and Mr. Hawkins aren't fugitives, that they haven't been charged with any crime and that investigations are under way into the gentleman we've just bested. I hope you'll be good enough, sir, to tell me you'll abide by that tale when we return to Bristol."

I expected my uncle to take umbrage at this. But he did not. He said, "Of course," and I realised he understood all this from a legal point of view. In fine, the captain wished to be exonerated from any possible accusation.

"Now—the advantage we've had from that adversity has been the addition of four men. I've looked at them. Some care will restore two of them almost immediately. Some more days—the other two. They need rest, food, water, sleep. A little warmth of nature."

I never thought to hear such words from Captain Reid's lips.

"With such crew as we have, and these men, we can rig the ship to half-sail in some days. I know Mr. Coll. I know Bo'sun Noonstock. They are not men who give in easily. On account of them I wish to circumnavigate the island. It is my belief that they've been unable to find the pathway back to this side and the land has proven impassable. That is the reason for the delay."

Seeing me about to blurt, the captain raised his hand.

"Mr. Hawkins, I don't believe you can have looked effectively."

"Captain!" I had noted that the use of his title caught his attention more than the use of the word "sir." He paused.

"Captain, I believe my uncle doesn't know what went on ashore. You have asked me not to speak of it."

"Tell him now. It'll refresh my mind to hear of it again."

I told my tale, with ever greater diligence in being accurate. My uncle listened and said kindly the old words he had taught me. "People do not vanish into thin air."

"That's my thought," responded the captain.

"But it is a mystery," said my uncle to him.

"I don't believe in mysteries, sir, I am a Scotchman." He continued, "I believe in solutions. The men took a wrong turning. Mr.

Hawkins was perhaps away from them longer than he thought. They moved onwards, seeing something new perhaps."

"Where do you truly believe they went?" my uncle asked me.

Captain Reid butted in. "It'll be as I say. Inhospitable land. Unfamiliar pathways. These are mariners, Mr. Hatt, not geographers."

Uncle Ambrose said, "But surely we should stay here, this being the point whence they left?"

"Captain, may I offer a different remedy?" I said. Again I caught his attention. "May I suggest that I be permitted to recover a little of the ground I have lost?"

My uncle was pleased with me; I saw it from his face.

"What do you propose?"

"Let me go ashore. Ben Gunn will be there already with the most recent party. He knows the whole island and he trusts me."

From where I sat I could see the captain's feet beneath his table. The shiny shoes with their strong black laces shifted. Then they settled. He had thought to tell me an untruth, then changed his mind.

"Gunn is not ashore."

I said, "What?!"

"He is in detention. For a misdemeanour. For theft."

I was about to ask whether it had been the theft of cheese when the captain said, "It is a crime at sea to take more than your ration."

My heart lifted. "But Captain—this is excellent! No man knows the island better. Let me take him ashore. We can at a single move resolve all.

He hesitated.

"Captain, please. Put us ashore. When we return—have the ship within hailing distance of the land. One man, the cook, can use the canoe."

"By Jove, Jim, you have thought it out," exclaimed my uncle.

Neither man knew my deeper motivation, though Uncle Ambrose must have guessed at it. Were I ever to impress Grace Richardson again, I could not do so under the cloud at present hanging over me.

I grew forceful. "Captain, what do you say?"

Uncle Ambrose added his weight.

"It has much to recommend it, Captain, a solution to all aspects. Jim knows where he last saw Mr. Coll. Gunn knows the island beyond that. If they have been lost—or ferrying silver—they will be found—or helped."

"Nor," I added, "is there a very great problem putting us ashore. If I managed to take the longboat through the reef—"

This galled the captain. Stung, he agreed.

"Take provisions. Leave some where you put ashore—against a return. They can be recovered later. Bear some with you into the interior of the island. The men have no food by now. That's also a worry."

At that moment I saw something—that the tide of credibility had begun to flow my way. Up to then, in the captain's eyes, Coll and those men had vanished unreasonably. Reid still resisted any idea of mystery but the bald fact now stood out—a second, greater party of crewmen had not returned either. How relieved I felt to be given a chance to redeem myself!

"Mr. Hawkins," called the captain as my uncle and I left. "You understand that you will not depart until dawn. And of course it may yet be that you have no need of going."

But I knew from his voice he did not expect his men to return so soon. Or perhaps at all. How does a man learn how to conceal such concern? How does a man learn how to endure such concern as I felt at that moment and all that night? Further danger lay ahead, of what shape I knew not. Which was as well.

———◆———

Ch. 17—

The Smell of Death

It was always devilish hard to get Ben Gunn moving in one simple direction. Fix him to a point and he darted all round it. First, he forgot his cheese. Then he forgot the laces of his shoes. He always carried extra laces, for fear, he said, of his shoes falling off. The deeper truth had a more poignant ring. He had been so long marooned without shoes that he feared losing them ever again.

When freed from his detention he thanked me. "Ben's only friend is Jim."

"Nonsense, Ben. Everyone likes you."

"Not the captain, Jim. The captain has no liking for Ben Gunn."

"Where are the rest of your stores? You will need your tunic. It was cold where I stood."

"Spyglass Hill be's made of ice, Jim. Of ice."

I refrained from telling Ben the full story. He might have panicked and hid. Or run away. In any case he would have delayed our departure. I wished to give the captain no chance to change his mind.

Grace Richardson approached me as I checked the stores before loading. "What are you doing?"

I told her I was going ashore, then asked, "Madam, will you go and talk to my uncle? He will explain the dilemmas facing us."

She said, with a most direct look, "I believe I can state them myself."

Something took hold of me and I spoke as I had not intended to. "Madam."

She looked at me and I hoped she guessed by now that I held deep feelings for her.

"I know you are angry towards me. But I will explain all—when this is resolved."

She nodded, a little easier. If anyone should understand an embargo on information!

"And also when that moment comes, Madam . . . may we speak . . . of other things? I have . . . there is something . . . I wish to say."

She listened carefully and I saw that she softened.

My voice lost a little breath as I said, "Louis has a place in my heart. I never expected that. As for you—that is what I wish . . . what I wish to speak of. Now is not the time, but I wish you to know that (my tone was unsteady) that, well . . . Madam, I shall want to speak."

She replied carefully, slowly and with respect for the struggle she had seen in my face. "Louis loves you. I know that. I have seen how you have quelled his unruliness. And I see daily your other kindnesses, your care for us, your courage on my behalf." She now took a considerable moment before she spoke again. I, who had hoped for encouragement in her words, was suddenly cast down—because she said, "In fairness, you must know that Dr. Jefferies has asked if he may speak to me when he returns."

For a moment I felt the grim triumph that comes when one knows one has been correct in guessing something unlikeable. "Madam, what Dr. Jefferies wishes to say or do must be his affair. For my part, my deep concern for your beloved son is echoed no less in my feelings—"

Oh! The irritation! At that delicate moment Ben Gunn returned, saying he had mislaid the compass. I had to go with him and find it where it lay—in the middle of his bunk, clear to all.

My heart was rising and swooping like a bird in the sky; I was now near to trembling with a variety of fears—fear of how my clumsy speech seemed to Grace Richardson, fear of Jefferies's pursuit of her and the puzzling fear that lay ahead on the island.

Finally Ben Gunn seemed as ready as ever he might be. To my surprise Captain Reid attended our departure. The men from Maltby's brig, my uncle said, were recovering well. They told a bad tale of villainy and brutal treatment.

"Enough," he said, "to get Sir Thomas Maltby stripped of any privilege. They suspect he killed one of their number."

"He caused one to drown," I said with some sharpness, "in front of our eyes."

"So he did," marvelled my uncle. "On the plank."

Louis came forwards gravely; his bearing suggested that he was generally perturbed. Without a word (his usual manner) he crooked a finger to me and I followed him to a private corner of the deck.

"Here." He handed me a small package. I opened it to find two rich biscuits and a wonderful red-and-blue feather. "This is my lucky feather. I found it with Mamma in Scotland. By the sea. It always brings me luck."

Waiting for suitable words to come into my mind, I tried to guess which bird surrendered such a feather. But that thought would not come easily either and I tapped him gently on the shoulder.

"Thank you, Louis. Keep watch while we're gone. And if you sense danger, tell Captain Reid. I believe he likes you."

Louis held out his hand and I shook it—a boy endeavouring to be as brave as a man.

With the cook's fat arms pulling, the tides ran the canoe in from the *Hispaniola*. We reached the shore quickly and were discharged with our provisions. I had long known all the work would fall to me. Ben danced around like a man in a fix, trapped between a loathing of the island and pride in his knowledge of it. I secured all the provisions beneath a tree—a mound of canvas piled with stones to keep them safe from animals, birds and, I hoped, insects.

The canoe pulled away from us and there we were—the former cabin boy, Jim Hawkins himself, who, near here, ten years ago had met the old maroon, Ben Gunn, with his voice like a rusty lock and his passion for toasted cheese but who had lived solitarily here for three years on goats and berries and oysters.

"Well, Ben, here we go," I cried, jollying him along.

We looked back at the ocean. Light dappled the water at the departing oars of the canoe.

"A lovely ship," said Ben wistfully. Indeed the *Hispaniola* looked a picture, her spars gilt with sun, her sails rolled neat as cheroots.

"Yes, well, come along, Ben, we have travels ahead of us."

I determined that my tone throughout should be cheerful, whatever I felt. Give Ben one glimpse of my gloom and he might bound off like one of his goats. We set out.

"Must ye go this way, Jim?" asked Ben after about half an hour. He pinched me and I worried for him—he had not done that since the day I first met him.

"D'you know of another?"

"Not this way to the silver, Jim. Do we stop soon for vittles, Jim? We could go over to the spring."

"Now, Ben. We've only just left the ship. You ate before we left. We may be here a day or two."

"Jim, where be us bound?"

"Spyglass Hill, Ben. I said."

"Ben doan't want Spyglass Hill, Jim, and ye doan't neither. A bad place."

"Nevertheless, Ben, that is where we have to go."

He relaxed a little and began to tell me of his history in the island. Places we passed as we climbed reminded him of storms he saw while he was here, or ships that passed the shore but did not stop.

"One day, Jim, a ship, she did put summun' ashore. I seed him and I hid. He went away. Niver seed him again. Heard him that day crashing through the bushes and wailin' fierce. Niver seed him again."

"Was that long before we came here, Ben?"

"'Bout a year, Jim, or mebbe weeks. Ben doan't know."

"The island took him, Ben, but it didn't take you. See, the Almighty likes you too, Ben."

"An' he were big, Jim, a big, big feller. Red hair on him."

At another turn he told me how he ferried the silver. "Figgers, Jim,

Ben didn't have nuthin' else to do. So, begins by takin' a bar at a time. Then Ben makes a sling, like, over the shoulder. See?"

We had to stop while he showed me his shoulder. Impatiently I looked and then recoiled. A groove like a cart track remained where the sling made of creepers had cut a deep scar into him. He must have suffered from that cut.

"Your mother, Ben? She was . . . she had passed away before you got home?"

"Doan't know, Jim. Niver knowed. She were gone when I went lookin' for her. I has her Bible. It was her Bible made me pious, Jim."

"Who was your father, Ben?"

"Doan't know, Jim. Ben niver knowed. My mother, she were nice to Ben."

"How did you get to sea?" We had a few yards to go before the big climbing began.

"Rum, Jim, when I were too young. A press gang took me. Beat me. Allus gets beaten, Ben does."

I wanted to touch his arm and make some show of compassion.

"Then I were in Flint's crew, with Billy Bones and Silver like I told ye. Beaten again. But this 'ere place, it were the worst. I were pious again after bein' on my ownsome three years, Jim."

The image of Ben Gunn as a boy, being made drunk by a press gang, carried to some ship and spending his life at sea on the wrong end of a rope's end, getting flogged every day by some drunken cook or mate, hurt my soul. I resolved there and then that Ben must come and live at the Admiral Benbow when we returned. The dear old fellow had never been cared for in his life and he had not one ounce of harm in him.

By now the place grew dark under the trees. Where sunlight had never reached, it was colder than I had remembered. The ground gave way to the rocks Mr. Coll and his men had found so difficult. I felt a little ashamed that recently I had raced back over these outcrops as though some beast chased me.

After hard climbing, we reached the base of the vertical stone path.

From here we could see the corner of the wooden building. I heard Ben gasp behind me, so loudly and emphatically I thought he had seen something.

I turned sharply. "What's the matter, Ben?"—but why did I whisper, and why did he whisper when replying?

"The smell, Jim. Bad smell."

I sniffed the air. No odour reached me other than greenness and damp, cold foliage. But then I and my friends know that I possess only the feeblest sense of smell. I am a man for whom flowers are pleasing only to the eye.

"Nonsense, Ben," but I felt not as cheerful as I pretended. Furthermore, I recollected Coll holding his nose.

"Jim! That smell! It be bad, Jim."

Had there been room on the crag Ben would have danced his little dance of agitation. He made to go back and I grabbed his arm.

"Ben! I need you! Come on!"

He subsided, and we stepped forwards to the rocks whence the last path, if I may call it such, ascended. Here we stood again and Ben began to clutch at me and pluck my clothing as he had done when first we met on the island. "Jim, Ben begs thee. Doan't ask of 'im to go up there!"

"Have you been up here before, Ben?" Still we whispered.

"No, Jim, no. Oh, Jim, that smell."

Now I did whiff something, and could not place it. If it reached Ben more severely than me, I now caught enough of it to pity him. What was it? A dead animal? A goat fallen down a defile nearby? But yet it was too sweet a smell for that, a heavy and sickly aroma. It began to repel me and I believed I could smell it now because my senses were more sharpened than before.

"Ben—one last climb. Come with me to prove I was not mad. Come with me to prove there is no other way from that plateau. We have to make a search, Ben. Captain Reid won't like us if we don't."

I had to tell him without telling him, so to speak, why we had come. As I looked in the dear old boy's eyes I saw the dilemma of fears. Which would win? Captain Reid's discipline, or the nameless smell and the spooked place?

Behind me, Ben took my arm like a child crossing a stream and we reached the last few half-level "steps." Soon we stood by the rude wooden structure. Ben recoiled at the skull on the earth. I recoiled too but for a different reason—Tom Morgan's red tunic cloth had disappeared. Had the bo'sun and his party taken it? I gazed skyward. Could some bird, a magpie or its equal in these climes, have swooped and taken it away? I had heard of exotic birds who, in order to attract mates, lay out nests constructed of all they can find.

My fear rose higher than before. Now I had the extra responsibility for poor Ben's fate. It would be too cruel if, having survived the island for so long, he had again been taken back here by me and made victim to it. I resolved to do our duty and take us out of there swiftly. We would have to follow Captain Reid's plan and search by sailing around the island.

"Ben." I spoke bravely to dispel any mood that had come upon us. "This is what I need you to verify. Come here."

I took him first to one drop on one side, then the other.

"Now, Ben, do you see any sign of human life here? Or of human accident?"

I had scanned every inch we had travelled to this point and saw no trace whatsoever of the bo'sun's party. Ben also looked all around. He did so carefully, to give him his full due.

"No, Jim. Nuthin' mortal, no, Jim."

"Now, Ben, survey this," and I took him to the wall of vines, ivies and shrub growths that formed the rear wall of the plateau. "Look up, Ben, and look down and look all around, as I did. I need your witness."

Ben obliged me as fully as I could have wished. He gazed up to the point of the Spyglass; he looked across to the Spyglass shoulder; he scrutinised the shoulder-high bush spreading through the lone pines that had once grown singularly across the mountain; he inspected the floor of the rock we stood on; he walked hither and thither like a scout and, seeking some remote bravery in himself, attempted to do so without haste.

"No, Jim. Ben sees nuthin', Jim."

"Thank you, Ben. I think we can go now."

In truth I did not know what to do, or what must follow next. We—I—had lost a small company of men; the ship had lost most of its crew. Two parties of able seamen under competent leaders had come here and vanished. How on earth could Captain Reid return to Bristol with such a tale to tell? And now with but poor resources to help him?

Suddenly, Ben called. "Jim! See, Jim!" He knelt and pointed.

I joined him. In the rock gleamed a fresh white scar as if scraped hard by something heavy.

"Jim—see!" Inches away glowed another scar—and then another. I stood to advise myself whether a pattern might be seen. Ben stayed on his hands and knees and began to crawl across the rock floor to the rear wall as though on a path.

"What do you think they are, Ben? Could goats have made them?"

"No, Jim, too deep, too hard. Goats is light on their feet." He foraged some more. "Eee! and another!"

By now he had all but reached the foot of the rock escarpment at the rear. He pressed back a shrub or two and withdrew his hand sharply, sucking his fingers, "Owwww!" Thorns had got him, thorns as big as ships' nails.

"Be careful, Ben!" The odour on the rock had now thickened and was frightful.

He stood and, worse agitated than I had yet seen him, said, "Jim, enough now? Enough, Jim?"

"Yes, Ben. In a moment."

For how many bitter days and nights, noons and sad mornings did I regret those three words—"In a moment."

Ben plucked at me and I shrugged him off—because something at the shrub which had torn him excited my attention. The growth— but only on the closest inspection—seemed less attached to the rock than its neighbours. I took my knife from its sheath and poked through the thorny branches. No wall was found—my blade struck no rock.

"Ben. Come here. See. Tell me what you find."

Ben did likewise, then stood back. He said nothing and I saw from his clothing that the poor old fellow had been unable to control his bladder.

My mind raced. In an instant I flashed to what I thought must have happened. Our companions—in both parties—had discovered this entrance to some deep caves and either languished still inside, or had traversed them and even now awaited rescue on the far and most inhospitable side of the island.

"Ben, I think we have a discovery here."

He made to run and I grabbed him. "No, Ben. We're all right"— and he stood.

With my knife I forced back the shrub and found a veritable archway. Now I met the strange odour as fully as Ben must have been describing it to me. Today, when I hear mention of dead human flesh, that smell assails my nostrils.

"Ben—it's a cave!" I forced my way inwards and held the shrub apart for him. With all the reluctance in the world he followed.

We stood for a moment, trying to allow light from outside into the gloom. But we could not advance without letting the shrub fall back into its place and my knife was not strong enough to cut it away from the entrance.

Ben took a step forwards, peering beneath cupped hands. I began to adjust myself to the pitch dark. We edged inwards; there might have been an abyss at our feet for all we knew. At once, hands from Hell seized us both and my knife fell from my grasp.

—⚓—

Ch. 18—

The Pit of Evil

Everything stopped—my thoughts, my feelings and maybe my heart. The darkness did not allow me to see Ben's attacker—and mine came from behind with a blade at my throat. Nobody spoke. All I could see of Ben in the darkness was his white trousers—and beneath my own chin a blade wide enough to slice off my head.

Next I saw that Ben began to shuffle sideways like a crab, being impelled that way, no doubt, by the blade held at his craw. He disappeared into the gloom. Sure enough, I was now pushed likewise—but only by the blade; I had no consciousness of a body behind it, of a hand pressing it. Yet it drove me steadily sideways very slowly for some paces. I heard breathing behind me and at a height that suggested a being of at least my own stature.

The cavern did brighten. All I could make out was that I shuffled along a broad path of stone. Ahead of me, darkness spread like a thick black sheet.

Soon the path seemed to broaden and I was stopped. The blade was taken from my throat and I next felt it on my head, pressed downwards into the highest point of my skull: its point felt like a needle. The pressure indicated that I should sink to the ground; first I knelt and then I sat. The blade was withdrawn and my throat and crown hurt from the metal.

From behind me came the noise of scraping—a flint or a match. A dim light glowed and was held above me. I waited until the beam spread. Ben was just ahead of me, also sitting, and I heard him gasp. We sat on a thin shelf of rock. Beneath us lay an abyss. Now the smell identified itself. A decaying human arm lay across a crag. I felt sure we had been lured into a charnel house where men had recently perished. Poor Ben looked paralysed.

I tried to listen to my surroundings. Since I could not see far, since I dare not touch, since the sense of smell proved so repellent, my ears proved my most useful faculty.

First I heard the silence of that cave—I hear it to this day. Every place has a sound of some nature. I have been on the headland above Kitts Hole on the mildest dawns of Christendom when not a breeze nor a songbird trembled—yet there was always a sound, if only the sound of the world. I have stood on the laneway outside the Admiral Benbow on nights when the frost iced the stars, when the waves had gone to sleep—yet there was a sound, if only the sound of the night and its darkness.

Here, deep beneath Spyglass Hill on Treasure Island, this cave too had its own sound. It was the world's most frightening sound—the sound of nothing.

But the closing of our other faculties improves those left to us (which is why blind men make clocks). Now my ears took on extra powers and I began to hear other sounds. First I heard the breathing of my captor, quiet, easy, a yard behind my back, the breathing of a man in control. Next I heard a distant moan, too far away to come from Ben Gunn whose stricken silence was that of the cave itself. Finally I heard something which aroused the faculty of touch—the whisper of a breeze.

But it did not come from the door (if such it may be called) through which we had recently come; my face felt this breeze and it came and went in such a fashion that I knew it was not the cold air of the cave itself.

What had gone on in this place? Others too must have found their way in here and been taken. Some at least, and perhaps many, had been dispatched to the pit below, an easy matter of a shove from this path on which we knelt. But one, perhaps more, had survived, hence the distant moan.

I also reasoned that the absence of human thoroughfare on the plateau outside gave leave to believe the usual entrance to the cave lay elsewhere. This would account for the breeze; the cave must have an easier, more accessible entry.

Dare I say my spirits rose? It seems a fancy to claim so, for at any moment I might be pitched headlong to join the wretched carcasses below. Dr. Livesey told me a long time ago that when he ever found himself in an intolerable situation, he either departed it or altered it. I had no such choice—and only one resource: I began to talk.

"Whoever you are. I and my friend mean you no harm. We have merely come to search for our missing companions. If you tell us where they might be, that is if you know where they are—you will render us a good service. We shall be grateful."

I heard my voice echo a little along the walls. I sounded quavery at first and then firmer. This gave me heart and I continued.

"I will tell you who I am. My name is Jim Hawkins. I have been on this island before. Now I have returned to find someone we left behind. The man's name is Joseph Tait. It may be that you are Joseph Tait. It may be that you know Joseph Tait. It may be that you *knew* Joseph Tait. If it be within your Christian means to find Joseph Tait for us or enable us to bring news of him to those who, in no spirit of harm, seek him—then we will trouble you no more."

I received a result but not one I would have wanted: Ben's captor, still hidden in the shadows, yanked the old chap to his feet by the hair. Ben did not utter—and directly following, I felt a similar brutal clutch on my head. I rose, trying not to stumble forwards: the edge of the pit lay less than half a pace from my shoes. The knife returned, this time to my temple, resting on the top of my ear where it joins my skull. One slip, either of my footing or that of the blade, would sever the ear from the head.

By watching Ben in the dim light, and then by pressure of the blade, I divined we must shuffle sideways again, along the ledge. We were not being pushed into the pit—we were being taken somewhere. New light glimmered. It grew brighter from time to time, then faded, confirming my belief that a wind entered this cavern from an opening somewhere ahead of us.

We edged along, Ben and I, like men stepping sideways into eternity. Once, a stone was dislodged by my shoe and I heard it fall, but its landing was muffled; I imagined that it fell upon the corpse of one of our poor sailors. A moment later I heard a squeal and saw from the corner of my eye that Ben almost lost his footing. That was when I caught the first sign of a captor. A hand, large and rough, I can give no better description than that, reached out and steadied him, but with force and by the hair.

"It's all right, Ben," I called. "You shall be safe."

But the blade at my ear pressed downwards and I gasped at the sting of a sharp cut in that most tender place.

On we inched, sideways and sideways. I heard the moan again, now nearer, and it seemed that the draught of wind grew keener. The ledge widened to a path and we seemed to withdraw from the direct edge of the precipice. As I could not look ahead, I could not see where we were being taken. From time to time I glanced down and saw that the pit had begun to end—but even where its slopes were shallow I saw bones and the remains of clothing. And still there hung that smell, that awful odour.

Who could know how long that journey took—in such fear and trembling, amid such pernicious gloom? There came a moment—perhaps it was a quarter, perhaps half an hour—when at last Ben and I were conducted backwards in unison and we saw the edge of the pit recede. From the walls on either side I saw that we were being led along a broad passageway. This was some relief; at least we would not now by misadventure fall into that pit. But was there another such hole—to which we were being led?

Soon a fuller light gleamed. Then I perceived a torch aflame on the wall above my head, but daylight was mixed in too. To my right I saw a human hand, then a head, then a body—of a man. I could not tell whether I knew him; he was being held to the ground by a large boulder resting squarely between his shoulders; in a moment I saw another rock resting on the backs of his knees. Both were of such a weight that he could not attempt to release himself from beneath them without causing a noise. Next we passed another man similarly imprisoned, then another.

After a minute or so we were halted and Ben was forced to his knees—but I was not. I stood and watched as he was made to lie face-down by the stone wall of the passageway. My head was forced away from my view of him but the noise of grunting and then of Ben in pain, suggested that he had been similarly weighted to the stone floor of this cave.

Why was I not thus pinned? Instead I was walked forwards and with prods of the knife point instructed to spread my hands high above my head and place the palms flat on the cold wall, then spread my legs wide apart, so that I stood in the shape of a large "X," with the dank stone wall for support.

My captor retreated—that I knew. When someone has been so close to you, especially in such awful circumstances, you become immediately knowledgeable of their absence. I believe they left the cave—for presently there arose from the ground all around me the sound of moaning.

I heard Ben among them and called softly, "Ben. It's Jim. Here. Are you safe?"

"Pinned, Jim. Dreadfully pinned."

"What injuries will the poor fellow have?" I asked myself. "*If* he gets out of here."

"A Christian voice," came another call.

"Yes," I answered. "Who are you?" The man seemed near at hand.

"Able seaman Moore, sir, late of the *Hispaniola* out of Bristol."

I had not known the names of all the crew; never troubling to read the manifest, I had been content with Captain Reid's command.

"Moore, I come from the *Hispaniola*. What has happened to Mr. Coll?"

"Dead sir. They cut his eyes out and pushed him off the path, sir. They will us all."

A fury rose in me, and although fury is a danger in such circumstances, it may also be a salvation. Coll was an excellent man, whom I liked and admired, a man I would have hoped to remain acquainted with long after the end of our voyage.

I listened for a moment. No captors' footsteps returned. No doubt they conferred somewhere.

"Moore," I murmured. "How many have died?"

"I know not, sir."

"And how many strong are they?"

"I know not, sir. There are certainly two."

"Do they know the King's English?" I asked.

"Two of them speak it, sir. I have heard a word here and there. But it is all deadly secret. We have seen but their feet as they kick us."

He hissed as his words ended and then he squealed, from which I guessed that a blow had landed on him. As did on me. My head felt as if it had been hit with something of a hardness greater than I had encountered, something harder than stone, than iron. I staggered and, as I fell—backwards—I saw above me the face of Joseph Tait.

———— ✎ ————

Part Four

—✦—

The Impenitent Thief

Ch. 19 —

The Savagery of Man

Tait did not want me to see his face—and rued that I had. He seized my hair and by the force and shape of the grip I recognised that he had been my captor all along. Therefore he had heard my desperate words. They had no effect on him. He pressed my face so savagely to the wall that the bridge of my nose still bears the scar.

But I had remembered the face. He was now heavily bearded and much weathered, but without doubt it was Joseph Tait. I had the fleeting thought, "Give thanks that his sweet son resembles the mother rather than the father." (Seeing Tait again, I realised I had been wrong about Louis's nose!)

Did he step away from me in the darkness? I do not know; I was too stunned. For several minutes I half-lay, half-knelt, crumpled against the wall. My neck was ricked badly, and I had been kicked in the spine. I felt blood trickle both from within and upon my nose, and one eye hurt like a spike.

But I tried to gain some advantage. By seeming stunned I could think myself to this new position in which I found myself. Yes, I had seen Tait—but I had also glimpsed daylight!

Some sort of entrance to the cave lay fifteen or twenty yards away. A shallow natural arch, like a rough bridge, curved up from the stone floor where I lay. I saw the sunlight and the branch of a tree. To take in all of this needed time; I continued in my act of being stunned.

Next, I thought of the several men from the *Hispaniola* who lay in this cave or somewhere in the darkness nearby. Maybe not all had been killed. If I could get to them maybe I could overturn Tait. Indeed were I to swing my boots around in a whirl, I might knock him off his feet into the pit below.

But then I realised I did not know how many accomplices Tait had. I reasoned that if they had overcome all the men from the *Hispaniola*, my chances were few. Nothing left, I thought, but to escape—if I could.

My head throbbed and I thought my nose bone broken. First I had the idea of getting back to the ruined shack on the little plateau. Ben and I had left our weapons there. But how could I return through the cavern—in the pitch blackness? Along the edge of a deep abyss that was full of rotting human flesh and bones? Watched by an unknown number of murderous captors who had developed the cat's gift of seeing in the dark?

I thought again. Not daring to look around me, I kept my mind on that rough arch. Maybe I could overcome my fear and move swiftly enough to get to it. When I got there I might find nothing but the open air, that the arch opened high on the side of a sheer cliff. For all I knew those were the very tops of trees I looked at. It did not matter; I had no other possibility.

The first thing I needed was subterfuge. I stirred myself enough to provoke an attack from Tait or his gang. This would do things for me. It would tell me whether I was still being guarded and how closely.

"Look," I cried. "I know who you—"

Tait hit me; he struck my head hard with what I took to be the hilt of his knife. My forehead bounced off the crag in front of my face. The double injury hurt terribly and I was easily able to feign senselessness.

For long, long minutes, maybe half an hour, I waited. I allowed my body to subside, as if in utter collapse. Soon I heard a stealthy scrape and I figured that Tait believed he had cancelled any threat I might offer.

Slowly, slowly, I eased my position. In this alleyway of our wild prison there was no sound, not even from poor Ben. Slowly, slowly, I concentrated my hearing until I fancied I could hear rustling noises and hoped it was the wind in the trees outside the cave. Somewhere I heard other moans, but they were faint and I did not wish, however callous it must make me seem, to be distracted. I had to gather all my strength for one swift movement. Assuming the ruffians guarded the cave mouth I should have to dive between them or past them in order to escape.

By the smallest portions of an inch I turned my body around. It may have taken a hour, or so it seemed, but presently I was lolling my head against the wall in such a fashion as to eye cautiously the arc of daylight. As I expected, two of them sat by it—Tait and another whom I could not see clearly. They fixed something between them; it seemed to be a rope that they made from long, supple branches. Neither spoke; both bent to the task, plaiting the twigs back and forth.

I watched them closely—and I also watched the sky. Was that a treetop? If so, then I had some chance of safety after my proposed dive. Yet the way seemed hopeless—until I looked in the opposite direction. Using the glimmer of light through the arch and the accustomedness my eyes had now acquired to the dark I could make out some details of the cavern.

What I saw was awful. Down one side, to the bottom of the pit lay bodies and bones. I recognised the long shape and uniform of Noonstock, the bo'sun. His neck slewed at an angle, broken like a matchstick. Beneath him I could see the body of an able seaman, a burly, sullen man I only knew as Sexton, black-haired and young. His head had been cleft open with frightful force.

No sign of poor Coll—not that I wished to look upon that fine, open face now so mutilated. I stretched as much as I dare but only saw limbs. Had Tait and his ruffians killed all our men? How many had survived with Moore? And why?

Ben Gunn was groaning. He would not last, I reckoned—his bones were too brittle to bear those huge stones that pinned him down. But it was his plight that decided me. His face was about three yards from mine. I peered through the gloom and saw tears on his cheeks.

I whispered to him, "Ben, I'm going to try and escape." He never answered; he couldn't.

My immediate task was of the greatest difficulty—how to get myself into a position where I could launch myself with hard momentum. I might get one movement undetected—in this narrow space to get two unnoticed movements would be a gift from the Almighty.

Where I sit now, as I write this down, is as tranquil as any place on earth. The sea is shimmering in the distance; some lobsterman is out beyond Kitts Hole in a small fishing boat, fingering the satin waters. And when I return to my page of writing and think back on the last moments of that morning, I still cannot comprehend how I did it. But somehow I twisted myself, rose from the floor and launched myself, running low, all in one effort, soft on tiptoes. Moving hard, bent double, I aimed myself like an arrow at the arc of light.

Tait saw me first and moved quickest—but even then contrived only to raise his length of creeper that he wove. It tripped me—and I fell out into the blinding day. Tait grabbed my shirt and I dropped half over a ledge. My heart sank—this was a sheer drop beneath me, not firm ground; the tree I saw grew out of some ledge in the cliff's side.

I grasped, more with instinct than sense, at the stone ledge. Tait reached down to grab my hair and a second pair of hands grasped my other shoulder. Then Tait stood so firm on my hand I could not move it. There I swung, half on and half off the ledge, torn between a drop of what proportions I knew not and the hands of the most villainous pair of men outside captivity.

My mind raced, and looked for another trick. I found the trick—I let them half-haul me back up so that they thought they had me. Then I wriggled, flung myself about and escaped their grip. I began to fall very horribly.

But not very far. I collided with a thing that grunted and I bounced off it and crashed into the cliff face. It was a human body, still alive. Next, instead of falling headlong I began to slide down, banging into stones and scrubs. Soon I came to a stop by the bulk of a great rock. I was horribly bruised, and I looked upwards whence I had come.

The body that had stopped me was one of about ten—all men from the *Hispaniola*! They had been placed on a narrow ridge and tied by their wrists to the roots and trunks of shrubs that grew from the rockface. A sorry sight they made, like some row of bedraggled statuary, whitening in the sun, and all heavy with dried blood. I had overshot this ledge, their prison, and collided with the one on the extremest edge. Out at the farthest extremity it broke my heart to see Tom Taylor: Tom's dear head drooped on his shoulder as though he might already have died.

What a bizarre kingdom of evil I had found! What a frightful return to this diseased isle! But I had no time to contemplate. After a loud explosion, a musket ball whizzed past my hand where it rested on the rock behind me and a splinter of stone stung my arm.

After the quickest of glances at the terrain I guessed I must go right. Correct decision: to my left I heard the crashing of the undergrowth. I knew not where to run, but reasoned that a flight downwards would bring me to the water's edge. I was now completely in the hands of Providence; there would be no life if Tait caught me. Another crack, another whizzing bullet past my ear: one man fired at me while the other pursued.

No journey of mine will ever again be so hazardous. Never again shall I run so headlong. I had come out on the other side of Spyglass Hill and was now on the Cape of the Woods, racing down through land so rough and uncertain both my legs could have been broken. Branches and plants slapped my face and neck and arms and hands; roots writhed from the earth to grasp at my ankles and knees.

I have heard it said that when engaged in furious activity a man feels no difficulty within his gut. This is not true. As I raced I felt nausea as I had never known in my life, not aboard ship nor on dry land.

Behind me, the crashing of my pursuer grew louder as he gained ground on me. And he had every advantage; he knew the island and the route to the sea. Indeed he did not even follow directly behind me but on an easier way and soon I heard his loud puffing. What to do? Should I stop a moment and play cat-and-mouse? Or should I trust to my impetus for safety?

I chose the latter course and tried to increase my speed. Suddenly I was in open ground and there ahead spread the sea. But this onrush of freedom brought the worst danger—it placed me in the open where my follower could see me. I saw him too—over to my right, racing to converge: it was Tait.

He threw something and it hit my shoulder with a wounding, piercing pain and lodged there. Was it a knife? He threw again. The second missile pierced me just behind and above the knee, but did not lodge there.

A patch of scrub, low and awkward, remained between me and the spit of sand before the waves. I tried to leap across it and came down. Up again, I felt his hand on my shoulder. I lashed backwards and caught him somewhere with more force than I knew I possessed. This blow won me a temporary ease.

The scrub gave way to soft sand, so soft I sank to my ankles immediately and my boots filled. Now what to do? Here I was, the ocean ahead of me and no way back.

Tait closed in again and I half-turned and swung at him, but more like a boy does at play with a friend than with any viciousness that might save my life. Tait's force spun me around and I saw his hand try to grab at me. He carried a knife.

I ducked under his arm and, twisting him around, broke his grip on my shoulder and got away again. An insect flew into my eye, large and hot, blinding me. In my heat and distress I ran I knew not where, but found firm sand. I was running along parallel to the waves—and ahead of me, as though anchored specially for my use, floated a rude raft. Of course! flashed my mind. Were I cast away here I should also build a raft.

Tait saw me make for it and roared. We got to the raft together and bestrode it. Again as unskilled as a boy, I pushed him and he fell backwards into the shallow waters. This delayed him a little and I, kneeling, pushed the raft away. I cast off the rope of creeper that led to a small peg in the soft sand.

Like a Triton, Tait rose bellowing from the waters and slashed at me with his knife. The blade missed me and tangled in the crude slats of the raft. As he struggled with it I kicked his arm and I fell back onto the raft with the force of my kick. But I had been effective and he fell back too.

He rose again and stood in water now to his waist as I knelt on the raft. Some vicious spike in its timbers tore at my shin but I cared not. I looked around for a paddle—none, nor oar nor propulsion of any kind. And Tait lurched forwards again. Spray flecked his beard and rage lit his eyes. He grabbed the knife from the slats.

I retreated to the corner of the raft furthest from him. He tried to board and I rocked the raft dementedly to upset his balance. The craft tipped him back again into the sea; its edge caught him a mild blow to the face and he half-fell, then stood once more in the waves, roaring like a creature.

The raft began to float outwards on the waves to where the water deepened. Tait tried to stalk around the raft's perimeter, but a small wave slowed him. By now I saw that unless he swam he should soon be shoulder-high in the ocean. Some lucky current had caught me—and I remembered the treacherous speeds of these waters.

Tait debated with himself. I saw him stop and look. He measured the distance between him and the raft which was being pulled away from him by the tides. With each second his dilemma increased. For a moment he half-lunged forwards, then drew back; then drew further back until he stood steady on the seabed. He half-lost his balance—I could see that he was trying to judge his chances against the sea.

He made his decision—he raised his knife to a point high above his shoulder. I saw the blade flash in the sunlight as it flew from his hand and I knew I had not moved quickly enough to evade it.

———✦———

Ch. 20 —

Escape into Peril

When I awake in these days of my life (and I am by anyone's measure a young man) I first ask myself by instinct the question, "Am I safe?" Since I am usually abed in the Admiral Benbow, my answer comes swift and sure: yes, I'm safe. That morning, Tait's knife knocked me senseless and when I awoke, on that makeshift, shambling raft, I knew I had never been less safe.

My eyes were pained, and one eye blurred; my head was desperately sore and dizzy and I bled from shoulder, nose and thigh. Add to this that I had been seized on a fast tidal current and was sweeping out to sea. In short I was beleaguered to a point of serious danger.

My mind was in a fair jumble. I had done the right thing in escaping, because I had no hope of influencing the horrible state of affairs in the cave. Also, I had been correct in attempting my escape so soon, while I was still a matter of surprise to Tait. But what now? Not even the heavens, it seemed, could answer that.

Uncle Ambrose's face came to me. My concern swerved to include all those for whom I had taken responsibility. Poor Ben Gunn—I had enticed him from a life of safety. And Louis—what a fate to be the son of such a degenerate brute!

Far behind me the figure of Tait grew smaller. He had remained on the shore, perhaps hoping for a quirk of the tide that would deliver me back to him. My race down to the sand had taken me in a transverse direction and I could catch no sight of the cave mouth or the men strung out in the sun.

Now I must see to it that I survived to help them—or as many of them as might still be alive if I ever got back. A hot tropical glare bore down on me and salt water lashed me. I was wounded, perhaps grievously, and adrift without sail or rudder on an ocean I knew to be pitilessly whimsical. That was the size, energy and savagery of my misfortune.

Soon, all fortitude and sense deserted me and for several unseeing minutes I watched the distant line of the Spyglass—accursed hill! The belief that had sustained me—of experience through former hardship—was nowhere to be found within my mind. I sat on the raft and watched the waves; then I lay down and must have lapsed from consciousness again.

When my senses returned I felt new alarm. My distance from the island told me that I must have been unconscious for many minutes. Where had Tait's knife struck me? On my head, without a doubt; I felt the place without needing to place fingers to it.

Hauling myself to my knees, I felt another infernal sharpness, as if stabbed again. I looked down; I was kneeling on the villain's dagger where it had lain after hitting my head. At least he had furnished me with a weapon. I lifted it from the boards of the raft and inspected it. No blood marked the blade—but the handle bore stains and what seemed like a rib or two of my hair. The knife's ivory hilt, rather than the steel of its blade, had connected.

Now I had the courage to reach for the wound. It gaped to my finger—what depth it would have been, had the blade found home, gave me cause to shudder. My fingertips had also found where blood had begun to crust on my neck and ear.

Not trusting my legs for steadiness (nor the motion of the raft) I rose to a full kneeling position. No sign of Tait could I see. But there, now, stood Spyglass Hill; the tide had carried me around. I strained but it was too far to define the cave mouth or the poor wretches stretched out there on their ridge above eternity.

A wave struck the raft and almost knocked me over, making me think I must inspect this rough conveyance. It was made of boards whose kind I had seen on the shed, a few paling-posts that might have come from our old stockade which the squire, the doctor and all of us had defended so vigorously. These timbers were lashed together with ropes made of vines or woven with supple branches. I could not think that Tait or anybody might ever have done more than poke along the shore of Treasure Island in this regrettable barque; she was not built for the high seas.

Therefore I had the dim thought that I must immediately take her towards the shore, but away from my most recent point of embarkation. As my head cleared I thought better and told myself I must head for the *Hispaniola*. Navigation in her direction presented no difficulty—she lay at anchor by the northeasterly point, an easy course to divine using Spyglass Hill as my landmark; indeed as I faced the isle I could now see to my left hand—that is to say, west of me—Mizzenmast Hill.

But the currents were taking me in a southerly direction and soon I should be by Haulbowline Head. To get to the *Hispaniola* I should have to propel myself all around the south of the island and then northwards along the eastern side. A prodigious distance in my circumstances and condition—and how was I to direct the raft? I looked around me, in case an oar or paddle of some kind had been stowed in some lashed fashion. Nothing. Must I paddle with my hands?

Why, then, I must—and I manoeuvred myself to a corner of the raft thinking to place her at an angle to the waves by paddling from one corner and making the opposite corner into a point so that she would sail like a diamond-shaped craft.

My plan failed because I had not the use of one arm. Where Tait's first, unseen weapon had struck my shoulder, I had taken a numbing wound; a muscular damage had been inflicted and I could scarcely move my arm; that side of me was growing stiffer by the minute.

Next I tried to read the tides. Perhaps I could clamber off the raft and, while clinging to her, push her, swimming with my legs into a current that would prove favourable. This I attempted and it almost proved my undoing. When the saltwater struck into the wound on my leg the pain was so excruciating I almost let go of the raft—on which I had but a poor hold. The raft bucked and then my good hand was also forced from it and I was thrust beneath a wave.

When I came up I was three feet from the raft—which was then wallowed back at me, but with force rather than precision. And, though its return enabled me to clamber aboard, it also struck me severely on the chest. I climbed up and was grateful to sprawl on my face, hoping the sea would not unhorse me.

For several minutes I lay there, and tried to assess my condition. None of my wounds seemed mortal; some would, I felt certain, prove troublesome. (One discomfits me to this day, particularly when frost arrives.)

My mental state was worse than my physical. I was in the midst of severe and extraordinary failure; my companions had fallen among the most appalling circumstances; and now I drifted out to sea in uncharted waters, unable to bring any influence to bear on my condition. It seems not unmanly to confess that when I measured the situation and the extent of my failure, I wept.

The grief brought a kind of stupor to me. I lay without moving for a span of time that I cannot reckon, even today. It may have been several hours. The sun seemed to blaze directly upon my back and the sea grew strangely calm.

In time the raft began to sink a little and generally floated about three inches beneath the surface. Now and then a flick of salt wave would lash me and it always seemed to find its way into a wound. One cut—on my thigh—was still bleeding profusely. It is a measure of my stupor that I removed my shirt and bound the wound— thereby leaving my back and shoulders bare to the sun. I was to regret that bitterly.

The night fell and I drifted on, away from Treasure Island—and away from the *Hispaniola*. My direction, to judge by the setting sun, was more or less due south. I grew further and further exhausted. Whether I had any clear senses I cannot say, but I remember the cold.

It should not have been unexpected; we had all, Dr. Livesey and the others and, lately, Uncle Ambrose and Captain Reid, remarked upon the contrast in the temperatures of day and night in these seas. But it took me by surprise. Also, my skin had been severely burned by the sun. I shivered so much that night that I wished to die.

The next day brought the same unpitying pattern, with hot, unrelenting rays burning me to cinders—after which a cold night froze me. My mouth swelled, my tongue bulged out beyond my teeth. I tried to ease matters by lying first on my face, then on my back or side. No relief ensued. Thirst overcame me so greatly that I made that greatest of castaways errors—I tasted the water of the sea. I was immediately repelled by the harshness of it and within minutes the curse of its saltiness tormented me and my last state of need was worse than my former.

Ch. 21—

A Safety of Sorts

How curious that conditions we find usually difficult, even shameful, can be our salvation. By which I mean what we call "dementia." That is the state, I believe, settled upon me on that raft. No food, no water, no horizon—perhaps dementia was created by the Almighty to be Man's saviour until fresh hope arrives. The last act I remember was a sensible one, and it came from a memory of another bad occasion when all seemed lost. Just as Israel Hands's dirk had pinned me by my flesh to the mast of the *Hispaniola* long ago, I used Tait's broad dagger, which had wedged itself between two planks of the raft, to pin myself to the slats by the cloth of my serge breeches.

That way, I should at least be held above water, were I to lose my senses through pain, starvation, thirst or the general oppression of my circumstances.

From the times that followed—and I believe it must have been about six or seven days—I have a memory of waves. I have a memory of burning skin tightening on my shoulders, of burning lips, of a tongue that would not work; of stiffness in my limbs and agonies of stinging waters, salt being rubbed, as it is said, in my wounds. Sometimes I thought monsters came by to sweep me off the raft, and sometimes I thought great, beating birds swooped low to pluck at me and carry me off as carrion. I heard noises, almost musical; they can only have been the cries of birds—can't they? Or the songs of the deep?

Of my pain, the stings linger longest in my mind; seawater splashing into my eyes and my cuts, which now felt legion all over my body. I seemed unable to move my leg, not only where I had pinned myself to the boards of the raft but where the wound was, and every time the raft tipped and yawed on the surface of the ocean I felt the horror of great pain in those parts where I was torn.

Then there was hunger, which returned like the waves. My bones felt hollow and I began to imagine the foods of England, the beef and the mutton and the cream and the syllabub that my mother so enjoyed providing. Their pictures seemed to dance in my mind and the juices of my palate tried to rise—and failed, because they, like my brain fluids and my blood, had all but ceased to flow.

And over and above all this came the sensation of floating. By this I do not mean floating on the surface of the water; that calmness came to me but rarely. More common was the feeling that I floated somewhere above my own body and that I looked down and saw myself in my own plight. There I lay, sprawled and pinned, arms outflung, on this coarse raft, all the corners of which I could almost reach, and I was tossed and tossed by each wave, great or impudently small.

To see that vision now is to see a young man in his twenties spread out like a victim under a burning sun, his body marked with sores and scalds from seawater and the skin around great wounds blackening and whitening as the sea washed away his dried blood.

In this condition did I drift and the only shores I neared were those of the sea of my Maker—until one morning early, when a cold wind fought with the hot sun for mastery, an object loomed at me and human hands grabbed at me and dimly heard voices asked me questions. They told me later I did not answer them—I could not.

My next memory also concerns touch—clean touch, of hard but decent cloth, and of rough wood. Of sight's faculty I had to be patient: I could not open my eyes; they had been too afflicted with seawater and the eyelids had encrusted themselves shut, as though to protect my sight.

They also told me later they found that small creatures of the sea had found pathways into my ears—as they had into my wounds. But in the case of my wounds, they had been protected by the cleansing processes of salt water and greater damage was thus avoided. As for my ears, a constant washing with clean water for several days slowly gave me back my excellent hearing. When I was a boy I loved to press a seashell to my ears, thinking to hear the ocean's roar. I cannot play that sweet game now; the thought of it causes me to tremble.

From the sensation of touch, and from the blurred voices around me I soon understood that I must have been taken aboard a ship rather than a landfall. No taste came yet, nor smell; my nostrils were all but closed with seawater sores. Touch assisted me most. I was able to move all of my limbs and feel my extremities—for that I was grateful. Any sudden movement caused great pain, as when I retched and brought up, as they told me, pints of brine.

A new unconsciousness took me over and one that I welcomed— the cure of sleep. I believe I slept most of two days. When I awoke, matters had improved. I could not yet open my eyes; my nostrils, my ears and my wounds still hurt frightfully. But my spirits had much lightened and by dint of a small sponging, applied by a kind hand, I tasted broth on my tongue. Nectar, stolen from the cup of each and every god, cannot have tasted sweeter.

Nobody asked me questions, yet the persons who tended me chattered to me as amiably as taproom drinkers. They were rough but— and this is what made the miracle—they were English. As I could not speak I could not yet ask them questions and they knew nothing of me, for I heard them consider whether I be Spanish or French; my skin they thought dark enough to be Portuguese, yet they wondered whether this had not been wrought by the sun.

Nor could they tell my age, and from their talk, always dimly heard, I began to measure my own dreadful state. In short, to them I was a male human creature, found adrift on the ocean high, a man of no determinable nationality who was exceedingly fortunate to be alive. And so they often said.

Thus informed, I began to cure myself; I firmly believe that knowledge brings results.

Bit by bit I began to take some strength. My tongue's swelling subsided and my wounds stung a little less each day with whatever potions they applied. The shape and nature of the damage led them to consider that I might have been a buccaneer on the worst end of a rowdy cutlass or a mutiny. But they concluded that my clothes, what was left of them, seemed too fine bred to match such a supposition.

It was clear that I was in the crew's quarters, among the sailors of this English vessel. They joked in terms I knew, they spoke of the King and of their own native places. Of their captain they said—and thought—little. I never learned his name and from their dismissive talk I gleaned that he was no more than a journeyman master mariner whose ticket permitted him to accept charters.

I also heard the name of a harbour to which they headed and where they hoped to put me ashore—a place for provisions, repairs (they had grazed a reef) and some new canvas, for they had been subject to a gale; in short the normal hazards of long voyages. And I thought I recognised the name of this port, but I should have been as hazy had they been talking of Plymouth. Again sleep drifted in and took me with it.

One day, when it seemed to me as if I might soon open my eyes again (some dulling of the pain and stiffness made the eyeballs seem to grow easier) a new voice floated among the bunks where I lay. My senses, though not yet returned to their fullest, jumped to the alert. The voice, thin and high, enquired how I progressed. An answer was given, by the sailor I thought most attentive to me, that I recovered reasonably, though slowly.

"Has he spoken?"

"Not a word, sir. He 'as tried. The tongue's too much swollen in itself, it takes only foods that pours."

"Is he French?"

"We think so, sir. No means of recognition, I fear. Nothing in the pockets. Well, sir, no pockets, to be truthful, almost no garments left."

"Ye-es."

My mother, not a woman who races forwards with a compliment, marvels at the keenness of my ear. She has told neighbours that I can hear a bird landing in a field. And therefore and thereby—I know voices.

I knew this voice too well—even though I had heard it but on one occasion. It was the voice of Maltby's clerk; I had heard it outside the Admiral Benbow as they drew up their drumhead court. Maltby was the master of this brig, in everything but marine qualification.

How fortunate proved my injuries! Had it not been for their severity I would have made my name plain to my rescuers before I knew that I had landed aboard Maltby's ship.

Maltby's ship! The black brig! My wounds hurt afresh!

"Inform me when you believe he may be recovered enough to be spoken to."

"Aye, aye, sir."

"On another matter. What about Raspen? Sir Thomas has enquired as to his humour."

"A little calmer, sir. And, I believe, calming steadily."

"And the boy?"

"Still poorly, sir. It were—it were severe, sir."

"Yes. I know," and the thin voice departed.

The man who attended me closest, who had long since begun to chatter to me, even though he expected no response, turned to me and said, "We 'ad an unfortunate event on board, we 'ave a strange fellow with us, name of Abel Raspen, with a great 'ump on his back and 'e thought the cabin boy laughed at him so he flogged 'im. To near death. It were your luck too. This be Raspen's bunk you lies in."

Oh, my Creator! I sleep in the hunchback's bed! Is that his name—"Abel Raspen"? He should have been christened "Cain." What else will Fate throw at me? My mind gave a weary sigh. On top of the wildest imaginable chance that I had been plucked from the sea by Maltby and his gang: how must I now think?

When Maltby's brig came alongside the *Hispaniola*, I gave myself the comfort that he had not seen me—but it had slipped my mind that the hunchback had once encountered me on the road. True, he did not know that I was the landlord of the inn to which he and his cohorts then laid siege—but if he saw me he must recognise me from our one brief meeting. I lay there, all but overwhelmed but with enough sense to rest and then think my way back into the fray.

What stratagem must I now employ? Was there to be no end to my terrors? How should I contrive to come safely off this ship without further harm? I had the advantage of time. Until I felt so, I had no need of speaking, and I had no need of showing my face about the ship.

If, as I surmised from what I had overheard, the hunchback was being held in some restraint aboard due to his violent act, I could safely meet Maltby. What other ruse might secure me? I might write everything down and not speak, giving my tongue as a reason.

But, knowing he would kill me the moment he recognised me, I must guard against the day when the hundchback would again walk free. How should I do that? I knew from the ministrations served upon me that my eyes gave my protectors some concern. Perhaps it would be practical to have much of my face bandaged—not too unusual a request for a man in my state.

My fear subsided a little and my mind raced on and on. If I could be said to feel pleased at anything, I commended myself for the quickness with which my senses restored themselves.

From the conversation that took place about me, I divined that they expected harbour within five to seven days. My mind toyed and tossed with something that snagged my memory: the name, the *name*—of the port they were bound? Why did I know it? But I did not yet have the key that would open that lock and, tired, I abandoned the effort to recall its familiarity. Instead I began to exercise my body in small ways, flexing my shoulder and leg, turn and turn about, and willing my poor eyes to heal themselves.

To spur my mind and spirit I began to think of my companions, all of them—imprisoned in the cavern, the wretches pegged and bleached out on the cliff side and the anxious, powerless ones waiting aboard the *Hispaniola*.

My dear Uncle Ambrose? How stood he now aboard the ship—

what was he counselling the captain? On the island, how many good men had fallen to Tait's murderous villainy? Was it right that young Louis, that child who had taken a lease upon my heart, should be brought face-to-face with his brute father? And Grace Richardson, whom I now knew I loved as dearly as if she had been chosen for me by God Himself—would it not be beastly beyond contemplation that she should encounter such a man as he now stood, the blood of many on his vile hands?

As is ever the case with me, my judgements give way to practical concerns. I told myself sharply that it would help everybody were I to consider how I might rectify all the troubles I now knew. The tasks were mighty—to save as many of the men on that island as I could possibly hope to save—Tom Taylor, any of the crewmen, Dr. Jefferies (even if he is my rival); to fetch Ben Gunn (were he still alive, and how I shuddered at *that* thought!) back to his peaceful green lanes and hedges; to bring Tait to justice, whatever the pleas of Grace Richardson; to put right all the damage and trouble I had brought into the life and fine seamanship of Captain Reid; and to get us all home safely.

Any one of those tasks must have tried a Hercules. I say that with no sense of grandeur—rather to point out that I saw them all as my duty.

My next thought was the most natural one. In order to accomplish any, not to say all, of these endeavours, I must take care that I myself recovered from my injuries. Also, that I must use all cunning and guile to keep myself out of any new danger until I could put my plans in motion.

And that was the instant at which my mind gave me the cleverest idea of my young life thus far. I recalled why I knew the name of the port and the beautiful landlocked gulf to which this ship was bound—and felt the skin of my face crack a little at the first smile I dared since my rescue. And I thanked fervently the dear Admiral Benbow whose heavy door concealed me during our siege.

Ch. 22—

The Jaws of Danger

The days passed; I was now able to count the minutes as well as the hours—and I had also become increasingly aware of the roughness of this crew. They were disciplined and experienced, certainly, but they came from the harsher side of marine employment. They meant or caused me no harm and in their society I had the freedom to implement the plan whose first inkling had caused me to smile.

It began with the grunting sounds I made one morning as my "physician" squeezed warm broth between my lips.

He said to me, "Can you speak yet?"

I shook my head.

"But you know what I say?"

I nodded.

"Are you English?" An intelligent man, he began to ask questions that could be answered wordlessly.

Again I nodded.

"Can you see?"

I made the facial grimace that suggested I struggled with my eyelids.

"No matter, no matter. And 'ave we given you food that is good with you?"

I nodded and made an affirmatory gesture with my hand; then I added what I had carefully thought out—a gesture that indicated I wished to write.

"Wait 'ere," said my companion—at which I half-smiled, being in no condition to run away, nor having anywhere to run.

I knew what was about to happen and was pleased to be proven right. The clerk with the thin voice came back.

"They tell me you begin to feel recovered?" he enquired.

I nodded.

"And that you wish to write?"

I nodded again.

They sat me up, and I allowed the experience to display more pain than it cost—though it must be said that this was not such an effort; knives of fire seemed to stab into my flesh. In my left hand they placed a logbook; in my right a quill or a stylus of some kind.

My hand trembled; I knew it did so from my fear of my own daring—they will have thought it owed to injury. I wrote in a scrawl, "M-I-L-L-S. B-R-I-S-T-O-L."

The clerk, evidently reading my words, asked in his thin singsong, "What ship, Mister Mills?"

I scrawled, "H-I-S-P-A-N-" and he stopped me.

"The *Hispaniola*?"

I nodded—and could hear him thinking.

At length he asked, "What became of her?"

I scrawled, "P-L-A-G-U-E."

"She got the plague?"

I nodded.

"Did you get the plague?"

I shook my head and wrote, "B-U-R-I-A-L-S. T-O-O-K R-A-F-T."

"You are a deserter?" hissed the thin clerk.

I shook my head and wrote, "P-E-R-M-I-S-S'N. S-T-A-Y O-R G-O."

Now I gave the impression that the effort was proving strenuous. Remember, my eyes had not yet been recovered enough to open wide without severe pain.

"Mister Mills, do you know what the voyage of the *Hispaniola* intended?"

I nodded—reticently.

He sensed my mood and thought himself (as I wished him to think) on a trail; he changed tack.

"What was the purpose of the voyage?"

I remained motionless.

"Do you wish to tell me, Mister Mills?"

I wrote, "P-R-I-V-A-T-E," halted a moment then added, "S-E-C-R-E-T."

"I see." He could scarcely keep the excitement from his thin voice.

I sighed as if in fatigue. The clerk affected kindness then.

"You must rest, Mister Mills. We are glad to have you aboard, you seem like a fine fellow and we shall move you to better quarters. Get you tended better. But I must ask one question. Do you know if your ship—do you know if she found, or thought she found, what she came for?"

I took thought (as it were) and nodded, then, with a pause, nodded again.

The clerk said to the sailor in charge of me, "Move him to the officers' quarters. Find Vail. Instruct him that this man is to be cared well and rested—and given all comfort. Sir Thomas will think us fortunate to have saved such a man." To me he said, "Mister Mills, Vail is a manservant, well trained in all manner of caring duties. He will tend you well."

As he left I felt my face wishing to smile sardonically. I knew what Sir Thomas would think fortunate. And I knew also my importance to them; it could be measured from the way they had moved me up in the world, given me one of their manservants. It certainly did not mean they thought me a gentleman, like them!

But I wished I understood the true, deep reason they had followed us. I knew Grace (as I now began to call her) and Louis were the objects of their pursuit. But what was it about them? What did Grace mean, or own, or harbour, or know? Something very powerful evidently: a man had died on our lane for it and his kinsman had chartered a ship and followed us three-quarter ways round the world.

But, because Grace had not answered my questions, I still languished in ignorance of the fullest reasons that lay at the root of this
mystery. What did the clerk's question mean: "Do you know if your
ship—do you know if she found, or thought she found, what she
came for?" Did Maltby also seek Tait? And, if so, why? Or had they
merely got wind of the bar silver? No, I doubted that a trove by itself
could have pulled them so far.

Thus I battled, to and fro, to and fro, but nothing came clear to
me—except the supreme consideration that I must conceal my true
identity from everyone on this brig.

The "raising" of my lowly status began immediately. A litter appeared, carried by two sailors. Next came a small, round man with
jowls so smooth he never shaved. He was dressed unlike any mariner I
had ever seen—tight black breeches, a white shirt with what seemed
like a fantail collar and a waistcoat of gold-and-claret stripes. He directed the sailors to lift me on the litter and they did so with surprising
gentleness.

"I am called Vail," said the small, round, smooth man.

They took me to a good cabin and gently transferred me to a low,
wide bunk. I lay, breathing stiffly from the experience. With my
hands I gestured.

"Bathe your eyes, Mister Mills? Is that it?"

I nodded.

Vail fetched cool water and gently dabbed each poor eyelid. I
winced as he did so—a little more than I felt, though the eyes still suffered horribly.

"Better, sir?"

I nodded, took his hand and gestured it towards my eyes, indicating that I would like him to cover the eyelids.

"Shall I fold something on the eyes, sir? Is that it?"

I nodded. Vail went away and came back presently with a piece of
good linen which he laid tenderly across my eyes and forehead. I adjusted it so that it covered my nose too. Then I asked him, by ges-
tures, for some alabaster ointment. When he brought it to me I

applied it slowly to my lips—but again winced, and not falsely, at the pain induced thereby.

After that I lay back, well pleased. My plan truly excited me—an immodest fellow would have called it a glorious inspiration, or a wickedly sharp scheme. I liked it so much it caused me almost to laugh out loud as I contemplated its intricacies and possibilities.

At no stage did I think that I would not succeed—and I am now, in general, certain that the first requirement of success is to believe profoundly that one's plans will be fruitful.

Next morning, as I fully expected, Sir Thomas Maltby came to where I lay. The clerk came with him, Vail stood by and into my hand were pressed the instruments of writing.

"Mills, I believe?"

I nodded.

"I am Sir Thomas Maltby"—and I needed no such introduction, but of course he did not know that.

At his words I attempted a better sitting position and he said, "No need, my good man. I understand your injuries have been severe. We are, however, a little puzzled as to the nature of some of the wounds."

I wondered whether someone would move towards this enquiry.

"We would have thought you to have been injured in a brawl. But Vail here, who tends you—he suggests sea creatures did the damage."

I nodded and allowed my face a contortion as if at the memory.

"Now, Mills." Someone brought Maltby a chair; I heard the legs scraping on the wooden floor. "What I have to ask you may prove important, even serious. I am on the King's business. This ship of yours, the *Hispaniola*—was she gravely affected by the plague?"

I nodded.

"Did she carry civilians?"

I nodded.

"Who were they?"

I wrote, "L-A-D-Y" and "B-O-Y."

"Scotch woman?" he asked. "Boy of almost twelve years, brown eyes?"

I nodded.

"What became of them?"

I wrote, "D-E-A-D."

He grunted. "Any others?"

I nodded.

"Their names?"

I wrote, "H-A-W-K-I-N-S."

"A landlord?"

I nodded.

The duke asked, "Others?"

"H-A-T-T."

"A lawyer?"

"Hatt? And Hawkins? The plague get them?" He spoke hopefully.

I nodded, a trifle rueful at killing off poor Uncle Ambrose and inordinately pleased at my own death.

"What was the purpose of their voyage? You may speak plainly."

I held back.

"Come, man. We know what it is, we merely need confirmation."

I made as if to write, but again held back.

"I respect your loyalty, Mills, but I must have your verification. I shall ask you the questions and if you nod or shake your head you cannot stand accused of dereliction of duty in having written down or spoken anything. Did they seek a fugitive called Tait?"

I nodded—reluctantly.

"Did they find him?"

I nodded—with the same reluctance: I was beginning to enjoy this grim playacting.

"Did he speak to them? Were there witnesses?"

I nodded.

"Did this Tait write anything down?"

I made a gesture to indicate I didn't know.

"But he spoke to people? To the ship's captain?"

I nodded.

"You are certain of that?"

I nodded vigorously—then winced as though at the effort.

Maltby created a long pause. I could not see what he was doing; he may merely have been thinking. At last I heard his chair creak as he rose.

"Thank you, Mills. I am most grateful to you. You have been indeed helpful. We must speak again when you feel better." He made to leave, then turned in afterthought. "I must ask you yet another question. Is the captain's plan—should he survive—is it his plan to await a relief ship?"

I nodded.

"And be crewed thus back to England with this fellow, Tait?"

With my last nod I now affected extreme fatigue; I had become quite the actor.

"You have done well, Mills."

Maltby left the cabin and Vail, decent man, came to my side.

"Mister Mills, I am worried. You must be very tired."

I waved a feeble hand and asked for a fresh cloth over my eyes. What a marvellous plan this was proving!

———— ✌ ————

Ch. 23 —

Dry Land Once More

Although they never thought me such, I was now included as a gentleman. Wine was brought to me, to take with the fine foods, very different from the crew's rations. I did not drink the wine—my senses needed all their steadiness; but I did welcome the excellent clothing they supplied and which I pulled on with Vail's help and the greatest of slow, painful caution.

My eyes had begun to work again, yet while walking on the decks I took care that the bandage was larger and wider. I had not yet seen myself in a looking-glass and so I did not know how recognisable I was to the hunchback. Although he still seemed to be confined, his presence aboard terrified me.

We reached our port—and I recognised the place. So far, so good! I understood from Vail that the necessary repairs would take a number of weeks. Work did not proceed in these warm climes as swiftly as in Bristol Docks.

I understood also from Vail that the delay pleased Maltby not at all, that he chafed when told and that "great, secret plans' were being drawn against the calendar and the seasons. This did not immediately point to the black brig's returning to Bristol and I believed my ploys were maturing—that my false informations were impelling Maltby towards a return to Treasure Island.

The dangers in such an eventuality would have frightened me out of my wits had I not kept a steady faith in what I planned. Does great hope spring from instinct? I believe it does. Had my spirit not told me in its mysterious way that all the parts of my plan—including the next, key part—would come to pass, I would not have undertaken it; it was prohibitively dangerous.

When we had been some days in port, I made a request to Maltby by means of Vail and my writing book. Vail was at my side while I rested by the poop deck and contrived to scribble the words, "A-S-H-O-R-E?" and then "I-N-N?"

"Mister Mills, you wish to go ashore?" Vail and I had become the best of intimates; I liked him. "Visit an inn? Some ale?"

I nodded.

"Of course you do, Mister Mills, of course you do. What gentleman wouldn't?"

Then I wrote, "R-O-O-M? S-T-A-Y?"

"Aha, Mister Mills, you want a rest in an inn? Just like Bristol?"

I nodded. Pausing, I finally wrote slowly, "D-O-CT-O-R?"

"Certainly," he said.

He took my request to Maltby and next day I was accompanied ashore by Vail to a place that seemed to offer the services of an inn but was unimaginably different from the Admiral Benbow or the Royal George. I longed afresh to return home if only to tell John Culzean of what passes for a tavern in these parts.

By now I had learned (at night while alone) how to stretch the linen that covered my eyes, so that I could see through it. Not as fine as gauze or the cloths we use for covering cheeses, it nevertheless gave me a sufficient view of the world as to take an accurate measure of what went on. Also, I knew for certain that my plan was on course—yes, I had been in this port before.

The inn, hung with flowers, and with a rackety roof of red tiles, had a name in a language I could not make out. Vail took me inside its lively porch and we went slowly up short marble stairs of faded grandeur, along a corridor of green and yellow tiles to a room with ochre walls. A great bed awaited me and a chair by the window—but I had the presence of mind to have Vail conduct me to all these things.

He sat me by the window in some style and then went downstairs to await a physician that he said had been summoned. My request was for a doctor who would understand English. I would have to work out a means of contriving that he speak to me alone.

When he came, he was a tidy and authoritative man, a neat yet burly person called Ballantyne. Not only did he understand English— he spoke it perfectly: he was Scotch. Vail showed him my wounds and this man praised the care I had already received. He listened attentively while Vail told him all my circumstances. I learned something new—that I had been without consciousness for two whole days after they landed me like a sea animal from the raft.

Doctor Ballantyne took my hand and greeted me as "Mister Mills." His voice had that respect in it of the true believer in the equality of men, again a characteristic I have noted among the Scotch. From the way I pressed his hand he guessed that something more lay behind my tale—and he was a man who gave an air of having plenty of time at his command.

Turning to Vail, he said, "It's my professional habit to examine all my patients alone. No personal offence, you understand." He said it so amiably that no man could have taken offence, not even the choleric Maltby himself. Vail, by nature a respectful if somewhat mealy-mouthed man, withdrew, leaving Dr. Ballantyne and me alone.

He drew a chair forwards. "Now, sir. What shall it be first—your wounds, or what really ails you?"

I reached up and took the linen from my eyes.

Beckoning him close, lest Vail listened at the door, I whispered, in the first normal voice I had used since I had heard myself scream at Tait, "I have a story to tell you. But before I tell it I must ask you a question."

I asked my question. He looked at me gravely and curiously—but he gave me the answer I had hoped for, that I had prayed for. When, in my pleasure, I sighed, "Oh, thank the *Lord!*" he leaned back and smiled a dry smile. Then I told him my story. He gave me his complete attention and belief—two of the finest gifts any man can give to another.

My tale lasted some time, after which he and I had a lengthy talk, and during which he asked many questions. At last, in a loud voice, he said, "Now, Mister Mills. What am I to do with you?"

Briefly he examined all the damage he could see in me, then went to the door and summoned Vail who, in a truer respect than I had hoped for (because I feared he had been also asked to spy on me), had waited some way along the corridor, therefore well out of our conversational earshot.

Dr. Ballantyne asked Vail to help turn me over that he might examine my shoulder, back and thigh. Vail remained in the room and Dr. Ballantyne concluded his inspection. From his case he took some writing-paper and sat at the table.

Vail bathed my forehead; I had sweated in the worry of confiding my story to this stranger. But there are times when our lives have sunk so low that all we have left to us is the wild factor of chance—and Dr. Ballantyne was my good fortune.

He finished writing and, rising from the table, handed both envelopes to Vail.

"There is an apothecary of sorts, a Portuguese fellow. By the steps that lead to this parade of buildings. Give him this: he knows me well. While he prepares it, I should be grateful if you would take this letter to your master, whoever he be. I beg an audience with him."

"Sir Thomas Maltby, sir, a gentleman, sir, friend of the King." The words were so well-rehearsed he must have spoken them often.

Vail went and Ballantyne turned to me.

"I'm asking to have you put in my care at my house. To safeguard your eyes and heal your tongue. I also want a look at friend Maltby. This is a terrible tale you tell me."

Although he was a calm, untroubled man, something in him caught fire; it showed in the urgency of his speech.

"My wounds?" I asked.

"No lasting damage," said this sharp and excellent Scotchman. "You will be sore for many a day. But no more than that. The leg concerned me. I feared for a tendon but it seems to have been gashed, not severed."

Now he began another inspection, this time of my head and face, paying especial attention to my eyes, my ears, my nostrils, lips and tongue.

"Indeed, tale or no tale, I should have asked to take you into my care in any case. And when you have had some full, unworried sleep, we'll talk about your other request." He shook his head and smiled, this man who said but little.

For several minutes we sat there in silence, a period of comfort for me. I did not need to be watchful.

Then Dr. Ballantyne said thoughtfully, "On that island. What is it the ruffians eat?"

He gave me an odd look, as of a man reluctant to plant an offensive thought in the mind of another, however true the thought might prove.

I closed my eyes as his question sank in.

He said, "I'm sorry to raise such offensive matter. We have heard tales. In this end of the world, people stay but a little distance from the savage end of things."

If he had wished to strengthen my resolve regarding all my friends he could not have chosen more powerful methods.

From his bag he took a phial of small pellets and placed one on my tongue. It had sweetness beyond what I ever knew and soon it made me feel benign. I lay back in the chair, he drew the linen over my eyes again and I rested while he sat by.

Presently Vail returned and helped the doctor spread a perfumed unguent on my eyelids, my ears, my nostrils and my lips, and a different one on the head, shoulder and leg wounds. Their attentions completed, Vail said, "My master instructs that I am to take you there now."

"I shall return, Mister Mills," said Dr. Ballantyne.

While they were gone I tried my legs and body in an essay of movements—short steps or slow strides, to and fro across the room. I wanted to recover a mobility unsuspected by those around me lest, in emergency, I might need the asset of surprise. My leg, though dreadfully sore, worked well and my shoulder loosened a little with every attention I paid it.

From the window I could see the harbour and I watched, when safe to do so, the bright blue coat of Dr. Ballantyne walking with Vail towards the brig. Then I examined my room and found in its annexe a large looking-glass.

But who was this stranger I saw in the glass?! I could not have expected what I found: anyone, my mother included, would have hard guessing of it to make me out as the man they knew. My skin had burned black-brown, with the top of my nose scarred from blisters. I had little left by way of eyebrows or eyelashes. Some rearrangement seemed to have occurred at one of my ears, giving my head a different shape. Most of all, my hair had bleached snow-white in the sun. I looked foreign and older, in no wise the young and cheerful landlord of the Admiral Benbow inn on the coast of Devon.

It is the truth that I accommodated my appearance in a mixed way. On the one hand I rejoiced at the disguise it gave me: the hunchback would not have known me. On the other hand I grew upset for the loss of such looks as I had had. To be true to myself I had never thought I looked a gallant. But neither had I thought that I needed a bucket over my head lest I frighten children and animals. I also reckoned I should be in no haste to speak again; for some people (and I am among them) the ear's memory lasts longer than the eye's.

Dr. Ballantyne returned—alone. He entered my room after knocking discreetly. Looking at me he nodded.

"You are to come with me. I have seen your Sir Thomas Maltby. And I marvel that you are alive."

Resting on Dr. Ballantyne's arm and with my gauze overhanging my face, we left the hotel and walked slowly to the steps, below which the doctor's open carriage awaited. A young native man helped me most considerately into the seat and at a gentle pace we set out.

Some hundreds of yards beyond the dockside (did I shudder a little as we passed the black brig's anchorage?) the road became countryside, with great trees, wonderful, huge, bright foliage and birds of many colours swooping and clattering in the hot sunshine. We bowled along by the shore and then the route took a turn upwards. Little habitation occurred along here, save now and then what seemed like a temporary edifice roofed with heavy leaves; or, once or twice, a great white or pink house, some with colonnades.

As we rounded a sharp bend on the rutted lane Dr. Ballantyne gained my attention. He pointed upwards.

"There. And there." He pointed to two houses, one grander, both pleasing. About two miles, I thought, separated them.

"The first is mine. Where you will stay. The second—that is the house you wish to visit."

At Dr. Ballantyne's house we were greeted by a number of beautiful children, all splendidly dressed and merry. They thronged to their father in so sweet a way as to give me pangs of young Louis—and for children of my own one day. A wife appeared, elegance itself, French by birth, the daughter, as it would turn out, of an ambassador. She greeted me as though I too were a man of state, yet at the same time I might have been one of their oldest friends.

Over dinner she, not her husband, told me the story of their romance. He had been a ship's doctor and she a passenger. She became ill with respiratory problems on a voyage from Bordeaux to Liverpool. He had recommended that she live in warm, dry air and he mentioned this port, whose waters we now observed from their veranda. Her rejoinder was thought bold by everybody who knew her —except the doctor: "I shall go there only if you accompany me."

Since their arrival here she had not known a day of the old ill health which had plagued her.

"Now tell me your story," she said in tones I could not resist.

The tale I told her was in part only that of the *Hispaniola* and my dreadful mission. I wished to spare her ears the worst details—but I found a greater wish within me: to speak of my feelings for Grace.

Mrs. Ballantyne listened closely. When I had ended she said to me, "I believe you'll be successful, Mr. Hawkins. Your concern is more for others than for yourself. As I have seen in my husband's life, that produces excellent results."

A nightbird sang somewhere nearby as I settled to sleep that night. I was excited at my plan but I was also calm with the safety of this house. The calm won and I had the best night's sleep since the *Hispaniola*. With no fearful dreams.

———— ✦ ————

Ch. 24 —

And We Meet Again

The Ballantynes gave me care, peace and rest. I found a pleasing contrast in my life with them. It seemed that my strength came back as with a rush, yet I was spending lazy days, on their veranda, or in their shaded rooms, or walking slowly in their gardens beneath huge trees with wide, thick leaves. The quickness with which I felt recovered seemed counter to the slow pace at which I convalesced—a most pleasant opposition.

Messengers from the doctor brought to the ship word of my progress. In return we were informed as to the likely sailing date. Dr. Ballantyne and I talked many times—of my adventure so far and, above all, of the venture I now wished to accomplish. Of that, he had the gravest doubts at the beginning, continued to express those misgivings and then slowly made a judgement that he should support me. I think he did so out of concern for my survival—but I also think he was intrigued by the nature and shape of my plan.

Regarding the name I had given him—of his neighbour as I had hoped and discovered—the doctor sent a message as I requested, asking if he might pay a social call "with a visitor to the island": he did not mention my name. The first answer refused our visit and I felt set back. We thought again and Dr. Ballantyne sent a new message, this time with stronger and more confident words, assuring the person that there might be much advantage in our visit.

That same day we received a reply asking us to come immediately and we climbed into the landau.

"At the least I've made you aware," the doctor said, "of my reservations at this."

I replied, "As you know—I have them too."

"But I accept your reasoning," he replied. "It seems to me in every way sound. If in some ways reprehensible."

The landau climbed. How brilliant the sea looked, with the fat table mountain that gives such shelter to this gulf. Mrs. Ballantyne had described for me the storms they see rampaging across the sky between their hill and the harbour below. When first I came here long ago, I had been too drowsy—and too young—to retain much detail. Now I sat back, very excited and, as happens when the spirits are running high, drinking in the scene with more intensity than usual.

Soon the track worsened, yet at the same time the foliage on either side took on a kind of half-trimmed look. We reached a high gate, white-painted and with twin characteristics of cheerfulness and forbiddingness. Two native men approached; one held the gate open a little while the other stood and glowered; both wore a sort of erratic footman livery.

The doctor said, "Your master expects us."

We waited while one man departed and the other closed the door against us.

Soon the gate swung open and we were permitted to enter. Both servants walked ahead of our carriage. We rounded a dark corner overhung with branches and the house came into view. I had seen it from our journey upwards and now I admired it again—a small mansion with some columns and a handsome portico. On the lawn a fountain played—the house of a prosperous citizen.

We climbed down and I stood calmly on the steps by Dr. Ballantyne's side as the carriage was led away. Nothing happened for several minutes; one servant stood by as though to prevent us from entering the house. Then I heard a tune being whistled and I have to say my heart shivered—both with pleasure and the return of ancient fear.

He appeared on the steps like a sultan. Something much changed about him caught my attention and it took a moment—then I knew it. Before, his crutch had been made of rough wood like that of any old sailor; but this crutch was made of silver. Its lovely filigree work had all the tendrils of the forest; the block under the armpit was made of gleaming ebony and bordered with wide silver bands.

The face was still as large as a ham and the eyes had the same old glint of Life itself. Prosperity's air rose from him like a song from a bird. But in truth, Long John Silver looked very little different from the man I had first seen when I was the lad sent by Squire Trelawney to Silver's tavern by the Bristol docks—the man his fellow pirates called "Barbecue."

"Well, well, me hearties!"

Still the same voice, with a laugh like the sound of cracking walnuts. Still the same habit of cocking the head to one side and looking hard out of those eyes. The hair had changed colour a little; there was more salt and pepper in it, but the sun had changed part of it to the colour of tea.

I was surprised that he was so little surprised. He came down the steps more agilely than younger men with all their faculties. Slipping his crutch under his arm, as I had so often seen him do, he grabbed my shoulders with both hands.

"Jim, lad! You'll not believe this! But John's been half-expecting you!"

I made a laughing sound of disbelief and he stepped back, growing serious.

"No, Jim. I swear it! I been thinking about you and about old times and thinking I never got the chance to thank you for all my doings. I went a sort of sudden-like, didn't I, Jim lad?!"—and he chuckled.

It was always part of Silver's gift to get himself believed, no matter how preposterous his claims. That was how he managed to dupe all of us, including Doctor Livesey when the first crew of the *Hispaniola* was being assembled. But I was inclined to give credence to his claim that he had been "half-expecting" me; he had an uncanny knack of divining turns of fate.

"And good-day to you, Doctor Ballantyne, I allus likes to know my neighbours, John's allus been a hospitable cove, right, Jim?"

"And you are rich, John!" I exclaimed. "Look at all this!" and I cast my eyes in admiration around his house and grounds.

My delight at seeing him must have nonplussed Dr. Ballantyne. He looked drily but respectfully on this almost comic reunion—beneath whose surface lay a deadly serious purpose.

"But—Jim! You've been in the wars! What's become of you?"

He inspected the traces of damage on my face and then turned us towards the house. We walked indoors to rooms that were spacious and cool, lavishly but haphazardly furnished with myriad articles purchased more from money than taste. On a wide terrace at the rear, tall plants gave shade. The house had every appearance, whatever its owner's taste, of being well tended and clean.

"Sit down, sit down!" He laughed. "We'll drink to many things, Jim—I still likes my rum."

Silver seemed delighted to see me and I thought, yes, perhaps he had, in some strange way, been expecting to see me again. While we sat, I examined him closely. As well as wealth—he must have made his ill-gotten gains expand—he seemed to be in the best of health. His spirits were excellent and his general demeanour so affable and welcoming that it remained difficult for me to remember him as one of the most treacherous villains in the world.

That arrangement in him, of pleasantness and villainy, was indeed the very reason I had come to see him. When I realised that the brig had landed me in the same port where Silver jumped ship that long-ago night, I took it as an omen. It set in motion a chain of thought and that chain rattled at me until I polished its links into a plan.

To put it simply, I meant to fight fire with fire—set a villain to trump a villain. Silver, who now sat before me in his brocade cloth with his glittering eye and his cheerful smile, was as evil as I took Maltby to be, and unafraid to kill. Therefore I believed him capable of overcoming both Maltby and the hunchback, Abel Raspen.

By now my plan had been honed to clarity. Doctor Ballantyne had asked me many defining questions about it. It was my intention to offer Silver a huge reward should he come and recover the awful situation I had recently escaped.

I hoped he would take the bait. The adventurer in him had always seemed very strong. I also knew he had failed himself in his own eyes when he lost to the good forces of Dr. Livesey and Squire Trelawney. In addition, however villainous he knew himself to be, he might dearly love an opportunity to cancel the death sentence that faced him should he ever reach England again.

A pretty, native maidservant brought rum. Silver had become a lord in his own manor. We talked about our old journey to Treasure Island. He asked about everyone who had come home with us and he recollected names and personages so clearly that I believed he must have an excellent memory—or else he often relived that time, sitting up here on his grand hillside.

"And now, Jim, I wants you to meet an old friend."

He saw my alarm and guessed I feared a pirate—some old ruffian from the Bristol docks or some other criminal of his acquaintance. But he patted my arm soothingly and whistled.

A young servant came from the dim interiors of the house and on his arm perched that vile old parrot, Captain Flint. The bird hopped to its master's outstretched fingers and then to his shoulder, where it sat looking at me, beady and malevolent. In a moment, at a "coo!" from Silver, it burst forth its horrid old scraping chant, "Pieces of eight! Pieces of eight!"

"And you see, Jim, Cap'n Flint's prospered too." Long John pointed to the silver bands that adorned the bird's legs like gaiters.

"Stand by to go about," the parrot screamed.

We came, in time, to the point. After two draughts of the fine, if thin, rum, Silver leaned forwards and patted my arm.

"Now, Jim, lad. You wants something offa John. And it has to do with the wars you been in? Am I right?"

I said, very simply and clearly, "John, I need your help." It had been Dr. Ballantyne's advice that I say no more than those words and fill them with feeling.

As briefly as I could, I told Silver the whole story—the arrival of Grace and her boy, the death of Berwick, Maltby, the hunchback, the siege at the Admiral Benbow, our flight, the brig, my experiences on the island (which I described indefinitely as "some misadventures") and the means by which I came hither. He listened like a round-eyed child—and I, like a good storyteller, kept the most powerful information until last.

"So, John—all you see in my face and my general visage—this walking-stick, these wounds—they were caused by one man."

I always thought of Silver as having liked me, for all his villainy. He credited me, I also knew, with having saved his skin. Time, ten years, had not altered this perspective; now I would test it.

"Then you been in bad company, Jim." He looked at me in that old way that could bring comfort or disturbance—and usually both at once.

"You know the man who did it, John. You recruited him."

He waited, his eyes darkening a little. It is a measure of his strength that he did not hasten me, nor did he seem puzzled.

"Must I name him, John, or shall you guess?"

Still he waited.

"Do you not remember, John? We left him behind."

But he wanted me to say it—and so I did.

"How does the name 'Joseph Tait' lie on your memory, John?"

Silver sat back in his chair. As I looked at him I understood something about him for the first time. He had by repute a youth spent in good schooling and had once been of better character. Although he had regrettably chosen to use it for evil, this was a man possessed of extraordinary natural powers, who could have been or done anything he chose.

He rubbed his hand across his mouth as a man does when reckoning whether he should shave. "Joseph. Tait."

He spoke the name as two words. And repeated it—"Joseph. Tait."

"He still lives on that island, John."

As he had done so often before and as he would again, Silver surprised me.

"Aye. So I've heard. It crossed my mind his was the name you'd say."

I looked at him in amazement. Treasure Island lay far south of here and yet he knew of Tait and his survival. Had he tried to go back there? Or had others tried and failed, yet brought back bad tales? Or was this Silver's combination of uncanny shrewdness and wishing to be seen as knowledgeable? Did he have spies out in the world? I let it pass and asked him a direct question.

"What opinion do you hold of Tait, John?"

Silver puffed his cheek a little, the prelude in him to a strong expression.

"I niver liked Tait. I niver took an eye off him. I rec'llect him as the silent one, niver said much, and, Jim, as you knows well, I holds little with men as keeps too much o' their own counsel. Don't trust 'em. Now the doctor here, Doctor, you be known as a man of few words, but that ain't the same as I mean about Tait."

He stopped—and thought again.

"Jim, this here's my verdict on Joe Tait. I wants the claim to hanging him myself, I does. John Silver'll pull that rope hisself. I don't care if they hangs me right after him. Well, I does care, o'course, but manner of speaking—no, Tait's the worst sorta man."

This outburst surprised me for its force, length and intemperate expression and I was about to ask him whether a personal reason—from beyond our times together—lay beneath his vehemence when he interrupted me with a beam.

"And here comes the lady herself—'Lady Silver' I calls her. You remembers her, Jim?"

So he had made it after all, as he said he would—he had made it to safe harbour with his "old black missis" as he once called her and now he smiled at her with the fondest of looks.

Silver was still so shrewd. He knew how to control his own situation. That ended our conversation for that day—which meant that we had to come back or he must come to us. With the distracting arrival of "Lady" Silver, who offered fruit and sweetmeats, the old buccaneer purchased the time he required to think on everything I had told him.

Now that we knew how he regarded Joseph Tait, our only question hung over the way Silver would react to Maltby. His response to the nobleman was crucial to our plan. I felt evil to evil must surely produce a conflagration, with the righteous Maltby clinging to his good opinion of himself.

In the landau on the way back, Dr. Ballantyne and I tried to measure whether we had engaged Silver's interest—and we agreed that we did not know. It had been a curious encounter and I feel that I should be ashamed at how much I enjoyed seeing Silver again. But shame is not what I felt; excitement, satisfaction that my plan had the properties of inspiration, a sense of being empowered—those were my emotions as we turned into Dr. Ballantyne's shaded avenue.

Silver kept us waiting. Indeed, he kept us waiting so long that I persuaded the doctor to write him another letter but on the very morning he sealed it, a manservant arrived, inviting us to luncheon with Silver next day.

His second greeting was warmer than his first. Under the wonderful foliage of the terrace at the rear of his house we ate fruits I had never seen and a succulent meat like pork. We drank only rum: as Dr. Ballantyne said on the way home, "A sailor may leave the sea but he never leaves his rum."

I was most pleased at how things fell out—and I think Dr. Ballantyne was impressed at how accurately I had judged my man. Everything we intended to put to Silver came from his lips first. In fact, he drafted all the strategy. It was exactly what we wanted and more, with many details added.

Maltby had told Dr. Ballantyne of the island and his plan to return there—"on the King's business." The doctor, said Silver, must impress upon Maltby that a local citizen, once master of a vessel out of

Plymouth now retired from the sea, a man of fine standing (and here Silver grinned) had sailed those seas and knew Treasure Island well. This "Cap'n Silver" had available to him his own small militia of sailors, many of whom had retired to this port, and he would wish them in his company.

But Maltby, a shrewd man, would wish to know why a well-to-do retired man such as Silver—already very obviously infirm, no matter how agile—should wish to return to this pestilential isle for the sake of a stranger. Silver would then play his trump card; he would tell Maltby—and Maltby alone—of the remaining treasure.

Indeed, when I put that final piece of strategy to Silver, I could almost swear he did not know or recall that we had left so much—or indeed *any*—treasure behind, even though he pretended otherwise. The Long John Silver of old would have lifted that treasure long ago if he felt it worthwhile going there.

All the initial strategy in place, Silver took over the plan. He outlined in detail how we must proceed when we reached the island and had thought out a contingency for each situation. If the *Hispaniola* were still there we must do this-and-this; were she absent we should do that-and-that. Every step of the way from the shore to Spyglass Hill and back again, and every action likely to be demanded of us, every danger, every way of escape, had been considered by him and anticipated so expertly we could not fault him.

The doctor and I knew that a portion of the remaining treasure must be offered to Silver: this was the only point on which we did not reach agreement.

"Jim, we has time-and-a-half to ourselves to figger that divvy."

And I replied, "But you haven't met Captain Reid."

"Reid, Jim? You say his name's Reid?"

"Yes."

"Red-haired swab?"

"Hardly a swab, John," I said sharply. "A fine captain."

"Scotch? With a lady's hands?"

I said, "Yes. Do you know him?"

"Not personally. But him it was hung Blue Jackson. Hung Pete Ackham. Near to pulled the rope hisself, he did. Strutted up and down Execution Dock like a turkey. Hung Ned Haley and he only a lad of seventeen, and no mutineer was he, you can't have a mutineer and he only seventeen."

"'Tis clear you're an expert on mutineers," said Dr. Ballantyne, but he said it in a way that made Silver chuckle.

Yet at Captain Reid's name I saw the cold ice enter Silver's pale eyes and worried whether this scheme might not take an awful turn— for all of us. But I reasoned that Reid seemed above all else a practical man and so long as Silver did not wish to return to England with us, Reid, who would certainly guess at Silver's past, or perhaps know of it, would accommodate him in return for services rendered.

Again and again that day we discussed every part of our plan. It required assiduous effort and made arduous demands. Silver referred over and over to the hostility we would surely encounter, given what we meant to do. He also murmured questions concerning his own age.

"I'm probably gone soft by now, Jim."

"You're fine, John," I encouraged.

He looked me up and down and never taking his eyes off me said, "How fit's Jim now, Doctor?"

"Let us ask him, Mr. Silver."

"I feel quite well, thank you," I said.

"You'll need to," said Silver.

He leaned back and, winking at me, called out in a chant I had heard before, in very different times, "Here's to ourselves, and hold your luff, plenty of prizes and plenty of duff."

— ✦ —

Part Five

— x —

Gentlemen of Spirit

Ch. 25 —

A Motley Crew

Eight days later, with Dr. Ballantyne by my side, I watched from the quay as Long John Silver sailed again. He arrived with an entourage, a potentate now; the bearers lowered his carriage steps to the stone wharf. No longer the somewhat uncombed sea cook I had first seen in England, he was still plain and intelligent; and no longer pale—his skin had taken a light mahogany sheen from the sun and he seemed to have oiled it a little; he wore a competent wig.

"He's not inconsiderable, is he?" murmured Ballantyne, more to himself than to me.

"Wait 'til you see him move quickly," I said. "You'll be surprised at his agility."

"But not at his strength."

Silver saw us and called us over. My arm upon Dr. Ballantyne's (we had enjoyed our planning of such strategic details), we strolled to his open carriage. He lorded it there, high and expansive, the parrot on his shoulder. We admired his baggage: two great teakwood chests bound in copper; a very large leather valise and two gun cases decorated in brass.

"You carry a pouch or two, I see?" observed Ballantyne in that dry, uplifted tone of his.

Silver took the joke with his quick-eyed smile and then grew serious.

"This"—he tapped the valise—"is all the necessaries I shall need. Man like me likes his comforts at this age. These"—he slapped hard

on the chests—"will bring home my share of what we find. I've reckoned it close enough for accuracy, I shouldn't think."

"We shall have need of clerks to do the counting," murmured the
doctor.

Silver, seeing Ballantyne's glance change direction, swooped to the
brass-bound gun cases.

"And these," he said, "I shall use to get me what I deserves."

With Silver the menace was never far behind the cheer. He cradled
one case in his large hands, opened it, showed us the pistols inside and
grinned that grin I have seen on his lips when planning more than
mischief. Fortunately my face remained covered with the muslin cloth
(which I had restored for the sake of life aboard the brig) and I was
able to conceal my anxious expression.

Silver dominated the quayside that morning. This was a man with
no difference between the life he wanted and the life he lived. His
booming voice, the pleasantries he uttered in his mixed bits of lan-
guages to all who passed or dallied, showed him to be a man of note
in this harbour town, known to many and respected by most. He told
everyone that he was going to sea again, that the land had "grown
blessed hard under my leg" and that he was looking for one more
"worthy voyage."

For a moment I trembled that his tongue might slip and include
me, his "old shipmate," as the reason for this new embarkation. But
Silver was too deep for such an error and he contented himself with
roaring a variety of exchanges up and down the dock.

Soon he had assembled his trappings, and in his booming voice he
commanded two sailors from the brig. They hesitated and I saw that
they took orders from someone on board; then I saw the pointed head
of the thin clerk and the men ran down to escort Silver.

Dr. Ballantyne and I followed. Not for a moment should we have
dreamed of going before Silver, although in truth, breeding, and
moral standing we both had a far better right to the stature he now
commandeered. He went up that gangplank like a ship's owner,
squinting appraisal to left and right, tapping timbers here, whistling re-

flectively there, eyeing canvas and yards and reefs like a man who means to have a profound say in how this vessel will sail.

On board, the thin clerk came forward and shook Silver's hand. The doctor and I had by then walked about halfway up the gangplank. Silver turned, his face gleaming with the exertion and the heat and called out to me.

"Mister Mills! You best come in out o' this sun. In your poor state."

I felt Dr. Ballantyne chuckle to himself.

"Not at all, Captain Silver," he replied for me. "He shall be in the cool shade below within minutes."

As we walked past where Silver and the clerk stood, Silver said, loudly enough for me to hear, "I bin talking to Mister Mills down there on the dock and I do believe I knew his father in Bristol, a decent man, a shipwright with a good hand to turning wood."

The clerk said, in thin affirmation, "This Mister Mills seems a very brave man."

"Ay. The doctor's been describing his injuries, haven't you, doctor? Not many'd live that long on a raft in them seas."

At this point a curious juggling of people seemed to begin and I, from some instinct or extra sense, placed myself halfway behind Dr. Ballantyne and at the head of the brig's main companionway. Silver turned his head at some noise that came from the bow. His face took on an irritated frown and he muttered something under his breath. I looked in the direction and went cold.

The hunchback, Abel Raspen (how I gave thanks that I had concealed myself), strutted about the foredeck, in an exaggerated mime of a man with one leg. He clearly meant to give an imitation of John Silver and he laughed as he did so, hopping from place to place, his foot caught up in one hand and his hump shivering beneath the brown broadcloth I had always seen him wear.

Silver turned away and then looked back again. He murmured some comment to the thin clerk—who then steered Silver in another direction and intended, I believe, to take him below for a welcome from Maltby.

Dr. Ballantyne and I made for the companionway near us; it led to my cabin which I was now, I understood, to share with the doctor—much to my pleasure. I looked one more time at the hunchback. He still hopped about but less vigorously, because he laughed so much at his own joke he had grown short of breath. I felt relief that his capering distracted him from looking too closely at me.

In the cabin, to my surprise, Dr. Ballantyne ordered me to bed immediately, even though it had scarcely passed noon.

"This is not mere strategy," he said in his quiet voice. "You must take account of your condition. You still need to rest. And after all, great exertions may yet lie ahead."

Earlier, my respect for him had grown when I understood that he had taken his leave of his wife in private. The children, however, had run cheerfully after the landau and waved to us many times until we disappeared from their sight.

I lay down as bidden. When I awoke some considerable time later I knew I had been in a deep sleep. We were under way; I heard the waters slap the sides of the brig.

Ships know who they are. In the country, the creak of one farm cart, wagon or mail coach seems much like another as they wince and rattle along our lanes. Ships, though, describe themselves to those who sail in them. When the brig hauled me from the raft, one of my earliest moments of clearheadedness came when I knew that, wherever I lay, it was not on board the *Hispaniola*. The brig had a lighter voice, a tenor, where the *Hispaniola* had deep bass notes in the timbers, and a fuller, richer crack to her canvas when she moved to the persuasion of the winds.

By now, I figured, Silver had installed himself well. Dr. Ballantyne and I knew we had taken a great risk. The man was a pirate, a mutineer, a murderer, capable of savage violence without a tremor of conscience. I doubt his soul gave him any unease; I doubt he ever lay awake and enumerated his sins.

Ten years ago, Squire Trelawney greeted him when we came back from the stockade and all the fights: "John Silver—you're a prodigious villain and monstrous impostor," to which Silver saluted and said, "Thank you kindly, sir." That was the man we had now enlisted.

As for Silver and Maltby, on an afternoon some days after we agreed our plans with him, Dr. Ballantyne had taken the old pirate down to the brig. We decided that I should best remain a "convalescent" and not be seen in Silver's company until we all embarked again.

When Dr. Ballantyne came home that evening he said Maltby had played very much the large fellow, known to King George, Court Counsellor, of high birth, all of that. I knew enough of John Silver to recall his dislike for those who dwelt upon their rank in order to keep him down. Maltby had not made a natural friend there—no, not by any means. I finally knew that all had gone well for us when at dinner that night the doctor remarked, "Your old sea cook certainly has a giant's spirit."

It was that spirit which we sought to harness on behalf of everything and everyone. But I knew of a difficulty which faced us. It was also in the "giant's spirit" to need paying more than any other man would think decent. That was bad enough—but if Silver thought he might not get as much of the haul as he asked for, his great force would as easily turn against those who thought him on their side.

For that reason I took a certain delight that Silver had seen the mocking antics of the hunchback. I needed him to feel as much animosity as possible on board the brig. All to our good if he did. And I depended upon his natural dislike for authority to throw him into opposition against Maltby.

Next I began to imagine how it would be when the two ships drew close again. Dr. Ballantyne would be spokesman: that fact remained crucial. Beyond that, we expected little resistance from Maltby in allowing events to take their course. Dr. Ballantyne said he had Maltby down for a valetudinarian; apparently he had plied the doctor with questions on numerous ailments. In the doctor's experience, men who fuss so anxiously about their health and well-being rarely put themselves in the arena of disease—and the *Hispaniola*, after all, had been "a plague ship"!

Therefore, for the second phase of our plan, we expected—and needed—Maltby to stay rigidly aboard the brig. The doctor, in the guise of measuring the general health on board the *Hispaniola*, could alert Captain Reid and my uncle to our plans while Silver and I went ashore with Silver's "militia" to force matters on Tait. With Tait subdued and the treasure secured we would then return at night to load the *Hispaniola* and slip away before the brig was awake.

It was in that business I had the most confidence in Silver. The fact that Tait had almost certainly laid hold of the remaining treasure incensed him—even though he used the language of a superior officer to express his dislike, going so far as to call Tait "a common pirate." This detail gave Dr. Ballantyne and me a good smile later.

As all these plans and whimsies sailed across my mind, my good-natured "nurse," Vail, came to my cabin and told me that a small celebration was being held on the afterdeck.

"Sir Thomas says we must celebrate our sailing, Mister Mills, and very much hopes to have your company."

I walked slowly up. The sky seemed bluer than Heaven should have allowed. A calm descended upon me, and I felt assured that I had contemplated well and planned intelligently. I also felt quiet and strong that my decision to go and do such good as I might for people beloved of me had been the one most likely to yield the best fruit. For the moment I should not give a morose thought to all that might go wrong.

Vail led me out from the companionway onto the deck of the brig. Astern of me I saw something whose memory I still relish—for its incongruity, for its memorable scenery and for its very liveliness.

Maltby's little party had gathered. Behind them, as a painted curtain in a playhouse, rose a wonderful scene—of table mountain, rich, distant foliage, terracotta harbour and blue sky. Here and there on the slopes stood the fine houses of Dr. Ballantyne, John Silver and their scattered neighbours; the distance was too great to make out which was which.

As I moved along the deck another ingredient was added to this tableau—a flotilla of motley, misshapen craft, which followed us and waved, and from whose ragged sides boys and young men hung and waved and sometimes flung themselves into the sea to swim apace with us. The scene was altogether delightful.

By the afterdeck, I was welcomed into the little celebratory party. This was the first time I had been in all their company. The hunchback did not attend, being, I presumed, a man too coarse for such a gathering. But the soldier fellow with the red face and the thin clerk stood there and, of course, Maltby himself.

The rest of the party included Silver, Dr. Ballantyne, one or two men who looked civil enough and a dashing, strong fellow in a coat of burgundy. I, remember, had not been recovered enough to enter any company aboard until now and these figures, although on board, Vail told me, since Bristol, were new to my eyes.

Maltby and the clerk, the civil gentlemen, Dr. Ballantyne and Silver all wore wigs; this burgundy man had raven-black hair pressed close to his skull and pulled back in a rakish horsetail. He stared at me, at my hat, from beneath which fell the cream muslin which curtained my face. Then he looked enquiringly at Maltby.

—⁂—

Ch. 26—

In Sinister Times

Maltby greeted me.

"Mister Mills. Welcome, sir. To you we owe this celebration and of all the toasts we may give, I can think of none righter than your health. Doctor, is your patient permitted to charge his glass?"

The doctor looked at me and said, "With regret, no. I have him on a strong physic."

Silver, the virulent parrot on his shoulder, watched this and said nothing. I perceived that Maltby had a difficulty with me; I was, in his eyes, a mystery and yet he felt so much in need of my competence and goodwill that he must treat me as an equal.

"Then you shall have something cordial," Maltby said and a sailor hurried to my side with a pitcher. I waved a hand to decline.

"Thank you, but no," I murmured, not much above a whisper, but yet carrying across the little group. We had worked out, Dr. Ballantyne and I, that to speak softly would best disguise my voice.

Maltby looked hard at me and for a dreadful moment I believed he must have recognised my tones. I knew he had never seen me because I had remained behind the door throughout the siege—but he had heard my voice. When he spoke I understood that he had been surprised by something else.

"Mills, your voice says you are no seafarer."

I nodded.

"What are you, sir?"

It was time to shut the trap tight—and my reply set off that glint in Silver's eyes.

"Sir, I am an assay clerk."

"In Bristol?"

"The same, sir."

"For whom do you work?" I had prepared enough scraps of knowledge to satisfy his appetite.

"I have the fortune to be in the employ of Mr. Cale and Mr. Goodman."

I needed to say no more. The look on Maltby's face was that of a man for whom the pieces had clanked sweetly into place. He believed that Ambrose Hatt, whom he knew as a lawyer out of Bristol, had hired an assay clerk called Mills from Cale & Goodman's offices to sail with him in order to value the treasure on the island. This chimed exactly with the reason why Silver might have come "out of retirement." The man in burgundy smiled like a bear.

From that moment I thought it tactful to subside. Dr. Ballantyne altered the conversation to consider the weather that might lie ahead. Silver added one or two yarns of great storms assailing the gulf, which was now slipping away astern.

Soon the little party dissolved and Vail reappeared to escort me to my cabin. Safely below again, I asked him the question that had burned me.

"Who was that man in the burgundy coat, Vail?"

"Sir, did you not know? Oh, he's well known in certain parts, I even heard of him." Vail lowered his voice. "By name, sir, a Mister Egan, a famous swordsman, sir, by reputation the most dazzling blade in the kingdom—and he's a particular companion of Sir Thomas. Sir, they say he's never lost a fight, that his blade flashes so fast his enemy never sees it 'til he feels it."

"And the others, Vail, who are not mariners either?"

"All gentlemen, sir, all duellists by all accounts. With the blade or the pistol. Sir Thomas likes strong company."

Vail, having seen me among the drinking men, deferred afresh.

That night, I told Dr. Ballantyne Vail's words. I still dined in my cabin and the doctor joined me before his customary (as it would become) dinner with Maltby and the rest—a company which also included Silver.

"Egan?" he reflected. "I have too long been out of England. There was a time when I knew the name of every such brilliant swordsman. Because I treated their handiwork. And sometimes their bodies, if they had an unlucky night. Egan? Sounds Scotch."

It endeared him further to me that Dr. Ballantyne constantly thought every unfamiliar name Scotch.

"He's well known, it seems," I ventured.

"I wonder what Silver thinks?" and Dr. Ballantyne went to dinner.

Later, I found out what Silver thought. He came to see me that night. I shivered when I heard him approach—remembering when I had last heard the sound of that crutch, stumping and pegging its way along a ship's timbers. The bird gave soft *crawks!* as it lurched with him.

These sounds brought back many memories—the man was sixty now; ten years ago I heard him say he was fifty. That was when I had been hidden, riven with fear, in the *Hispaniola*'s apple barrel, overhearing their mutinous debates. I remembered his force, his violent words; I remembered his clever means of commanding them—how he had organised and encouraged them by example, by telling them of his own life, how he had closed everything down in Bristol and sent his wife to meet him at some secret destination when the voyage ended.

Now this unusual man stooped as he entered my cabin and looked around. The parrot's wings flapped.

"Eh, shipmate, this be a tidy little berth they've given you." He closed the door and legged himself closer to me. "Jim, I don't much like 'em," said he in a rough whisper. "I don't like 'em at all," and he dragged a chair to get closer.

"Have you heard of this swordsman?" I asked.

"No, but I can guess which one he be—the swab with the coat colour of wine. Am I right?" When I nodded he continued, "Now, he looked at me like he were either a judge or a cutpurse and I lay you I don't take much difference between either, they're all the same to John Silver, I says. But I shall be keeping a weather eye on that 'un, I shall so."

I said, "It's very good indeed to have you on board, John."

My remark had the intention of drawing him forth a little because he wore a sombre look, not something I had seen on his face in the past. I have seen Silver urgent and merry and devious—but never sombre and it made me anxious. He shifted in the chair, the silver crutch stretched ahead of him and he leaned forwards, his face inches from me.

"Jim, you knows me. And you seen me downface all manner of swabs."

"Yes, John."

"You seen me call Tom Morgan to heel. Stupid ol'" Morgan."

"I did, John."

"You seen me close the eyes on that swab George Merry, them eyes that was the colour of lemon peel with the ague."

"I recall it well, John."

"And you niver seen me afeard of any man jack of them?"

"No, John, you were never a man afraid."

"Well, Jim, mebbe John Silver's getting old. Mebbe the old wounds is stabbing and throbbing. Mebbe the world's a bit heavier on my shoulders than I known it. But I be a uncomfortable sort of a ship-mate, now."

I waited—and I had to wait for a long moment.

"You see, Jim—there's folks says I was evil. I niver agreed with them. Now, I niver says I was any sort of a angel outa the Lord's garden Hisself, but I were niver evil. Not Silver. Tough, mebbe. And a hard man, if crossed. And, I own, mebbe a bit bad now and then. But I were niver evil like Satan."

I thought the dry thought that Dr. Livesey and Squire Trelawney would give him a vigorous debate on this point—but naturally I did not say so.

This was a strange development—Long John Silver feeling apprehensive. I took the risk of lifting the cloth from my face (I always kept it down against a sudden incursion from Vail or someone).

"John—you're a worried man? I've not seen that before."

He retreated a little, as though affronted. "No," he drawled, "not worried, exactly, more like—well, more like being certain, with no known reason for it, that true evil could come from that there quarter."

This outburst from him pleased me oddly. It confirmed my view that I had been right to seek him; I had never encountered anyone else who could have cancelled Maltby's force.

As he left the cabin, he turned to me and whispered, "Mark you, Jim, there'll be a long day of reckoning yet. Peel open your eyes and empty your ears!"

I have observed about people, that some—who may not be supposed to—leave one feeling good and warm, while some, who have better repute, make one feel worse. Why is this? I began to list the people whose company always improved both my mood and my spirit: Uncle Ambrose, John Culzean, Louis—but not his mother; Grace Richardson had so disturbed me that at first, other than confusion and protectiveness, I could get no clear view of how she made me feel. Now, my ardour for her made me want to be near her all the time—as much for how rich in spirit she made me feel, as well as for the privilege of looking upon her lovely face.

My list ran on: I always liked being in the company of Dr. Livesey and the squire; likewise Dr. Ballantyne and his wife, although that is not surprising; and Nathan Coll, but not Noonstock.

And, although folk might dislike me for it, I stoutly confess that John Silver's company always made me feel better in myself whereas Maltby made me feel my skin was clammy as slime.

Once clear of the gulf we sailed well, the brig being lively and the wind mostly following. For some time we remained in sight of a lush coastline and then we seemed to change direction, from due south to southwest. Life brought no alarms; I saw few people—Vail; Silver now and then and, of course, Dr. Ballantyne. On all of those days I held myself prudently, secretly improving my physique, outwardly keeping a gentle pace, especially when I saw Maltby or any of his claque on deck. Silver liked that part of our plan which included keeping my true faculties unknown, so that I might provide some surprise in a crisis.

One night, when we had been long out on the widest sea, Vail entered the cabin. He prepared my nightly physic and my linen, and then disturbed my hopes of sleep.

"Sir Thomas wants to see you in the morning, sir. He said to me I was to tell you he'd very much like the opportunity to share his coffee with you before noon."

My mind racing I asked, "Has Dr. Ballantyne said I may?"

Vail whispered, "Sir Thomas says he's not to know."

When Dr. Ballantyne came in some time later, I naturally told him. The tot of brandy after his dinner had feisted his spirits a little; his cheeks glowed.

"What's his trick?" he thought aloud. "Divide and rule us? Or is it suspicion founded on he-knows-not-what, a vapour he has caught in the air, or some such?"

"But I must do it. I have no choice."

"Risky," said the doctor. "Risky. But I have to say, Jim, this is a tense ship. We should have sailed easier on a powder keg."

"Have you yet met this Egan?"

"Indeed I have. He showed me how to run a blade through a man's throat avoiding any bone. Said he thought I, as a physician, should find it interesting."

Dr. Ballantyne slept; I heard him snore; I had no such somnolent good fortune.

At four in the morning I heard the watch's call. My renewing skin itched me and my spirit fretted over the meeting ahead with Maltby. Bad if I went to it—bad if I didn't: but I had to. My mind was tossing both sides of this unpleasant coin when a sudden and curious noise disturbed me.

First, someone opened our cabin door—perhaps by a chink, but not yet wide enough to look in upon us. I puzzled, thinking the door had blown open in a mild draught of wind. What happened next dismissed that notion.

The door slammed shut, from the outside, and a silent, furious struggle took place. Nobody spoke but bodies slammed against the walls, two voices grunted and raged softly and the sheer force of the affray could be felt like a secret power. I half-rose. Dr. Ballantyne stirred himself too and I shushed him before he could speak. His cleverness kept him silent as he sat up and cleared the sleep from his brain.

The fracas continued—heave here, heave there, blows, gasps and not a coherent word spoken. It was as though two huge, dumb bears had entered a fierce, silent grapple in the tiny space outside the cabin. Then came a dull sound, awful and final, a significant *crack!* In the gloom Dr. Ballantyne and I could now see each other plainly. He looked at me and made a right-handed gesture towards the back of his neck, the kind of sideways chop with which a farmer kills a rabbit.

———⚓———

Ch. 27—

A Fearful Reunion

The victor in this awful, soundless affray leaned back against our cabin door so heavily I thought he might burst in upon us. He sighed after his exertion and for a moment or two stayed against the door, sometimes shifting a little.

Next he moved, having as I supposed got his breath back. I heard no footsteps; then came the sound of a heavy object dragged. Slowly the weight was towed from our hearing and the brig's noises took command of the night once more.

My face and neck sweated—which I did not like, since the sweat whipped a sting across those last, unhealed patches of my broken skin. Ballantyne looked at me, astonishment on his face.

"Lord above! What d'you suppose—?" he whispered but did not finish.

I shrugged, short of words.

"Now you *must* see Maltby," whispered the doctor—and that ended the night's faint hopes of any sleep.

In the morning Dr. Ballantyne went up on deck after his customary inspection of my condition and his advices to Vail, who set about his tasks nursing me.

I said, "Tell Sir Thomas I shall be pleased to see him and thank him for his kind invitation."

Vail looked at me, even more a rabbit's face than usual and nodded—and then I realised that, untypically, he had not yet spoken a word that day. He seemed frightened; he must have heard something about last night's fight.

After some hours, during which I tried to plan my demeanour for this interview, Vail took me along and knocked at the door. Maltby sat alone at a table with charts, the master who was no mariner. With a click of finger and thumb he retained Vail's services to pour coffee and then bade the manservant wait outside. Maltby indicated a divan and I sat; his manner was ingratiating and mild.

"Mills," he began. "I have been taught to value the opinion of any man who has cheated Death. And you, sir, have cheated Death and no mistake."

He had that habit I find both compelling and offensive: everything he said could have two meanings, as though he were a man who knew one's secrets and addressed them.

"I am complimented by you, sir," said I, remembering to keep my voice low.

"Tell me, Mills—and this is a private conversation—what's your opinion of this fellow, Silver?"

"In what sense, sir, do you wish me to answer?" I needed time to try and assess Maltby's direction.

"In a general sense—but in a particular sense too. You see, we have on board an excellent fellow, old friend of mine. He says he feels he's heard the name 'Silver' mentioned in certain dispatches."

"Dispatches, sir?"

"Yes—revenue."

"Sir, I've never heard the name of Silver mentioned in any assaying business."

It gave me pleasure to say something that would mislead while not being a lie. But Maltby was as quick as a man who uses such devices himself.

"Or in any business?"

I replied, "I believe my father knew of him"—which was true: my father had heard violently from Cap'n Billy Bones of "the sea cook with one leg."

"Did your father offer opinion of his character?"

"Sir, it's part of my remembrance of his goodness that my father only spoke well of every man."

"Ye-es." Maltby looked hard at me. "Ye-es."

He rose and paced a little.

"What say you of the doctor—Ballantyne?"

"Sir, how could I say other than the best? I count up daily what I owe him. The full use of my limbs, the healing of my skin, the—"

"Of course, of course." I could sense Maltby's irritation. Then he rapped at me, "What d'you think of this brig—of our life aboard?"

"She's tidy, sir, she spins well before the wind."

"Mills, when we were leaving England we sailed for a time, not more than a quarter of a day, behind the *Hispaniola*. Your ship. To which we now sail. I possess a very sound spyglass. Made by Germans, very clear. Unclouded."

"I'm told, sir, the Germans make such things excellently." My brain shouted: He knows! He knows it's me! He saw me!

I contrived to sit as still as ever. Maltby waited and, I can tell you, that was a long moment.

Then he said, "And I formed the impression—" he made my heart sweat with his pauses—"Yes, I formed the impression—now that we shall have, I hope, the opportunity—that I should prefer to sail home on her than on this. A brig's too small for me, Mills."

I nodded, not trusting my voice. In any case, he spoke again and this time his voice had a cut like a whip.

"Of course, I have been lucky, Mills." By now I had begun to fancy that he mocked the name by which he called me—but I had enough sense to know this might be fear tricking my imagination.

"Lucky, sir?" I said, the very echo of respect and attention.

"I had feared that when the time came to settle the matters on this island, and of course on this ship to which we sail—"

He paused again and I ventured, "How soon shall we reach—" but stopped when I saw that Maltby looked at me as though I were insubordinate. He ignored my question.

"There were people aboard her, Mills, who were fugitives. Murderers, to be plain. The plague took them—that's what I mean when I say I have been lucky. Otherwise I should have had to act on behalf of His Majesty the King for whom I have the privilege to be Counsellor. And I know His Majesty would not have me trouble his courts with them. With any of them."

I nodded. "That seems an . . . understandable . . . wisdom, sir." I hesitated, playing his game.

He said, "One of them—comprehend this, Mills—one of them was a child, a young boy. Already turned to evil." Maltby glittered. "I reserve, Mills, a most particular hatred for Papists. But there's a point where I agree with them. They claim a person's character is formed from the age of seven, when, it is said, we may tell good from evil. It is that boy's good fortune that the plague reached him before I did."

He would kill Louis! Silver's view of Maltby was true! This man embodied villainy.

When Vail led me back to my cabin, Dr. Ballantyne was waiting. I gave him a full account of my ghastly interview—and from that moment I began to count the hours until I could depart this vile ship.

However, I watched the life aboard closely. The brig's first crew, whose faces and voices I recognised from my rough stay among them, went about their business with a briskness I think was born of fear. Silver's "militia" mixed in with them and shared duties but also reserved themselves. As did Maltby's "gentlemen," although I did see that they looked at me closely, especially Egan, the swordsman. I never saw the hunchback, except at a distance, and for this I gave daily thanks.

The mood changed as the days wore on. I cannot say the feelings aboard had ever been of a light nature, but any natural ease ebbed hourly. That is how I knew we must be nearing our destination—although it somehow seems to me, on the experience of both my voyages, that at sea one can, in a mysterious way, without land or landmark, know where one is.

Late one forenoon we finally sighted the *Hispaniola*. She remained where I had last seen her, due north of North Inlet, east of Foremast Hill. During my absence I had wondered often what Captain Reid had done. Circumnavigated? I thought not. His surprise at Ben Gunn's failure to return must have given him pause; if one who knew the island so well had also failed to reappear, then something very seriously amiss had been confirmed.

All in all, I guessed that, given the undermanning of the *Hispaniola*, the captain had set himself to wait for his relief vessel. This also meant, as my uncle had pointed out, that the ship could easily be found should any of his missing crew return.

I remember the moment we saw her again as one of mixed and strong feelings. Vail came for me urgently; Maltby had requested my presence—and was in a fair stew of excitement, brandishing his spyglass. In that way in which land always materialises when seen from the sea, Treasure Island appeared, but as indistinct as a long, low cloud or a trick of the light. Slowly it defined itself and I felt safe in thinking, "There she is." At that moment I also began to look for the *Hispaniola*, because we sailed in from a northeasterly direction and she should lie in our path.

Maltby with his spyglass saw her first—and then tried what I presumed was a trick.

"There's something!" he exclaimed, twisting the telescope this way and that. Then—and this was the trick—he handed it to me. "See, Mills!"

Fortunately I had the presence of mind not to become caught up in his liveliness. With a regretful gesture I indicated my eyes behind the muslin face covering and, after a hard look at me, he nodded, "Ah, yes!" and returned to his spyglass, then walked away.

The ruse did not deter me: on the contrary, I watched more diligently and soon I began see the distant spars touching the faraway sky. Even at this distance and through the gauzy, indistinct fabric, I felt quite overcome to see her again.

My feelings became very troubled. On the one hand I should soon meet all those dear people again; on the other hand I sailed towards them on the back of a most awful danger—I might cost them their lives. The seriousness of my gamble came up in my throat like gorge.

However, at that moment, as though my mind had sent him a message, the main trump of my gamble slid to my side. Silver stood and looked ahead with me.

"She were allus a purty ship, Jim. I had a mind to own her myself. Often sat many's the morn on the dockside at Bristol and looked at her and wished she were mine. Purty."

Silver murmured low but his passion came across. I couldn't answer: my feelings would have cracked my voice. But Silver's next words, spoken in a lower tone, jolted me.

"I've lost a man."

My head almost spun from my shoulders as I turned to look at him. He spoke casually, while gazing straight ahead at our old ship on the horizon.

"I sent a messenger to your cabin last night, Jim—he niver came back. It were a test."

"John, that's frightful. I heard a scramble—"

He cut across me. "He were a youngish lad. Had a pretty wife and baby and what am I to tell her? That's what I wants to know."

"But John—"

"We shall be silent as the grave on this one, Jim, but I knows my score and it shall be settled."

"Was it Rasp—"

"Say no more. Just—he'd better be nimbler than he looks when the long day comes."

He stopped. The thin clerk had walked by and looked at us curiously. Silver slipped away and as he went he murmured, "The game's afoot now, Jim—in earnest. You may lay to it."

I leaned back, all words fled from my mind.

In the early evening we dropped anchor some few hundred yards from the *Hispaniola*. A watch of the brig hailed her.

"Ahoy!"

Nobody answered.

"Ahoy there!!"

There came no sound. Nobody hailed us in reply. She looked as still as a ghost ship and it felt impossible to divine whether she had seen us. I, luckily, had been through this experience before and thought that perhaps Captain Reid was playing tricks again.

Doctor Ballantyne came to where I stood.

"I understand you are to come with me."

I nodded. "Yes."

"How pleasant and yet vicious for you."

The man of few words had summed it up.

Within minutes he and I were under way. The brig's longboat moved swiftly on a sea of glass. I observed that Maltby had sent one of his "gentlemen" with us, no doubt as an observer.

As we drew alongside the *Hispaniola*, Dr. Ballantyne hailed—and again the ship made no reply. One of our boatmen threw a grapnel to secure a rope. When we had steadied ourselves upon the rope ladder, the doctor some feet below me, the longboat stood away. Her crew—and the duellist—showed no signs of wanting to board with us.

Dr. Ballantyne and I heaved ourselves over the rail. Oh, that was such a good feeling, to tumble out on her deck, even though laden with apprehension.

The *Hispaniola* looked as clean as if fully crewed: Captain Reid had found a way to keep spirits high. We went for'ards, Ballantyne and I, and when we rounded the fo'c'sle hatch I did two things.

First, I took a natural glance astern towards the brig. As I expected, Maltby stood far for'ard, spyglass at the ready, watching our every move. Next I called out in a low voice, "Captain Reid, it is I, Jim Hawkins—returned but advising caution. If you hear me, do not answer loud, but indicate where we may find you."

I heard a distant cough and Ballantyne nudged me. Ahead, on the first step of the main companionway and below the level of any sighting from the brig or the waiting longboat, a hand slapped the deck vigorously—a white hand, rather like a girl's but most certainly a man's.

We both breathed relief; the slapping indicated energy and command and we straightened ourselves to give the watching Maltby an impression of casual inspection. Moments later we stood at the head of the companionway and then went down, one after the other, into the gloom.

Gathered in waiting and all armed with swords or knives, were Captain Reid, Uncle Ambrose, the cook, the cabin boy and the four men we had rescued when Maltby threw them into the sea. My heart turned upside down to see my people safe.

Ch. 28—

The Game's Afoot

Words burst from me: "But you all look so well!"

Captain Reid put out an arm to impede Dr. Ballantyne.

"Friend or foe?" he rapped.

"Friend and fellow countryman!" replied the patriotic Scotchman. I introduced them and had told Dr. Ballantyne a great deal about Captain Reid.

My eyes caught a movement in the shadows behind Captain Reid. Grace and Louis came forwards and from power of feeling I was almost unable to look at them. As Louis grasped my arm and wound it about his shoulders, I turned to Uncle Ambrose—tall, lean, kindly Uncle Ambrose, with his head and neck and face like some lanky, gentle bird. My eyes were full of tears.

His hands took my hand and held it. "Oh, Jim, how good this is, how good this is! We thought you were lost." He seemed unable to speak either.

Louis said, "I knew you'd come back."

"And now," I heard Captain Reid say, "there's some plan afoot, no doubt? I take it that is why you are masked, sir."

I say that I heard him—but it was a dim voice and distant, because I was looking at Grace. She had taken a little, not much, of the sun; her face had browned and her freckles multiplied. I lifted my muslin veil the better to see her—and I regretted that I did, for I made her gasp.

"Ohhh! What brought this on you?"

She held my gaze and her eyes enchanted me and I knew that I would have gone through ten thousand more such travails, had my face reamed raw ten times more, for the value of that look.

Louis said, "Captain Reid has been teaching me the sabre."

"We shall be in need of it," said the same captain. "What are we to know? What is to happen now?"

He led us to his stateroom. There we had room to move a little. The cat, Christmas, graciously stepped down to allow us more room and Ballantyne began to tell him who was on the brig.

"Did you say Silver?" asked Captain Reid.

We all whispered, as if afraid of being heard; not such an outlandish notion—sound travels far over water.

"John Silver. He knows who you are, sir," I said.

The captain almost smiled. "Well, well. Who knows how paths may cross. Providence works odd tricks."

I looked around; we might have been in Bristol so calm was everything.

"Sir, you have kept the ship in the most remarkable way," I exclaimed, but did not feel true surprise.

"It could be argued, Mr. Hawkins (how enchanting to hear my own name again), that we had little else to do."

"Did you venture to the isl—" I began.

"Not a jot of it, wouldn't have it, we stayed here. Relief ship and such."

"I hope you'll have no need of the relief ship, sir."

But I could not concentrate my mind. My heart was overflowing with feeling and I was unable to cease looking at Grace. How I had missed her! She looked back at me many times, clear and generous of gaze, and Louis held my hand as though I were the most significant person he had ever known.

In all the circumstances is the word "happy" too strange for such a moment?

Dr. Ballantyne established that he was to stay on board. My stay among my dear friends had to be brief. Seeking a moment's privacy with the captain, I told him briefly the full plan—but begged his leave to go, saying that Dr. Ballantyne would explain more fully. All I required for the moment was to know that none of it seemed so unacceptable to the captain that we should abandon it. He raised his eyes at our daring and, as he put it, our "optimism" but he seemed excited and almost pleased.

"So you hire one villain to cancel another? Be careful, Mr. Hawkins. 'The man who shouts "Stop, Thief" is often the one who steals.' Have you heard that proverb?"

"Indeed," I said hastily, not wishing an ethical investigation at the hands of Captain Reid.

"Very well. I may say that this voyage is not what I expected. But I am with you and we shall prosper."

"How have they all been—in themselves, I mean?" I dared to ask.

He looked shrewdly at me. "The lady has been distressed. The boy grows apace and is of good stuff. And I have taken to asking Mr. Hatt many questions about the law."

With no more than a wave of my hand to the others I left, went up on deck and returned to the rope ladder. The yellow evening sky was streaked with black; the longboat saw me, made its way across and I was helped. In the process I had a mishap: when I jerked my head downwards to see where I placed my feet in the rungs, my hat slipped and my face covering blew away on the wind. The men in the longboat pursed their lips at the sight of my healing skin.

I had a different concern—and it surged like a flood around my heart. On my return the hunchback might now see and recognise me. As we drew nearer and nearer the brig, that concern turned to near panic; from the side of my eyes I could see Raspen's vile shape on the poop-deck and I knew he watched us.

We boarded. When climbing the ladder I kept my head down and my hat clamped tight on my head and did not lift it even when the thin clerk approached—he too had been watching our arrival: "Sir Thomas desires an immediate interview."

Behind me I heard Raspen's heavy foot and heavier breath, as he wandered over to get—I presumed—a look at me. But the clerk hurried me below.

Maltby waited, spread fat on his divan. My thoughts still lurched around the problem of how to conceal my face from the hunchback. Maltby solved it—by saying, "Blazes, man, I see why you covered your face. Where is your—?" and he gestured.

"I regret I lost it, sir."

He whipped a silk kerchief from where it lay on the arm of the divan.

"Take this, Mills. That face looks bad to me"—and I knew he meant that he had no wish to look at it. Dr. Ballantyne judged Maltby well: this was a man repelled by any ailment.

I gave him my report of the *Hispaniola*—an account of conditions so plausibly uncertain as to keep him from wanting to board her. Dr. Ballantyne believed, I said, he could clean the ship's air sufficiently for the safe conduct of her back to England but it would take several days before he could be sure she was plague free. When I listed the people I found (omitting, naturally, Grace, Louis and my uncle), his eyes narrowed.

"And none has the plague?" He sounded like a hangman afraid of being cheated.

"No, sir."

Maltby then asked me a strange question. "Did the doctor give any opinion as to the health of the island itself?"

I puzzled at his reason—then knew why he had asked: he wanted to know how many men he might risk on our morrow's journey to the Spyglass, especially his "gentlemen." This meant, as I guessed it, that he intended the mischief Silver warned about—namely, send us out and grab what we bring back.

I answered with a lie decked out like the truth.

"Dr. Ballantyne doesn't know the island, sir. But when I sailed here, Hawkins, the landlord—he who had been here before—he told all on board about a flying insect here, a fly or mosquito or some such, whose sting is extremely injurious. The fever it carries may strike immediately or not for many months. Hawkins told me that one of the crew who returned from that voyage has received paralysis from that sting."

I waited to see whether my lie had taken root. Maltby looked at me.

"But the ship—she's been standing near the isle. Is that not dangerous?"

"It's an insect that doesn't fly over water. Not uncommon, sir."

He accepted this. "These are your orders, Mills. Speak to Captain Silver tonight. For the purposes of this expedition he is now your leader. I believe you are to be ready in the hour before dawn. Bring proof of the contraband to this table."

And he sagged back on his divan, his large eyes bulging slightly, his sharp little teeth bared like a dog. I found his presence and his physique quite intolerable.

Outside, the night was falling in her sudden tropical way—one moment long rays from the west, the next, a deep darkness. A cold tremor ran through my shoulders: I should miss Dr. Ballantyne's company. I walked carefully to the stern and stood looking into the water; not far away I could hear the *Hispaniola* creak on her anchor but could not see her.

Restless, I walked to the bows. Nobody was about; the brig had fallen silent, as they say a soldiers' camp does before a battle. Leaning over the rail I blinked my eyes—and blinked them again. What's this? To the south, in the darkness, I saw a light. Had another ship happened by?

I felt a body slide to the rail beside me. Silver placed a finger to his lips and pointed to the light. We looked together; it beamed steadily, if not very brightly, like a house on land seen from the sea.

I whispered, "But that's where the reef is."

"Course it is, Jim," he replied. "That's what he wants."

"Who?"

"Joe Tait. I reckon he's made a living out of wrecking ships. Many a man has done. I seen it with my own eyes. Bad men, wreckers. They lights a light and a ship sails for it. I hate wreckers more'n I hate judges."

At last I understood the number and variety of bodies I had glimpsed in the pit. And at that moment I needed John Silver in my life more than I had ever needed another living being. I also reflected again and more powerfully that in the decade since my return from Treasure Island, I had generally missed him and his cold reality.

Later that night, Silver came to my cabin by arrangement. We spoke little and many of those words were formal—to confirm the time and place of our muster on deck; to confirm the strength of company he would take.

Our intent—which Silver, as he told me, had allowed Maltby to refine—was to get close to Spyglass Hill in the early shadows. The island's foliage meant that the sun's rays did not light our route: this too was Silver's choice—part of our ruse was the impression that he be the only one who knew the island.

We rowed ashore as the dawn, of rose-pink and lemon streaks, lazed like a skeleton's fingers along the horizon of the eastern sky. I looked down the length of the longboat, past the men who strained at the oars. Silver sat in the stern, a man born again, alight with energy, brimming with importance and excitement. Although his militia had been augmented with some of the brig's crew, none of Maltby's "gentlemen" had come with us and therefore I concluded my insect story had rooted.

On the veranda of Silver's house we had talked and talked of the reasons Maltby pursued Grace and her boy. I said repeatedly how puzzled I remained; I kept asking what could a man possess that made him so wanted by another. Silver had a good answer.

"Shipmates, what be the most powerful thing a man can own?" He meant to answer the question himself so we let him. "Not an army, though I should much like to have such. Or for me p'raps, better to have a navy—*Admiral* Silver!" He chuckled; it was one of the reasons people liked him, that chuckle. "Nor a garden full o' money—I'm a comfortable man in that respect, no complaints there. No, the thing a man has that's the most powerful—why 'tis also the thing that's the most dangerous to him. And that thing be—a *secret*. That be the most powerful thing. Believe you me. I knows, I'll lay to that—John Silver knows the power of a secret. And here we has, mebbe, a secret wrapped in a secret. The lady, she has a secret, that's why she's been followed. And the secret she wants is the secret Joe Tait has. Oh, yes, our old shipmate Tait—there's a swab as has a secret, I'll warrant you. Or he may be part of her secret. And it'll be connected to that swab who died on your lane, Jim, who was he again?"

"Berwick."

"Aye, Berwick. Makes sense, shipmates, don't it? Most men'd go halfway round the world for a secret if it were powerful enough. That's my wager."

I thought out that speech of Silver's many times in my mind and matched it against what I knew about Grace, Louis, Maltby, Tait and all our misadventures. It fitted—because Silver also told us that when he recruited Tait, he did not believe the man to be a "gentleman of fortune, take my meaning"—but rather a fugitive, who needed to get out of England and therefore, as Silver said, "a gentleman of fortune ready-made." As our longboat nosed the soft sand and we stepped ashore, I said to myself, "Perhaps this is when we'll discover the secret."

Silver was in command that day: no doubt whatever of that. With quiet orders he formed us up, distributed the weaponry (arming himself and me like dragoons) and gave the order to march. He and I took up the rear.

The men, eight of whom each carried a long stout pole but who had not been advised of its eventual purpose (the slings to carry the treasure), set off briskly. My hard companion, his hat at its usual tilt and his bandanna flying in the dawn breeze, surprised me again with his agility. Goodness knows how spry I shall be at the age of sixty—but even with two good legs I'll scarcely match this athlete.

Our march to the base of the Spyglass was crisp and unimpeded. I shivered when I looked up at it and I knew it was not the morning's cold. Would this time on Spyglass Hill be my last? I fervently hoped so but for the best reasons, not the worst.

Silver distributed his little force—sixteen men in all. He placed his own furthest from the rude plateau and ordered two of the brig's four sailors to take up positions nearer.

Then he and I climbed to the stones that formed the crude steps. He beckoned the other two sailors upwards to stand like sentries on the plateau, above the sheer drops at either side. I waited, as bidden, just below the lip of the shelf, where I could see and hear everything.

All of this operation had been conducted in the greatest silence. Now he changed that principle. With little bubbles of effort at his lips, Silver at last hoisted himself on his silver crutch and clambered on to the plateau. He strode across to the rude shed, his crutch and boot making noises I knew could only be deliberate: he must have clattered so loudly in order to be heard.

Pausing at the decrepit timbers of the failed building, he looked around, poking here and there. Tom Morgan's skull had vanished—which I regretted: I wanted Silver to see it. We all stood still in the half-light; so far not a bird had we heard; only a sad sort of wind hissed in the leaves; it blew from behind us, which explained why we had not yet met the awful smell.

Silver leaned back his great head and looked towards the top of the Spyglass. And then he jerked further back: what had he seen?

He began to laugh and to shake his head like a man who has discovered something both intriguing and engaging. Stepping back a yard or two he took off his hat and gazed up again—more directly this time, more concentratedly. He rested on the crutch and I started at what he did next.

"Hah, there!" and his voice rang around the rocks. "I seed you, Joe Tait, I seed you! Playin' hide-'n-go-seek like a child! Come out like a man."

———⚓———

Part Six

—x—

Let the Blow Fall

Ch. 29 —

Steel Meets Fire

So much became plain to me at that moment. Tait had worked out a spyhole through the dense growth above our heads. From inside the cavern he could get to a point above the little plateau and appraise who or what visited him below. No wonder our search parties had been overcome.

Silver waited. I adjusted my mind to this surprise and tried to squint through the gloom to the place where Tait had been glimpsed. Then Silver called again.

"Joe Tait! I allus had you down for a lily-liver—a girl, you were! Look again from your spyhole. See how I've prospered! I've come with my friends for the rest of what's due to me that's hid here. You can trade with me—or my militia can run you down like a dog. But I've come to c'llect my claim, I have, and unless you trade with me, your life won't go on long. I'm not for goin" into that infernal pit you hides in—so come out and talk!"

At that Silver made an impudent move: he found a place to prop his crutch and, rooting in the great pockets of his magnificent coat, began to assemble a pipe of tobacco. Nobody else moved. The leaves rustled in the breeze and I caught a whiff of that awful charnel smell. The men grasped their noses.

Soon it was replaced by something more congenial—the aroma of tobacco. I began to consider the way Silver managed these circumstances—and I marvelled at him. In one move he had closed down every possibility Joseph Tait possessed, except the possibility of leaving the island. Silver had made it clear he would work with Tait—or he would hound the man and kill him.

Not only that, he had further confused matters by introducing a factor that would have tormented the barbarian inside the mountain. Every sailor loves his tobacco—Tait, I recalled, was no exception. I thought to myself, "It will have been a long time since Joseph Tait smelled such a good smell. I wonder what he'll be reminded of." Now I knew why Silver had glittered with such interest when I told him of the vile odour coming out of Tait's cave.

My eyes danced between three points: Silver, leaning on his crutch and savouring his long, thin, curved, white pipe and the blue smoke rising from its bowl; the roughness of the growth high above the plateau where Silver had glimpsed Tait—and the wall of thorn and scrub that concealed the awful aperture, that doorway to Hell behind the rude shed. I had a clear view of all that bushy, thorny wall and from it I expected Tait would sidle into this new situation.

That supposition proved wrong. Tait appeared—but he did not sidle, he burst upon us. I saw him first. Like a squatting fiend, he perched high on the crag above the shed, but over to one side—and then he jumped down like some great, mad cat. He landed on all fours beside one of the two sentries Silver had posted by the sides of the plateau.

As Tait straightened, he grabbed the unfortunate sailor, a Kentish man called Hayward, by the hair and—as he had done with me—ran a broad knife to the man's knobbled throat.

Silver looked across at Tait and the terrified Hayward. Nobody else moved. Silver fiddled with his pipe. Hayward's eyes bulged as Tait forced his head back. I had the thought, "Kill him—kill him!"— meaning Tait, and I knew the accuracy with which Silver could strike. But Silver drew afresh on his calm pipe and the whole place remained rigid and still.

My eyes devoured Tait. When he and I fought during my escape on the raft I never formed a clear view as to his current appearance. Now I could look at him. There is a man in our parish whose company is much relished by the womenfolk. They hail him, they spoil him with beverages and cakes—women of all ages. I have never liked him, in part because he has a face of roughness and cunning. He came to my mind that morning, as being in that category of men whom women like inexplicably.

Tait had similar looks, when I first saw him ten years earlier. He had a lout's face; as I told Dr. Ballantyne, "a surly fellow, lowbred, with a rough look to him, curly-haired and silent." As I saw him now, he carried no extra flesh; each limb of him looked like direct bone; his hardships had made him abominably strong; the arms and legs were those of a Hercules.

I doubted that those sullen looks could prove winsome now. His hair was greased back with some vegetable stuff, perhaps squeezed from leaves, and his beard ran unchecked, with traces of occasional hacking; he wore some common shirt and trousers, culled, I supposed, from men he had killed. All in all, he looked what he had become—a murderous near savage.

Silver sucked on his pipe and spoke. From his tone he might have been pursuing a tavern conversation that had been interrupted some time earlier.

"Regard, Joe Tait, that nobody has threatened you. You've chose to threaten—with your knife there—a man as has done you no harm. But nobody's threatened you. Regard that. And nobody will. Don't it feel you should ask yourself why? I'll ask it—and I'll answer it for you. "Cause nobody *will* threaten you. That's why."

Silver drew again on his pipe and it became most odd to smell that sweet aroma in those conditions—especially as I knew what lay within the hill.

A new thought disturbed me. All our concentration had been on Tait but I also recalled that when I leapt from the cave, my dive had taken me between Tait and an accomplice. Where was that gentleman now? And doing what?

I was not allowed to develop the thought—because what happened next shocked even John Silver, a man who had often reminded me that he quartermastered "the roughest crew," that of the barbaric pirate, Captain Flint—"and Flint his own self were afeared of me."

Tait gave a kind of grunt, manoeuvred the terrified Hayward two yards forwards, so that the man's face was a yard from Silver's shoulder. Then, with a deep, mighty and wide swipe, as Silver looked directly at him, Tait cut Hayward's throat.

The blood spurted out and hit Silver's hand; I saw it splash on the white pipe and on the silver crutch. Hayward tried to scream and failed. Instead the blood welled and bubbled from the slash like a dark and terrible fountain.

As Hayward sought to sag, Tait more or less lifted him by the hair, dragged him at a run to the edge of the plateau and heaved him over. Then Tait turned and stood there, glaring at Silver.

I know Silver well; I know his responses. He was shocked—but he had enough inner power not to show it. Therefore, he made no move. He took the pipe from his mouth, inspected the blood spatters on the bowl, wiped them on his sleeve and put the stem back in his teeth.

No other person among us attempted to attack Tait. Such was the force coming off him that I think all of us would have run away; this man would have fought off a regiment. I could not take my eyes off him, but soon received a rude shock to see him staring at me as though he contemplated my throat next. He owed me retribution—I knew that; now I also knew he would do whatever he liked to whomsoever he chose.

Silver moved his body a little on its prop. He pointed with his pipe to the other sentry. Then Silver spoke.

"See that man over there. Name of Hall, London-born. Due a mate's ticket soon, I'll warrant. You can take him too, should the fancy strike you, Joe Tait. But you'll still have to reckon with me. And you'll know from the old days—if you foul John Silver there's only one person does the reckoning. So what's it to be, shipmate?"

What Silver did next amazed me. He turned his back on Tait; how broad a target must his shoulders have seemed. He hauled himself over to the edge of the plateau and called down to me.

"See Jim, I told you. Joe Tait's a girl. Never square, eh? Why, even Dick Johnson, poor loon—Dick were square."

Tait was hovering, like an animal that can't make up its mind to strike. Silver now spoke back to him, over the shoulder, not giving Tait the benefit or courtesy of looking at him.

"There you be, Joe Tait, and look at you! Not even a thought as to how you'll go on. I comes here—you already know why Jim comes—and I've combined the two bits of business. But we was wasting our time. Come on, Jim, let's make our other plans. Joe Tait, you're a dead man, you are! Any man who can't parley his way out of his own trouble—he don't deserve living."

Silver lowered himself from the plateau. Confusion took over. I moved towards Silver, whose face wore a most intense concentration. Our little militia was uncommonly disturbed and I could see the men's eyes ask why we had not shot Tait. Then Hall, who had been staring beseechingly at Silver's departing back, half-moved and the thing Hall must most have feared happened: Tait grabbed him too. Silver heard the shuffle and half-turned.

"Go on! Kill him into the bargain! Slice his throat the same way as you did the other. But it won't gain you the respect of John Silver—and John Silver had the respect of Flint hisself!"

He hissed the last words and to my utter amazement—it astounds me yet—Joseph Tait took a pace back from Hall; he even dropped the hand with which he had been about to knife the sailor. Now Silver turned fully back to face him and played his ace card.

"If you want to, Joe Tait—this here's my hand to shake. 'Tis a hand as held the Black Spot—as you well know. But them days is over long ago. There be no more gentlemen of fortune in the world—only true gentlemen by nature—and them as would be such gentlemen. Like me, John Silver, now a comfortable and comforted man. And like Jim here, in his pleasant inn, with his fire and his ale and his trade. Which be you, Joe—a dying gentleman of fortune or a man as could be a calm gentleman?"

And he turned away again, hand still outstretched behind him.

Tait retreated a step or two, until he felt the firm planks of the old shed at his back. He looked at every man there, coming to me and Silver last. Then he shipped his knife from one hand to the other and padded forwards on his bare feet.

Silver's hand remained outstretched. He did not look at me or at anyone there—he looked into the distance with that concentrated frown of his like wrinkled stone. When next he moved his head to look back, Joseph Tait reached down from the little stone plateau and lodged his hand in Silver's palm.

The men turned to each other and shook hands vigorously. But this was an unequal handshake, of two men requiring different things. Tait wanted Silver's friendship again, his respect and approval, and he looked up at him with that kind of appeal. Silver wanted—well, he wanted what he wanted and nobody ever knew what that might be.

Each inspected the other; I saw Tait reach forward gingerly and stroke the blue silk of Silver's sleeve. Silver looked at every part of Tait's face and head, especially the eyes. He spoke, so softly only Tait and I were near enough to hear.

"You're a young man, Joe. You should long ago been off of here to a better life somewhere."

Tait looked at him, almost like a dog looks at his master. But he didn't speak and I wondered whether he had lost the power of speech. Again I marvelled at the mismatch between Grace and this wild, sun-darkened cutthroat.

Silver put a hand on Tait's shoulder. The younger man flinched. Silver said, "Joe, put your hand in my pocket, that long pocket down there. See? And note, Joe Tait—my old wooden crutch's gone, 'tis made of silver nowadays, Joe, that's how good a man's life can get. That's it, down there, that deep pocket. Now draw out what you finds there, see if you remembers it."

To my horror Joseph Tait drew slowly up out of John Silver's coat pocket a long knife in a thin sheath. The ivory hilt had floral carvings and the sheath had been worked ornamentally. Tait looked at it in wonder.

"See, Joe? John Silver—he don't forget. That's the very knife you bought, you told me, from a ship's cook in the port o' Leith. You lent it to me in the stockade afore Smollett's men took me. I allus kept it for you and now my mind can rest a little easier. 'Cause I've kept my word to myself, my word being that some day I'll give Joe Tait back his knife that he bought in the port o' Leith."

Tait looked at Silver wonderingly and I knew he was thinking what Silver wanted him to think—"A man who gives me back my own weapon does not mean to kill me." With his next move Silver then won the whole gamble.

He said, "And I've something else for you too, Joe. Put your hand in this next pocket and draw out what you see."

Tait did so while Silver continued, "I thought to myself, I thought—what's the one thing I'd pine after if I were out here like Joe Tait, cut off from all. Oh, I'd miss my rum. And my old missis. But I'll lay to it I'd miss my pipe-and-baccy more'n anything."

Thereupon Tait drew out of Silver's pocket an object wrapped in rough sleaze cloth, and from it he unwrapped a pipe as long and white and slender as the one Silver smoked. Silver put an arm around him, led him down the rocks a little, out of earshot, and sat down. Tait, the knife in one hand and the pipe in the other, stood, uncertain what to do. Silver patted a crag invitingly but Tait chose to crouch and Silver handed him the makings of a smoke.

I looked towards them. At such extraordinary moments, how we reach for the inconsequential: my mind idled as to whether Tait had ever taken tobacco from the ships or bodies he had wrecked. Within minutes the two old comrades were puffing together as if they had last met the day before yesterday. Silver called out to us, in a military voice, "Stand easy, men," and we all tried to obey.

———✦———

Ch. 30 —

Dishonour Among Thieves

Other than Silver, I alone knew what would happen next. Long John, sitting there, was outlining a proposition to Tait. The offer gave Tait safe passage from the island with a worthwhile share of the treasure, in return for Silver receiving his own share. As to the "other matter," as Silver called it, should it transpire that Louis were Tait's son—and worse, that Grace had either been Tait's wife, or meant to marry him for Louis's sake—Silver meant to show Tait how life could work out for a man who had once been a pirate.

Silver believed Tait would show interest in this: all pirates, he said, crave respect—and we also counted on the factors of Grace and Louis.

But I knew that Silver meant to trick Tait of all this, that he would take him captive and haul him to the *Hispaniola*. Once there, and once we discovered at last the exact nature of this mystery, the next decision would be arrived at.

In different circumstances I would have thought to feel sorry for Tait at this dupery, but the savage and unconcerned way in which he killed poor Hayward, a man he had never known and who had never harmed him, made it easier for my harder feelings to gain sway. And that was before I dared recollect my wretched friends and companions inside the cave.

We stood there about an hour. Silver did the talking, long and deep. I watched without looking, so to speak. Somewhere a bird began to sing, an unexpectedly sweet note, and I fancied I might take that as a good omen. Each man smoked two full pipes and Joseph Tait looked almost calm, were such a thing possible.

But I knew from his visage that this was a man who, inside his soul, had gone wrong in himself. There was something appalling in those eyes, something I believed too far removed from the nature of the world ever to be brought back to it.

Silver, that great if warped judge of human nature, must have known the same, but to his credit he never behaved as though Tait were anything other than a man bounding back into the everyday world of ordinary folk.

They rose. Silver took a moment or two to ease his stiff limbs; I saw that he made Tait laugh with some saying or other. We fell into line as he and Tait headed, not upwards again, but down from the rocks at the base of the plateau.

I, guessing at our reason for this departure, beckoned the men to follow. When we reached the level ground beneath the climb to the Spyglass, Tait walked to his right. I knew where this direction led— due east, to an awful swamp, the place where, in Dr. Livesey's opinion, Dick Johnson contracted his fever. Should I baulk at this turn? Should I remind Silver? As I tossed these queries, Tait turned right again and at Silver's gesture we followed like children.

We marched for half an hour; we were beneath Spyglass shoulder and just as I had begun to imagine I should soon get a view up to that awful ledge with its poor bleached figures, Tait stopped and we walked deep into the shadows. Ahead, in the very overhang of the hill, lay an acre or so of flat, large rock, a sort of table by way of foothill to the greater heights. Tait made a gesture to Silver who stopped us and who then, after looking enquiringly at Tait, bade us all turn our backs. We had evidently reached the treasure.

I had supposed it lay elsewhere but Silver assured me that Tait would have moved it from Ben Gunn's hiding place. Silver and Tait began a deep talk. Immediately by, I had a view of nothing but scrub and dense trees. The same high roots were indigenous up here and the sun came through to them in shafts, making their coils look like serpents. I looked to my right and left and saw that the men nearest me, from Silver's militia, sweated more than the weather of the day warranted.

Again I had that same unease as when first I returned to Treasure Island—that from deep within these trailing creepers and trees, eyes watched me and only me. I shook off the feeling and returned to what I supposed myself to be—a sentry, protecting the negotiations between Tait and Silver.

There was to be no protecting of their talks. Behind me came the noise of a hard, sharp scuffle and we all turned.

"Jim!" called Silver. "Quick!"

We had also rehearsed this. Silver had told me of someone he had discovered. This was a man from the East, who taught him the way of the Cathay fighter, an unarmed method of hand-to-hand combat which could overwhelm an opponent.

As I looked, Silver had Tait on the ground, helpless, both arms pinioned; the point of Silver's crutch, on the nape of Tait's neck, pinned the man's face to the earth: it was a wonder to look at.

I and others rushed. From my pockets I drew special cords Silver had given me with careful instructions. These, he told me, were hangman's cords; tie a man with these and the more he pushed the tighter they became; they were made of silk and sisal mixed together. I called four militia men to help me, each to take a wrist or an ankle.

But how Tait fought! He rolled over, kicked each man away in turn and almost rose to overpower Silver. Eventually he was only subdued by Silver placing the ferrule of his crutch on Tait's upper lip at that point directly beneath the nose where, if a man be struck hard enough, he is killed at once—another oriental device.

Silver tied the cords himself and then we knew the first purpose of the poles we carried—Tait was strung on two of them and four of the militia became his bearers. And still he had not, so far as I knew, uttered a word.

"Has he spoken?" I asked Silver, who took off his hat and shook his head in weary wonder.

"Only grunts, Jim, A nod here and there. I niver met a mortal man so dangerous. There were a fellow sailed with Flint, name of Davis—

he were bad when riled. But this 'un—no, Jim, niver!" and he laughed that wonderful, inspiring laugh.

It didn't matter that Long John Silver would gyp his own children if he had any: the size of his spirit guaranteed his place in the world.

He beckoned to me, his lopsided grin like a gap-toothed quarter moon. I followed as he heaved himself up onto the low, wide table of rock. He began to pace one way and then another, then a third; a diagram of his footsteps would have made a pretty geometry. Then Silver stopped and tapped his silver crutch on the stones. He tapped again, his head cocked to one side, and I thought of his horrid parrot (now, happily, in a cloth-covered cage on the brig). Silver listened some more and then in one place he tapped his heel, hard. Next he dropped to his knees and looked at the flat rock as if reading the pages of some book. He smiled up at me like a child.

Evidently he had elicited from Tait the burial place of the silver bars. I thought as I watched him—"Silver to silver: that's a natural match."

He called me over and I knelt beside him. Never saying a word he stroked the ground we looked at. When I examined it closely I saw that the stone he caressed, a long, regular, natural rectangle, had clear edges and did not bed in quite so smoothly as the others did.

Silver called for "a spike." A man ran forward with an iron pin, the sort used for the thickest rope on the largest canvas, where a wooden marlin would snap. Most sailors carry them—a mariner's spike is as personal to him as his pipe or tobacco knife. Silver inserted the spike into an edge of the slab; I came round to his side and lifted the stone with him. It had not been disturbed for some time but it came up easy.

Directly beneath opened a space and I was about to poke a hand down into the darkness when Silver grabbed me and pushed me back. It flashed through my mind that he meant to stay me from the bullion but that was (for once) to misjudge him.

"Wait," he said. "Watch!"

One by one four spiders came climbing out of the hole, large as mice, black as jet and quilled with rough hairs. We stood and moved back. Fortunately they scuttled up the rocks away from us all and into the scrub.

"The 'Devil's Friend'," gasped Silver, more shaken than I think I had ever known him. "One scrape, Jim, and 'tis all up with a man. Die roaring, we would"—and he gaped after them: he had gone quite pale. The sweat on his upper lip came not from exertion.

He calmed himself. It took a moment or two: his hands trembled. Now we both knelt again to the rectangle of darkness. When we grew accustomed, and adjusted where we lay so as not to darken the hole, we saw that the place was broad and deep, a natural space beneath the ground, not unlike a ship's hold. We also saw that huge parcels of things lay down there, perhaps eighty, ninety massive packages, most of them wrapped in the hardest of sailcloth.

"John, this isn't what we left behind!"

Silver replied, "There's more than we ever had in the first day."

"What do we do?"

Silver looked around at the men. He called the smallest, neatest of them and the man, a foreigner whose language Silver understood, came running. At Silver's direction—he called him "Manolo"—the man dropped down into the hole. With difficulty, because the space was tight, he began to hand up the smallest packets. Silver stopped him after we had received four; we began to open them.

At first I felt keen disappointment. As the sailcloth yielded (breaking one or two of my fingernails), I saw flat packets of waxed paper. These did not yield at all and Silver, who had the same between his hands, grunted, "We must cut them, I fear."

With my teeth I began to saw; the paper had a waxy taste but also a little salt of the sea. As I pressed the interior of the packet, it began to yield and fragment.

"Careful, John," I warned. "I think I've broken this one."

He stopped and watched me. The paper began to dismantle in my fingers and I laid the packet on the stones to spread it apart.

It is to my shame that I swore. Never, not in peril of death, not even alone, has my voice put an oath on the air. It did now. This was an excitement too great to contain, this was like catching a star that had fallen from the night skies. The packet did not contain goods which I had broken in my haste or clumsiness; it contained a wonderful, shining gravel. Without ever having seen such stones before, I knew they were diamonds.

John Silver repeated the oath he had just heard from me. Then he repeated it again—but in the brightness of my dazzle it dawned on me that he did so with a different, an urgent, resonance.

I glanced across at him—he had straightened and begun to rise. He was staring warily at something, like a man about to be attacked. Had Tait escaped? No—but hurtling towards us, with the same speed and menace with which a squall hurtles over the surface of the sea, came a man wilder than Joseph Tait and a great deal larger. He was ten feet away and running hard to where we stood; he carried a sabre in one hand, a machete in the other and he whirled them like windmills.

Silver and I scattered. The interloper came after me. What instinct in him made that selection I cannot say: did I look more incapable than any other man there? In my vanity I sometimes think that perhaps he singled me out as the most dangerous of the company and therefore the one to be attacked first.

I scrambled to a higher place and, as I did so, felt the wind and heard the *chinnngg!* of a machete slicing at my ankle but hitting the rock. Had it caught me I should now perhaps be the second one-legged man I know. But the closeness of the blade made me turn to face the danger—and it was as well that I did.

He had begun to ascend the rock, this giant whose hair had once been red; his face had a kind of roaring look. Inside the cave I had never seen him fully, had merely felt his presence and glimpsed his silhouette. Those experiences had not prepared me; this man was huge. Something or someone—Tait perhaps?—had split his chin long ago and it seemed to have formed two chins; half of one ear was gone and he missed the thumb of his right hand.

But it was the look in his eyes that put the terror in my heart. I have often heard of men having red eyes and sometimes, if I have slept awkwardly on my face, one of my own eyes will be sore and red when I awake. But not red like this—this was dawn red, this was storm red, as when the clouds boil in summer and the heat of the sky crashes to the earth.

I backed away from him—what else could I do? He and I had covered so much ground so fast we had distanced ourselves from the others and therefore no one could get close enough to help me. Not that anyone showed such an inclination; back in the old days, when I, hidden not a mile from here, spied on a dispute between Silver and a young sailor called Tom who defied him and marched away, Silver felled the man by throwing his crutch like a projectile (and then killed the man with two knife blows). Would that Silver now threw his crutch!

But he didn't and this savage advanced. I scrambled higher and higher—cowardly, I know, but putting discretion ahead of valour. He came after me—and came after me—and came after me. I ducked and dodged and he slashed at my legs—now I was on a smooth slope and the steepness of the climb promised to tip me backwards. So I did what I could—I used the place's natural advantages and, turning, hurled myself back down the sliding face of rock, going past my assailant so fast and just out of his reach that I won the advantage of surprise.

And now I began to bound, like one of Ben Gunn's goats, from rock to rock. My intention was to reach my weapons which lay on the ground beside the open trove, or get back among the militia for the safety of numbers.

The giant, as I had hoped, proved slow in turning and hesitant in bounding down these rockfaces. But he lacked no courage and once he had made up his mind he came thundering after me. I made for the flat rocks but couldn't see Silver and I raced to try and get my gun.

Oh, I still feel sadness at what happened next—and I feel responsible for it and it makes me clasp my arms around myself and say, "No, no, no!" Why does it touch me so much? Perhaps because he was such a willing and mild-faced person. This is what happened.

As I bent to grab the gun—and hoped as I ran to try and prime it—the little man we had, Manolo, lifted his head from the treasure hole. The giant bent low and swept at him with the machete in his left hand and then the sabre in his right. What the first blade began the second blade completed, and the little dark-eyed smiling man died in an instant, decapitated. My fingers froze on my gun's priming rod.

The giant halted a moment, as though to admire his dreadful cleavering. I thank the Lord that it became his last moment.

He did not have the opportunity to see who attacked him. Silver eased from the concealment of a tall shaft of rock. In his hand he held a stone big as a boy's head and he crashed it on the giant. Curiously he did not aim—and he had time to—for the top of the giant's skull. Instead, in a slanting, upwards blow, he hit for the ear, the bone that protrudes just behind. The giant went down—for eternity. He rolled a little, twitched, half-bucked—and subsided.

Silver, who almost staggered off his crutch with the force he gave his blow, looked at me, then at the militia. To my astonishment not one man had readied his gun or drawn his cutlass. I ascribed this to fright and, feeling my own legs go weak, sat down on the ground. Silver stood above me—he might have been the Colossus, so great did he bulk in my eyes.

I heard him swear, then swear again. He turned, righted himself and went to the giant's body. Bending low he picked up the fatal stone and hurled it down on the giant's head again.

"Vile swab!" he shouted and swore again; I cannot think that I ever saw him so out of himself. He came lurching back to me and stood, shaking his head from side to side; he swore softly all the time and then gasped, "Jim, I'm getting old and I likes it not."

My shame at having run from the giant had begun to afflict me and I thought I had better do something of value. I rose, called the men and ordered two of them to haul the giant's body into the brush; two more took Manolo's corpse from where it slumped headless and bloody across the aperture that led down to the treasure and two others began to dig a grave.

I did something that I should never have thought myself capable of doing. But I did it and it is part of me now, and I believe—although I am not sure of it—that I rejoice in having done it out of respect and remorse. By its sleek black hair, now slippery with blood, I picked up Manolo's severed head. Not quite having the range of bravery to look at it, I led the way to a wide piece of soft earth some hundred yards on, and indicated where his grave must be dug.

There, I rooted with my foot and placed the unfortunate head tenderly on a piece of ground; I tore off some wide leaves to cover it. Then I bowed my face and said a prayer. And when I had done all these things, I walked to where Joseph Tait lay trussed like a pig for the roast, hanging between two poles from the shoulders of four men.

Looking down into his eyes I said nothing—but I had the satisfaction that he looked away from me, admittedly only after many, many seconds.

Silver sat on a high rock, the silver crutch stretched out beside him; that implement seemed to have a soul of its own. He was quiet and staring; he removed his hat and rubbed his head; he looked at nobody.

———✿———

Ch. 31—

Of Deepest Inhumanity

The advantage of a plan lies not merely in its execution, nor in the undeniable pleasure at its clean and successful completion. Its greatest recommendation is that it lies there, waiting to be fallen back upon.

In steps as measured as arithmetic, I knew what must happen next and I set out to bring it all about in a most orderly way. It was still very early in the day—we benefited from the advantage of our early rising. Conversely, that meant we also had a long day to get through with many tasks to be completed, before we could return to the safety of the longboat and the next—and, I hoped, final—stage of this compromising adventure. My instinct told me (and I was proven right) that Tait and the dead giant had been the only ones commanding Treasure Island.

A different hunch suggested that Silver had no stomach for what must now be done. I stood before him in a way that did not interrupt his thoughts but nevertheless gained his attention.

"John," I began.

He squinted up at me. I saw in his face his liking for me. It is a feeling I have never understood—except perhaps to wonder whether he saw in me a son whose company he might have enjoyed.

"It has been a hard morning," I continued. "You have done extraordinary things—and in a very short piece of time. If I suggest you take some rest now—would you feel offended? I mean it well. I know how to do this next task—I don't enjoy the contemplation of it, but I expect it won't take long."

Silver said nothing and I pressed on. "We have some stores to leave with you. The four men holding Tait will be here. Do you need extra assistance? Perhaps you could—should you wish some occupation—perhaps begin to have the trove raised to the surface of the ground?"

I knew my man. He shook himself and stood.

"Jim, there be a kindness in you. I recollect you told me once your father were a kind man. I reckon you gets it from him, God rest his soul." He eased his limbs and looked around. "I'll take you at your word. Give me two more men and while you're gone I'll oversee the heavy work."

"Good," I said, turning away from him. "Good."

He called me back.

"Jim—there's a thing I wants to say." He hesitated but then looked me full in the eyes. The sun glinted on the long strut of silver beneath the crutch's ebony rest. "There be them as has called me evil. But I niver killed a man and liked doing it. I'm a man has to try and get his sleep many a night. And doesn't."

He took my nod as a kind of absolution.

"I'll be here, waiting for you," he said.

A dilemma faced me now. Should I tell the men I took with me something about the horrors they faced? I decided not. Instead, I gave myself a hard visage and took on the demeanour of a brusque officer. We marched back the way we had come with Tait and I led them to the plateau at the foot of Spyglass Hill.

Once on that little platform, I gave an order for the rear wall to be stripped of all its wild and thorny growth. I watched as the men hacked it. It cost them some effort but soon the stone face of the hill lay as naked and cold as a plucked fowl. The entrance then opened to us—it was as wide as the door of the Admiral Benbow.

Two of the men had been placed in charge of such ordnance as we carried and I instructed them to make us some torches. I told them all that unpleasant sights and smells awaited us. In a matter of minutes we were ready to enter and I went first. Not until the others had crowded in behind me and our torches shone lights brighter than had ever been seen inside that place, did I measure the horror of Spyglass Hill.

I have been told, both by Dr. Livesey and Dr. Ballantyne, that he who witnesses horrors may be worse off, in some strange way, than he who suffers them. Dr. Ballantyne made me tell him many times the sights I saw that morning, in the lights of many torches. When, one day, I asked him why he held such a morbid curiosity as to make me talk about it over and over again, he replied, "It is for you—not for me."

I believe I know what he meant. Had I never been able to speak of it, I should have succumbed to it—and it proved so horrible I should have been able to speak of it to very few.

Indeed, I propose to glide over some of the more terrible details of the sight and content myself with telling of the physical structure of the place and, then, of the good we were able to do.

To begin with, I do not know how Ben Gunn and I did not fall off into the pit below, when Tait and the giant first took us. The path was as narrow as a forearm and we wore leather shoes. Easy for Tait and his ogre to walk it—they knew it familiarly and they felt it with their bare feet. Now I grew dizzy merely looking down at it. One of my men stumbled and another steadied him lest he fall.

I cannot say how deep that pit was—perhaps the depth of a large barn. There was nothing down there that could be saved—and the activities which had made that infernal pile had, I could tell, been going on for many years. I should guess that Tait had begun this awful work within months of being marooned by us. In among the scraps of cloth—and sometimes entire suits or uniforms—I saw, as well as skeletons, single bare bones and every time I saw one I turned away.

Behind me, along the line a little, I heard a man sobbing and for a moment I thought it might be one of Tait's captive wretches—but it was one of my own men, stricken by the awfulness of what we saw.

I spoke, as much to bring a human and warm sound into that place as to give an instruction.

"Follow me. I believe we may have good work to do," and I led the way very slowly, counselling those behind me to look neither to right nor left. Soon, as Ben and I had done, we emerged onto a wider place and there I saw the bloodstained rocks Tait had used to keep people pinioned. Nobody lay here now—but again I spied one or two long, single bones.

It may seem strange to report that I felt a sensation of pleasure in such a ghastly place—but I can honestly state that was my next sensation. It came when I looked across this wide stone area and saw the shallow arch with the light of day peeping through.

"Look," I called. "That is the arch through which I escaped."

"Sir," came the voice of one of our men. "Were you a prisoner here?"

"I was—and there may be others alive here. That's why we've come."

"No, sir," said another man's voice, in lugubrious tones, "there be no person alive in here."

I led them to the arch and one by one we crouched and looked. Was it possible that I shot out through here? My father's spirit, my mother's prayers—they are the only reasons I can give for my survival. The drop was near to sheer—and I fancied I could still see a small trail of broken shrubs where I had crashed downwards all those weeks ago. To my chagrin I saw that a perfectly good path wound down to the left and that was how Tait had followed me.

But my most abiding memory of that archway was the one I had come to redeem. I looked to left and right, in the places where I had seen the men standing, strapped upright, in the blazing sun on the ridge outside the cave. Nobody stood there now.

Where were they? I asked someone to hold my arm while I eased myself out. Then I saw the better way—there was a slight opening, tall as a thin man, through which I could ease myself from the cave and this led to the steep path down which Tait had run. The others crowded out behind me through this "door"—and who could blame them for not wishing to stay in that hole of evil. Soon we stood halfway down the hillside, in a place from which I could look back up.

Nobody was there. No mortal being stood pegged out and bleached. And with no person alive inside the cave—that must mean that Dr. Jefferies and, sadder still, Ben Gunn were dead. I had already figured that Tom Taylor had died—but, although the shock speared my heart, I had no time at that moment to engage with the fabric of such sadness.

One of the men called me: "Sir!"

I looked at him and he pointed. Across from the path, in deep scrub, was a rude shelter and beneath its rough woven awning we saw some human legs. We cocked our weapons and after some moments of thought we set off. I decided we would follow the path to its lowest levels and then ascend to approach the shelter from the rear. Nothing impeded or alarmed us.

Soon we stood in shoulder-high brush a few feet from the shelter's rear wall. I moved forwards gingerly and peeked through the weave of branches. What I saw would not have threatened a child. Three bodies lay on the earthen floor. They were in the saddest decrepitude—but I sensed they were alive. Beckoning the men to follow and then take guard, I rushed around to the entrance. The three figures, supine and torn, were Dr. Jefferies, Bo'sun Noonstock—and Ben Gunn.

It was Ben to whom I stooped first. "Ben! Dear fellow. Are you all right? It's Jim."

He didn't open his eyes. It is said that if you begin your life by being beaten, it will go on. Ben had been badly beaten about the face and head and his poor, thin shoulders wore such terrible bruises that I had to contain my anger.

"Ben, can you hear me? It's Jim."

He murmured, "Jim—" He reached—or tried to; I took his hand and almost wept at how thin it was.

"Oh—Ben. Poor Ben. What happened?"

No answer.

Still holding his hand, I looked at the other two. Noonstock was a man I had remarked upon when I met him, for his gauntness, and Jefferies, I recall thinking, had a waist as slim as a girl. As I reflected on the possible—and awful—reasons why they survived I knew one thing for sure: Joseph Tait must die. I did not know by what means, or by whose hand, and I did not care.

Silver's men had been like sheep, staring open-mouthed as I first spoke to Ben, then to Jefferies who made no reply and to Noonstock who had a tithe of vigour. Working out a new and simpler route by the breast of the Spyglass I dispatched four of them to the longboat to fetch litters, medicaments and stores. A fifth I sent along the same route, but with orders to divert and inform Silver where we were and how we had become occupied.

Then I enlisted the others to help me, and with our limited means make my grievously violated comrades as comfortable as possible.

Their wounds were terrible. One of my men found a source of clean water; this part of the island, just up the crest from the Cape of the Woods, abounds in springs and streams. We began by painting the lips of each of the three with water and then allowed them slow constant sips for many minutes.

I found something incongruous under branches inside the shelter—a pile of clothing including, disturbingly, a woman's dress. Some mate's wife from a ship wrecked by Tait? Or a captain's daughter? Or a hopeful passenger? The garments had been dropped here recently and I dared not dwell upon their suggestions. From them I ripped strips of cloth with which to clean wounds and then found full items of clothing to try and dress the devastated trio.

This proved appallingly difficult, because their own clothes—or what remained of them—stuck to their caked blood. To tell how severe their injuries were, Dr. Jefferies gasped in pain when a drop of cold water fell on his naked thigh. Not an inch of his body had not been beaten in some way or other. I guessed they had been used as slaves.

The day's gruesome work was not eased by the heat of the sun, which was now well risen and had come round the shoulder of the hill. Yet, I worked on and the others, unskilled as me, helped valiantly; I believe we wrought an improvement on the awful plight of each victim. Noonstock touched me curiously. As I bathed him and eased his limbs here and there as softly as if with a baby, I heard him trying to say something. It turned out that he was whispering, "I'll be good, I promise."

Jefferies attempted one word before he lapsed into a deeper and, I think, safer unconsciousness—he half-spoke, "Thank—" and then cut himself off.

By the time our litter bearers returned, two hours later, we had rendered as much help as we were able. How I longed for Dr. Livesey or Dr. Ballantyne; both men together would have achieved miracles and I wished with all the pain of a man disappointed in his own lack of skill that I had some knowledge of physic or some light training in it.

But I knew one thing: I knew as we loaded the men gently on the litters and set off on the calmer route to find Silver and the others, that the tooth of this island's serpent had been drawn. There was now nothing left to fear here. This thought consoled me—until the next thought warned me with the certainty of a Bible prophet that the worst, meaning Maltby and his retinue, was to come.

Silver, when we reached him, was composed again and he showed a great tenderness for the men we carried. I watched, anxious to see and remember forever, his reunion with Ben Gunn, who sometimes became conscious and then fell away again. Silver came to each litter and looked closely down. He saw Ben second; I had not told him who it was but he knew. Adjusting the silver crutch, he lowered himself a little to speak softly.

"Ben Gunn. You varmint! Is this where you fetch up?" I was astonished at his tenderness. "See what happens to a man who wants too much cheese."

Perhaps it was the appetising word that woke Ben; he flickered his eyes.

"Ben, 'tis John. John Silver."

Ben's scrawny hand fumbled a little and Silver took it like a baby's.

"Oh, Ben. You were allus a droll one."

Ben's eyes closed again. When Silver turned to face me, his own eyes had turned to flames and he shook his head like a man lost for words. He pointed to each litter in turn. At Jefferies he shook his head. Over Noonstock he gave a thumbs-up. And at Ben he gave a gesture of uncertainty. I trusted his judgement—he had, Heaven knows, seen enough to know when a man might live or die.

Ch. 32—

The Faces of Our Enemies

We made our arrangements quickly. Silver would stay to complete the hauling up of the trove. I would take the trussed Tait and our three invalids to a point of shelter near the longboat. This would free the litter bearers to return and help with the treasure. Silver agreed to this plan; he was in a thoughtful mood and I believe he had been deeply touched by the harm done to Ben Gunn.

Although we went gently so as not to shake our injured ones (for Tait's comfort we cared not), it took no more than an hour to reach the trees behind the beached longboat. I set up elaborate protection to ensure the comfort of my ill companions. Also, I did a vicious thing and although I blush to tell it, I feel defensive of it too.

I went to where we had propped Tait, the handles of his trussing poles suspended a little crazily between the branches of trees—and I bound him further. This time I bound him with tighter cords, in a way that hurt, and I neither looked at his face nor spoke to him as I did so.

But that was not the viciousness to which I refer; that came when I walked back to the little sheltered area I had created with tenderness so that these three decent men might be helped to recover. I looked down at them, watched for a moment their struggle for life and their shattered bodies and of a sudden I ran back to Tait's rig and kicked him so hard I near broke my foot. He grunted—and then I remembered myself and introduced some control of my spirit in case I repeated the act. Violence teaches violence.

In some ways that was the most curious day of my whole life so far—and I have had many abnormal times, from the whimsical to the ridiculous to the terrifying. Consider where I was—in a quiet grove, some fifty yards from the shore. Were I to step out of the shade, I could see and be seen by the *Hispaniola* to my left and the black brig to my right. On the one waited my beloved friends and, I hoped, my future; on the other, perdition.

By my side, under the shade of branches, lay three men on litters, each covered with incongruous clothes and each with some medical salve spread on more wounds and bruises than a man should ever be obliged to suffer. From time to time one groaned and when he did I took a soft piece of cloth, suffused it with clean, cold water and held it to his lips.

I confess that much though I tried to remain impartial, I attended Ben more than the others, although all my rivalry with Jefferies vanished in smoke when I saw how the poor man had been used by Tait. (It must be understood here that all three bore wounds of a nature I shall not and, in delicacy, must not reveal.)

Now consider what else met my eye in that grove. Trussed and suspended, and sometimes swinging himself violently as if to escape, lay Joseph Tait. His rage had not abated; his force seemed to turn the air about him red. I could scarcely look at him because he made me boil—my rage at him ran nearly as high as his rage at the world.

But think of the dilemma he posed me. I had looked afresh at Louis, the boy I took to be his son, when I went back to the ship with Dr. Ballantyne—and how warmly Louis greeted me and with such affection!

As for Grace: she must remove from her mind all trace and memory of ever having associated with this brute. I made up my mind that were I to return to England safely, I would attempt to make her my wife. To make it possible I would enlist in my suit the help of Uncle Ambrose, my mother, Mrs. Ballantyne, every ally I could find. Nothing Grace had shown me suggested she might consider me. But only the brave merit the fair and I was learning daily how to be braver.

She had, after all, said she needed the help of a brave man. I could point to the great feats and labours I had lately undertaken on her behalf. But perhaps, I feared, she might be a woman who took such things as her due. Maybe she had been reared to believe that men effect such deeds for ladies as part of the natural order. Still, my hopes were high—especially when I considered the riches John Silver and I had seen, and of which I would get a large share.

These giddy thoughts became sober when I then contemplated the brig and the dangers she threatened. I wound my excitement down.

Sometime in the afternoon I heard the first "halloo!" and saw the men trudge through the trees bearing the first canvas-wrapped wedge of treasure. By nightfall everything had been brought to our little grove: it was a very large pile. The men worked extraordinarily hard.

Silver came last of all and he looked weary. I offered him refreshment and he surprised me by saying he should enjoy some but, "First things first," and he went to Ben again, stooped low and spoke softly. I was too far away to hear what he said.

The rest of our plan went smoothly. When night fell, and I reflected thankfully on the absence of a wind, we began to load the longboat. Our calculations suggested at least seven journeys to the *Hispaniola*. Silver had his own men take the rowing duties, with the remaining crewmen from the brig hauling everything to the spit of sand between turns. Silver supervised them and I knew that he did so lest they thieved. I continued with my duties of care.

We worked all night. Back and forth went the longboat, back and forth. The oarsmen brought reports from the *Hispaniola* of swift, efficient help. Our last journey of all was preceded by a small and hard scenario. Silver called together the three remaining brig sailors. He beckoned me to join them. I wished he would hurry because the night would soon lose its darkness and the dawn's habit in those seas is to split open very fast.

"We've changed our plan," he told them. "We're not going back to the brig. Nor are you. You're now part of the crew of the *Hispaniola* and as such, you'll sail her back to England. If there be one man among you who finds that not to his taste, let him step over here to me."

Not a man moved. Even I, who knew Silver well, shivered at the menace in his calm voice. And I think I knew he would have easily killed me too, had I gone against him at that moment. We turned and walked to the longboat which had come back from the *Hispaniola* with fewer hands—in order to accommodate Silver, our three wounded friends, the hog-tied Joseph Tait and me. Tait kicked hard as we rolled him in the scuppers.

When we arrived at the anchorage, I sighed with relief. All was ready for us and Captain Reid's power was foremost. He supervised each embarkation quietly and decisively, and took particular interest in Noonstock. Dr. Ballantyne worked with him, the very picture of medical industry. Helpers were rallied to take the men below. All was done in strict silence. Now my weariness began to take account—but I was revived by the captain's quiet remark.

He walked to Tait and murmured to him, "Whoever your friends are, I shall be the one who pulls the rope around your neck. And I shall not pray God to have mercy on your soul." The captain spoke so evenly he might have been ordering marmalade from the cabin boy.

"Lock him in the foc's'le. Arrange for him to be fed. I want him in London alive. Do it quickly." Reid walked away in contempt.

Next came a moment which was as comic as the circumstances could allow. The last person aboard was Silver and he came with the hoisting of the longboat. When she was alongside he hauled himself out, stood on the deck of the *Hispaniola* and looked around with genuine pleasure.

"I love this here ship," he whispered.

When he saw Captain Reid he yanked himself forwards and half-bowed.

"Cap'n John Silver reporting for dooty, cap'n. I can be a mate or a cook—or a skipper should it come to that."

Captain Reid looked at this pirate and mutineer. I tried to follow the thoughts that must have run through his head and I could not keep up—but it amused me to see his face and hear his softly murmured words.

"Welcome aboard, sir. 'Cap'n Silver' is it, these days? Well, sir, the world does change itself round and about," and he walked away while Silver winked at me.

I held my breath and let it out slowly. So far so good: we had stolen the march we wanted to steal. I had rescued some of our men and could now help them fight for their lives. The treasure and Tait had come aboard the *Hispaniola* and we already knew she was a faster ship than the brig. We had another advantage—of surprise; and of that Captain Reid meant to make the most.

The ship set about a bustle such as I had never seen. Silver's men, not all of them mariners, rushed softly here and there and tried to get up the rigging as best they could.

I knew Dr. Ballantyne had taken the three wounded men below. Tait was shifted quickly and I took with me the key of the foc's'le. With every bone weary and my own old wounds hurting like darts, I climbed on deck again, thinking what to do next. My thoughts were scrambled to dust by the sudden assault on my arm by Grace.

"Where is he?!" Her cry broke the silence.

"Shhh, Madam. He's under lock and key."

"Who has the key?"

"Captain Reid's orders. I have the key but—"

"Give it to me!" and she began to wrestle with me.

"Madam, please! We need silence!"

Louis arrived and stopped dead before us, nonplussed at his mother's trying to grapple at my pockets.

"Madam, listen!" I managed to stop her.

"Give it!"

"Madam—it is best you not see him—"

"Oh, you've wounded him, I know it—"

"Listen, Madam—Grace—please—"

She tried to dive at me again but at that moment I saw something which gave me alarm. A man had gone to the ship's rail and stood there. He was one of the brig's crew and I knew what he meant to do. I tore myself from Grace's grasp and ran to him. She half-halted me with her final grab—and in that moment the man got away. I heard the splash and ran to tell Captain Reid.

Now we had found trouble—because even though we had numerous men, they were neither sufficiently skilled nor unwearied to rig the *Hispaniola* quite fast enough. We had lost our advantage. The man in the water began hallooing the brig and the first person to hear him would see us raising sail.

Though it was not yet fully light, Maltby prepared within minutes. I suspected he had been standing ready—or meant to get under way with all speed once he had got what he wanted. But, instead, we had it all—and now he therefore wanted us! Could we set off with enough immediate force to leave him behind?

I looked for Silver—and knew where to find him: on the poop, watching the great piles of the canvas hoard being stowed in the *Hispaniola*'s aft hold. He had an air of contentment about him—and I an air of agitation about me.

He looked at me. "They knows, I expect?"

"Yes, John."

"Allus happens. Allus some swab to blow the gaff. Better git ready. They'll be afire when they gits to us."

I took off my coat, as if to obey his order or at least show myself alert. All around me, our ship teemed with labour and some of the men on the yards seemed so hasty I thought they might fall into the sea. We yawed and swung as our canvas broke out unevenly—while behind, against the breaking light, the brig's sails unfurled as smoothly as a man unrolling a chart; Maltby had held back from the island a good number of crew. I fell to one side as the *Hispaniola* lurched and I heard Captain Reid berate the man whose lack of rhythm in his work caused the imbalance.

Up by the foredeck, I saw Grace in excited conversation with my uncle, whose hands were outstretched as though soothing her, but she was not heeding him. I climbed to the poop, where Silver had turned himself round to look at the brig.

"What will they do, John?"

"They'll board us," he said. "Leastways 'tis what I'd do."

"Are we finished—"

"Don't say sich a thing, Jim," he cut in. "Never say sich a thing! Sharper! Sharper!" he called down to his loading men.

"But—"

"Your cap'n'll do what a sensible master'll do—he'll begin a parley and if them there don't like the sound of the parley—then there'll be wigs on the deck, Jim."

He seemed so unconcerned I felt nettled—but now I know that this was Silver's means of keeping himself calm before the great effort ahead. And, naturally, he was proven right; we had no chance and soon the brig drew alongside like a swan to a bridge.

Hooks and grapnels bit into the pretty timbers of the *Hispaniola* and the two vessels made crushing, grinding noises. Silver jumped up and, using bulwarks and lines to steer himself, followed me to the point of the grab. I saw Grace look in dismay and turn to my uncle who instantly hurried her below. Why did she wish Tait released? The question annoyed me. She had hidden something, some motive, all through this crazy venture.

Matters squared off fast. On the brig, proud as a cock, Maltby stood nearest the *Hispaniola* and I wondered that he had no fear of a gun or a thrown knife. His bravado worked: he was permitted to stand there and hail Captain Reid.

That gentleman walked towards him, calm as a man accustomed to crisis.

"Sir, you are trespassing. Take your ship away from mine. Know you not the law of the sea?"

"I know the King's law!" roared Maltby and I was tired of that tune in him

"The King's law is also the law of the sea—when we sail under the King's flag. I believe I told you that when you came calling once before." Captain Reid's dry tone exuded command.

"Heave to, sir," cried Maltby. "I will not be duped by common villains."

"We may all see who the common villain is, sir. This is the action of a pirate."

Maltby stood alone. Apart from his sailors at their posts, nobody else could be seen. On our side, Silver's men began to gather around him; he had evidently alerted them to the likelihood of attrition. John himself leaned back as though at a fête.

Both Maltby and Reid gave orders to take in sail. When the vessels had come to a full halt, though yet juddering and swinging, the captain resumed his dialogue.

"Now, sir, state your purposes."

"You know what I want, you rogue," and to Maltby's gesture a sailor ran forward and ran a large wide plank from the brig to us. Maltby stood on this when it was steady and began to cross—alone.

Silver muttered to me, "Give him the palm for bravery, at any rate."

Now Maltby stood like an emperor, one foot on the *Hispaniola*'s rail. Why did we not take him down? I shall never know—but I must honestly admit that I myself did not think to do so, so mesmerised was I by his presence. He took a pace forwards and dropped his bulk on our deck; the curls of his black wig jiggled.

"I claim this ship and all on her for His Majesty the King."

"Claim what you like, sir," said Captain Reid, cool as morning. "In point, sir, get back out of here and to rot with you."

As if at a signal, a host of figures broke from the gloom of the dawn light behind Maltby and within seconds they swarmed in single file across the plank towards us.

Captain Reid yelled, "*Hold*! I have men primed to cut you down like pigs!"

———— ✦ ————

Ch. 35 —

The Wonder of Battle

They halted, some in a line on the plank and the rest waiting behind them. Maltby hesitated. He looked along our decks.

"Sir, give us what we claim and we shall depart."

Though the words rang of diplomacy, his voice had not dropped in force.

"I'll give you and your cohorts the end of a rope, that's what I'll give you," said the captain, his Scotch accent growing thicker with every word.

Maltby assumed an air of peace, dropping one hand to his hip and stretching out the other like a friend.

"We have much in common and we are both much pressed," he said. "We should work together."

"Aye, we'll work together," replied Reid. "We'll work my hands to your neck, sir. Now get off my ship!"

I heard Silver chuckle.

Nobody who has not seen such a thing can know the likes of what happened next. We were hit by a wave—a torrent—of armed men intent on killing. They poured onto the *Hispaniola* and I saw the "gentlemen" at last in their true colours, with Egan the master swordsman foremost among them. This time he wore no coat of burgundy but a tight shirt of a sleek, grey silk that seemed stuck to his body and I remembered hearing this to be the hallmark of the journeyman sword—a garment by which he cannot get caught.

In that first wave they almost had the best of it. Silver's men came forwards and made a hard-fought stand. I confess I hovered at the edge of the action, not entering but not retreating and I felt comforted that Silver himself had not moved either.

Then the event changed. One-on-one battles raged along the deck until Maltby called out.

"Stop! Cease this!"

His men fell back and everyone on our side able to stand upright showed cuts or wounds of some variety. Three of our men were down; of Maltby's, two had been felled, two heavily wounded—although the "gentlemen" showed no sign of trouble except a mild shortness of breath.

I worried that Maltby had more men in reserve: where, for example, was the hunchback? But, given such resources, another question arched above all: why had Maltby called a halt?

Today I know why. He feared losing so many men and killing so many of ours that he should not have enough to crew a voyage home with either ship, let alone both; indeed, if many died he might not get away from these waters.

"Sir, I'm a man who likes to discuss," Maltby said to Captain Reid.

"Not on my ship," replied Reid.

"We are here now, sir, and we ought to make the most of it."

"I find your posture absurd, sir."

"Then *you* propose a remedy." The captain did not answer and Maltby continued. "Sir, what am I to say? I seek to avoid a little war here and I find you dumb."

I was almost knocked aside as Silver loped forwards to the captain. He whispered urgently in Reid's ear and I saw the captain's quizzical glance. Silver whispered again and such words as he used made the captain halt. They conferred, this unlikely pair, the tall, rugged pirate and the stocky, composed martinet. Maltby looked with knowing mockery at Silver; then Captain Reid called out.

"Sir, I propose we settle this as the French do. We each send in our champions against each other."

"I know the French," said Maltby, "and I know their *pareil* methods," but I could see that he was taken with the idea. The thought seemed mad; when it came to swordplay they had the experts, we the yokels. But I trusted Silver enough to watch this unfold. "Declare your rules of engagement, sir."

Silver whispered again and Captain Reid called back, "Simple. As in all *pareil* fighting. One faces one. We each nominate our own champion. No free-for-all. Whoever wins one wins the day."

Some yards away I saw Uncle Ambrose; he looked most worried and I saw him restrain someone; I took it that he was still attempting to keep Grace from the scene.

Silver lurched back to me and winked.

"This is fine, Jim. Just dandy. It battens down our hatches and draws their teeth."

But I knew their strength better than he did and I felt no such ease.

This morning, now, as I look out of the Admiral Benbow, I can see the "white horses," the little dancing, foamy waves of the sea. All around me is quiet and bright—but my mind's eye can only see that moment on the deck of the *Hispaniola*. It was now early morning; Silver and I had departed for the island and Tait and the treasure a little more than twenty-four hours ago; twelve hours before that, I had come back to find Grace and Louis, my Uncle Ambrose, Captain Reid and the good ship *Hispaniola* where I had last seen them. The volume of incident packed into that thirty-six hours remains a wonder to me.

In front of my mind's eye I see two ships jammed together, some canvas flapping, backdrop to a row of ruthless faces. These are the faces of confident men, who stand with the blades of their swords pointing to the sky, small smiles on their lips, as they await the certain outcome.

At their head stands a fleshy man with a black curly wig and round, cruel eyes—but he's a deceptive man; he has small feet and like many heavy men can move like a dancer. Near him leans a rugged, jowled man, ale-red in the face and plump too—but battle hardened.

Nearest of all to the leader I find a figure of some elegance, a man neither tall nor short, a slim man, as balanced as a goldsmith's scale.

His grey, silk cuffs are bound tight to his wrists and he has a toss to his thoroughbred head as he looks up and down the opposing ranks and he senses—and he is right—that without doubt he belongs to the superior side.

He jigs a little and the light of the southern sun catches the buckles on his shining black shoes. Then he preens some more, because he knows he will be first into the fray and if he wins—and he expects to—the game is up for all of us. Those are the rules of *pareil* fighting.

Now I look along my side. You can tell most about a man from the rear, whether he feels safe, whether he is strong, whether he is lonely. And from the profile you can tell if he is a worried man—because the jaw betrays so much. All on our side knew anxiety that morning. Except Silver—but Silver did not come into this world to worry. As I look, he has done something clever: he has fixed his gaze upon the prancing swordsman and Silver's force has made the man flinch, not much, just a little.

Maltby waved his kerchief like a small cloud. This signified the start.

"I nominate the man the King calls his Champion," he shouted. "I name Henry Egan."

This was why I blanched when our combat changed. In a wild mêlée we stood some chance of ruse, ambush, raid. But one to one—who could match this? Captain Reid looked up and down our ragged line. He stepped forward a pace—and it was a pace as decisive as I had ever seen this firm man take.

"And I nominate Captain Alastair Reid, namely myself."

The murmur that went up contained a deal of surprise. I had never known the captain as a particular swordsman, nor had I heard that he was so reputed. Yet for some reason I felt a rush of good feeling. Reid had surprised me again and again; he was a man from whom one did not know what next to expect. Then I allowed reason into my mind and reminded myself that a duellist who did little else in life except practise his swordsmanship was certain to make a fool of a stocky, thoughtful and severe man who had dedicated his life to seamanship and the good trade of marine commerce.

The pair squared off. Reid took off his coat and Silver held it. The captain next did something exceptional—he ripped the sleeve from his shirt, so that his right arm was bare to the shoulder. Only four people there, I believe, knew the significance of that gesture: Reid, Silver, myself—and Egan.

If, in a knuckle fight, the man who faces you begins to remove his rings—beware. He is an experienced brawler who knows the tricks of the alehouse and understands that if he strikes his enemy with his rings on, his own finger bones may break. Likewise, be wary of a swordsman who bares his arm to leave it as free as possible. That man knows the darker side of duelling.

Next Captain Reid chose his weapon—a sabre.

Egan shouted, "Foul!" and wagged his rapier.

"No foul, sir—I do not object to your weapon and I have the choice. You can have your rapier."

Egan smiled his bear's smile again. To put a sabre up against a rapier was as crude as putting a catapult against a pistol.

As I was watching these moments, I had the diversion of seeing Grace move closer to my right and stand at a vantage point. My irritation that she should expose herself to a scene of dangerous fighting made me miss the first parry—and I also felt a stab of wariness about her actions but did not know why. As my uncle had evidently not succeeded in calming her, I wanted to make my way to her. But I was hemmed in by supporters of the swordsmen and I did not want to cause a distraction.

The clash of steel called me back and I saw both men locked to each other, a foot apart, each hilt hard to the other. This is not an unusual moment in such a fight—it is when the swordsmen test each other. Often, the test includes the decision as to which breaks first.

Egan broke away and Reid, surprisingly, did not follow him. I watched Egan's face. He was trying to reckon Reid: should he fight him fast or slow? He decided on slow and came circling back in, pointing, flicking and waving but not thrusting. Reid scarcely moved. I watched his feet. He did not stand flat on the ground but rather stood halfway on his toes. With his right foot he levered himself around in a circle, eyeing Egan all the time. And yet neither man thrust: they merely circled and watched.

The mood changed. Our opponents had expected Egan to move in immediately with, say, a drive to the captain's throat. I watched the other duellists, the "gentlemen," and they looked more closely at this match than they expected they should have to. And still Egan circled, sometimes jigging up and down, sometimes making his blade sing in the air. When he did that, Reid blocked and fended Egan back.

Then Egan attempted to change the tempo of the fight. One! Two! Three! Four! Five! He rammed a volley of thrusts at Reid's middle. The captain blocked each one and never moved back an inch. Egan turned his back; he sweated but the captain remained dry, still stood there with his bare, sleeveless sword arm. The sun had come up and the crosstrees of the ships were lit as with gold. I dared a glance at Silver, whose face showed how he loved all of this.

Egan remained with his back turned and I knew what he meant by this. He hoped Reid would aim a foul thrust, as tavern fighters do. But I could have told him different: Captain Reid did not fall for other men's bait. The Scotchman stood there, his sword only half-raised, waiting, as he had done from the outset, for the fight to come to him.

For the next three or four minutes they went at each other. Once or twice Reid changed his tactic and carried the fight—and then I knew why Egan had his reputation: he possessed superb defence. I saw Reid's face acknowledge this and when he failed to get through he returned to his first position.

They fought and locked; they locked and fought; it was a long fight, so absorbing that everyone on both sides became entranced. I enjoyed that they used so little space—in all I reckon they moved within a circle no more than three yards across. No clumsy blows fell, no accidental cuts or stumbles—they were so accomplished and evenly matched that I almost forgot to marvel at Reid's rough brilliance. I expected it from Egan; that was his life and it has to be said his finesse was admirable, a wonder to view. But Reid astounded all.

And then came the fatal error.

It was born of vanity, and these were both vain men. Also, it came of mockery—and I was the butt. Egan tried once more to penetrate Reid's guard. This time the captain's parry caused Egan to spin around and he danced quite happily to Reid's tune, because as yet the match had been equal and he had no concerns. But his dance brought him face to face with me and with a cry of "*Mister* Mills—huzzah to you, sir" he flicked my cheek with the tip of his blade.

The cut he made was tiny; when today I tell my tales in the parlour of the Admiral Benbow I regret I have no scar to show. But the error was grievous.

Captain Reid shouted at him, "Foul, sir!" and Egan grew enraged. He ran at Reid who stepped back a little and kicked Egan on the knee. Egan stumbled and fell and Reid was on him.

Maltby shouted, "Hold!"

The captain looked up, his sabre point on Egan's neck, beneath the jawbone.

"Will you retreat from my ship, sir?" called Reid.

Maltby snarled, "You are fighting foul!"

At this, Reid ran his blade simply into Egan's neck, twisted it and took it out. Maltby started forward and Reid lifted the dripping sword.

"Come on! Come on!"

Maltby stopped.

"What became of rules?—" but he didn't know what to say or how to say it; Egan's dying body twitched two feet away from his legs, the grey, silk shirt already darkening with blood. "Sir—we are fighting rules, here."

"He broke the rules," shouted Reid.

I stood back, a tiny sting on my cheek and no blood worth the description. Nobody else knew what to do either. Everyone moved, yet never left their places. The "gentlemen" seemed stunned and angry. Maltby turned for support. The beery-faced soldier said something to him and Maltby turned back.

"Rules, sir—what about rules?"

"Yes! Rules! Retreat sir, you are defeated according to your own rules! Therefore leave us. And take away your dead."

I saw Silver's look of amazement—not even he, I think, might dare be as hard in such generally unequal circumstances.

Maltby, trying to regain a level sense, shouted once again, "If you do not obey rules—why should we?"

As though these words were a signal, from behind Maltby a figure lumbered out of the shadow of the brig's mainmast and hurled something through the air. It hit Captain Reid hard, not on his head where it had been aimed, but on his bare shoulder. I saw it fall to the ground—it was one of the hunchback's shiny hammers and now Raspen himself came thundering forward.

Reid was helpless. He had dropped his sabre and I knew his arm was hurt. I moved towards him and picked up his blade. The hunchback saw me, recognised me, stopped, puzzled over me and then roared. I stepped back.

Maltby asked, "What's this?"

Raspen pointed at me. "I seen him! On the road near that inn. That's 'Awkins, I figger."

To which Maltby merely said, "Yes, we know. Enjoy him."

And to which Silver called, "You great swab! You misshaped lump of jelly."

Raspen turned and threw a hammer at Silver: he drew those things from his pouch like other men draw knives. Silver ducked it easily and sneered again, "You be blind as well as humped!" and stepped forwards. At a gesture from Maltby, two sailors hauled Egan's body back to their side and Raspen lumbered across the open space towards Silver. My mind was in a daze and not least of my feelings was the tang of sadness at the death of Egan, whose skill was so wondrous and whose figure so elegant.

Silver stood to face Raspen, who pulled a larger hammer from his pouch. I had seen Silver fight before and when he reached for support to a spar by the hatch, I kept my eye on the silver crutch.

He didn't disappoint me. As the hunchback raised the hammer, Silver brought the leg of the crutch up like a shining bolt and rammed it high between Raspen's thighs. The hunchback screamed so loud that I have a clear memory of hearing the birds over on the island screech in alarm.

Raspen doubled over and Silver came at him—but Raspen came up fast and butted Silver in the mouth. He sent Silver staggering, then grabbed at the leg of the crutch. He caught hold of it—until Silver twisted it and the leg came apart to release a hidden blade which cut deep into Raspen's hand. Silver sawed it this way and that, until Raspen dropped the crutch and stepped back.

Figuring out what had cut him caused Raspen to delay and Silver was upon him, trying to sink a knife. Raspen threw him off and the men grappled.

Silver got a thumb into Raspen's eye and the hunchback wrestled himself away. He hit Silver a great, dazing punch to the side of the head and then grabbed Silver's face and bit into it. He used the bite to begin rocking Silver from side to side—a one-legged man has scant balance. Silver bellowed and cast him off: his face had begun to bloody—but worse, his composure had been disturbed and in all Silver's actions that I had seen, he had been victorious on account of his calm.

Raspen sensed this and strode in. Silver flicked a hand to me and tried to reach the sabre I handed him. The hunchback kicked his hand, the sabre fell to the deck and with every violent movement that huge mound of flesh between the man's shoulders wobbled sickeningly.

Silver threw him back again and there came that moment which all fights have—a moment's stillness when nothing happens: the fighters glare at each other and then, customarily, break out into some new and wilder violence. As did this pair—with Raspen carrying himself forwards like a mountain.

Silver's cunning came to his aid. He employed the hunchback's momentum—by grabbing his hair and propelling him forwards. Raspen slammed face first into a bulwark and quick as I had ever seen him move Silver whipped up his sabre and speared him through the hump on his back, pinning him to the timber. Raspen screamed and screamed and tried to release himself. At the same time Silver now had no weapon.

I shouted, "John!" He turned and I bent, picked up the shiny hammer that had struck Captain Reid and lobbed it to Silver. He caught it, but as he tried to hit Raspen on the head the hunchback, with a mighty heave, freed himself and began to lurch about the deck, blood staining the darkness of his coat. He flailed so much that Silver could not get a clean blow.

The beery soldier came running forwards. Silver hit him full in the face with the hammer. We all heard bones crack and the man went down. Silver, now using Raspen as his prop, grabbed the hilt of the sabre where it protruded from the awful hump and he used it to run the hunchback at Maltby—who jumped back.

Indeed, they all jumped back, they parted like a bow wave, and next I heard a smashing of timbers and I knew that Silver had propelled Raspen into the rail of the *Hispaniola*. I couldn't see fully and ran forwards to another part of the rail. Then I heard the scream and the splash—and I saw Raspen hit the water, Long John Silver's sabre protruding either side of his hump.

Silver had now got himself into trouble: two of the brig's crewmen attacked him, doubtless to impress Maltby. I ran down towards them and began to cut at them. Silver fought back too, took a knife from somewhere and almost sliced one man's face in half. We got Silver back to his corner by the hatchway where, as I stood before him swishing and screaming like a madman at anyone and everyone, Silver put his crutch back together and stepped to a safer place.

But the relative control of the whole circumstance had changed. Egan's death, and then Raspen's and, by all appearances, that of the beery-faced man had added up to a declaration of war. In numbers we seemed evenly matched—but not in skill; and I now knew that Maltby's crew was also more military than marine. They began to come at us again, with Maltby shouting at them to give us no quarter, to cut us all down.

And then above the noise, I and everyone else there heard a new screaming, of a different, almost bestial order. I knew straightway why my wariness had been excited when I saw Grace. She had found the keys in my coat pocket and released Joseph Tait.

Ch. 34—

The Last, Longest Moments

What makes men so fierce? Is it given to us all, if we have lived in the fires of the sun, to fight like wild things? These questions often drift through my mind—and some mornings I think I have encountered such savage men because I have asked such questions. No matter: I have seen too many of them. I do not want to see any such men again.

I know why they puzzle me. It is because I glimpse beneath the savagery, the wildness and the rage, a kind of innocence, a simplicity, as though this were a soul that has found only one, violent way of calling attention to itself, of making its way through an uneven world.

Tait had this quality; I saw it. Silver had it too, though less obviously so. I cannot say whether Raspen did, but there was something in him during the last throes of his life that touched me deeply. He was like a bull that is being slaughtered and he went down that way, his great shaven head and body and gaitered legs heaving and bucking.

With Tait I saw it in another way. I had already perceived it in the simple fashion Silver had tricked him on the island and I was baffled that such a fighter could so easily have been caught. Now I saw it again as he came roaring up the deck from the fo'csle companionway, a broad knife in his hand. Where did he get the knife? I dared not ask—I never have.

When he reached the thick of the fray every contestant fell away to look at him, Tait stopped and gazed around him in wonder. It was a kind of half-smile he had on his face and he peered at us all, like some sort of rustic come to town. But he gave off such ferocity that those nearest to him fell far back.

Then he saw Maltby—and he sprang forward like an ape. Maltby shouted some kind of command and three crewmen attacked Tait. He slashed the first with a sweep of the blade across the eyes, the second got the hilt on the bridge of the nose and the third took beneath his ribs the swiftest thrust that was ever made. All of them dropped or retreated, anguished or dying.

Maltby's remaining "gentlemen" came forwards now and they, professional fighters, knew something—they knew not to engage Tait at close quarters. All three of them formed a circle around him, swords pointed at him so that he became the hub and they the spokes of a wheel. Tait looked as though they had contained him, especially when two others joined in.

But you cannot fight a man who has no sense of what constitutes damage to himself. Those who contained him did not taunt him, as they might have been tempted to do; rather, they respected him and tried to hold him still. In vain: he grabbed one sword by the blade and, though it cut into his hand, whisked it out of the owner's grip. The gentleman ran backwards. Tait thought to follow him but didn't.

Fast on the heels of this action, as Tait looked at his cut palm, another sword thrust at him. It was the fittest of these duellists, alert and bright-eyed, and otherwise a civil man if appearances may be relied upon. Tait raised his own arm so that the blade passed beneath and ran towards the man and hammered his knife blade somewhere into the man's face, beneath the right eye, I think. We all heard the thudd! The duellist fell and Tait took his sword.

A third gallantly attacked, trying to run Tait through—but he died, there and then, with a thrust to the neck; he died quickly and with a desperate look on his face.

Throughout all this I endeavoured to watch everything, lest my own life fall into danger—and I owed it to John Silver to see that he was not attacked. He and Captain Reid had found a place that could be defended—the small arena before the hatch to the main companionway and later, when I came to dwell on it all, I felt much amused to think of those two becoming comrades-in-arms.

But Tait was now loose again; and this meant that his next port of call could be Silver or myself. That did not happen. He aimed for Maltby—who had taken refuge behind as many men as he could find. Tait stopped, his way blocked. Then a tall man that I had seen earlier came forwards with two pistols and held them not more than a yard from Tait's face. I could see the guns and they looked like two dark eyes staring at Tait's.

At the same time something snaked through the air above everyone's head and a man ran out behind Tait and caught it. It was a long, thin rope, the kind natural to all ships. The man whipped his end of it into a loose loop and threw it once around Joseph Tait's neck.

I say "once" because that was the nature of the torment. Inside the crowd of his supporters, Maltby took the other end and together, from opposite directions, he and the sailor pulled Tait this way and that by the neck until the man knew he was caught. He spun around to try and whirl from the rope but each time he did they tightened it.

Slowly, as though he were a beast in a glade of the forest, they got him under control and stood him there, twitching or flicking the rope if he dared to move. After some minutes Tait stopped, standing on his bare feet, his knife in one hand, the sword he had snatched in the other but unable to move. Swiftly he raised the knife to cut at the rope, but swifter Maltby and his man tightened their pull and Tait's eyes bulged like a man being strangled.

I moved forwards; my bones sang with an instinct that something was about to happen. A question had been tearing at me, a question to which I could not, in the heat of everything, give words: *Where is Louis?* If there's anyone I must protect it is he.

Tait looked from one to the other. He looked at Silver; he looked at me. Behind me I heard a gasp and then Grace came running through—Uncle Ambrose tried to stop her and failed.

She got as far as Tait and Maltby shouted, "Cut her down!"

I shouted, "*No!*" Luckily, Maltby's words and mine shocked those whom he ordered and they froze.

Now Maltby shouted, "Hold her! I'll do it!" Two men grabbed

her—one did so in a vulgarly ungallant fashion and I marked him as a target for myself. Circling Tait, still maintaining his tight grip on the rope, Maltby edged towards Grace.

"A sword!" he cried. "Give me a sword!" and from the ranks behind him a cutlass was thrust, hilt first, into his hand. With the hindrance of the rope Maltby could not move fast. And the rope was long, therefore he had to walk in a wide circle in order to keep it taut. Step by step, not hurrying, watching Tait and then looking at Grace where she was held brutally, Maltby came forward. I swear that any wind blowing across the seas of the south that day held its breath during those minutes.

Tait, wild and mad, looked down at the rope around his neck. Again he brought his knife up to try and cut at it but again Maltby and the other man tightened the rope so savagely they almost jerked Tait off his feet. The movement required Maltby to stop. He waited until Tait was again settled and began to move once more towards Grace.

Then Joseph Tait spoke. I had never heard his voice and, though half-strangulated as he was, it surprised me with its richness, this man who had tortured other men to death—who had violated beyond description dear old Ben Gunn and respectable Doctor Jefferies and countless others, who had killed Tom Taylor, a sleepy harmless man in the service of my family at the Admiral Benbow since he was a boy.

"Truth," Tait called, and it was extraordinary to hear a sacred word come from such a profane being. "I tell you all," he shouted. "This man—" he pointed the knife he held at Maltby.

But Maltby nodded to the sailor holding the other end of the rope and that man was watching Maltby's face for commands. They stood, those two, legs spread for balance and each pulled on that rope as though bringing down a young horse—and they pulled and pulled. I have a memory of seeing the shocked faces of everyone, even those hard men lined up against us.

I looked to the sky, my eyes unable to watch—and what I saw changed the scene. Louis had been watching everything from the rigging; indeed he squatted not far from where I had fled to escape Israel

Hands. The conjunction of Louis sitting where I had once almost died and the look on his face as he held out one hand to me beseechingly snapped something in me. I ran forwards and cut into the wrist of the sailor who, with Maltby, held the rope.

The man screamed and staggered back. The rope slackened and although Maltby tugged with all his might he merely had the effect of spinning Tait in the opposite direction. Then Tait, eyes bulging, face blued, fell—but I knew by the way his body hit the bleached timbers of the deck that he had either died, or soon would.

This gave me a new problem. Tait had evidently been about to spill the secret. Now only one witness to this truth, this mystery, remained, and Maltby was completely free of any other encumbrance. Faster than a man of his girth should be able to move, he ran on his small feet to where Grace screamed. I moved too and did not move fast enough.

Or so I thought: Maltby got there but a clumsiness among the men holding Grace did not provide him with the open target he needed. I saw her turn her face and head away, I heard Louis, high above us all, scream "Mama!" and I heard one of the deadliest sounds in the world, the swish of a blade through the air.

But it was my own sword I heard and as I struck I did not feel the customary jarring of the arm when a weapon strikes. Nor did I see whether I had wounded anyone because I had my eyes closed in fear as I delivered the blow. I opened my eyes. All I saw was Maltby stepping back a little, unhurt, but my attack had placed me in front of Grace and he could not now strike her without passing me.

Maltby screamed again, "Cut her down! I command you— cut her down!"

I shouted, "No! She knows the truth." In this I took my lead from Tait—because after all I did not know what truth Grace knew.

Maltby came at me, swiping and swishing, dancing on one forward-raised foot, and I went back and back and back. I am no swordsman and it shows. Maltby had been trained by the best. Fortunately for me he stumbled over Tait's body and I gained a second or two.

Behind me I heard a voice, speaking quite low. "Be calm. You will win. You're the one fighting the good cause. Be calm. Stand still and he will stand still. Watch him."

It was Dr. Ballantyne. I didn't see him but I heard his voice again.

"Watch everything he does. Move only when you want to. That is the core of all defence. If you are still, if you are calm—you will win."

Maltby disentangled his feet from the sprawled figure of Tait. I saw Silver and Captain Reid make a move towards the men who held Grace. They were at a loss, those captors, rude and coarse, with never an experience of holding a lady of such quality in danger. They released her—not wholly, but enough to give me courage. If she now presented an easier target, Maltby knew he could not get her without first dispatching me.

He stood before me: we were directly by the thickest part of the mainmast. Now I could see Dr. Ballantyne as well as hear him; he stood a little way off as serene as a church on Sunday.

"Gently, Jim. Calmly." It was the first time he had used my name.

All around the faces watched and I watched Maltby's. It was easy to see how clever a man he must be; those eyes knew how to take in knowledge; that brow fronted a large, well-stocked mind. And I also saw how he cared about no other human being on earth. All that mattered to him was what he believed in, and what he wanted, for himself.

He stepped closer, simply looking at me. Suddenly, he thrust twice and twice I parried, but my parry was like an ox pawing the ground. Men groaned, either in pleasure for Maltby or despair for me.

Another voice behind me spoke.

"This is fine. You will have him. Your bravery will win it for you."

My heart lifted: this was Captain Reid. There and then I would have fought a war single-handed for him.

Maltby came again at me. This time, more confident, I twisted away and his thrust ran past me but I no longer looked like a girl fleeing a gander. I turned around to face him on the return and saw his eyes. He believed that he had me.

Except that he did not. Sometimes I have heard that, among the ancients, retribution came from the skies. It did now. Something fell on Maltby—no, not fell; something hit him from Heaven. It was a small round iron ball, used for the only cannon on board the *Hispaniola*. It landed on the top of Maltby's head, thrown I knew with his accurate aim by Louis overhead.

How clearly I remember the thought that flew into my brain at that moment. Maltby stopped and the colour of his eyes changed. The ball had killed him outright. But how can a boy of twelve go through the world knowing he has killed a man, even though he has done so to save his own mother's life? I have seen enough of death to know that our mortality must be fiercely protected and preserved where possible.

I myself had taken a man's life—on this very ship, that of Israel Hands; he fell here, on this same spot where Maltby now swayed. And even though I was defending my own life, I had been haunted by that act and that is why I know that the taking of another's life is the most grave event on earth, something from which, no matter how a man speaks to himself in the deepest folds of the darkest night, he can never get ease.

And that is why at that moment I ran my sword through Sir Thomas Maltby half a second before he fell, although I knew he was already dead. Anybody there that day will believe for ever that I was the one who killed him.

———⚓———

Epilogue

A Bed of Roses?

Calm has a texture we never forget once it has touched us. I think of it as feeling like wool on the skin—soft, safe and intended for warmth. That is the calm I know today in this parish, one year and some weeks after all those terrible events.

When, with Maltby's death, the affray ended, I saw the same calm in the faces of the brig's men—relief, a greeting for safety. They were dignified enough not to slink away; they were noble enough to come forward and hand themselves into the command of Captain Reid. He, in turn, made a gesture which, they knew, absolved them of any guilt or complicity—he broke out rations and called up food and drink.

Before that happened, my last position was one of a man paralysed. I let go my sword and it swayed, buried in Maltby's gut. A sound like a sigh went up from all the people and then I heard nothing. I raised my head and looking around the circle saw the eyes of Doctor Ballantyne, Captain Reid, Long John Silver; I saw the men assembled against us, the men with us and finally I saw Grace, beside whom stood my dear Uncle Ambrose. They all looked at me and I looked at them and we had no need of words.

A parting came in the circle and through it squeezed Louis, who flung himself at me and wrapped his arms around my waist. All I could do was reach down and smooth his hair and stroke his shoulders. His mother came forwards but he clung to me and I saw Doctor Ballantyne smile and I knew I had not done wrong. My hands were shaking.

Captain Reid walked about, inspecting everything but hurrying nobody. It was strange to see men, who had earlier been hacking at each other, mingle easily, if a trifle sullenly, eating ship's rations and drinking the (admittedly meagre) tot of rum granted by the captain.

One man busied himself: Doctor Ballantyne. With sleeves rolled up he went from corpse to corpse, verifying death. He knew, I expected, that Captain Reid would demand the full record required by law. When he finished with Maltby's body he shot me a shrewd glance. The doctor knew the truth of how Maltby had died and I suspect he guessed what had taken place—he never discussed it with me.

When Louis released himself, and when I promised him we would speak at endless length, Silver strolled to my side with his lopsided smile.

"Jim, lad. You downfaced that swab!"

His manner contained a congratulation I was embarrassed to enjoy—his old charming warmth was working its spell again. And then the other Silver came through, as he lowered his voice.

"Jim, lad—what d'you suppose might be the ownership of that there brig? She's a tidy piece, I mean, she'd not be to my own choice, if I had a choice, but—she's tidy, like I say."

I could almost hear the bargaining begin.

From Captain Reid I received no congratulation. He called together my uncle and me and spoke to us as the charterers of the *Hispaniola*—and the captain also had a bargain to strike.

He said, "I have not had a voyage like this before, although I have been on the sea since I was twelve. But it may prove possible, gentlemen, by means of discourse, to remove the necessity of tedious enquiry. Shall we debate in, say, a few days? When matters are more resolved and we're under way for home."

Uncle Ambrose and I agreed readily. We walked away from the captain and my uncle said to me, "By Jove, Jim—what?! You've become quite the hero!"

"No, Uncle. There's so much to be attended. And I still don't know what caused this mystery."

He exclaimed, "Oh, I do!"

My uncle, naturally, had spent more time with Grace than had been my good fortune.

"How much do you know, Uncle?"

"Jim, a lady will always talk to a lawyer."

"Then can you answer me how she came to—how such a man came—?" I exploded with the question that had troubled me most. "Uncle, that's what baffles me! I can't believe it! That she had a child by him! *Grief!*"

He put his hand on my arm. "No, Jim. That is not the case. It's all simple and human. Give matters a day or two and I will answer as I have heard." When eventually he told me, he silenced me.

I will now convey to you what my uncle narrated—which is what Grace Richardson told him. The information has not answered all my questions. For example, neither I nor my uncle have ever discovered how Grace knew Tait was still alive. Or how she had heard that information a year before she came to me. Or indeed, how she found me. I shall have to live with those questions unanswered.

But I know—as you now shall know—the main thrust of her motive, and I understand finally what sparked off such an extraordinary and conflagratory and discommoding and plain risky adventure.

Tait was not Louis's father. How that information soothed my mind, because I am primitive about breeding and I believe in what passes down through the blood. In truth I had never been led by anyone to believe that Tait was the father: I, Jim Hawkins, have never needed a helping hand to jump to a wrong conclusion. But Tait knew who had fathered Louis. This is what came about.

The old Duke of Berwick, kin to the Maltby family but vastly richer, had two sons: one was called Louis and the younger one called William. Louis had a delicate nature and William, the one who died on our lane, was robust and warlike (as I had cause to know). At the age of sixteen, Grace, of a good but insufficient family—the Richardsons were Scotch landowners but not aristocratic—fell in love with the elder brother and he loved her too. Louis's coachman was Joseph

Tait and Tait alone knew of the trysts; he had driven the lovers hither and yon.

When Grace knew she was to bear a child, she told her lover—and Louis, being an unworldly man, confided in his younger brother. Uncle Ambrose, with his lawyer's mind, understood and explained all this clearly.

"William, the younger brother, whom you encountered, had always hoped his brother would die of poor health, in which case he would inherit. Jim, he *needed* to inherit. He had large—impossible— gambling debts, indeed he was generally in the grip of costly addictions. But although he felt alarm at the news of the confinement, William still had, as I'm sure he'd put it, a card or two left to play."

This revelatory conversation, I may say, took place one night after supper, on deck in the balm after a hot day, when all had become quiet again and we sailed peacefully.

"Even if the brother's child were female, William would still come into the inheritance if and when his older brother died. But the older boy, Louis, married Grace secretly and then the child was born—a son, also named Louis. This marriage created a new succession, from the father Louis to the legitimate son, Louis. The witness to the legitimising marriage was—as you may guess—Joseph Tait. The old Duke of Berwick and his wife had not yet been told of Grace, or the birth, or any of this. That meeting was planned to take place within days of the birth. But, as you can imagine, William had now had his most powerful hopes dashed. The newborn was not female, therefore William would not inherit. And, worst of all, the heir was correct under the law."

"Uncle, this is lawyer's work. I merely seek to know why we came to the South Seas—"

Uncle Ambrose smiled. "Patience, Jim. That is how one hears secrets. Patience. Two nights after the birth of the baby, Louis the father was killed by his younger brother, William, assisted by Maltby. Tait witnessed the murder—and took Grace and the infant away from there. She later tried and tried to reach the old Duke and his wife—

but William, the villainous son, in newfound solicitude, erected a veritable garrison around his parents. Grace tried everything—but she had to be careful not to reveal to William where she was, where her attempted messages came from. She knew he would kill her and young Louis. Eventually I think—though she has not said so—despair set in. Her father tried to help—she has no brother or uncle—but he could not get an interview with the old Duke alone. And William threatened Mr. Richardson's life. Or so Grace believes."

The remainder of the story became simpler to follow. Uncle Ambrose told it clearly.

"Grace knew she and Louis were to be killed so that William could inherit. With money conveyed legitimately by bankers from her parents to a relative in France but intended for Grace, she began to lead a fugitive's life. France concealed them for a number of years; but Berwick discovered that connection. Then she went to Italy and Portugal—but always with, she believed, the hot breath of danger on their necks. Fugitives, as you probably know (my uncle smiled), believe they are always followed. They fled to Poland and as far as Greece. During their travels she heard that her parents, one after the other, died, and William was installed as, to all intents and purposes, the rightful Duke of Berwick. So now she had nothing. Matters like this have often occurred, Jim, believe me."

My heart was almost unable to bear this tale. I wanted it to end.

"Uncle, why has Grace not told me this tale? There is no shame in it."

Ambrose shifted a little. "Well, who knows?" he said vaguely. "For some time, while she toured these islands, Tait was her protector. She had to be disguised. A woman of her birth—she'd not like that she had to, well, adopt certain postures."

My uncle shook himself clear of these thoughts and raced back to the main tale.

"Then a rumour reached them that William had died soldiering and the wanderers came home to England. But the rumour was a lure. Berwick laid a trap in London, Grace fled to Bristol, then Yeovil—all the time pursued again. And that is how she came to the Royal George and to you, Jim."

"Uncle, I shall never forget the moment she arrived."

Uncle Ambrose smiled at me indulgently and finished his tale—or, should I say, Grace's.

"Tait, by now, was long gone, as you know. In fact he had travelled with her only a year or two. She will not say why he left. That was when she went abroad. Young Louis was about two years old."

I reckoned the times. This tallied with Tait joining Silver's band.

"As the years went on and Louis grew, Grace knew that her only hope resided in Joseph Tait. He had witnessed the marriage—and the murder. He knew Louis was the rightful Duke of Berwick. But Tait was gone. There, Jim, it is as simple as that."

"And how did Maltby come into all this?"

Uncle Ambrose laughed and rubbed his hands.

"Aha, Jim—a lawyer's delight, that question. Do you know why Maltby followed Grace, wanted her dead? Wanted Tait dead? Wanted young Louis dead?"

"Tell me, Uncle." I felt irritation growing.

"The law of entail again, Jim. A woman may not inherit. First of all, Maltby, Berwick's first cousin and a man of little enough means, had, I believe, been promised lands by William for help in any conspiracy to succeed to the title and estates. But when William died in your lane—who was the heir in line after young Louis?"

"Maltby!"

"Right, Jim. That doubled the reason why Grace needed to find the one witness in the world."

"But, Uncle!" I cried. "The game's up! Tait's dead. It's all been for nothing. He can't witness now." I struck the rail of the ship in rage.

Ambrose smiled at me, a strange, slow smile.

"While you were gone away on your unfortunate adventure, I tried to think prudently, Jim. I prepared a statement—and Tait signed it. That is why Grace was so desperate to release him. And I witnessed it."

At last I knew most things and I thanked my uncle—although I felt a little bridled when he asked me not to discuss it with Grace.

"Uncle, why did she not tell all this to me?"

"She feels shame, Jim. I have told her she must not feel any such—"

"Shame? What is there to be ashamed of?"

"I think she feels shame that you might have thought Tait the father of Louis. And therefore shame that you might think so little of her—"

"Uncle," I interrupted. "If I thought so little of her would I have made such efforts?"

"People reach unusual conclusions, Jim. Grace is no different from any of us."

"But I can't leave off speaking to her forever. There are things I have to say."

"Jim—wait until you have had some more rest. You've been a wonder. You have brought it off handsomely."

"So our young Louis is now the Duke of Berwick." I laughed. "Oh, how I shall delight in calling him 'Your Grace'—oh, yes!"

My uncle laughed too. "We knew you'd say that, Jim."

"And is his title, all that, his succession, the estates—that is all safe, or will be?"

"Beyond doubt, Jim."

I left him, utterly pleased for the outcome—but uneasy, which I put down to my exhaustion. And I told Ambrose before I went below, "Uncle, I couldn't have done anything without the good sense you bring with you. And your care and protection."

He beamed—and of us all, he showed the least wear and tear: in fact he looked like a man who had come to the southern seas for his health.

The practical details of that homewards voyage are simple to relate, if sad. After the fray, Captain Reid ordered that the corpses be stitched into canvas, as is the sailor's custom at sea, and, saying the Prayers for Burial at Sea, he conducted a mass burial to a watery grave: Maltby,

Tait, Henry Egan, the beery-faced man, those "gentlemen" who died and many others whose names I never heard: he prayed with, I thought, a special little edge for Raspen, the hunchback. The thin clerk assisted him, reading some prayers in French. He, the clerk, had made a formal request to be allowed ashore when convenient and Captain Reid told him he would give it consideration.

Vail once again attached himself to me. I fell ill, not gravely so but enough to keep me in bed, feverish, for three days. Vail kept me informed as to what took place on board—including reports of arguments between Captain Reid and Silver. I laughed to hear the root of those.

Christmas, our cat from the Admiral Benbow, had taken a murderous interest in Silver's old parrot and Cap'n Flint was screeching the place down—to Captain Reid's annoyance. I cheered silently for Christmas—he's on my side, I thought. And Captain Reid would not let Silver have Christmas locked away, telling Long John that he of all men should know how a cat brings luck to a ship.

There was, however, another root to this dispute, I reckoned. Silver was using a tactic of displacement—because we had taken the brig under tow and that, I believe, was Silver's main target of negotiation.

When I felt better I sought Dr. Ballantyne. He daily ministered to our wounded, none of whom were in danger. More intently, he attended the three men I had brought from the island. Of these, Noonstock proved the quickest to show recovery, Ben gave cause for concern and Jefferies had not regained consciousness: Silver's assessment was accurate again.

The doctor worked night and day for Jefferies. At first I thought he was so strenuous because Jefferies came of the same profession. Then I saw him attend the others, and his tenderness and robust care dispelled that notion—although it is perhaps true to observe that he showed greater distress over Jefferies.

In the end he lost him. I was there—it was in the middle of the afternoon. The doctor had rigged up a hammock in his own cabin (a bunkroom provided an infirmary for most of the others) and we stood watching Jefferies who, at the last, half-turned for a moment, almost the only movement we had seen in him. The face, the bruises now fading, contorted like a man trying to puzzle out something; spittle came from the side of his mouth. Dr. Ballantyne wiped it away and Jefferies sighed and expired.

I shook Dr. Ballantyne's hand and walked out. Yet facing me at home lay the tasks of telling Clara and Josh Taylor about Tom's death—and now I must face Squire Trelawney about his cousin, but the squire takes a more cursory view of death. Dr. Ballantyne came and stood with me on the deck.

"This was all so terrible it had to be expunged," he said. "That greed, that evil. It needed the sacrifice of a good life."

I made no answer—and on we sailed. The *Hispaniola* felt sluggish and we rolled too much . . .

Our voyage to the landlocked gulf in general ran badly; for a number of days I had little to say to anyone, but took my meals alone and walked alone. My mind was utterly occupied with the approach I planned to Grace. Now I was at last a man who had proven himself and I had at least doubled my means. Also, I had demonstrated—and she had acknowledged—my capability to father Louis; as everybody knew, the boy and I loved each other. I planned to speak to Grace when we left Dr. Ballantyne and Silver back at their port, before we ourselves headed at last for Bristol.

One morning I saw Silver; he sat ill humoured and remote, the same John Silver who always wished to speak to everybody.

"Jim, lad, this ain't good. I want to beard Reid."

"What is it you need, John?" I asked, thinking he was chafing for his share of the trove.

"We'd sail quicker if that brig were crewed."

I jumped up and almost ran to Reid.

"Captain!"

"I am busy, Mr. Hawkins."

This was the old Captain Reid, his arm now in a sling from Dr. Ballantyne.

"Captain, my uncle and I pay for any damage to this ship."

"Do you presume to challenge my care of her?"

"Captain, should a storm blow up—"

He understood at once—and also knew my purpose. And he gave in; without any objection he said, "Let us arrange for *Captain* (how he emphasised the word!) Silver to take her to harbour. But before us, always. The cargo stays here until we meet him again."

Silver said when I told him, "A mixed pronouncement, to be sure, Jim. But I'll weather it. Will you sail with me?"

"John—as you probably understand, I have business here. You know what I mean."

He smiled, that sly, fast smile.

"Good luck on it, Jim. I'm looking ahead to seeing my old missis," he said.

It took most of a day to separate and crew the brig and the two skippers conferred. Agreement, drawn up by my uncle, had us all meet in Silver's—and Dr. Ballantyne's—home port. That afternoon, as we stripped some canvas and thus fell behind the brig, we buried Dr. Jefferies at sea. Grace and Louis appeared, the first time I had seen them at any leisure since the great fracas.

After the rite I approached her, merely to enquire for her well-being—but she fluttered her hand at me and called, "This is such a sad business. I am overcome."

Care of those whom one loves is founded, I believe, on tact as well as warmth of feelings, so I withdrew. Thereafter a kind of torpor fell on us all until we reached the port we aimed for.

I have little to report from that day onwards. A mighty conference took place to distribute the treasure, which consisted of diamonds and other jewels, innumerable coins and ingots, the bar silver we had left there and all manner of valuables taken from ships which Tait had lured onto the reef. It was altogether a fabulous hoard—or so I was told; I could not bring myself to look at it and my share sat here in the inn stables a full nine months before my mother prevailed upon me to take advantage of it and collect its value. It has made us very rich.

Captain Reid prospered out of it too, as did Dr. Ballantyne—to my uncle who had taken charge of the dividend I insisted that the doctor be handsomely compensated. Silver fought his corner tooth and nail but he was forced to count the brig as part of his spoils. (Captain Reid observed to my uncle afterwards that he shouldn't be surprised to hear of a black brig sailing the southern hemisphere under the Jolly Roger!)

Uncle Ambrose asked me what share I wanted and did I desire anything in particular. I told him merely to be fair to himself and to me—and most of all to Grace and Louis. He agreed with me in his sage way and I knew that his share, added to the old money he already had, would finally make him one of the wealthiest men in the South-West of England.

One evening, on the quayside of that quaint and lovely harbour, with the table-mountain in the background, everything divided and agreed, and all who wanted to go ashore dispatched (mostly with good riddance)—we all shook hands.

Silver came to me. "I won't forget what you said, Jim."

"What's that, John?"

"About putting in a good word for me in England."

"And now of course," I replied, "you will have the good word of Captain Reid too. He isn't making any report of all this."

The Captain looked uncomfortable—the first time I had seen such a turn in him.

Silver smiled. "I'm glad you looked up an old shipmate, Jim," he said.

I walked with him to his carriage. He breathed heavily, as if the silver crutch gave him too much work to do.

"Jim," he said. "We had us a brave time, eh, lad? 'Course I can't call you 'lad' no more, can I, and you such a dab hand with the cutlass?"

He turned to me. The bitemarks on his face from the hunchback's teeth had healed well. I held out my hand and he grabbed it with such strength I winced.

"If a man's right company be men, then, Jim, you be company I shall think about day by day"—and for the first time I saw his loneliness.

"But we shall meet again, John," I said. "I feel certain of it."

He lit up. "Shall we, Jim? Oh, I hopes so!"

With a hand clap to my shoulder that almost knocked me, he climbed up to his seat and his carriage bore him away, with his crammed trunks; a cart followed, high with canvas packets. I looked after him—and I missed him there and then, as I do now, villain though he may always be.

Dr. Ballantyne's wife and children came down in the landau. Such a greeting has never been seen. When the doctor extricated himself from the many joyous embraces, Mrs. Ballantyne invited Grace, Louis and me, as though we were already a family, to come and stay in their house. But Captain Reid wished to catch a morning tide and I had to take my leave of this remarkable doctor, this man of few words who had given so much to me.

"Come to the Admiral Benbow one day," I pleaded.

Mrs. Ballantyne smiled and said, with large meaning, "And good luck."

The doctor shook my hand. "Thank you, Jim," and he pointed to the *Hispaniola*. At the rail appeared a small, frail and heavily bandaged grey head. "You'd best go back and give him his cheese," he smiled.

Ben Gunn lives here now, at the Admiral Benbow, and irks my mother. He is still spry and can perform useful tasks if supervised—but I know he is not as lively as he was; he is fearful and, if that were possible, more timid. But he is a gentle companion and I need him and I have told him so, though I wish he did not follow me everywhere like a puppy.

I have bought more lands, up by the heath. Soon we start to build afresh here, in the field beside the inn where I will make Ben a small cottage all for himself and he can have as much cheese as he wants. Squire Trelawney loves to see him and he always amuses Dr. Livesey.

Those gentlemen cannot hear enough about my return to that ac-cursed island and I have had to write all this down so that, I hope, I may be allowed to cease speaking of it, for although the exploit strengthened me and gave me courage, the memory frightens and discommodes me, and it was my boasting of the first adventure to Treasure Island that surely provoked the second.

But I must be respectful to its outcome because I profited so greatly from it, although I would never choose such a path towards riches—and I gained one reward with which mere riches may not be compared. It reached me in a mixed way but it lights my life every day.

About a week after we had left Silver and Dr. Ballantyne in their land-locked gulf, I was walking on the deck of the *Hispaniola*. My thoughts roamed across their usual subject, upon which I brooded every moment I was awake—and in my dreams too. Louis was ahead of me and he saw me and waved, then went on with whatever occupied him. I had an impulse that this was the moment to seize those brooding fancies—to ask his mother to be my wife.

Rushing forwards I exclaimed, "Louis, I must speak to your Mamma! Louis—'tis most important!"

He saw my urgency and ran. Grace returned with him.

"Madam—Grace." She smiled and melted my heart again. Louis ran away and I stuttered on. "We have not spoken since everything—"

She interrupted: "And I have been too—distressed, surprised, overcome—I have not thanked you. But how could I have been so churlish, so tardy? You have done so much—for me—and for Louis."

I took a deep breath. "I am now considerably well placed," I began. "I believe my profit from this voyage will be great. Therefore I shall soon buy land and I am twenty-five years old and I love your boy deeply—I feel he and I may be the closest of friends—"

"But you are! You are his very hero!"

"Grace—Madam—I told you once that I wished to speak my heart to you. But I have no practice at what I am about to say—"

She held up a hand. "Please say nothing. Say nothing more. I know the words on your lips and you must not say them!"

Her words were strong but her look was considerate. She stepped back from me, watching me.

"I want to tell you—I want to tell you something." She was unusually hesitant and my heart leaped with joy. She was experiencing the same difficulty in speaking her heart as I was! "There is something in my heart too—something I hope you will understand—"

I recall thinking: this wonderful information will change me and my life for ever and ever. My very brain and bones thrilled.

She spoke again, looking at me in the closest, deepest of ways—she seemed so anxious at speaking her heart I longed to assuage her, to let me speak for both of us. I waited. She spoke.

"Now I must call you 'Jim,' I suppose. But it will be easy. Louis uses it."

I thought, Yes, and you will, I hope, call me "beloved" and "dearest" and all the other sweet names of a husband and wife.

She spoke again. "Now that you and I are to be kinfolk."

"What?" My brain was tired.

At that moment I saw him; he wandered gently round a corner and being a lawyer took in at once the circumstances. He came forwards, smiling carefully.

"Jim! Imagine—at my age. What will your mother say?" He watched me anxiously and then took my hand. "But—congratulate me, Jim!"—and he took Grace's hand tenderly and folded it in his arm. We stood on either side of him and I was stricken to my soul and Uncle Ambrose knew it and it hurt him too, whatever his joy.

My mother, when I told her, looked impatient and said, "There's no fool like an old fool" and added, with a close, significant look at me, "Forty years is too wide between them."

It is darkening a little out on the sea, a rain cloud, I think, coming in over the Western Approaches. I returned to my cabin after that conversation with Grace and Ambrose and I lay face down on my bunk. Nowhere within me could I find the words to tell me what I should feel. Someone knocked on my door and entered unbidden. It was Louis and he asked, "Jim, may I come and live in your house? Until I must go back to Scotland. It will be many years."

That was the blessing in which I rejoice every day. One day, I know, he will have to go and live on his estates, take up his place as the Duke of Berwick. But, for now, Louis is my closest, dearest friend and I also enjoy the affection in which he holds his mother—and she him.

Soon Louis and I shall visit Bristol and I know that my uncle and his bride will come and visit us often and I shall see Grace and hear her and converse with her and my feelings will not have changed, whatever the pain that she did not become mine.

As well as Ben Gunn's cottage I shall also build a larger, finer house, to welcome all such visitors—to encourage them here more often. I have also engaged Dr. Livesey's older sister to tutor Louis and, with the squire's eye on him, Louis has become the makings of an excellent horseman. The inn has become so prosperous that Black Cove is no longer a byway and the rooms overflow often. Indeed, someone has now come to the door of the parlour and I must cease writing.

—— ❧ ——

CENTRAL

DATE DUE

6-28-02			

GAYLORD

PRINTED IN U.S.A